The Dirk Gently Omnibus

The
Dirk Gently
Omnibus

Dirk Gently's Holistic Detective Agency
The Long Dark Tea-Time of the Soul

Douglas Adams

WILLIAM HEINEMANN : LONDON

First published in the United Kingdom in 2001 by William Heinemann

13 15 17 19 20 18 16 14 12

The novels comprising *The Dirk Gently Omnibus* were originally published
separately: *Dirk Gently's Holistic Detective Agency* (1987), *The Long Dark
Tea-Time of the Soul* (1988) by William Heinemann.

William Heinemann
The Random House Group Limited
20 Vauxhall Bridge Road, London SW1V 2SA

Random House Australia (Pty) Limited
20 Alfred Street, Milsons Point, Sydney,
New South Wales 2061, Australia

Random House New Zealand Limited
18 Poland Road, Glenfield,
Auckland 10, New Zealand

Random House (Pty) Limited
Isle of Houghton, Corner of Boundary Road & Carse O'Gowrie,
Houghton 2198, South Africa

The Random House Group Limited Reg. No. 954009

www.randomhouse.co.uk

A CIP catalogue record for this book is available
from the British Library

ISBN 9780434009190

The Random House Group Limited supports The Forest Stewardship
Council (FSC®), the leading international forest certification organisation.
Our books carrying the FSC label are printed on FSC® certified paper.
FSC is the only forest certification scheme endorsed by the leading
environmental organisations, including Greenpeace. Our
paper procurement policy can be found at
www.randomhouse.co.uk/environment

Printed and bound in Great Britain by Clays Ltd, St Ives PLC

Contents

Dirk Gently's Holistic Detective Agency

to my mother,
who liked the bit about the horse

Author's Note

The physical descriptions of St Cedd's College in this book, in so far as they are specific at all, owe a little to my memories of St John's College, Cambridge, although I've also borrowed indiscriminately from other colleges as well. Sir Isaac Newton was at Trinity College in real life, and Samuel Taylor Coleridge was at Jesus.

The point is that St Cedd's College is a completely fictitious assemblage, and no correspondence is intended between any institutions or characters in this book and any real institutions or people, living, dead, or wandering the night in ghostly torment.

This book was written and typeset on an Apple Macintosh Plus computer and LaserWriter Plus printer using MacAuthor word-processing software.

The completed document was then printed using a Linotron 100 at The Graphics Factory, London SW3, to produce a final high-resolution image of the text. My thanks to Mike Glover of Icon Technology for his help with this process.

Finally, my very special thanks are due to Sue Freestone for all her help in nursing this book into existence.

Douglas Adams
London, 1987

Chapter One...

This time there would be no witnesses.

This time there was just the dead earth, a rumble of thunder, and the onset of that interminable light drizzle from the north-east by which so many of the world's most momentous events seem to be accompanied.

The storms of the day before, and of the day before that, and the floods of the previous week, had now abated. The skies still bulged with rain, but all that actually fell in the gathering evening gloom was a dreary kind of prickle.

Some wind whipped across the darkening plain, blundered through the low hills and gusted across a shallow valley where stood a structure, a kind of tower, alone in a nightmare of mud, and leaning.

It was a blackened stump of a tower. It stood like an extrusion of magma from one of the more pestilential pits of hell, and it leaned at a peculiar angle, as if oppressed by something altogether more terrible than its own considerable weight. It seemed a dead thing, long ages dead.

The only movement was that of a river of mud that moved sluggishly along the bottom of the valley past the tower. A mile or so further on, the river ran down a ravine and disappeared underground.

But as the evening darkened it became apparent that the tower was not entirely without life. There was a single dim red light guttering deep within it.

The light was only just visible – except of course that there was no one to see, no witnesses, not this time, but it was nevertheless a light. Every few minutes it grew a little stronger and a little brighter and then faded slowly away almost to nothing. At the same time a low keening noise drifted out on the wind, built up to a kind of wailing climax, and then it too faded, abjectly, away.

Time passed, and then another light appeared, a smaller, mobile light. It emerged at ground level and moved in a single bobbing circuit of the tower, pausing occasionally on its way around. Then it, and the shadowy figure that could just be discerned carrying it, disappeared inside once more.

An hour passed, and by the end of it the darkness was total. The world seemed dead, the night a blankness.

And then the glow appeared again near the tower's peak, this time growing in power more purposefully. It quickly reached the peak of brightness it had previously attained, and then kept going, increasing, increasing. The keening sound that accompanied it rose in pitch and stridency until it became a wailing scream. The scream screamed on and on till it became a blinding noise and the light a deafening redness.

And then, abruptly, both ceased.

There was a millisecond of silent darkness.

An astonishing pale new light billowed and bulged from deep within the mud beneath the tower. The sky clenched, a mountain of mud convulsed, earth and sky bellowed at each other, there was a horrible pinkness, a sudden greenness, a lingering orangeness that stained the clouds, and then the light sank and the night at last was deeply, hideously dark. There was no further sound other than the soft tinkle of water.

But in the morning the sun rose with an unaccustomed sparkle on a day that was, or seemed to be, or at least would have seemed to be if there had been anybody there to whom it could seem to be anything at all, warmer, clearer and brighter – an altogether livelier day than any yet known. A clear river ran through the shattered remains of the valley.

And time began seriously to pass.

Chapter Two...

High on a rocky promontory sat an Electric Monk on a bored horse. From under its rough woven cowl the Monk gazed unblinkingly down into another valley, with which it was having a problem.

The day was hot, the sun stood in an empty hazy sky and beat down upon the grey rocks and the scrubby, parched grass. Nothing moved, not even the Monk. The horse's tail moved a little, swishing slightly to try and move a little air, but that was all. Otherwise, nothing moved.

The Electric Monk was a labour-saving device, like a dishwasher or a video recorder. Dishwashers washed tedious dishes for you, thus saving you the bother of washing them yourself, video recorders watched tedious television for you, thus saving you the bother of looking at it yourself; Electric Monks believed things for you, thus saving you what was becoming an increasingly onerous task, that of believing all the things the world expected you to believe.

Unfortunately this Electric Monk had developed a fault, and had started to believe all kinds of things, more or less at random. It was even beginning to believe things they'd have difficulty believing in Salt Lake City. It had never heard of Salt Lake City, of course. Nor had it ever heard of a quingigillion, which was roughly the number of miles between this valley and the Great Salt Lake of Utah.

The problem with the valley was this. The Monk currently believed that the valley and everything in the valley and around it, including the Monk itself and the Monk's horse, was a uniform shade of pale pink. This made for a certain difficulty in distinguishing any one thing from any other thing, and therefore made doing anything or going anywhere impossible, or at least difficult and dangerous. Hence the immobility of the Monk and the boredom of the horse, which had had to put up with a lot of silly things in its time but was secretly of the opinion that this was one of the silliest.

How long did the Monk believe these things?

Well, as far as the Monk was concerned, forever. The faith which moves mountains, or at least believes them against all the available evidence to be pink, was a solid and abiding faith, a great rock against which the world could hurl whatever it would, yet it would not be shaken. In practice, the horse knew, twenty-four hours was usually about its lot.

So what of this horse, then, that actually held opinions, and was sceptical about things? Unusual behaviour for a horse, wasn't it? An unusual horse perhaps?

No. Although it was certainly a handsome and well-built example of its species, it was none the less a perfectly ordinary horse, such as convergent evolution has produced in many of the places that life is to be found. They have always understood a great deal more than they let on. It is difficult to be sat on all day, every day, by some other creature, without forming an opinion about them.

On the other hand, it is perfectly possible to sit all day, every day, on top of another creature and not have the slightest thought about them whatsoever.

When the early models of these Monks were built, it was felt to be important that they be instantly recognisable as artificial objects. There must be no danger of their looking at all like real people. You wouldn't want your video recorder lounging around on the sofa all day while it was watching TV. You wouldn't want it picking its nose, drinking beer and sending out for pizzas.

So the Monks were built with an eye for originality of design and also for practical horse-riding ability. This was important.

People, and indeed things, looked more sincere on a horse. So two legs were held to be both more suitable and cheaper than the more normal primes of seventeen, nineteen or twenty-three; the skin the Monks were given was pinkish-looking instead of purple, soft and smooth instead of crenellated. They were also restricted to just the one mouth and nose, but were given instead an additional eye, making for a grand total of two. A strange-looking creature indeed. But truly excellent at believing the most preposterous things.

This Monk had first gone wrong when it was simply given too much to believe in one day. It was, by mistake, cross-connected to a video recorder that was watching eleven TV channels simultaneously, and this caused it to blow a bank of illogic circuits. The video recorder only had to watch them, of course. It didn't have to believe them all as well. This is why instruction manuals are so important.

So after a hectic week of believing that war was peace, that good was bad, that the moon was made of blue cheese, and that God needed a lot of money sent to a certain box number, the Monk started to believe that thirty-five percent of all tables were hermaphrodites, and then broke down. The man from the Monk shop said that it needed a whole new motherboard, but then pointed out that the new improved Monk Plus models were twice as powerful, had an entirely new multi-tasking Negative Capability feature that allowed them to hold up to sixteen entirely different and contradictory ideas in memory simultaneously without generating any irritating system errors, were twice as fast and at least three times as glib, and you could have a whole new one for less than the cost of replacing the motherboard of the old model.

That was it. Done.

The faulty Monk was turned out into the desert where it could believe what it liked, including the idea that it had been hard done by. It was allowed to keep its horse, since horses were so cheap to make.

For a number of days and nights, which it variously believed to

be three, forty-three, and five hundred 'and ninety-eight thousand
seven hundred and three, it roamed the desert, putting its simple
Electric trust in rocks, birds, clouds and a form of non-existent
elephant-asparagus, until at last it fetched up here, on this high
rock, overlooking a valley that was not, despite the deep fervour
of the Monk's belief, pink. Not even a little bit.

    Time passed.

Chapter Three...

Time passed.

Susan waited.

The more Susan waited, the more the doorbell didn't ring. Or the phone. She looked at her watch. She felt that now was about the time that she could legitimately begin to feel cross. She was cross already, of course, but that had been in her own time, so to speak. They were well and truly into his time now, and even allowing for traffic, mishaps, and general vagueness and dilatoriness, it was now well over half an hour past the time that he had insisted was the latest time they could possibly afford to leave, so she'd better be ready.

She tried to worry that something terrible had happened to him, but didn't believe it for a moment. Nothing terrible ever happened to him, though she was beginning to think that it was time it damn well did. If nothing terrible happened to him soon maybe she'd do it herself. Now there was an idea.

She threw herself crossly into the armchair and watched the news on television. The news made her cross. She flipped the remote control and watched something on another channel for a bit. She didn't know what it was, but it also made her cross.

Perhaps she should phone. She was damned if she was going to phone. Perhaps if she phoned he would phone her at the same moment and not be able to get through.

She refused to admit that she had even thought that.

Damn him, where was he? Who cared where he was anyway? She didn't, that was for sure.

Three times in a row he'd done this. Three times in a row was enough. She angrily flipped channels one more time. There was a programme about computers and some interesting new developments in the field of things you could do with computers and music.

That was it. That was really it. She knew that she had told herself that that was it only seconds earlier, but this was now the final real ultimate it.

She jumped to her feet and went to the phone, gripping an angry Filofax. She flipped briskly through it and dialled a number.

"Hello, Michael? Yes, it's Susan. Susan Way. You said I should call you if I was free this evening and I said I'd rather be dead in a ditch, remember? Well, I suddenly discover that I am free, absolutely, completely and utterly free, and there isn't a decent ditch for miles around. Make your move while you've got your chance is my advice to you. I'll be at the Tangiers Club in half an hour."

She pulled on her shoes and coat, paused when she remembered that it was Thursday and that she should put a fresh, extra-long tape on the answering machine, and two minutes later was out of the front door. When at last the phone did ring the answering machine said sweetly that Susan Way could not come to the phone just at the moment, but that if the caller would like to leave a message, she would get back to them as soon as possible. Maybe.

Chapter Four...

It was a chill November evening of the old-fashioned type.

The moon looked pale and wan, as if it shouldn't be up on a night like this. It rose unwillingly and hung like an ill spectre. Silhouetted against it, dim and hazy through the dampness which rose from the unwholesome fens, stood the assorted towers and turrets of St Cedd's, Cambridge, a ghostly profusion of buildings thrown up over centuries, medieval next to Victorian, Odeon next to Tudor. Only rising through the mist did they seem remotely to belong to one another.

Between them scurried figures, hurrying from one dim pool of light to another, shivering, leaving wraiths of breath which folded themselves into the cold night behind them.

It was seven o'clock. Many of the figures were heading for the college dining hall which divided First Court from Second Court, and from which warm light, reluctantly, streamed. Two figures in particular seemed ill-matched. One, a young man, was tall, thin and angular; even muffled inside a heavy dark coat he walked a little like an affronted heron.

The other was small, roundish, and moved with an ungainly restlessness, like a number of elderly squirrels trying to escape from a sack. His own age was on the older side of completely indeterminate. If you picked a number at random, he was probably a little older than that, but – well, it was impossible to tell. Certainly his face was heavily lined, and the small amount of hair that escaped from under his red woollen skiing hat was thin, white, and had very much its own ideas about how it wished to arrange itself. He too was muffled inside a heavy coat, but over it he wore a billowing gown with very faded purple trim, the badge of his unique and peculiar academic office.

As they walked the older man was doing all the talking. He was pointing at items of interest along the way, despite the fact that it was too dark to see any of them. The younger man was saying "Ah yes," and "Really? How interesting ..." and "Well, well, well," and "Good heavens." His head bobbed seriously.

They entered, not through the main entrance to the hall, but through a small doorway on the east side of the court. This led to the Senior Combination Room and a dark-panelled anteroom where the Fellows of the college assembled to slap their hands and make "brrrrrr" noises before making their way through their own entrance to the High Table.

They were late and shook off their coats hurriedly. This was complicated for the older man by the necessity first of taking off his professorial gown, and then of putting it back on again once his coat was off, then of stuffing his hat in his coat pocket, then of wondering where he'd put his scarf, and then of realising that he hadn't brought it, then of fishing in his coat pocket for his handkerchief, then of fishing in his other coat pocket for his spectacles, and finally of finding them quite unexpectedly wrapped in his scarf, which it turned out he had brought after all but hadn't been wearing despite the damp and bitter wind blowing in like a witch's breath from across the fens.

He bustled the younger man into the hall ahead of him and they took the last two vacant seats at the High Table, braving a flurry of frowns and raised eyebrows for interrupting the Latin grace to do so.

Hall was full tonight. It was always more popular with the undergraduates in the colder months. More unusually, the hall was candlelit, as it was now only on very few special occasions. Two long, crowded tables stretched off into the glimmering darkness. By candlelight, people's faces were more alive, the hushed sounds of their voices, the clink of cutlery and glasses, seemed more exciting, and in the dark recesses of the great hall,

all the centuries for which it had existed seemed present at once. High Table itself formed a crosspiece at the top, and was raised about a foot above the rest. Since it was a guest night, the table was set on both sides to accommodate the extra numbers, and many diners therefore sat with their backs to the rest of the hall.

"So, young MacDuff," said the Professor once he was seated and flapping his napkin open, "pleasure to see you again, my dear fellow. Glad you could come. No idea what all this is about," he added, peering round the hall in consternation. "All the candles and silver and business. Generally means a special dinner in honour of someone or something no one can remember anything about except that it means better food for a night."

He paused and thought for a moment, and then said, "It seems odd, don't you think, that the quality of the food should vary inversely with the brightness of the lighting. Makes you wonder what culinary heights the kitchen staff could rise to if you confined them to perpetual darkness. Could be worth a try, I think. Got some good vaults in the college that could be turned over to the purpose. I think I showed you round them once, hmmm? Nice brickwork."

All this came as something of a relief to his guest. It was the first indication his host had given that he had the faintest recollection who he was. Professor Urban Chronotis, the Regius Professor of Chronology, or "Reg" as he insisted on being called, had a memory that he himself had once compared to the Queen Alexandra Birdwing Butterfly, in that it was colourful, flitted prettily hither and thither, and was now, alas, almost completely extinct.

When he had telephoned with the invitation a few days previously, he had seemed extremely keen to see his former pupil, and yet when Richard had arrived this evening, a little on the late side, admittedly, the Professor had thrown open the door apparently in anger, had started in surprise on seeing Richard, demanded to know if he was having emotional problems, reacted in annoyance to being reminded gently that it was now ten years since he had been Richard's college tutor, and finally agreed that

Richard had indeed come for dinner, whereupon he, the Professor, had started talking rapidly and at length about the history of the college architecture, a sure sign that his mind was elsewhere entirely.

"Reg" had never actually taught Richard, he had only been his college tutor, which meant in short that he had had charge of his general welfare, told him when the exams were and not to take drugs, and so on. Indeed, it was not entirely clear if Reg had ever taught anybody at all and what, if anything, he would have taught them. His professorship was an obscure one, to say the least, and since he dispensed with his lecturing duties by the simple and time-honoured technique of presenting all his potential students with an exhaustive list of books that he knew for a fact had been out of print for thirty years, then flying into a tantrum if they failed to find them, no one had ever discovered the precise nature of his academic discipline. He had, of course, long ago taken the precaution of removing the only extant copies of the books on his reading list from the university and college libraries, as a result of which he had plenty of time to, well, to do whatever it was he did.

Since Richard had always managed to get on reasonably well with the old fruitcake, he had one day plucked up courage to ask him what, exactly, the Regius Professorship of Chronology was. It had been one of those light summery days when the world seems about to burst with pleasure at simply being itself, and Reg had been in an uncharacteristically forthcoming mood as they had walked over the bridge where the River Cam divided the older parts of the college from the newer.

"Sinecure, my dear fellow, an absolute sinecure," he had beamed. "A small amount of money for a very small, or shall we say non-existent, amount of work. That puts me permanently just ahead of the game, which is a comfortable if frugal place to spend your life. I recommend it." He leaned over the edge of the bridge and started to point out a particular brick that he found interesting.

"But what sort of study is it supposed to be?" Richard had pursued. "Is it history? Physics? Philosophy? What?"

"Well," said Reg, slowly, "since you're interested, the chair was originally instituted by King George III, who, as you know, entertained a number of amusing notions, including the belief that one of the trees in Windsor Great Park was in fact Frederick the Great.

"It was his own appointment, hence 'Regius'. His own idea as well, which is somewhat more unusual."

Sunlight played along the River Cam. People in punts happily shouted at each other to fuck off. Thin natural scientists who had spent months locked away in their rooms growing white and fishlike, emerged blinking into the light. Couples walking along the bank got so excited about the general wonderfulness of it all that they had to pop inside for an hour.

"The poor beleaguered fellow," Reg continued, "George III, I mean, was, as you may know, obsessed with time. Filled the palace with clocks. Wound them incessantly. Sometimes would get up in the middle of the night and prowl round the palace in his nightshirt winding clocks. He was very concerned that time continued to go forward, you see. So many terrible things had occurred in his life that he was terrified that any of them might happen again if time were ever allowed to slip backwards even for a moment. A very understandable fear, especially if you're barking mad, as I'm afraid to say, with the very greatest sympathy for the poor fellow, he undoubtedly was. He appointed me, or rather I should say, my office, this professorship, you understand, the post that I am now privileged to hold to – where was I? Oh yes. He instituted this, er, Chair of Chronology to see if there was any particular reason why one thing happened after another and if there was any way of stopping it. Since the answers to the three questions were, I knew immediately, yes, no, and maybe, I realised I could then take the rest of my career off."

"And your predecessors?"

"Er, were much of the same mind."

"But who were they?"

"Who were they? Well, splendid fellows of course, splendid to a man. Remind me to tell you about them some day. See that brick? Wordsworth was once sick on that brick. Great man."

All that had been about ten years ago.

Richard glanced around the great dining hall to see what had changed in the time, and the answer was, of course, absolutely nothing. In the dark heights, dimly seen by the flickering candlelight, were the ghostly portraits of prime ministers, archbishops, political reformers and poets, any of whom might, in their day, have been sick on that same brick.

"Well," said Reg, in a loudly confidential whisper, as if introducing the subject of nipple-piercing in a nunnery, "I hear you've suddenly done very well for yourself, at last, hmmm?"

"Er, well, yes, in fact," said Richard, who was as surprised at the fact as anybody else, "yes, I have."

Around the table several gazes stiffened on him.

"Computers," he heard somebody whisper dismissively to a neighbour further down the table. The stiff gazes relaxed again, and turned away.

"Excellent," said Reg. "I'm so pleased for you, so pleased.

"Tell me," he went on, and it was a moment before Richard realised that the Professor wasn't talking to him any more, but had turned to the right to address his other neighbour, "what's all this about, this," he flourished a vague hand over the candles and college silver, "… stuff?"

His neighbour, an elderly wizened figure, turned very slowly and looked at him as if he was rather annoyed at being raised from the dead like this.

"Coleridge," he said in a thin rasp, "it's the Coleridge Dinner, you old fool." He turned very slowly back until he was facing the front again. His name was Cawley, he was a Professor of Archaeology and Anthropology, and it was frequently said of him, behind his back, that he regarded it not so much as a serious academic study, more as a chance to relive his childhood.

"Ah, is it," murmured Reg, "is it?" and turned back to Richard. "It's the Coleridge Dinner," he said knowledgeably. "Coleridge was a member of the college, you know," he added after a moment. "Coleridge. Samuel Taylor. Poet. I expect you've heard of him. This is his Dinner. Well, not literally, of course. It would be cold by now." Silence. "Here, have some salt."

"Er, thank you, I think I'll wait," said Richard, surprised. There was no food on the table yet.

"Go on, take it," insisted the Professor, proffering him the heavy silver salt cellar.

Richard blinked in bemusement but with an interior shrug he reached to take it. In the moment that he blinked, however, the salt cellar had completely vanished.

He started back in surprise.

"Good one, eh?" said Reg as he retrieved the missing cruet from behind the ear of his deathly right-hand neighbour, provoking a surprisingly girlish giggle from somewhere else at the table. Reg smiled impishly. "Very irritating habit, I know. It's next on my list for giving up after smoking and leeches."

Well, that was another thing that hadn't changed. Some people pick their noses, others habitually beat up old ladies on the streets. Reg's vice was a harmless if peculiar one – an addiction to childish conjuring tricks. Richard remembered the first time he had been to see Reg with a problem – it was only the normal *Angst* that periodically takes undergraduates into its grip, particularly when they have essays to write, but it had seemed a dark and savage weight at the time. Reg had sat and listened to his outpourings with a deep frown of concentration, and when at last Richard had finished, he pondered seriously, stroked his chin a lot, and at last leaned forward and looked him in the eye.

"I suspect that your problem," he said, "is that you have too many paper clips up your nose."

Richard stared at him.

"Allow me to demonstrate," said Reg, and leaning across the desk he pulled from Richard's nose a chain of eleven paper clips and a small rubber swan.

"Ah, the real culprit," he said, holding up the swan. "They come in cereal packets, you know, and cause no end of trouble. Well, I'm glad we've had this little chat, my dear fellow. Please feel free to disturb me again if you have any more such problems."

Needless to say, Richard didn't.

Richard glanced around the table to see if there was anybody else he recognised from his time at the college.

Two places away to the left was the don who had been Richard's Director of Studies in English, who showed no signs of recognising him at all. This was hardly surprising since Richard had spent his three years here assiduously avoiding him, often to the extent of growing a beard and pretending to be someone else.

Next to him was a man whom Richard had never managed to identify. Neither, in fact, had anyone else. He was thin and vole-like and had the most extraordinarily long bony nose – it really was very, very long and bony indeed. In fact it looked a lot like the controversial keel which had helped the Australians win the America's Cup in 1983, and this resemblance had been much remarked upon at the time, though not of course to his face. No one had said anything to his face at all.

No one.

Ever.

Anyone meeting him for the first time was too startled and embarrassed by his nose to speak, and the second time was worse because of the first time, and so on. Years had gone by now, seventeen in all. In all that time he had been cocooned in silence. In hall it had long been the habit of the college servants to position a separate set of salt, pepper and mustard on either side of him, since no one could ask him to pass them, and to ask someone sitting on the other side of him was not only rude but completely impossible because of his nose being in the way.

The other odd thing about him was a series of gestures he made and repeated regularly throughout every evening. They consisted of tapping each of the fingers of his left hand in order, and then one of the fingers of his right hand. He would then occasionally tap some other part of his body, a knuckle, an elbow or a knee. Whenever he was forced to stop this by the requirements of eating he would start blinking each of his eyes instead, and occasionally nodding. No one, of course, had ever dared to ask him why he did this, though all were consumed with curiosity.

Richard couldn't see who was sitting beyond him.

In the other direction, beyond Reg's deathly neighbour, was Watkin, the Classics Professor, a man of terrifying dryness and oddity. His heavy rimless glasses were almost solid cubes of glass within which his eyes appeared to lead independent existences like goldfish. His nose was straight enough and ordinary, but beneath it he wore the same beard as Clint Eastwood. His eyes gazed swimmingly around the table as he selected who was going to be spoken at tonight. He had thought that his prey might be one of the guests, the newly appointed Head of Radio Three, who was sitting opposite – but unfortunately he had already been ensnared by the Music Director of the college and a Professor of Philosophy. These two were busy explaining to the harassed man that the phrase "too much Mozart" was, given any reasonable definition of those three words, an inherently self-contradictory expression, and that any sentence which contained such a phrase would be thereby rendered meaningless and could not, consequently, be advanced as part of an argument in favour of any given programme-scheduling strategy. The poor man was already beginning to grip his cutlery too tightly. His eyes darted about desperately looking for rescue, and made the mistake of lighting on those of Watkin.

"Good evening," said Watkin with smiling charm, nodding in the most friendly way, and then letting his gaze settle glassily on to his bowl of newly arrived soup, from which position it would not allow itself to be moved. Yet. Let the bugger suffer a little. He wanted the rescue to be worth at least a good half-dozen radio talk fees.

Beyond Watkin, Richard suddenly discovered the source of the little girlish giggle that had greeted Reg's conjuring trick. Astonishingly enough it was a little girl. She was about eight years old with blonde hair and a glum look. She was sitting occasionally kicking pettishly at the table leg.

"Who's that?" Richard asked Reg in surprise.

"Who's what?" Reg asked Richard in surprise.

Richard inclined a finger surreptitiously in her direction. "The girl," he whispered, "the very, very little girl. Is it some new maths professor?"

Reg peered round at her. "Do you know," he said in astonishment, "I haven't the faintest idea. Never known anything like it. How extraordinary."

At that moment the problem was solved by the man from the BBC, who suddenly wrenched himself out of the logical half-nelson into which his neighbours had got him, and told the girl off for kicking the table. She stopped kicking the table, and instead kicked the air with redoubled vigour. He told her to try and enjoy herself, so she kicked him. This did something to bring a brief glimmer of pleasure into her glum evening, but it didn't last. Her father briefly shared with the table at large his feelings about baby-sitters who let people down, but nobody felt able to run with the topic.

"A major season of Buxtehude," resumed the Director of Music, "is of course clearly long overdue. I'm sure you'll be looking forward to remedying this situation at the first opportunity."

"Oh, er, yes," replied the girl's father, spilling his soup, "er, that is ... he's not the same one as Gluck, is he?"

The little girl kicked the table leg again. When her father looked sternly at her, she put her head on one side and mouthed a question at him.

"Not now," he insisted at her as quietly as he could.

"When, then?"

"Later. Maybe. Later, we'll see."

She hunched grumpily back in her seat. "You always say later," she mouthed at him.

"Poor child," murmured Reg. "There isn't a don at this table who doesn't behave exactly like that inside. Ah, thank you." Their soup arrived, distracting his attention, and Richard's.

"So tell me," said Reg, after they had both had a couple of

spoonsful and arrived independently at the same conclusion, that it was not a taste explosion, "what you've been up to, my dear chap. Something to do with computers, I understand, and also to do with music. I thought you read English when you were here – though only, I realise, in your spare time." He looked at Richard significantly over the rim of his soup spoon. "Now wait," he interrupted before Richard even had a chance to start, "don't I vaguely remember that you had some sort of computer when you were here? When was it? 1977?"

"Well, what we called a computer in 1977 was really a kind of electric abacus, but ..."

"Oh, now, don't underestimate the abacus," said Reg. "In skilled hands it's a very sophisticated calculating device. Furthermore it requires no power, can be made with any materials you have to hand, and never goes bing in the middle of an important piece of work."

"So an electric one would be particularly pointless," said Richard.

"True enough," conceded Reg.

"There really wasn't a lot this machine could do that you couldn't do yourself in half the time with a lot less trouble," said Richard, "but it was, on the other hand, very good at be'ng a slow and dim-witted pupil."

Reg looked at him quizzically.

"I had no idea they were supposed to be in short supply," he said. "I could hit a dozen with a bread roll from where I'm sitting."

"I'm sure. But look at it this way. What really is the point of trying to teach anything to anybody?"

This question seemed to provoke a murmur of sympathetic approval from up and down the table.

Richard continued, "What I mean is that if you really want to understand something, the best way is to try and explain it to someone else. That forces you to sort it out in your own mind. And the more slow and dim-witted your pupil, the more you have to break things down into more and more simple ideas. And that's really the essence of programming. By the time you've sorted out a complicated idea into little steps that even a stupid machine can deal with, you've certainly learned something about it yourself. The teacher usually learns more than the pupil. Isn't that true?"

"It would be hard to learn much less than my pupils," came a low growl from somewhere on the table, "without undergoing a pre-frontal lobotomy."

"So I used to spend days struggling to write essays on this 16K machine that would have taken a couple of hours on a typewriter, but what was fascinating to me was the process of trying to explain to the machine what it was I wanted it to do. I virtually wrote my own word processor in BASIC. A simple search and replace routine would take about three hours."

"I forget, did you ever get any essays done at all?"

"Well, not as such. No actual essays, but the reasons why not were absolutely fascinating. For instance, I discovered that ..."

He broke off, laughing at himself.

"I was also playing keyboards in a rock group, of course," he added. "That didn't help."

"Now, that I didn't know," said Reg. "Your past has murkier things in it than I dreamed possible. A quality, I might add, that it shares with this soup." He wiped his mouth with his napkin very carefully. "I must go and have a word with the kitchen staff one day. I would like to be sure that they are keeping the right bits and throwing the proper bits away. So. A rock group, you say. Well, well, well. Good heavens."

"Yes," said Richard. "We called ourselves The Reasonably Good Band, but in fact we weren't. Our intention was to be the Beatles of the early eighties, but we got much better financial and legal advice than the Beatles ever did, which was basically 'Don't bother', so we didn't. I left Cambridge and starved for three years."

"But didn't I bump into you during that period," said Reg, "and you said you were doing very well?"

"As a road sweeper, yes. There was an awful lot of mess on the roads. More than enough, I felt, to support an entire career.

However, I got the sack for sweeping the mess on to another sweeper's patch."

Reg shook his head. "The wrong career for you, I'm sure. There are plenty of vocations where such behaviour would ensure rapid preferment."

"I tried a few – none of them much grander, though. And I kept none of them very long, because I was always too tired to do them properly. I'd be found asleep slumped over the chicken sheds or filing cabinets – depending on what the job was. Been up all night with the computer you see, teaching it to play 'Three Blind Mice'. It was an important goal for me."

"I'm sure," agreed Reg. "Thank you," he said to the college servant who took his half-finished plate of soup from him, "thank you very much. 'Three Blind Mice', eh? Good. Good. So no doubt you succeeded eventually, and this accounts for your present celebrated status. Yes?"

"Well, there's a bit more to it than that."

"I feared there might be. Pity you didn't bring it with you, though. It might have cheered up the poor young lady who is currently having our dull and crusty company forced upon her. A swift burst of 'Three Blind Mice' would probably do much to revive her spirits." He leaned forward to look past his two right-hand neighbours at the girl, who was still sitting sagging in her chair.

"Hello," he said.

She looked up in surprise, and then dropped her eyes shyly, swinging her legs again.

"Which do you think is worse," enquired Reg, "the soup or the company?"

She gave a tiny, reluctant laugh and shrugged, still looking down.

"I think you're wise not to commit yourself at this stage," continued Reg. "Myself, I'm waiting to see the carrots before I make any judgments. They've been boiling them since the weekend, but I fear it may not be enough. The only thing that could possibly be worse than the carrots is Watkin. He's the man with the silly glasses sitting between us. My name's Reg, by the way. Come over and kick me when you have a moment."

The girl giggled and glanced up at Watkin, who stiffened and made an appallingly unsuccessful attempt to smile good-naturedly.

"*Well*, little girl," he said to her awkwardly, and she had desperately to suppress a hoot of laughter at his glasses. Little conversation therefore ensued, but the girl had an ally, and began to enjoy herself a tiny little bit. Her father gave her a relieved smile.

Reg turned back to Richard, who said, suddenly, "Do you have any family?"

"Er ... no," said Reg, quietly. "But tell me. After 'Three Blind Mice', what then?"

"Well, to cut a long story short, Reg, I ended up working for WayForward Technologies ..."

"Ah, yes, the famous Mr Way. Tell me, what's he like?"

Richard was always faintly annoyed by this question, probably because he was asked it so often.

"Both better and worse than he's represented in the press. I like him a lot, actually. Like any driven man he can be a bit trying at times, but I've known him since the very early days of the company when neither he nor I had a bean to our names. He's fine. It's just that it's a good idea not to let him have your phone number unless you possess an industrial-grade answering machine."

"What? Why's that?"

"Well, he's one of those people who can only think when he's talking. When he has ideas, he has to talk them out to whoever will listen. Or, if the people themselves are not available, which is increasingly the case, their answering machines will do just as well. He just phones them up and talks at them. He has one secretary whose sole job is to collect tapes from people he might have phoned, transcribe them, sort them and give him the edited text the next day in a blue folder."

"A blue one, eh? "

"Ask me why he doesn't simply use a tape recorder," said Richard with a shrug.

Reg considered this. "I expect he doesn't use a tape recorder because he doesn't like talking to himself," he said. "There is a logic there. Of a kind."

He took a mouthful of his newly arrived *porc au poivre* and ruminated on it for a while before gently laying his knife and fork aside again for the moment.

"So what," he said at last, "is the role of young MacDuff in all this?"

"Well, Gordon assigned me to write a major piece of software for the Apple Macintosh. Financial spreadsheet, accounting, that sort of thing, powerful, easy to use, lots of graphics. I asked him exactly what he wanted in it, and he just said, 'Everything. I want the top piece of all-singing, all-dancing business software for that machine.' And being of a slightly whimsical turn of mind I took him literally.

"You see, a pattern of numbers can represent anything you like, can be used to map any surface, or modulate any dynamic process – and so on. And any set of company accounts are, in the end, just a pattern of numbers. So I sat down and wrote a program that'll take those numbers and do what you like with them. If you just want a bar graph it'll do them as a bar graph, if you want them as a pie chart or scatter graph it'll do them as a pie chart or scatter graph. If you want dancing girls jumping out of the pie chart in order to distract attention from the figures the pie chart actually represents, then the program will do that as well. Or you can turn your figures into, for instance, a flock of seagulls, and the formation they fly in and the way in which the wings of each gull beat will be determined by the performance of each division of your company. Great for producing animated corporate logos that actually *mean* something.

"But the silliest feature of all was that if you wanted your company accounts represented as a piece of music, it could do that as well. Well, I thought it was silly. The corporate world went bananas over it."

Reg regarded him solemnly from over a piece of carrot poised delicately on his fork in front of him, but did not interrupt.

"You see, any aspect of a piece of music can be expressed as a sequence or pattern of numbers," enthused Richard. "Numbers can express the pitch of notes, the length of notes, patterns of pitches and lengths ..."

"You mean tunes," said Reg. The carrot had not moved yet.

Richard grinned.

"Tunes would be a very good word for it. I must remember that."

"It would help you speak more easily." Reg returned the carrot to his plate, untasted. "And this software did well, then?" he asked.

"Not so much here. The yearly accounts of most British companies emerged sounding like the Dead March from *Saul*, but in Japan they went for it like a pack of rats. It produced lots of cheery company anthems that started well, but if you were going to criticise you'd probably say that they tended to get a bit loud and squeaky at the end. Did spectacular business in the States, which was the main thing, commercially. Though the thing that's interesting me most now is what happens if you leave the accounts out of it. Turn the numbers that represent the way a swallow's wings beat directly into music. What would you hear? Not the sound of cash registers, according to Gordon."

"Fascinating," said Reg, "quite fascinating," and popped the carrot at last into his mouth. He turned and leaned forward to speak to his new girlfriend.

"Watkin loses," he pronounced. "The carrots have achieved a new all-time low. Sorry, Watkin, but awful as you are, the carrots, I'm afraid, are world-beaters."

The girl giggled more easily than last time and she smiled at him. Watkin was trying to take all this good-naturedly, but it was clear as his eyes swam at Reg that he was more used to discomfiting than being discomfited.

"Please, Daddy, can I now?" With her new-found, if slight, confidence, the girl had also found a voice.

"Later," insisted her father.

"This is already later. I've been timing it."

"Well ..." He hesitated, and was lost.

"We've been to Greece," announced the girl in a small but awed voice.

"Ah, have you indeed," said Watkin, with a little nod. "Well, well. Anywhere in particular, or just Greece generally?"

"Patmos," she said decisively. "It was beautiful. I think Patmos is the most beautiful place in the whole world. Except the ferry never came when it said it would. Never, ever. I timed it. We missed our flight but I didn't mind."

"Ah, Patmos, I see," said Watkin, who was clearly roused by the news. "Well, what you have to understand, young lady, is that the Greeks, not content with dominating the culture of the Classical world, are also responsible for the greatest, some would say the only, work of true creative imagination produced this century as well. I refer of course to the Greek ferry timetables. A work of the sublimest fiction. Anyone who has travelled in the Aegean will confirm this. Hmm, yes. I think so."

She frowned at him.

"I found a pot," she said.

"Probably nothing," interrupted her father hastily. "You know the way it is. Everyone who goes to Greece for the first time thinks they've found a pot, don't they? Ha, ha."

There were general nods. This was true. Irritating, but true.

"I found it in the harbour," she said, "in the water. While we were waiting for the damn ferry."

"Sarah! I've told you ..."

"It's just what you called it. And worse. You called it words I didn't think you knew. Anyway, I thought that if everyone here was meant to be so clever, then someone would be able to tell me if it was a proper ancient Greek thing or not. I think it's *very* old. Will you please let them see it, Daddy?"

Her father shrugged hopelessly and started to fish about under his chair.

"Did you know, young lady," said Watkin to her, "that the

Book of Revelation was written on Patmos? It was indeed. By
Saint John the Divine, as you know. To me it shows very clear
signs of having been written while waiting for a ferry. Oh, yes, I
think so. It starts off, doesn't it, with that kind of dreaminess you
get when you're killing time, getting bored, you know, just
making things up, and then gradually grows to a sort of climax of
hallucinatory despair. I find that very suggestive. Perhaps you
should write a paper on it." He nodded at her.

She looked at him as if he were mad.

"Well, here it is," said her father, plonking the thing down on
the table. "Just a pot, as you see. She's only six," he added with
a grim smile, "aren't you, dear?"

"Seven," said Sarah.

The pot was quite small, about five inches high and four inches
across at its widest point. The body was almost spherical, with a
very narrow neck extending about an inch above the body. The
neck and about half of the surface area were encrusted with hard-
caked earth, but the parts of the pot that could be seen were of a
rough, ruddy texture.

Sarah took it and thrust it into the hands of the don sitting on
her right.

"You look clever," she said. "Tell me what you think."

The don took it, and turned it over with a slightly supercilious
air. "I'm sure if you scraped away the mud from the bottom," he
remarked wittily, "it would probably say 'Made in Birmingham'."

"That old, eh?" said Sarah's father with a forced laugh. "Long
time since anything was made there."

"Anyway," said the don, "not my field, I'm a molecular
biologist. Anyone else want to have a look?"

This question was not greeted with wild yelps of enthusiasm,
but nevertheless the pot was passed from hand to hand around the
far end of the table in a desultory fashion. It was goggled at
through pebble glasses, peered at through horn-rims, gazed at
over half-moons, and squinted at by someone who had left his
glasses in his other suit, which he very much feared had now
gone to the cleaner's. No one seemed to know how old it was, or

to care very much. The young girl's face began to grow downhearted again.

"Sour lot," said Reg to Richard. He picked up a silver salt cellar again and held it up.

"Young lady," he said, leaning forward to address her.

"Oh, not again, you old fool," muttered the aged archaeologist Cawley, sitting back and putting his hands over his ears.

"Young lady," repeated Reg, "regard this simple silver salt cellar. Regard this simple hat."

"You haven't got a hat," said the girl sulkily.

"Oh," said Reg, "a moment please," and he went and fetched his woolly red one.

"Regard," he said again, "this simple silver salt cellar. Regard this simple woolly hat. I put the salt cellar in the hat, thus, and I pass the hat to you. The next part of the trick, dear lady ... is up to you."

He handed the hat to her, past their two intervening neighbours, Cawley and Watkin. She took the hat and looked inside it.

"Where's it gone?" she asked, staring into the hat.

"It's wherever you put it," said Reg.

"Oh," said Sarah, "I see. Well ... that wasn't very good."

Reg shrugged. "A humble trick, but it gives me pleasure," he said, and turned back to Richard. "Now, what were we talking about?"

Richard looked at him with a slight sense of shock. He knew that the Professor had always been prone to sudden and erratic mood swings, but it was as if all the warmth had drained out of him in an instant. He now wore the same distracted expression Richard had seen on his face when first he had arrived at his door that evening, apparently completely unexpected. Reg seemed then to sense that Richard was taken aback and quickly reassembled a smile.

"My dear chap!" he said. "My dear chap! My dear, dear chap! What was I saying?"

"Er, you were saying 'My dear chap'."

"Yes, but I feel sure it was a prelude to something. A sort of short toccata on the theme of what a splendid fellow you are prior to introducing the main subject of my discourse, the nature of which I currently forget. You have no idea what I was about to say?"

"No."

"Oh. Well, I suppose I should be pleased. If everyone knew exactly what I was going to say, then there would be no point in my saying it, would there? Now, how's our young guest's pot doing?"

In fact it had reached Watkin, who pronounced himself no expert on what the ancients had made for themselves to drink out of, only on what they had written as a result. He said that Cawley was the one to whose knowledge and experience they should all bow, and attempted to give the pot to him.

"I said," he repeated, "yours was the knowledge and experience to which we should bow. Oh, for heaven's sake, take your hands off your ears and have a look at the thing."

Gently, but firmly, he drew Cawley's right hand from his ear, explained the situation to him once again, and handed him the pot. Cawley gave it a cursory but clearly expert examination.

"Yes," he said, "about two hundred years old, I would think. Very rough. Very crude example of its type. Utterly without value, of course."

He put it down peremptorily and gazed off into the old minstrel gallery, which appeared to anger him for some reason.

The effect on Sarah was immediate. Already discouraged, she was thoroughly downcast by this. She bit her lip and threw herself back against her chair, feeling once again thoroughly out of place and childish. Her father gave her a warning look about misbehaving, and then apologised for her again.

"Well, Buxtehude," he hurried on to say, "yes, good old Buxtehude. We'll have to see what we can do. Tell me ..."

"Young lady," interrupted a voice, hoarse with astonishment, "you are clearly a magician and enchantress of prodigious powers!"

All eyes turned to Reg, the old show-off. He was gripping the pot and staring at it with manic fascination. He turned his eyes slowly to the little girl, as if for the first time assessing the power of a feared adversary.

"I bow to you," he whispered. "I, unworthy though I am to speak in the presence of such a power as yours, beg leave to congratulate you on one of the finest feats of the conjurer's art it has been my privilege to witness!"

Sarah stared at him with widening eyes.

"May I show these people what you have wrought?" he asked earnestly.

Very faintly she nodded, and he fetched her formerly precious, but now sadly discredited, pot a sharp rap on the table.

It split into two irregular parts, the caked clay with which it was surrounded falling in jagged shards on the table. One side of the pot fell away, leaving the rest standing.

Sarah's eyes goggled at the stained and tarnished but clearly recognisable silver college salt cellar standing jammed in the remains of the pot.

"Stupid old fool," muttered Cawley.

After the general disparagement and condemnation of this cheap parlour trick had died down – none of which could dim the awe in Sarah's eyes – Reg turned to Richard and said, idly:

"Who was that friend of yours when you were here, do you ever see him? Chap with an odd East European name. Svlad something. Svlad Cjelli. Remember the fellow?"

Richard looked at him blankly for a moment.

"Svlad?" he said. "Oh, you mean Dirk. Dirk Cjelli. No. I never stayed in touch. I've bumped into him a couple of times in the street but that's all. I think he changes his name from time to time. Why do you ask?"

Chapter Five...

High on his rocky promontory the Electric Monk continued to sit on a horse which was going quietly and uncomplainingly spare. From under its rough woven cowl the Monk gazed unblinkingly down into the valley, with which it was having a problem, but the problem was a new and hideous one to the Monk, for it was this – Doubt.

He never suffered it for long, but when he did, it gnawed at the very root of his being.

The day was hot; the sun stood in an empty hazy sky and beat down upon the grey rocks and the scrubby, parched grass. Nothing moved, not even the Monk. But strange things were beginning to fizz in its brain, as they did from time to time when a piece of data became misaddressed as it passed through its input buffer.

But then the Monk began to believe, fitfully and nervously at first, but then with a great searing white flame of belief which overturned all previous beliefs, including the stupid one about the valley being pink, that somewhere down in the valley, about a mile from where he was sitting, there would shortly open up a mysterious doorway into a strange and distant world, a doorway through which he might enter. An astounding idea.

Astoundingly enough, however, on this one occasion he was perfectly right.

The horse sensed that something was up.

It pricked up its ears and gently shook its head. It had gone into a sort of trance looking at the same clump of rocks for so long, and was on the verge of imagining them to be pink itself. It shook its head a little harder.

A slight twitch on the reins, and a prod from the Monk's heels, and they were off, picking their way carefully down the rocky incline. The way was difficult. Much of it was loose shale – loose brown and grey shale, with the occasional brown and green plant clinging to a precarious existence on it. The Monk noticed this without embarrassment. It was an older, wiser Monk now, and had put childish things behind it. Pink valleys, hermaphrodite tables, these were all natural stages through which one had to pass on the path to true enlightenment.

The sun beat hard on them. The Monk wiped the sweat and dust off its face and paused, leaning forward on the horse's neck. It peered down through the shimmering heat haze at a large outcrop of rock which stood out on to the floor of the valley. There, behind that outcrop, was where the Monk thought, or rather passionately believed to the core of its being, the door would appear. It tried to focus more closely, but the details of the view swam confusingly in the hot rising air.

As it sat back in its saddle, and was about the prod the horse onward, it suddenly noticed a rather odd thing.

On a flattish wall of rock nearby, in fact so nearby that the Monk was surprised not to have noticed it before, was a large painting. The painting was crudely drawn, though not without a certain stylish sweep of line, and seemed very old, possibly very, very old indeed. The paint was faded, chipped and patchy, and it was difficult to discern with any clarity what the picture was. The Monk approached the picture more closely. It looked like a primitive hunting scene.

The group of purple, multi-limbed creatures were clearly early hunters. They carried rough spears, and were in hot pursuit of a large horned and armoured creature, which appeared to have been wounded in the hunt already. The colours were now so dim as to be almost non-existent. In fact, all that could be clearly seen was the white of the hunters' teeth, which seemed to shine with a whiteness whose lustre was undimmed by the passage of what must have been many thousands of years. In fact they even put the Monk's own teeth to shame, and he had cleaned them only that morning.

The Monk had seen paintings like this before, but only in pictures or on the TV, never in real life. They were usually to be found in caves where they were protected from the elements, otherwise they would not have survived.

The Monk looked more carefully at the immediate environs of the rock wall and noticed that, though not exactly in a cave, it was nevertheless protected by a large overhang and was well sheltered from the wind and rain. Odd, though, that it should have managed to last so long. Odder still that it should appear not to have been discovered. Such cave paintings as there were were all famous and familiar images, but this was not one that he had ever seen before.

Perhaps this was a dramatic and historic find he had made. Perhaps if he were to return to the city and announce this discovery he would be welcomed back, given a new motherboard after all and allowed to believe – to believe – believe what? He paused, blinked, and shook his head to clear a momentary system error.

He pulled himself up short.

He believed in a door. He must find that door. The door was the way to ... to ...

The Door was The Way.

Good.

Capital letters were always the best way of dealing with things you didn't have a good answer to.

Brusquely he tugged the horse's head round and urged it onward and downward. Within a few minutes more of tricky manoeuvring they had reached the valley floor, and he was momentarily disconcerted to discover that the fine top layer of dust that had settled on the brown parched earth was indeed a very pale brownish pink, particularly on the banks of the sluggish trickle of mud which was all that remained, in the hot season, of the river that flowed through the valley when the rains came. He dismounted and bent down to feel the pink dust and run it through his fingers. It was very fine and soft and felt pleasant as he rubbed it on his skin. It was about the same colour, perhaps a little paler.

The horse was looking at him. He realised, a little belatedly perhaps, that the horse must be extremely thirsty. He was extremely thirsty himself, but had tried to keep his mind off it. He unbuckled the water flask from the saddle. It was pathetically light. He unscrewed the top and took one single swig. Then he poured a little into his cupped hand and offered it to the horse, who slurped at it greedily and briefly.

The horse looked at him again.

The Monk shook his head sadly, resealed the bottle and replaced it. He knew, in that small part of his mind where he kept factual and logical information, that it would not last much longer, and that, without it, neither would they. It was only his Belief that kept him going, currently his Belief in The Door.

He brushed the pink dust from his rough habit, and then stood looking at the rocky outcrop, a mere hundred yards distant. He looked at it not without a slight, tiny trepidation. Although the major part of his mind was firm in its eternal and unshakeable Belief that there would be a Door behind the outcrop, and that the Door would be The Way, yet the tiny part of his brain that understood about the water bottle could not help but recall past disappointments and sounded a very tiny but jarring note of caution.

If he elected not to go and see The Door for himself, then he could continue to believe in it forever. It would be the lodestone of his life (what little was left of it, said the part of his brain that knew about the water bottle).

If on the other hand he went to pay his respects to the Door and it wasn't there ... what then?

The horse whinnied impatiently.

The answer, of course, was very simple. He had a whole board of circuits for dealing with exactly this problem, in fact this was the very heart of his function. He would continue to believe in it whatever the facts turned out to be, what else was the meaning of Belief?

The Door would still be there, even if the door was not.

He pulled himself together. The Door would be there, and he must now go to it, because The Door was The Way.

Instead of remounting his horse, he led it. The Way was but a short way, and he should enter the presence of the Door in humility.

He walked, brave and erect, with solemn slowness. He approached the rocky outcrop. He reached it. He turned the corner. He looked.

The Door was there.

The horse, it must be said, was quite surprised.

The Monk fell to his knees in awe and bewilderment. So braced was he for dealing with the disappointment that was habitually his lot that, though he would never know to admit it, he was completely unprepared for this. He stared at The Door in sheer, blank system error.

It was a door such as he had never seen before. All the doors he knew were great steel-reinforced things, because of all the video recorders and dishwashers that were kept behind them, plus of course all the expensive Electric Monks that were needed to believe in it all. This one was simple, wooden and small, about his own size. A Monk-size door, painted white, with a single, slightly dented brass knob slightly less than halfway up one side. It was set simply in the rock face, with no explanation as to its origin or purpose.

Hardly knowing how he dared, the poor startled Monk staggered to his feet and, leading his horse, walked nervously forward towards it. He reached out and touched it. He was so startled when no alarms went off that he jumped back. He touched it again, more firmly this time.

He let his hand drop slowly to the handle – again, no alarms. He waited to be sure, and then he turned it, very, very gently. He felt a mechanism release. He held his breath. Nothing. He drew the door towards him, and it came easily. He looked inside, but the interior was so dim in contrast with the desert sun outside that he could see nothing. At last, almost dead with wonder, he entered, pulling the horse in after him.

A few minutes later, a figure that had been sitting out of sight around the next outcrop of rock finished rubbing dust on his face, stood up, stretched his limbs and made his way back towards the door, patting his clothes as he did so.

Chapter Six...

"In Xanadu did Kubla Khan
    A stately pleasure-dome decree:"

The reader clearly belonged to the school of thought which holds
that a sense of the seriousness or greatness of a poem is best
imparted by reading it in a silly voice. He soared and swooped at
the words until they seemed to duck and run for cover.

"Where Alph, the sacred river ran
    Through caverns measureless to man
        Down to a sunless sea."

Richard relaxed back into his seat. The words were very, very
familiar to him, as they could not help but be to any English
graduate of St Cedd's College, and they settled easily into his
mind.

The association of the college with Coleridge was taken very
seriously indeed, despite the man's well-known predilection for
certain recreational pharmaceuticals under the influence of which
this, his greatest work, was composed, in a dream.

The entire manuscript was lodged in the safe-keeping of the
college library, and it was from this itself, on the regular occasion
of the Coleridge Dinner, that the poem was read.

"So twice five miles of fertile ground
    With walls and towers were girdled round:
    And there were gardens bright with sinuous rills,
    Where blossomed many an incense-bearing tree;

> And here were forests ancient as the hills,
> Enfolding sunny spots of greenery."

Richard wondered how long it took. He glanced sideways at his former Director of Studies and was disturbed by the sturdy purposefulness of his reading posture. The singsong voice irritated him at first, but after a while it began to lull him instead, and he watched a rivulet of wax seeping over the edge of a candle that was burning low now and throwing a guttering light over the carnage of dinner.

> "But oh! that deep romantic chasm which slanted
> Down the green hill athwart a cedarn cover!
> A savage place! as holy and enchanted
> As e'er beneath a waning moon was haunted
> By woman wailing for her demon-lover!"

The small quantities of claret that he had allowed himself during the course of the meal seeped warmly through his veins, and soon his own mind began to wander, and provoked by Reg's question earlier in the meal, he wondered what had lately become of his former ... was friend the word? He seemed more like a succession of extraordinary events than a person. The idea of him actually having friends as such seemed not so much unlikely, more a sort of mismatching of concepts, like the idea of the Suez crisis popping out for a bun.

Svlad Cjelli. Popularly known as Dirk, though, again, "popular" was hardly right. Notorious, certainly; sought after, endlessly speculated about, those too were true. But popular? Only in the sense that a serious accident on the motorway might be popular – everyone slows down to have a good look, but no one will get too close to the flames. Infamous was more like it. Svlad Cjelli, infamously known as Dirk.

He was rounder than the average undergraduate and wore more hats. That is to say, there was just the one hat which he habitually wore, but he wore it with a passion that was rare in one so young. The hat was dark red and round, with a very flat brim, and it appeared to move as if balanced on gimbals, which ensured its perfect horizontality at all times, however its owner moved his head. As a hat it was a remarkable rather than entirely successful piece of personal decoration. It would make an elegant adornment, stylish, shapely and flattering, if the wearer were a small bedside lamp, but not otherwise.

People gravitated around him, drawn in by the stories he denied about himself, but what the source of these stories might be, if not his own denials, was never entirely clear.

The tales had to do with the psychic powers that he'd supposedly inherited from his mother's side of the family who, he claimed, had lived at the smarter end of Transylvania. That is to say, he didn't make any such claim at all, and said it was the most absurd nonsense. He strenuously denied that there were bats of any kind at all in his family and threatened to sue anybody who put about such malicious fabrications, but he affected nevertheless to wear a large and flappy leather coat, and had one of those machines in his room which are supposed to help cure bad backs if you hang upside down from them. He would allow people to discover him hanging from this machine at all kinds of odd hours of the day, and more particularly of the night, expressly so that he could vigorously deny that it had any significance whatsoever.

By means of an ingenious series of strategically deployed denials of the most exciting and exotic things, he was able to create the myth that he was a psychic, mystic, telepathic, fey, clairvoyant, psychosassic vampire bat.

What did "psychosassic" mean?

It was his own word and he vigorously denied that it meant anything at all.

> "And from this chasm, with ceaseless turmoil seething,
>   As if this earth in fast thick pants were breathing,
>   A mighty fountain momently was forced:
>   Amid whose swift half-intermitted burst
>   Huge fragments vaulted ..."

Dirk had also been perpetually broke. This would change.

It was his room-mate who started it, a credulous fellow called

Mander, who, if the truth were known, had probably been specially selected by Dirk for his credulity.

Steve Mander noticed that if ever Dirk went to bed drunk he would talk in his sleep. Not only that, but the sort of things he would say in his sleep would be things like, "The opening up of trade routes to the mumble mumble burble was the turning point for the growth of empire in the snore footle mumble. Discuss."

> "… like rebounding hail,
> Or chaffy grain beneath the thresher's flail:"

The first time this happened Steve Mander sat bolt upright in bed. This was shortly before prelim exams in the second year, and what Dirk had just said, or judiciously mumbled, sounded remarkably like a very likely question in the Economic History paper.

Mander quietly got up, crossed over to Dirk's bed and listened very hard, but other than a few completely disconnected mumblings about Schleswig-Holstein and the Franco-Prussian war, the latter being largely directed by Dirk into his pillow, he learned nothing more.

News, however, spread – quietly, discreetly, and like wildfire.

> "And 'mid these dancing rocks at once and ever
> It flung up momently the sacred river."

For the next month Dirk found himself being constantly wined and dined in the hope that he would sleep very soundly that night and dream-speak a few more exam questions. Remarkably, it seemed that the better he was fed, and the finer the vintage of the wine he was given to drink, the less he would tend to sleep facing directly into his pillow.

His scheme, therefore, was to exploit his alleged gifts without ever actually claiming to have them. In fact he would react to stories about his supposed powers with open incredulity, even hostility.

> "Five miles meandering with a mazy motion
> Through wood and dale the sacred river ran,

Then reached the caverns measureless to man,
And sank in tumult to a lifeless ocean:
And 'mid this tumult Kubla heard from far
Ancestral voices prophesying war!"

Dirk was also, he denied, a clairaudient. He would sometimes hum tunes in his sleep that two weeks later would turn out to be a hit for someone. Not too difficult to organise, really.

In fact, he had always done the bare minimum of research necessary to support these myths. He was lazy, and essentially what he did was allow people's enthusiastic credulity to do the work for him. The laziness was essential – if his supposed feats of the paranormal had been detailed and accurate, then people might have been suspicious and looked for other explanations. On the other hand, the more vague and ambiguous his "predictions", the more other people's own wishful thinking would close the credibility gap.

Dirk never made much out of it – at least, he appeared not to. In fact, the benefit to himself, as a student, of being continually wined and dined at other people's expense was more considerable than anyone would expect unless they sat down and worked out the figures.

And, of course, he never claimed – in fact, he actively denied – that any of it was even remotely true.

He was therefore well placed to execute a very nice and tasty little scam come the time of finals.

"The shadow of the dome of pleasure
Floated midway on the waves;
Where was heard the mingled measure
From the fountain and the caves.
It was a miracle of rare device,
A sunny pleasure-dome with caves of ice!"

"Good heavens ...!" Reg suddenly seemed to awake with a start from the light doze into which he had gently slipped under the influence of the wine and the reading, and glanced about himself with blank surprise, but nothing had changed.

Coleridge's words sang through a warm and contented silence that had settled on the great hall. After another quick frown, Reg settled back into another doze, but this time a slightly more attentive one.

> "A damsel with a dulcimer
>   In a vision once I saw:
>   It was an Abyssinian maid,
>   And on her dulcimer she played,
>   Singing of Mount Abora."

Dirk allowed himself to be persuaded to make, under hypnosis, a firm prediction about what questions would be set for examination that summer.

He himself first planted the idea by explaining exactly the sort of thing that he would never, under any circumstances, be prepared to do, though in many ways he would like to, just to have the chance to disprove his alleged and strongly disavowed abilities.

And it was on these grounds, carefully prepared, that he eventually agreed – only because it would once and for all scotch the whole silly – immensely, tediously silly – business. He would make his predictions by means of automatic writing under proper supervision, and they would then be sealed in an envelope and deposited at the bank until after the exams.

Then they would be opened to see how accurate they had been *after* the exams.

He was, not surprisingly, offered some pretty hefty bribes from a pretty hefty number of people to let them see the predictions he had written down, but he was absolutely shocked by the idea. That, he said, would be *dishonest* ...

> "Could I revive within me
>   Her symphony and song,
>   To such a deep delight 'twould win me,
>   That with music loud and long,
>   I would build that dome in air,
>   That sunny dome! Those caves of ice!"

Then, a short time later, Dirk allowed himself to be seen around town wearing something of a vexed and solemn expression. At first he waved aside enquiries as to what it was that was bothering him, but eventually he let slip that his mother was going to have to undergo some extremely expensive dental work which, for reasons that he refused to discuss, would have to be done privately, only there wasn't the money.

From here, the path downward to accepting donations for his mother's supposed medical expenses in return for quick glances at his written exam predictions proved to be sufficiently steep and well-oiled for him to be able to slip down it with a minimum of fuss.

Then it further transpired that the only dentist who could perform this mysterious dental operation was an East European surgeon now living in Malibu, and it was in consequence necessary to increase the level of donations rather sharply.

He still denied, of course, that his abilities were all that they were cracked up to be, in fact he denied that they existed at all, and insisted that he would never have embarked on the exercise at all if it wasn't to disprove the whole thing – and also, since other people seemed, at their own risk, to have a faith in his abilities that he himself did not, he was happy to indulge them to the extent of letting them pay for his sainted mother's operation.

He could only emerge well from this situation.

Or so he thought.

> "And all who heard should see them there,
>   And all should cry, Beware! Beware!
>   His flashing eyes, his floating hair!"

The exam papers Dirk produced under hypnosis, by means of automatic writing, he had, in fact, pieced together simply by doing the same minimum research that any student taking exams would do, studying previous exam papers and seeing what, if any, patterns emerged, and making intelligent guesses about what might come up. He was pretty sure of getting (as anyone would be) a strike rate that was sufficiently high to satisfy the credulous, and sufficiently low for the whole exercise to look perfectly innocent.

As indeed it was.

What completely blew him out of the water, and caused a furore which ended with him being driven out of Cambridge in the back of a Black Maria, was the fact that all the exam papers he sold turned out to be the same as the papers that were actually set.

Exactly. Word for word. To the very comma.

> "Wave a circle round him thrice,
>   And close your eyes with holy dread,
>   For he on honey-dew hath fed,
>   And drunk the milk of Paradise ..."

And that, apart from a flurry of sensational newspaper reports which exposed him as a fraud, then trumpeted him as the real thing so that they could have another round of exposing him as a fraud again and then trumpeting him as the real thing again, until they got bored and found a nice juicy snooker player to harass instead, was that.

In the years since then, Richard had run into Dirk from time to time and had usually been greeted with that kind of guarded half smile that wants to know if you think it owes you money before it blossoms into one that hopes you will lend it some. Dirk's regular name changes suggested to Richard that he wasn't alone in being treated like this.

He felt a tug of sadness that someone who had seemed so shiningly alive within the small confines of a university community should have seemed to fade so much in the light of common day. And he wondered at Reg's asking after him like that, suddenly and out of the blue, in what seemed altogether too airy and casual a manner.

He glanced around him again, at his lightly snoring neighbour, Reg; at little Sarah rapt in silent attention; at the deep hall swathed in darkly glimmering light; at the portraits of old prime ministers and poets hung high in the darkness with just the odd glint of candlelight gleaming off their teeth; at the Director of English

Studies standing reading in his poetry-reading voice; at the book of "Kubla Khan" that the Director of English Studies held in his hand; and finally, surreptitiously, at his watch. He settled back again.

The voice continued, reading the second, and altogether stranger part of the poem ...

Chapter Seven...

This was the evening of the last day of Gordon Way's life, and he was wondering if the rain would hold off for the weekend. The forecast had said changeable – a misty night tonight followed by bright but chilly days on Friday and Saturday with maybe a few scattered showers towards the end of Sunday when everyone would be heading back into town.

Everyone, that is, other than Gordon Way.

The weather forecast hadn't mentioned that, of course, that wasn't the job of the weather forecast, but then his horoscope had been pretty misleading as well. It had mentioned an unusual amount of planetary activity in his sign and had urged him to differentiate between what he thought he wanted and what he actually needed, and suggested that he should tackle emotional or work problems with determination and complete honesty, but had inexplicably failed to mention that he would be dead before the day was out.

He turned off the motorway near Cambridge and stopped at a small filling station for some petrol, where he sat for a moment, finishing off a call on his car phone.

"OK, look, I'll call you tomorrow," he said, "or maybe later tonight. Or call me. I should be at the cottage in half an hour. Yes, I know how important the project is to you. All right, I know how important it is, full stop. You want it, I want it. Of course I do. And I'm not saying that we won't continue to support it. I'm just saying it's expensive and we should look at the whole thing with determination and complete honesty. Look, why don't you come out to the cottage, and we can talk it through. OK, yeah, yes, I know. I understand. Well, think about it, Kate. Talk to you later. Bye."

He hung up and continued to sit in his car for a moment.

It was a large car. It was a large silver-grey Mercedes of the sort that they use in advertisements, and not just advertisements for Mercedes. Gordon Way, brother of Susan, employer of Richard MacDuff, was a rich man, the founder and owner of WayForward Technologies II. WayForward Technologies itself had of course gone bust, for the usual reason, taking his entire first fortune with it.

Luckily, he had managed to make another one.

The "usual reason" was that he had been in the business of computer hardware when every twelve-year-old in the country had suddenly got bored with boxes that went bing. His second fortune had been made in software instead. As a result of two major pieces of software, one of which was *Anthem* (the other, more profitable one had never seen the light of day), WFT-II was the only British software company that could be mentioned in the same sentence as such major U.S. companies as Microsoft or Lotus. The sentence would probably run along the lines of "WayForward Technologies, unlike such major U.S. companies as Microsoft or Lotus ..." but it was a start. WayForward was in there. And he owned it.

He pushed a tape into the slot on the stereo console. It accepted it with a soft and decorous click, and a moment or two later Ravel's *Boléro* floated out of eight perfectly matched speakers with fine-meshed matte-black grilles. The stereo was so smooth and spacious you could almost sense the whole ice-rink. He tapped his fingers lightly on the padded rim of the steering wheel. He gazed at the dashboard. Tasteful illuminated figures and tiny, immaculate lights gazed dimly back at him. After a while he suddenly realised this was a self-service station and got out to fill the tank.

This took a minute or two. He stood gripping the filler nozzle, stamping his feet in the cold night air, then walked over to the small grubby kiosk, paid for the petrol, remembered to buy a couple of local maps, and then stood chatting enthusiastically to the cashier for a few minutes about the directions the computer industry was likely to take in the following year, suggesting that parallel processing was going to be the key to really intuitive productivity software, but also strongly doubting whether artificial intelligence research *per se*, particularly artificial intelligence research based on the ProLog language, was really going to produce any serious commercially viable products in the foreseeable future, at least as far as the office desk top environment was concerned, a topic that fascinated the cashier not at all.

"The man just liked to talk," he would later tell the police. "Man, I could have walked away to the toilet for ten minutes and he would've told it all to the till. If I'd been fifteen minutes the till would have walked away too. Yeah, I'm sure that's him," he would add when shown a picture of Gordon Way. "I only wasn't sure at first because in the picture he's got his mouth closed."

"And you're absolutely certain you didn't see anything else suspicious?" the policeman insisted. "Nothing that struck you as odd in any way at all?"

"No, like I said, it was just an ordinary customer on an ordinary night, just like any other night."

The policeman stared at him blankly. "Just for the sake of argument," he went on to say, "if I were suddenly to do this ..." – he made himself go cross-eyed, stuck his tongue out of the corner of his mouth and danced up and down twisting his fingers in his ears – "would anything strike you about that?"

"Well, er, yeah," said the cashier, backing away nervously. "I'd think you'd gone stark raving mad."

"Good," said the policeman, putting his notebook away. "It's just that different people sometimes have a different idea of what 'odd' means, you see, sir. If last night was an ordinary night just like any other night, then I am a pimple on the bottom of the Marquess of Queensbury's aunt. We shall be requiring a statement later, sir. Thank you for your time."

That was all yet to come.

Tonight, Gordon pushed the maps in his pocket and strolled back towards his car. Standing under the lights in the mist it had gathered a finely beaded coat of matte moisture on it, and looked like – well, it looked like an extremely expensive Mercedes-Benz. Gordon caught himself, just for a millisecond, wishing that he had something like that, but he was now quite adept at fending off that particular line of thought, which only led off in circles and left him feeling depressed and confused.

He patted it in a proprietorial manner, then, walking around it, noticed that the boot wasn't closed properly and pushed it shut. It closed with a good healthy clunk. Well, that made it all worth it, didn't it? Good healthy clunk like that. Old-fashioned values of quality and workmanship. He thought of a dozen things he had to talk to Susan about and climbed back into the car, pushing the auto-dial code on his phone as soon as the car was prowling back on to the road.

"... so if you'd like to leave a message, I'll get back to you as soon as possible. Maybe."

Beep.

"Oh, Susan, hi, it's Gordon," he said, cradling the phone awkwardly on his shoulder. "Just on my way to the cottage. It's, er, Thursday night, and it's, er...8.47. Bit misty on the roads. Listen, I have those people from the States coming over this weekend to thrash out the distribution on *Anthem* Version 2.00, handling the promotion, all that stuff, and look, you know I don't like to ask you this sort of thing, but you know I always do anyway, so here it is.

"I just need to know that Richard is on the case. I mean *really* on the case. I can ask him, and he says, Oh sure, it's fine, but half the time – shit, that lorry had bright lights, none of these bastard lorry drivers ever dips them properly, it's a wonder I don't end up dead in the ditch, that would be something, wouldn't it, leaving your famous last words on somebody's answering machine, there's no reason why these lorries shouldn't have automatic light-activated dipper switches. Look, can you make a note for me to tell Susan – not you, of course, secretary Susan at the office – to tell her to send a letter from me to that fellow at the Department of the Environment saying we can provide the technology if he can provide the legislation? It's for the public good, and anyway he owes me a favour plus what's the point in having a CBE if you can't kick a little ass? You can tell I've been talking to Americans all week.

"That reminds me, God, I hope I remembered to pack the shotguns. What is it with these Americans that they're always so mad to shoot my rabbits? I bought them some maps in the hope that I can persuade them to go on long healthy walks and take their minds off shooting rabbits. I really feel quite sorry for the creatures. I think I should put one of those signs on my lawn when the Americans are coming, you know, like they have in Beverly Hills, saying 'Armed Response'.

"Make a note to Susan, would you please, to get an 'Armed Response' sign made up with a sharp spike on the bottom at the right height for rabbits to see. That's secretary Susan at the office, not you, of course.

"Where was I?

"Oh yes. Richard and *Anthem* 2.00. Susan, that thing has got to be in beta testing in two weeks. He tells me it's fine. But every time I see him he's got a picture of a sofa spinning on his computer screen. He says it's an important concept, but all I see is furniture. People who want their company accounts to sing to them do not want to buy a revolving sofa. Nor do I think he should be turning the erosion patterns of the Himalayas into a flute quintet at this time.

"And as for what Kate's up to, Susan, well, I can't hide the fact that I get anxious at the salaries and computer time it's eating up. Important long-term research and development it might be, but there is also the possibility, only a possibility, I'm saying, but nevertheless a possibility which I think we owe it to ourselves fully to evaluate and explore, which is that it's a lemon. That's odd, there's a noise coming from the boot, I thought I'd just closed it properly.

"Anyway, the main thing's Richard. And the point is that there's only one person who's really in a position to know if he's getting the important work done, or if he's just dreaming, and that one person is, I'm afraid, Susan.

"That's you, I mean, of course, not secretary Susan at the office.

"So can you, I don't like to ask you this, I really don't, can you really get on his case? Make him see how important it is? Just make sure he realises that WayForward Technologies is meant to be an expanding commercial business, not an adventure playground for crunch-heads. That's the problem with crunch-heads – they have one great idea that actually works and then they expect you to carry on funding them for years while they sit and calculate the topographies of their navels. I'm sorry, I'm going to have to stop and close the boot properly. Won't be a moment."

He put the telephone down on the seat beside him, pulled over on to the grass verge, and got out. As he went to the boot, it opened, a figure rose out of it, shot him through the chest with both barrels of a shotgun and then went about its business.

Gordon Way's astonishment at being suddenly shot dead was nothing to his astonishment at what happened next.

Chapter Eight...

"Come in, dear fellow, come in."

The door to Reg's set of rooms in college was up a winding set of wooden stairs in the corner of Second Court, and was not well lit, or rather it was perfectly well lit when the light was working, but the light was not working, so the door was not well lit and was, furthermore, locked. Reg was having difficulty in finding the key from a collection which looked like something that a fit Ninja warrior could hurl through the trunk of a tree.

Rooms in the older parts of the college have double doors, like airlocks, and like airlocks they are fiddly to open. The outer door is a sturdy slab of grey painted oak, with no features other than a very narrow slit for letters, and a Yale lock, to which suddenly Reg at last found the key.

He unlocked it and pulled it open. Behind it lay an ordinary white-panelled door with an ordinary brass doorknob.

"Come in, come in," repeated Reg, opening this and fumbling for the light switch. For a moment only the dying embers of a fire in the stone grate threw ghostly red shadows dancing around the room, but then electric light flooded it and extinguished the magic. Reg hesitated on the threshold for a moment, oddly tense, as if wishing to be sure of something before he entered, then bustled in with at least the appearance of cheeriness.

It was a large panelled room, which a collection of gently shabby furniture contrived to fill quite comfortably. Against the far wall stood a large and battered old mahogany table with fat ugly legs, which was laden with books, files, folders and teetering piles of papers. Standing in its own space on the desk, Richard was amused to note, was actually a battered old abacus.

There was a small Regency writing desk standing nearby which might have been quite valuable had it not been knocked about so much, also a couple of elegant Georgian chairs, a portentous Victorian bookcase, and so on. It was, in short, a don's room. It had a don's framed maps and prints on the walls, a threadbare and faded don's carpet on the floor, and it looked as if little had changed in it for decades, which was probably the case because a don lived in it.

Two doors led out from either end of the opposite wall, and Richard knew from previous visits that one led to a study which looked much like a smaller and more intense version of this room – larger clumps of books, taller piles of paper in more imminent danger of actually falling, furniture which, however old and valuable, was heavily marked with myriad rings of hot tea or coffee cups, on many of which the original cups themselves were probably still standing.

The other door led to a small and rather basically equipped kitchen, and a twisty internal staircase at the top of which lay the Professor's bedroom and bathroom.

"Try and make yourself comfortable on the sofa," invited Reg, fussing around hospitably. "I don't know if you'll manage it. It always feels to me as if it's been stuffed with cabbage leaves and cutlery." He peered at Richard seriously. "Do you have a good sofa?" he enquired.

"Well, yes." Richard laughed. He was cheered by the silliness of the question.

"Oh," said Reg solemnly. "Well, I wish you'd tell me where you got it. I have endless trouble with them, quite endless. Never found a comfortable one in all my life. How do you find yours?" He encountered, with a slight air of surprise, a small silver tray he had left out with a decanter of port and three glasses.

"Well, it's odd you should ask that," said Richard. "I've never sat on it."

"Very wise," insisted Reg earnestly, "very, very wise." He

went through a palaver similar to his previous one with his coat and hat.

"Not that I wouldn't like to," said Richard. "It's just that it's stuck halfway up a long flight of stairs which leads up into my flat. As far as I can make it out, the delivery men got it part way up the stairs, got it stuck, turned it around any way they could, couldn't get it any further, and then found, curiously enough, that they couldn't get it back down again. Now, that should be impossible."

"Odd," agreed Reg. "I've certainly never come across any irreversible mathematics involving sofas. Could be a new field. Have you spoken to any spatial geometricians?"

"I did better than that. I called in a neighbour's kid who used to be able to solve Rubik's cube in seventeen seconds. He sat on a step and stared at it for over an hour before pronouncing it irrevocably stuck. Admittedly he's a few years older now and has found out about girls, but it's got me puzzled."

"Carry on talking, my dear fellow, I'm most interested, but let me know first if there's anything I can get you. Port perhaps? Or brandy? The port I think is the better bet, laid down by the college in 1934, one of the finest vintages I think you'll find, and on the other hand I don't actually have any brandy. Or coffee? Some more wine perhaps? There's an excellent Margaux I've been looking for an excuse to open, though it should of course be allowed to stand open for an hour or two, which is not to say that I couldn't ... no," he said hurriedly, "probably best not to go for the Margaux tonight."

"Tea is what I would really like," said Richard, "if you have some."

Reg raised his eyebrows. "Are you sure?"

"I have to drive home."

"Indeed. Then I shall be a moment or two in the kitchen. Please carry on, I shall still be able to hear you. Continue to tell me of your sofa, and do feel free in the meantime to sit on mine. Has it been stuck there for long?"

"Oh, only about three weeks," said Richard, sitting down. "I could just saw it up and throw it away, but I can't believe that there isn't a logical answer. And it also made me think – it would be really useful to know before you buy a piece of furniture whether it's actually going to fit up the stairs or around the corner. So I've modelled the problem in three dimensions on my computer – and so far it just says no way."

"It says what?" called Reg, over the noise of filling the kettle.

"That it can't be done. I told it to compute the moves necessary to get the sofa out, and it said there aren't any. I said 'What?' and it said there aren't any. I then asked it, and this is the really mysterious thing, to compute the moves necessary to get the sofa into its present position in the first place, and it said that it couldn't have got there. Not without fundamental restructuring of the walls. So, either there's something wrong with the fundamental structure of the matter in my walls or," he added with a sigh, "there's something wrong with the program. Which would you guess?"

"And are you married?" called Reg.

"What? Oh, I see what you mean. A sofa stuck on the stairs for a month. Well, no, not married as such, but yes, there is a specific girl that I'm not married to."

"What's she like? What does she do?"

"She's a professional cellist. I have to admit that the sofa has been a bit of a talking point. In fact she's moved back to her own flat until I get it sorted out. She, well ..."

He was suddenly sad, and he stood up and wandered around the room in a desultory sort of way and ended up in front of the dying fire. He gave it a bit of a poke and threw on a couple of extra logs to try and ward off the chill of the room.

"She's Gordon's sister, in fact," he added at last. "But they are very different. I'm not sure she really approves of computers very much. And she doesn't much like his attitude to money. I don't think I entirely blame her, actually, and she doesn't know the half of it."

"Which is the half she doesn't know?"

Richard sighed.

"Well," he said, "it's to do with the project which first made the software incarnation of the company profitable. It was called *Reason*, and in its own way it was sensational."

"What was it?"

"Well, it was a kind of back-to-front program. It's funny how many of the best ideas are just an old idea back-to-front. You see there have already been several programs written that help you to arrive at decisions by properly ordering and analysing all the relevant facts so that they then point naturally towards the right decision. The drawback with these is that the decision which all the properly ordered and analysed facts point to is not necessarily the one you want."

"Yeeeess ..." said Reg's voice from the kitchen.

"Well, Gordon's great insight was to design a program which allowed you to specify in advance what decision you wished it to reach, and only then to give it all the facts. The program's task, which it was able to accomplish with consummate ease, was simply to construct a plausible series of logical-sounding steps to connect the premises with the conclusion.

"And I have to say that it worked brilliantly. Gordon was able to buy himself a Porsche almost immediately despite being completely broke and a hopeless driver. Even his bank manager was unable to find fault with his reasoning. Even when Gordon wrote it off three weeks later."

"Heavens. And did the program sell very well?"

"No. We never sold a single copy."

"You astonish me. It sounds like a real winner to me."

"It was," said Richard hesitantly. "The entire project was bought up, lock, stock and barrel, by the Pentagon. The deal put WayForward on a very sound financial foundation. Its moral foundation, on the other hand, is not something I would want to trust my weight to. I've recently been analysing a lot of the arguments put forward in favour of the Star Wars project, and if you know what you're looking for, the pattern of the algorithms is very clear.

"So much so, in fact, that looking at Pentagon policies over the last couple of years I think I can be fairly sure that the US Navy is using version 2.00 of the program, while the Air Force for some reason only has the beta-test version of 1.5. Odd, that."

"Do you have a copy?"

"Certainly not," said Richard, "I wouldn't have anything to do with it. Anyway, when the Pentagon bought everything, they bought everything. Every scrap of code, every disk, every notebook. I was glad to see the back of it. If indeed we have. I just busy myself with my own projects."

He poked at the fire again and wondered what he was doing here when he had so much work on. Gordon was on at him continually about getting the new, super version of *Anthem* ready for taking advantage of the Macintosh II, and he was well behind with it. And as for the proposed module for converting incoming Dow Jones stock-market information into MIDI data in real time, he'd only meant that as a joke, but Gordon, of course, had flipped over the idea and insisted on its being implemented. That too was meant to be ready but wasn't. He suddenly knew exactly why it was he was here.

Well, it had been a pleasant evening, even if he couldn't see why Reg had been quite so keen to see him. He picked up a couple of books from the table. The table obviously doubled as a dining table, because although the piles looked as if they had been there for weeks, the absence of dust immediately around them showed that they had been moved recently.

Maybe, he thought, the need for amiable chit-chat with someone different can become as urgent as any other need when you live in a community as enclosed as a Cambridge college was, even nowadays. He was a likeable old fellow, but it was clear from dinner that many of his colleagues found his eccentricities formed rather a rich sustained diet – particularly when they had so many of their own to contend with. A thought about Susan nagged him, but he was used to that. He flipped through the two books he'd picked up.

One of them, an elderly one, was an account of the hauntings of Borley Rectory, the most haunted house in England. Its spine was getting raggedy, and the photographic plates were so grey and blurry as to be virtually indistinguishable. A picture he thought must be a very lucky (or faked) shot of a ghostly apparition turned out, when he examined the caption, to be a portrait of the author.

The other book was more recent, and by an odd coincidence was a guide to the Greek islands. He thumbed through it idly and a piece of paper fell out.

"Earl Grey or Lapsang Souchong?" called out Reg. "Or Darjeeling? Or PG Tips? It's all tea bags anyway, I'm afraid. And none of them very fresh."

"Darjeeling will do fine," replied Richard, stooping to pick up the piece of paper.

"Milk?" called Reg.

"Er, please."

"One lump or two?"

"One, please."

Richard slipped the paper back into the book, noticing as he did so that it had a hurriedly scribbled note on it. The note said, oddly enough, "Regard this simple silver salt cellar. Regard this simple hat."

"Sugar?"

"Er, what?" said Richard, startled. He put the book hurriedly back on the pile.

"Just a tiny joke of mine," said Reg cheerily, "to see if people are listening." He emerged beaming from the kitchen carrying a small tray with two cups on it, which he hurled suddenly to the floor. The tea splashed over the carpet. One of the cups shattered and the other bounced under the table. Reg leaned against the door frame, white-faced and staring.

A frozen instant of time slid silently by while Richard was too startled to react, then he leaped awkwardly forward to help. But the old man was already apologising and offering to make him another cup. Richard helped him to the sofa.

"Are you all right?" asked Richard helplessly. "Shall I get a doctor?"

Reg waved him down. "It's all right," he insisted, "I'm perfectly well. Thought I heard, well, a noise that startled me. But it was nothing. Just overcome with the tea fumes, I expect. Let me just catch my breath. I think a little, er, port will revive me excellently. So sorry, I didn't mean to startle you." He waved in the general direction of the port decanter. Richard hurriedly poured a small glass and gave it to him.

"What kind of noise?" he asked, wondering what on earth could shock him so much.

At that moment came the sound of movement upstairs and an extraordinary kind of heavy breathing noise.

"That ..." whispered Reg. The glass of port lay shattered at his feet. Upstairs someone seemed to be stamping. "Did you hear it?"

"Well, yes."

This seemed to relieve the old man.

Richard looked nervously up at the ceiling. "Is there someone up there?" he asked, feeling this was a lame question, but one that had to be asked.

"No," said Reg in a low voice that shocked Richard with the fear it carried, "no one. Nobody that should be there."

"Then ..."

Reg was struggling shakily to his feet, but there was suddenly a fierce determination about him.

"I must go up there," he said quietly. "I must. Please wait for me here."

"Look, what is this?" demanded Richard, standing between Reg and the doorway. "What is it, a burglar? Look, I'll go. I'm sure it's nothing, it's just the wind or something." Richard didn't know why he was saying this. It clearly wasn't the wind, or even anything like the wind, because though the wind might conceivably make heavy breathing noises, it rarely stamped its feet in that way.

"No," the old man said, politely but firmly moving him aside, "it is for me to do."

Richard followed him helplessly through the door into the small hallway, beyond which lay the tiny kitchen. A dark wooden staircase led up from here; the steps seemed damaged and scuffed.

Reg turned on a light. It was a dim one that hung naked at the top of the stairwell, and he looked up it with grim apprehension.

"Wait here," he said, and walked up two steps. He then turned and faced Richard with a look of the most profound seriousness on his face.

"I am sorry," he said, "that you have become involved in what is ... the more difficult side of my life. But you are involved now, regrettable though that may be, and there is something I must ask you. I do not know what awaits me up there, do not know exactly. I do not know if it is something which I have foolishly brought upon myself with my ... my hobbies, or if it is something to which I have fallen an innocent victim. If it is the former, then I have only myself to blame, for I am like a doctor who cannot give up smoking, or perhaps worse still, like an ecologist who cannot give up his car – if the latter, then I hope it may not happen to you.

"What I must ask you is this. When I come back down these stairs, always supposing of course that I do, then if my behaviour strikes you as being in any way odd, if I appear not to be myself, then you must leap on me and wrestle me to the ground. Do you understand? You must prevent me from doing anything I may try to do."

"But how will I know?" asked an incredulous Richard. "Sorry, I don't mean it to sound like that, but I don't know what ...?"

"You will know," said Reg. "Now please wait for me in the main room. And close the door."

Shaking his head in bewilderment, Richard stepped back and did as he was asked. From inside the large untidy room he listened to the sound of the Professor's tread mounting the stairs one at a time.

He mounted them with a heavy deliberation, like the ticking of a great, slow clock.

Richard heard him reach the top landing. There he paused in silence. Seconds went by, five, maybe ten, maybe twenty. Then

came again the heavy movement and breath that had first so
harrowed the Professor.

Richard moved quickly to the door but did not open it. The
chill of the room oppressed and disturbed him. He shook his head
to try and shake off the feeling, and then held his breath as the
footsteps started once again slowly to traverse the two yards of
the landing and to pause there again.

After only a few seconds, this time Richard heard the long
slow squeak of a door being opened inch by inch, inch by
cautious inch, until it must surely now at last be standing wide
agape.

Nothing further seemed to happen for a long, long time.

Then at last the door closed once again, slowly.

The footsteps crossed the landing and paused again. Richard
backed a few slight paces from the door, staring fixedly at it.
Once more the footsteps started to descend the stairs, slowly,
deliberately and quietly, until at last they reached the bottom.
Then after a few seconds more the door handle began to rotate.
The door opened and Reg walked calmly in.

"It's all right, it's just a horse in the bathroom," he said quietly.

Richard leaped on him and wrestled him to the ground.

"No," gasped Reg, "no, get off me, let me go, I'm perfectly all
right, damn it. It's just a horse, a perfectly ordinary horse." He
shook Richard off with no great difficulty and sat up, puffing and
blowing and pushing his hands through his limited hair. Richard
stood over him warily, but with great and mounting
embarrassment. He edged back, and let Reg stand up and sit on a
chair.

"Just a horse," said Reg, "but, er, thank you for taking me at
my word." He brushed himself down.

"A horse," repeated Richard.

"Yes," said Reg.

Richard went out and looked up the stairs and then came back
in.

"A *horse*?" he said again.

"Yes, it is," said the Professor. "Wait –" he motioned to

Richard, who was about to go out again and investigate – "let it be. It won't be long."

Richard stared in disbelief. "You say there's a horse in your bathroom, and all you can do is stand there naming Beatles songs?"

The Professor looked blankly at him.

"Listen," he said, "I'm sorry if I ... alarmed you earlier, it was just a slight turn. These things happen, my dear fellow, don't upset yourself about it. Dear me, I've known odder things in my time. Many of them. Far odder. She's only a horse, for heaven's sake. I'll go and let her out later. Please don't concern yourself. Let us revive our spirits with some port."

"But ... how did it get in there?"

"Well, the bathroom window's open. I expect she came in through that."

Richard looked at him, not for the first and certainly not for the last time, through eyes that were narrowed with suspicion.

"You're doing it deliberately, aren't you?" he said.

"Doing what, my dear fellow?"

"I don't believe there's a horse in your bathroom," said Richard suddenly. "I don't know what is there, I don't know what you're doing, I don't know what any of this evening means, but I don't believe there's a horse in your bathroom." And brushing aside Reg's further protestations he went up to look.

The bathroom was not large.

The walls were panelled in old oak linenfold which, given the age and nature of the building, was quite probably priceless, but otherwise the fittings were stark and institutional.

There was old, scuffed, black-and-white checked linoleum on the floor, a small basic bath, well cleaned but with very elderly stains and chips in the enamel, and also a small basic basin with a toothbrush and toothpaste in a Duralex beaker standing next to the taps. Screwed into the probably priceless panelling above the basin was a tin mirror-fronted bathroom cabinet. It looked as if it had been repainted many times, and the mirror was stained round the edges with condensation. The lavatory had an old-fashioned cast-iron chain-pull cistern. There was an old cream-painted wooden cupboard standing in the corner, with an old brown bentwood chair next to it, on which lay some neatly folded but threadbare small towels. There was also a large horse in the room, taking up most of it.

Richard stared at it, and it stared at Richard in an appraising kind of way. Richard swayed slightly. The horse stood quite still. After a while it looked at the cupboard instead. It seemed, if not content, then at least perfectly resigned to being where it was until it was put somewhere else. It also seemed ... what was it?

It was bathed in the glow of the moonlight that streamed in through the window. The window was open but small and was, besides, on the second floor, so the notion that the horse had entered by that route was entirely fanciful.

There was something odd about the horse, but he couldn't say what. Well, there was one thing that was clearly very odd about it indeed, which was that it was standing in a college bathroom. Maybe that was all.

He reached out, rather tentatively, to pat the creature on its neck. It felt normal – firm, glossy, it was in good condition. The effect of the moonlight on its coat was a little mazy, but everything looks a little odd by moonlight. The horse shook its mane a little when he touched it, but didn't seem to mind too much.

After the success of patting it, Richard stroked it a few times and scratched it gently under the jaw. Then he noticed that there was another door into the bathroom, in the far corner. He moved cautiously around the horse and approached the other door. He backed up against it and pushed it open tentatively.

It just opened into the Professor's bedroom, a small room cluttered with books and shoes and a small single bed. This room, too, had another door, which opened out on to the landing again.

Richard noticed that the floor of the landing was newly scuffed and scratched as the stairs had been, and these marks were consistent with the idea that the horse had somehow been pushed up the stairs. He wouldn't have liked to have had to do it himself, and he would have liked to have been the horse having it done to him even less, but it was just about possible.

But why? He had one last look at the horse, which had one last look back at him, and then he returned downstairs.

"I agree," he said. "You have a horse in your bathroom and I will, after all, have a little port."

He poured some for himself, and then some for Reg, who was quietly contemplating the fire and was in need of a refill.

"Just as well I did put out three glasses after all," said Reg chattily. "I wondered why earlier, and now I remember.

"You asked if you could bring a friend, but appear not to have done so. On account of the sofa no doubt. Never mind, these things happen. Whoa, not too much, you'll spill it."

All horse-related questions left Richard's mind abruptly.

"I did?" he said.

"Oh yes. I remember now. You rang me back to ask me if it would be all right, as I recall. I said I would be charmed, and fully intended to be. I'd saw the thing up if I were you. Don't want to sacrifice your happiness to a sofa. Or maybe she decided that an evening with your old tutor would be blisteringly dull and opted for the more exhilarating course of washing her hair instead. Dear me, I know what I would have done. It's only lack of hair that forces me to pursue such a hectic social round these days."

It was Richard's turn to be white-faced and staring.

Yes, he had assumed that Susan would not want to come.

Yes, he had said to her it would be terribly dull. But she had insisted that she wanted to come because it would be the only way she'd get to see his face for a few minutes not bathed in the light of a computer screen, so he had agreed and arranged that he would bring her after all.

Only he had completely forgotten this. He had not picked her up.

He said, "Can I use your phone, please?"

Chapter Nine...

Gordon Way lay on the ground, unclear about what to do.

He was dead. There seemed little doubt about that. There was a horrific hole in his chest, but the blood that was gobbing out of it had slowed to a trickle. Otherwise there was no movement from his chest at all, or, indeed, from any other part of him.

He looked up, and from side to side, and it became clear to him that whatever part of him it was that was moving, it wasn't any part of his body.

The mist rolled slowly over him, and explained nothing. At a few feet distant from him his shotgun lay smoking quietly in the grass.

He continued to lie there, like someone lying awake at four o'clock in the morning, unable to put their mind to rest, but unable to find anything to do with it. He realised that he had just had something of a shock, which might account for his inability to think clearly, but didn't account for his ability actually to think at all.

In the great debate that has raged for centuries about what, if anything, happens to you after death, be it heaven, hell, purgatory or extinction, one thing has never been in doubt – that you would at least know the answer when you were dead.

Gordon Way was dead, but he simply hadn't the slightest idea what he was meant to do about it. It wasn't a situation he had encountered before.

He sat up. The body that sat up seemed as real to him as the body that still lay slowly cooling on the ground, giving up its blood heat in wraiths of steam that mingled with the mist of the chill night air.

Experimenting a bit further, he tried standing up, slowly, wonderingly and wobblingly. The ground seemed to give him support, it took his weight. But then of course he appeared to have no weight that needed to be taken. When he bent to touch the ground he could feel nothing save a kind of distant rubbery resistance like the sensation you get if you try and pick something up when your arm has gone dead. His arm had gone dead. His legs too, and his other arm, and all his torso and his head.

His body was dead. He could not say why his mind was not.

He stood in a kind of frozen, sleepless horror while the mist curled slowly through him.

He looked back down at the him, the ghastly, astonished-looking him-thing lying still and mangled on the ground, and his flesh wanted to creep. Or rather, he wanted flesh that could creep. He wanted flesh. He wanted body. He had none.

A sudden cry of horror escaped from his mouth but was nothing and went nowhere. He shook and felt nothing.

Music and a pool of light seeped from his car. He walked towards it. He tried to walk sturdily, but it was a faint and feeble kind of walking, uncertain and, well, insubstantial. The ground felt frail beneath his feet.

The door of the car was still open on the driver's side, as he had left it when he had leaped out to deal with the boot lid, thinking he'd only be two seconds.

That was all of two minutes ago now, when he'd been alive. When he'd been a person. When he'd thought he was going to be leaping straight back in and driving off. Two minutes and a lifetime ago.

This was insane, wasn't it? he thought suddenly.

He walked around the door and bent down to peer into the external rear-view mirror.

He looked exactly like himself, albeit like himself after he'd had a terrible fright, which was to be expected, but that was him, that was normal. This must be something he was imagining, some horrible kind of waking dream. He had a sudden thought and tried breathing on the rear-view mirror.

Nothing. Not a single droplet formed. That would satisfy a doctor, that's what they always did on television – if no mist formed on the mirror, there was no breath. Perhaps, he thought anxiously to himself, perhaps it was something to do with having heated wing mirrors. Didn't this car have heated wing mirrors? Hadn't the salesman gone on and on about heated this, electric that, and servo-assisted the other? Maybe they were digital wing mirrors. That was it. Digital, heated, servo-assisted, computer-controlled, breath-resistant wing mirrors ...

He was, he realised, thinking complete nonsense. He turned slowly and gazed again in apprehension at the body lying on the ground behind him with half its chest blown away. That would certainly satisfy a doctor. The sight would be appalling enough if it was somebody else's body, but his own ...

He was dead. Dead ... dead ... He tried to make the word toll dramatically in his mind, but it wouldn't. He was not a film sound track, he was just dead.

Peering at his body in appalled fascination, he gradually became distressed by the expression of asinine stupidity on its face.

It was perfectly understandable, of course. It was just such an expression as somebody who is in the middle of being shot with his own shotgun by somebody who had been hiding in the boot of his car might be expected to wear, but he nevertheless disliked the idea that anyone might find him looking like that.

He knelt down beside it in the hope of being able to rearrange his features into some semblance of dignity, or at least basic intelligence.

It proved to be almost impossibly difficult. He tried to knead the skin, the sickeningly familiar skin, but somehow he couldn't seem to get a proper grip on it, or on anything. It was like trying to model plasticine when your arm has gone to sleep, except that instead of his grip slipping off the model, it would slip through it. In this case, his hand slipped through his face.

Nauseated horror and rage swept through him at his sheer bloody blasted impotence, and he was suddenly startled to find himself throttling and shaking his own dead body with a firm and furious grip. He staggered back in amazed shock. All he had managed to do was to add to the inanely stupefied look of the corpse a twisted-up mouth and a squint. And bruises flowering on its neck.

He started to sob, and this time sound seemed to come, a strange howling from deep within whatever this thing he had become was. Clutching his hands to his face, he staggered backwards, retreated to his car and flung himself into the seat. The seat received him in a loose and distant kind of way, like an aunt who disapproves of the last fifteen years of your life and will therefore furnish you with a basic sherry, but refuses to catch your eye.

Could he get himself to a doctor?

To avoid facing the absurdity of the idea he grappled violently with the steering wheel, but his hands slipped through it. He tried to wrestle with the automatic transmission shift and ended up thumping it in rage, but not being able properly to grasp or push it.

The stereo was still playing light orchestral music into the telephone, which had been lying on the passenger seat listening patiently all this time. He stared at it and realised with a growing fever of excitement that he was still connected to Susan's telephone-answering machine. It was the type that would simply run and run until he hung up. He was still in contact with the world.

He tried desperately to pick up the receiver, fumbled, let it slip, and was in the end reduced to bending himself down over its mouthpiece. "Susan!" he cried into it, his voice a hoarse and distant wail on the wind. "Susan, help me! Help me for God's sake. Susan, I'm dead ... I'm dead ... I'm dead and ... I don't know what to do ..." He broke down again, sobbing in desperation, and tried to cling to the phone like a baby clinging to its blanket for comfort.

"Help me, Susan ..." he cried again.

"*Beep*," said the phone.

He looked down at it again where he was cuddling it. He had managed to push something after all. He had managed to push the button which disconnected the call. Feverishly he attempted to grapple the thing again, but it constantly slipped through his fingers and eventually lay immobile on the seat. He could not touch it. He could not push the buttons. In rage he flung it at the windscreen. It responded to that, all right. It hit the windscreen, careered straight back though him, bounced off the seat and then lay still on the transmission tunnel, impervious to all his further attempts to touch it.

For several minutes still he sat there, his head nodding slowly as terror began to recede into blank desolation.

A couple of cars passed by, but would have noticed nothing odd – a car stopped by the wayside. Passing swiftly in the night their headlights would probably not have picked out the body lying in the grass behind the car. They certainly would not have noticed a ghost sitting inside it crying to himself.

He didn't know how long he sat there. He was hardly aware of time passing, only that it didn't seem to pass quickly. There was little external stimulus to mark its passage. He didn't feel cold. In fact he could almost not remember what cold meant or felt like, he just knew that it was something he would have expected to feel at this moment.

Eventually he stirred from his pathetic huddle. He would have to do something, though he didn't know what. Perhaps he should try and reach his cottage, though he didn't know what he would do when he got there. He just needed something to try for. He needed to make it through the night.

Pulling himself together he slipped out of the car, his foot and knee grazing easily through part of the door frame. He went to look again at his body, but it wasn't there.

As if the night hadn't produced enough shocks already. He started, and stared at the damp depression in the grass.

His body was not there.

Chapter Ten...

Richard made the hastiest departure that politeness would allow.

He said thank you very much and what a splendid evening it had been and that any time Reg was coming up to London he must let him, Richard, know and was there anything he could do to help about the horse. No? Well, all right then, if you're sure, and thank you again, so much.

He stood there for a moment or two after the door finally closed, pondering things.

He had noticed during the short time that the light from Reg's room flooded out on to the landing of the main staircase, that there were no marks on the floorboards there at all. It seemed odd that the horse should only have scuffed the floorboards inside Reg's room.

Well, it all seemed very odd, full stop, but here was yet another curious fact to add to the growing pile. This was supposed to have been a relaxing evening away from work.

On an impulse he knocked on the door opposite to Reg's. It took such a long time to be answered that Richard had given up and was turning to go when at last he heard the door creak open.

He had a slight shock when he saw that staring sharply up at him like a small and suspicious bird was the don with the racing-yacht keel for a nose.

"Er, sorry," said Richard, abruptly, "but, er, have you seen or heard a horse coming up this staircase tonight?"

The man stopped his obsessive twitching of his fingers. He cocked his head slightly on one side and then seemed to need to go on a long journey inside himself to find a voice, which when found turned out to be a thin and soft little one.

He said, "That is the first thing anybody has said to me for seventeen years, three months and two days, five hours, nineteen minutes and twenty seconds. I've been counting."

He closed the door softly again.

Richard virtually ran through Second Court.

When he reached First Court he steadied himself and slowed down to a walking pace.

The chill night air was rasping in his lungs and there was no point in running. He hadn't managed to talk to Susan because Reg's phone wasn't working, and this was another thing that he had been mysteriously coy about. That at least was susceptible of a rational explanation. He probably hadn't paid his phone bill.

Richard was about to emerge out on to the street when instead he decided to pay a quick visit to the porter's lodge, which was tucked away inside the great archway entrance into the college. It was a small hutchlike place filled with keys, messages and a single electric bar heater. A radio nattered to itself in the background.

"Excuse me," he said to the large black-suited man standing behind the counter with his arms folded. "I ..."

"Yes, Mr MacDuff, what can I do for you?"

In his present state of mind Richard would have been hard-pressed himself to remember his own name and was startled for a moment. However, college porters are legendary for their ability to perform such feats of memory, and for their tendency to show them off at the slightest provocation.

"Is there," said Richard, "a horse anywhere in the college – that you know of? I mean, you would know if there was a horse in the college, wouldn't you?"

The porter didn't blink.

"No, sir, and yes, sir. Anything else I can help you with, Mr MacDuff, sir?"

"Er, no," said Richard and tapped his fingers a couple of times on the counter. "No. Thank you. Thank you very much for your help. Nice to see you again, er ... Bob," he hazarded. "Good-night, then."

He left.

The porter remained perfectly still with his arms folded, but shaking his head a very, very little bit.

"Here's some coffee for you, Bill," said another porter, a short wiry one, emerging from an inner sanctum with a steaming cup. "Getting a bit colder tonight?"

"I think it is, Fred, thanks," said Bill, taking the cup.

He took a sip. "You can say what you like about people, they don't get any less peculiar. Fellow in here just now asking if there was a horse in the college."

"Oh yes?" Fred sipped at his own coffee, and let the steam smart his eyes. "I had a chap in here earlier. Sort of strange foreign priest. Couldn't understand a word he said at first. But he seemed happy just to stand by the fire and listen to the news on the radio."

"Foreigners, eh."

"In the end I told him to shoot off. Standing in front of my fire like that. Suddenly he says is that really what he must do? Shoot off? I said, in my best Bogart voice, 'You better believe it, buddy.'"

"Really? Sounded more like Jimmy Cagney to me."

"No, that's my Bogart voice. This is my Jimmy Cagney voice – 'You better believe it, buddy.'"

Bill frowned at him. "Is that your Jimmy Cagney voice? I always thought that was your Kenneth McKellar voice."

"You don't listen properly, Bill, you haven't got the ear. This is Kenneth McKellar. 'Oh, you take the high road and I'll take the low road ...'"

"Oh, I see. I was thinking of the Scottish Kenneth McKellar. So what did this priest fellow say then, Fred?"

"Oh, he just looked me straight in the eyes, Bill, and said in this strange sort of ..."

"Skip the accent, Fred, just tell me what he said, if it's worth hearing."

"He just said he did believe me."

"So. Not a very interesting story then, Fred."

"Well, maybe not. I only mention it because he also said that he'd left his horse in a washroom and would I see that it was all right."

Chapter Eleven...

Gordon Way drifted miserably along the dark road, or rather, tried to drift.

He felt that as a ghost – which is what he had to admit to himself he had become – he should be able to drift. He knew little enough about ghosts, but he felt that if you were going to be one then there ought to be certain compensations for not having a physical body to lug around, and that among them ought to be the ability simply to drift. But no, it seemed he was going to have to walk every step of the way.

His aim was to try and make it to his house. He didn't know what he would do when he got there, but even ghosts have to spend the night somewhere, and he felt that being in familiar surroundings might help. Help what, he didn't know. At least the journey gave him an objective, and he would just have to think of another one when he arrived.

He trudged despondently from lamppost to lamppost, stopping at each one to look at bits of himself.

He was definitely getting a bit wraithlike.

At times he would fade almost to nothing, and would seem to be little more than a shadow playing in the mist, a dream of himself that could just evaporate and be gone. At other times he seemed to be almost solid and real again. Once or twice he would try leaning against a lamppost, and would fall straight through it if he wasn't careful.

At last, and with great reluctance, he actually began to turn his mind to what it was that had happened. Odd, that reluctance. He

really didn't want to think about it. Psychologists say that the
mind will often try to suppress the memory of traumatic events,
and this, he thought, was probably the answer. After all, if
having a strange figure jump out of the boot of your own car and
shoot you dead didn't count as a traumatic experience, he'd like to
know what did.

He trudged on wearily.

He tried to recall the figure to his mind's eye, but it was like
probing a hurting tooth, and he thought of other things.

Like, was his will up-to-date? He couldn't remember, and
made a mental note to call his lawyer tomorrow, and then made
another mental note that he would have to stop making mental
notes like that.

How would his company survive without him? He didn't like
either of the possible answers to that very much.

What about his obituary? There was a thought that chilled him
to his bones, wherever they'd got to. Would he be able to get
hold of a copy? What would it say? They'd better give him a good
write-up, the bastards. Look at what he'd done. Single-handedly
saved the British software industry: huge exports, charitable
contributions, research scholarships, crossing the Atlantic in a
solar-powered submarine (failed, but a good try) – all sorts of
things. They'd better not go digging up that Pentagon stuff again
or he'd get his lawyer on to them. He made a mental note to call
him in the mor...

No.

Anyway, can a dead person sue for libel? Only his lawyer
would know, and he was not going to be able to call him in the
morning. He knew with a sense of creeping dread that of all the
things he had left behind in the land of the living it was the
telephone that he was going to miss the most, and then he turned
his mind determinedly back to where it didn't want to go.

The figure.

It seemed to him that the figure had been almost like a figure of
Death itself, or was that his imagination playing tricks with him?
Was he dreaming that it was a cowled figure? What would any

figure, whether cowled or just casually dressed, be doing in the boot of his car?

At that moment a car zipped past him on the road and disappeared off into the night, taking its oasis of light with it. He thought with longing of the warm, leather-upholstered, climate-controlled comfort of his own car abandoned on the road behind him, and then a sudden extraordinary thought struck him.

Was there any way he could hitch a lift? Could anyone actually see him? How would anyone react if they could? Well, there was only one way to find out.

He heard another car coming up in the distance behind him and turned to face it. The twin pools of hazy lights approached through the mist and Gordon gritted his phantom teeth and stuck his thumb out at them.

The car swept by regardless.

Nothing.

Angrily he made an indistinct V sign at the receding red rear lights, and realised, looking straight through his own upraised arm, that he wasn't at his most visible at the moment. Was there perhaps some effort of will he could make to render himself more visible when he wanted to? He screwed up his eyes in concentration, then realised that he would need to have his eyes open in order to judge the results. He tried again, forcing his mind as hard as he could, but the results were unsatisfactory.

Though it did seem to make some kind of rudimentary, glowing difference, he couldn't sustain it, and it faded almost immediately, however much he piled on the mental pressure. He would have to judge the timing very carefully if he was going to make his presence felt, or at least seen.

Another car approached from behind, travelling fast. He turned again, stuck his thumb out, waited till the moment was right and willed himself visible.

The car swerved slightly, and then carried on its way, only a little more slowly. Well, that was something. What else could he do? He would go and stand under a lamppost for a start, and he would practise. The next car he would get for sure.

Chapter Twelve...

"... so if you'd like to leave a message, I'll get back to you as soon as possible. Maybe."

Beep.

"Shit. Damn. Hold on a minute. Blast. Look ... er ... "

Click.

Richard pushed the phone back into its cradle and slammed his car into reverse for twenty yards to have another look at the signpost by the road junction he'd just sped past in the mist. He had extracted himself from the Cambridge one-way system by the usual method, which involved going round and round it faster and faster until he achieved a sort of escape velocity and flew off at a tangent in a random direction, which he was now trying to identify and correct for.

Arriving back at the junction he tried to correlate the information on the signpost with the information on the map. But it couldn't be done. The road junction was quite deliberately sitting on a page divide on the map, and the signpost was revolving maliciously in the wind. Instinct told him that he was heading in the wrong direction, but he didn't want to go back the way he'd come for fear of getting sucked back into the gravitational whirlpool of Cambridge's traffic system.

He turned left, therefore, in the hope of finding better fortune in that direction, but after a while lost his nerve and turned a speculative right, and then chanced another exploratory left and after a few more such manoeuvres was thoroughly lost.

He swore to himself and turned up the heating in the car. If he

had been concentrating on where he was going rather than trying
to navigate and telephone at the same time, he told himself, he
would at least know where he was now. He didn't actually like
having a telephone in his car, he found it a bother and an
intrusion. But Gordon had insisted and indeed had paid for it.

He sighed in exasperation, backed up the black Saab and
turned around again. As he did so he nearly ran into someone
lugging a body into a field. At least that was what it looked like
for a second to his overwrought brain, but in fact it was probably
a local farmer with a sackful of something nutritious, though what
he was doing with it on a night like this was anyone's guess. As
his headlights swung around again, they caught for a moment a
silhouette of the figure trudging off across the field with the sack
on his back.

"Rather him than me," thought Richard grimly, and drove off
again.

After a few minutes he reached a junction with what looked a
little more like a main road, nearly turned right down it, but then
turned left instead. There was no signpost.

He poked at the buttons on his phone again.

"... get back to you as soon as possible. Maybe."

Beep.

"Susan, it's Richard. Where do I start? What a mess. Look,
I'm sorry, sorry, sorry. I screwed up very badly, and it's all my
fault. And look, whatever it takes to make up for it, I'll do it,
solemn promise ..."

He had a slight feeling that this wasn't the right tone to adopt
with an answering machine, but he carried straight on.

"Honestly, we can go away, take a holiday for a week, or even
just this weekend if you like. Really, this weekend. We'll go
somewhere sunny. Doesn't matter how much pressure Gordon
tries to put on me, and you know the sort of pressure he can
muster, he is your brother, after all. I'll just ... er, actually, it
might have to be next weekend. Damn, damn, damn. It's just that
I really have promised to get, no, look, it doesn't matter. We'll
just do it. I don't care about getting *Anthem* finished for

Comdex. It's not the end of the world. We'll just go. Gordon will just have to take a running jump – Gaaarghhhh!"

Richard swerved wildly to avoid the spectre of Gordon Way which suddenly loomed in his headlights and took a running jump at him.

He slammed on the brakes, started to skid, tried to remember what it was you were supposed to do when you found yourself skidding, he knew he'd seen it on some television programme about driving he'd seen ages ago, what was the programme? God, he couldn't even remember the title of the programme, let alone – oh yes, they'd said you mustn't slam on the brakes. That was it. The world swung sickeningly around him with slow and appalling force as the car slewed across the road, spun, thudded against the grass verge, then slithered and rocked itself to a halt, facing the wrong way. He collapsed, panting, against the steering wheel.

He picked up the phone from where he'd dropped it.

"Susan," he gasped, "I'll get back to you," and hung up.

He raised his eyes.

Standing full in the glare of his headlights was the spectral figure of Gordon Way staring straight in through the windscreen with ghastly horror in its eyes, slowly raising its hand and pointing at him.

He wasn't sure how long he just sat there. The apparition had melted from view in a few seconds, but Richard simply sat, shaking, probably for not more than a minute, until a sudden squeal of brakes and glare of lights roused him.

He shook his head. He was, he realised, stopped in the road facing the wrong way. The car that had just screeched to an abrupt halt almost bumper to bumper with him was a police car. He took two or three deep breaths and then, stiff and trembling, he climbed out and stood up to face the officer who was walking slowly towards him, silhouetted in the police car's headlights.

The officer looked him up and down.

"Er, I'm sorry, officer," said Richard, with as much calmness as he could wrench into his voice. "I, er, skidded. The roads are slippery and I, er ... skidded. I spun round. As you see, I, I'm facing the wrong way." He gestured at his car to indicate the way it was facing.

"Like to tell me why it was you skidded then, exactly, sir?" The police officer was looking him straight in the eye while pulling out a notebook.

"Well, as I said," explained Richard, "the roads are slippery because of the mist, and, well, to be perfectly honest," he suddenly found himself saying, in spite of all his attempts to stop himself, "I was just driving along and I suddenly imagined that I saw my employer throwing himself in front of my car."

The officer gazed at him levelly.

"Guilt complex, officer," added Richard with a twitch of a smile, "you know how it is. I was contemplating taking the weekend off."

The police officer seemed to hesitate, balanced on a knife edge between sympathy and suspicion. His eyes narrowed a little but didn't waver.

"Been drinking, sir?"

"Yes," said Richard, with a quick sigh, "but very little. Two glasses of wine max. Er ... and a small glass of port. Absolute max. It was really just a lapse of concentration. I'm fine now."

"Name?"

Richard gave him his name and address. The policeman wrote it all down carefully and neatly in his book, then peered at the car registration number and wrote that down too.

"And who is your employer then, sir?"

"His name is Way. Gordon Way."

"Oh," said the policeman raising his eyebrows, "the computer gentleman."

"Er, yes, that's right. I design software for the company. WayForward Technologies II."

"We've got one of your computers down the station," said the policeman. "Buggered if I can get it to work."

"Oh," said Richard wearily, "which model do you have?"

"I think it's called a Quark II."

"Oh, well that's simple," said Richard with relief. "It doesn't work. Never has done. The thing is a heap of shit."

"Funny thing, sir, that's what I've always said," said the policeman. "Some of the other lads don't agree."

"Well, you're absolutely right, officer. The thing is hopeless. It's the major reason the original company went bust. I suggest you use it as a big paperweight."

"Well, I wouldn't like to do that, sir," the policeman persisted. "The door would keep blowing open."

"What do you mean, officer?" asked Richard.

"I use it to keep the door closed, sir. Nasty draughts down our station this time of year. In the summer, of course, we beat suspects round the head with it."

He flipped his book closed and prodded it into his pocket.

"My advice to you, sir, is to go nice and easy on the way back. Lock up the car and spend the weekend getting completely pissed. I find it's the only way. Mind how you go now."

He returned to his car, wound down the window, and watched Richard manoeuvre his car around and drive off into the night before heading off himself.

Richard took a deep breath, drove calmly back to London, let himself calmly into his flat, clambered calmly over the sofa, sat down, poured himself a stiff brandy and began seriously to shake.

There were three things he was shaking about.

There was the simple physical shock of his near-accident, which is the sort of thing that always churns you up a lot more than you expect. The body floods itself with adrenaline, which then hangs around your system turning sour.

Then there was the cause of the skid – the extraordinary apparition of Gordon throwing himself in front of his car at that moment. Boy oh boy. Richard took a mouthful of brandy and gargled with it. He put the glass down.

It was well known that Gordon was one of the world's richest natural resources of guilt pressure, and that he could deliver a ton on your doorstep fresh every morning, but Richard hadn't realised he had let it get to him to such an unholy degree.

He took up his glass again, went upstairs and pushed open the door to his workroom, which involved shifting a stack of *BYTE* magazines that had toppled against it. He pushed them away with his foot and walked to the end of the large room. A lot of glass at this end let in views over a large part of north London, from which the mist was now clearing. St Paul's glowed in the dark distance and he stared at it for a moment or two but it didn't do anything special. After the events of the evening he found this came as a pleasant surprise.

At the other end of the room were a couple of long tables smothered in, at the last count, six Macintosh computers. In the middle was the Mac II on which a red wire-frame model of his sofa was lazily revolving within a blue wire-frame model of his narrow staircase, complete with banister rail, radiator and fuse-box details, and of course the awkward turn halfway up.

The sofa would start out spinning in one direction, hit an obstruction, twist itself in another plane, hit another obstruction, revolve round a third axis until it was stopped again, then cycle through the moves again in a different order. You didn't have to watch the sequence for very long before you saw it repeat itself.

The sofa was clearly stuck.

Three other Macs were connected up via long tangles of cable to an untidy agglomeration of synthesisers – an Emulator II+ HD sampler, a rack of TX modules, a Prophet VS, a Roland JX10, a Korg DW8000, an Octapad, a left-handed Synth-Axe MIDI guitar controller, and even an old drum machine stacked up and gathering dust in the corner – pretty much the works. There was also a small and rarely used cassette tape recorder: all the music was stored in sequencer files on the computers rather than on tape.

He dumped himself into a seat in front of one of the Macs to see what, if anything, it was doing. It was displaying an "Untitled" *Excel* spreadsheet and he wondered why.

He saved it and looked to see if he'd left himself any notes and

quickly discovered that the spreadsheet contained some of the data
he had previously downloaded after searching the *World
Reporter* and *Knowledge* on-line databases for facts about
swallows.

He now had figures which detailed their migratory habits, their
wing shapes, their aerodynamic profile and turbulence
characteristics, and some sort of rudimentary figures concerning
the patterns that a flock would adopt in flight, but as yet he had
only the faintest idea as to how he was going to synthesise them
all together.

Because he was too tired to think particularly constructively
tonight he savagely selected and copied a whole swathe of figures
from the spreadsheet at random, pasted them into his own
conversion program, which scaled and filtered and manipulated
the figures according to his own experimental algorithms, loaded
the converted file into *Performer*, a powerful sequencer program,
and played the result through random MIDI channels to
whichever synthesisers happened to be on at the moment.

The result was a short burst of the most hideous cacophony,
and he stopped it.

He ran the conversion program again, this time instructing it to
force-map the pitch values into G minor. This was a utility he was
determined in the end to get rid of because he regarded it as
cheating. If there was any basis to his firmly held belief that the
rhythms and harmonies of music which he found most satisfying
could be found in, or at least derived from, the rhythms and
harmonies of naturally occurring phenomena, then satisfying
forms of modality and intonation should emerge naturally as well,
rather than being forced.

For the moment, though, he forced it.

The result was a short burst of the most hideous cacophony in
G minor.

So much for random shortcuts.

The first task was a relatively simple one, which would be
simply to plot the waveform described by the tip of a swallow's
wing as it flies, then synthesise that waveform. That way he

would end up with a single note, which would be a good start, and it shouldn't take more than the weekend to do.

Except, of course, that he didn't have a weekend available to do it in because he had somehow to get Version 2 of *Anthem* out of the door sometime during the course of the next year, or "month" as Gordon called it.

Which brought Richard inexorably to the third thing he was shaking about.

There was absolutely no way that he could take the time off this weekend or next to fulfil the promise he had made to Susan's telephone-answering machine. And that, if this evening's débâcle had not already done so, would surely spell the final end.

But that was it. The thing was done. There is nothing you can do about a message on someone else's answering machine other than let events take their course. It was done. It was irrevocable.

An odd thought suddenly struck him.

It took him by considerable surprise, but he couldn't really see what was wrong with it.

Chapter Thirteen...

A pair of binoculars scanning the London night skyline, idly, curious, snooping. A little look here, a little look there, just seeing what's going on, anything interesting, anything useful.

The binoculars settle on the back of one particular house, attracted by a slight movement. One of those large late-Victorian villas, probably flats now. Lots of black iron drainpipes. Green rubber dustbins. But dark. No, nothing.

The binoculars are just moving onwards when another slight movement catches in the moonlight. The binoculars refocus very slightly, trying to find a detail, a hard edge, a slight contrast in the darkness. The mist has lifted now, and the darkness glistens. They refocus a very, very little more.

There it is. Something, definitely. Only this time a little higher up, maybe a foot or so, maybe a yard. The binoculars settle and relax – steady, trying for the edge, trying for the detail. There. The binoculars settle again – they have found their mark, straddled between a windowsill and a drainpipe.

It is a dark figure, splayed against the wall, looking down, looking for a new foothold, looking upwards, looking for a ledge. The binoculars peer intently.

The figure is that of a tall, thin man. His clothes are right for the job, dark trousers, dark sweater, but his movements are awkward and angular. Nervous. Interesting. The binoculars wait and consider, consider and judge.

The man is clearly a rank amateur.

Look at his fumbling. Look at his ineptitude. His feet slip on the drainpipe, his hands can't reach the ledge. He nearly falls. He waits to catch his breath. For a moment he starts to climb back down again, but seems to find that even tougher going.

He lunges again for the ledge and this time catches it. His foot shoots out to steady himself and nearly misses the pipe. Could have been very nasty, very nasty indeed.

But now the way is easier and progress is better. He crosses to another pipe, reaches a third-floor window ledge, flirts briefly with death as he crawls painfully on to it, and makes the cardinal error and looks down. He sways briefly and sits back heavily. He shades his eyes and peers inside to check that the room is dark, and sets about getting the window open.

One of the things that distinguish the amateur from the professional is that this is the point when the amateur thinks it would have been a good idea to bring along something to prise the window open with. Luckily for this amateur the householder is an amateur too, and the sash window slides grudgingly up. The climber crawls, with some relief, inside.

He should be locked up for his own protection, think the binoculars. A hand starts to reach for the phone. At the window a face looks back out and for a moment is caught in the moonlight, then it ducks back inside to carry on with its business.

The hand stays hovering over the phone for a moment or two, while the binoculars wait and consider, consider and judge. The hand reaches instead for the A–Z street map of London.

There is a long studious pause, a little more intent binocular work, and then the hand reaches for the phone again, lifts it and dials.

Chapter Fourteen...

Susan's flat was small but spacious, which was a trick, reflected Richard tensely as he turned on the light, that only women seemed able to pull off.

It wasn't that observation which made him tense, of course – he'd thought it before, many times. Every time he'd been in her flat, in fact. It always struck him, usually because he had just come from his own flat, which was four times the size and cramped. He'd just come from his own flat this time, only via a rather eccentric route, and it was this that made his usual observation unusually tense.

Despite the chill of the night he was sweating.

He looked back out of the window, turned and tiptoed across the room towards where the telephone and the answering machine stood on their own small table.

There was no point, he told himself, in tiptoeing. Susan wasn't in. He would be extremely interested to know where she was, in fact – just as she, he told himself, had probably been extremely interested in knowing where he had been at the beginning of the evening.

He realised he was still tiptoeing. He hit his leg to make himself stop doing it, but carried on doing it none the less.

Climbing up the outside wall had been terrifying.

He wiped his forehead with the arm of his oldest and greasiest sweater. There had been a nasty moment when his life had flashed before his eyes but he had been too preoccupied with falling and had missed all the good bits. Most of the good bits had involved Susan, he realised. Susan or computers. Never Susan *and* computers – those had largely been the bad bits. Which was why he was here, he told himself. He seemed to need convincing, and told himself again.

He looked at his watch. Eleven forty-five.

It occurred to him he had better go and wash his wet and dirty hands before he touched anything. It wasn't the police he was worried about, but Susan's terrifying cleaner. She would know.

He went into the bathroom, turned on the light switch, wiped it, and then stared at his own startled face in the bright neon-lit mirror as he ran the water over his hands. For a moment he thought of the dancing, warm candlelight of the Coleridge Dinner, and the images of it welled up out of the dim and distant past of the earlier part of the evening. Life had seemed easy then, and carefree. The wine, the conversation, simple conjuring tricks. He pictured the round pale face of Sarah, pop-eyed with wonder. He washed his own face.

He thought:

"... Beware! Beware!
His flashing eyes, his floating hair!"

He brushed his own hair. He thought, too, of the pictures hanging high in the darkness above their heads. He cleaned his teeth. The low buzz of the neon light snapped him back to the present and he suddenly remembered with appalled shock that he was here in his capacity as burglar.

Something made him look himself directly in the face in the mirror, then he shook his head, trying to clear it.

When would Susan be back? That, of course, would depend on what she was doing. He quickly wiped his hands and made his way back to the answering machine. He prodded at the buttons and his conscience prodded back at him. The tape wound back for what seemed to be an interminable time, and he realised with a jolt that it was probably because Gordon had been in full flood.

He had forgotten, of course, that there would be messages on the tape other than his own, and listening to other people's phone messages was tantamount to opening their mail.

He explained to himself once again that all he was trying to do was to undo a mistake he had made before it caused any irrevocable damage. He would just play the tiniest snippets till he found his own voice. That wouldn't be too bad, he wouldn't even be able to distinguish what was being said.

He groaned inwardly, gritted his teeth and stabbed at the Play button so roughly that he missed it and ejected the cassette by mistake. He put it back in and pushed the Play button more carefully.

Beep.

"Oh, Susan, hi, it's Gordon," said the answering machine. "Just on my way to the cottage. It's, er ..." He wound on for a couple of seconds. "... need to know that Richard is on the case. I mean *really* on ..." Richard set his mouth grimly and stabbed at the Fast Forward again. He really hated the fact that Gordon tried to put pressure on him via Susan, which Gordon always stoutly denied he did. Richard couldn't blame Susan for getting exasperated about his work sometimes if this sort of thing was going on.

Click.

"... Response. Make a note to Susan would you please, to get an 'Armed Response' sign made up with a sharp spike on the bottom at the right height for rabbits to see."

"*What?*" muttered Richard to himself, and his finger hesitated for a second over the Fast Forward button. He had a feeling that Gordon desperately wanted to be like Howard Hughes, and if he could never hope to be remotely as rich, he could at least try to be twice as eccentric. An act. A palpable act.

"That's secretary Susan at the office, not you, of course," continued Gordon's voice on the answering machine. "Where was I? Oh yes. Richard and *Anthem* 2.00. Susan, that thing has got to be in beta testing in two ..." Richard stabbed at the Fast Forward, tight-lipped.

"... point is that there's only one person who's really in a position to know if he's getting the important work done, or if he's just dreaming, and that one person ..." He stabbed angrily again. He had promised himself he wouldn't listen to any of it, and now here he was getting angry at what he was hearing. He should really just stop this. Well, just one more try.

When he listened again he just got music. Odd. He wound forward again, and still got music. Why would someone be phoning to play music to an answering machine? he wondered.

The phone rang. He stopped the tape and answered it, then almost dropped the phone like an electric eel as he realised what he was doing. Hardly daring to breathe, he held the telephone to his ear.

"Rule One in housebreaking," said a voice. "Never answer the telephone when you're in the middle of a job. Who are you supposed to be, for heaven's sake?"

Richard froze. It was a moment or two before he could find where he had put his voice.

"Who is this?" he demanded at last in a whisper.

"Rule Two," continued the voice. "Preparation. Bring the right tools. Bring gloves. Try to have the faintest glimmering of an idea of what you're about before you start dangling from window ledges in the middle of the night.

"Rule Three. *Never* forget Rule Two."

"Who is this?" exclaimed Richard again.

The voice was unperturbed. "Neighbourhood Watch," it said. "If you just look out of the back window you'll see ..."

Trailing the phone, Richard hurried over to the window and looked out. A distant flash startled him.

"Rule Four. Never stand where you can be photographed.

"Rule Five ... Are you listening to me, MacDuff?"

"What? Yes ..." said Richard in bewilderment. "How do you know me?"

"Rule Five. *Never* admit to your name."

Richard stood silent, breathing hard.

"I run a little course," said the voice, "if you're interested ..."

Richard said nothing.

"You're learning," continued the voice, "slowly, but you're learning. If you were learning fast you would have put the phone down by now, of course. But you're curious – and incompetent – and so you don't. I don't run a course for novice burglars as it happens, tempting though the idea is. I'm sure there would be grants available. If we have to have them they may as well be trained.

"However, if I did run such a course I would allow you to enrol for free, because I too am curious. Curious to know why Mr Richard MacDuff who, I am given to understand, is now a wealthy young man, something in the computer industry, I believe, should suddenly be needing to resort to house-breaking."

"Who –?"

"So I do a little research, phone Directory Enquiries and discover that the flat into which he is breaking is that of a Miss S. Way. I know that Mr Richard MacDuff's employer is the famous Mr G. Way and I wonder if they can by any chance be related."

"Who –?"

"You are speaking with Svlad, commonly known as 'Dirk' Cjelli, currently trading under the name of Gently for reasons which it would be otiose, at this moment, to rehearse. I bid you good evening. If you wish to know more I will be at the Pizza Express in Upper Street in ten minutes. Bring some money."

"Dirk?" exclaimed Richard. "You ... Are you trying to blackmail me?"

"No, you fool, for the pizzas." There was a click and Dirk Gently rang off.

Richard stood transfixed for a moment or two, wiped his forehead again, and gently replaced the phone as if it were an injured hamster. His brain began to buzz gently and suck its thumb. Lots of little synapses deep inside his cerebral cortex all joined hands and started dancing around and singing nursery rhymes. He shook his head to try and make them stop, and quickly sat down at the answering machine again.

He fought with himself over whether or not he was going to push the Play button again, and then did so anyway before he had made up his mind. Hardly four seconds of light orchestral music had oozed soothingly past when there came the sound of a key scratching in the lock out in the hallway.

In panic Richard thumped the Eject button, popped the cassette out, rammed it into his jeans pocket and replaced it from the pile of fresh cassettes that lay next to the machine. There was a similar pile next to his own machine at home. Susan at the office provided them – poor, long-suffering Susan at the office. He must remember to feel sympathy for her in the morning, when he had the time and concentration for it.

Suddenly, without even noticing himself doing it, he changed his mind. In a flash he popped the substitute cassette out of the machine again, replaced the one he had stolen, rammed down the rewind button and made a lunge for the sofa where, with two seconds to go before the door opened, he tried to arrange himself into a nonchalant and winning posture. On an impulse he stuck his left hand up behind his back where it might come in useful.

He was just trying to arrange his features into an expression composed in equal parts of contrition, cheerfulness and sexual allurement when the door opened and in walked Michael Wenton-Weakes.

Everything stopped.

Outside, the wind ceased. Owls halted in mid-flight. Well, maybe they did, maybe they didn't, certainly the central heating chose that moment to shut down, unable perhaps to cope with the supernatural chill that suddenly whipped through the room.

"What are you doing here, Wednesday?" demanded Richard. He rose from the sofa as if levitated with anger.

Michael Wenton-Weakes was a large sad-faced man known by some people as Michael Wednesday-Week, because that was when he usually promised to have things done by. He was dressed in a suit that had been superbly well tailored when his father, the late Lord Magna, had bought it forty years previously.

Michael Wenton-Weakes came very high on the small but select list of people whom Richard thoroughly disliked.

He disliked him because he found the idea of someone who

was not only privileged, but was also sorry for himself because he thought the world didn't really understand the problems of privileged people, deeply obnoxious. Michael, on the other hand, disliked Richard for the fairly simple reason that Richard disliked him and made no secret of it.

Michael gave a slow and lugubrious look back out into the hallway as Susan walked through. She stopped when she saw Richard. She put down her handbag, unwound her scarf, unbuttoned her coat, slipped it off, handed it to Michael, walked over to Richard and smacked him in the face.

"I've been saving that up all evening," she said furiously. "And don't try and pretend that's a bunch of flowers you've forgotten to bring which you're hiding behind your back. You tried that gag last time." She turned and stalked off.

"It's a box of chocolates I forgot this time," said Richard glumly and held out his empty hand to her retreating back. "I climbed up the entire outside wall without them. Did I feel a fool when I got in."

"Not very funny," said Susan. She swept into the kitchen and sounded as if she was grinding coffee with her bare hands. For someone who always looked so neat and sweet and delicate she packed a hell of a temper.

"It's true," said Richard, ignoring Michael completely. "I nearly killed myself."

"I'm not going to rise to that," said Susan from within the kitchen. "If you want something big and sharp thrown at you, why don't you come in here and be funny?"

"I suppose it would be pointless saying I'm sorry at this point," Richard called out.

"You bet," said Susan, sweeping back out of the kitchen again. She looked at him with her eyes flashing, and actually stamped her foot.

"Honestly, Richard," she said, "I suppose you're going to say you forgot again. How can you have the gall to stand there with two arms, two legs and a head as if you're a human being? This is behaviour that a bout of amoebic dysentery would ashamed of.

I bet that even the very lowest form of dysentery amoeba shows up to take its girlfriend out for a quick trot around the stomach lining once in a while. Well, I hope you had a lousy evening."

"I did," said Richard. "You wouldn't have liked it. There was a horse in the bathroom, and you know how you hate that sort of thing."

"Oh, Michael," said Susan brusquely, "don't just stand there like a sinking pudding. Thank you very much for dinner and the concert, you were very sweet and I did enjoy listening to your troubles all evening because they were such a nice change from mine. But I think it would be best if I just found your book and pushed you out. I've got some serious jumping up and down and ranting to do, and I know how it upsets your delicate sensibilities."

She retrieved her coat from him and hung it up. While he had been holding it he had seemed entirely taken up with this task and oblivious to anything else. Without it he seemed a little lost and naked and was forced to stir himself back into life. He turned his big heavy eyes back on Richard.

"Richard," he said, "I, er, read your piece in … in *Fathom*. On Music and, er …"

"Fractal Landscapes," said Richard shortly. He didn't want to talk to Michael, and he certainly didn't want to get drawn into a conversation about Michael's wretched magazine. Or rather, the magazine that *used* to be Michael's.

That was the precise aspect of the conversation that Richard didn't want to get drawn into.

"Er, yes. Very interesting, of course," said Michael in his silky, over-rounded voice. "Mountain shapes and tree shapes and all sorts of things. Recycled algae."

"Recursive algorithms."

"Yes, of course. Very interesting. But so wrong, so terribly wrong. For the magazine, I mean. It is, after all, an *arts* review. I would never have allowed such a thing, of course. Ross has utterly ruined it. Utterly. He'll have to go. *Have* to. He has no sensibilities and he's a thief."

"He's not a thief, Wednesday, that's absolutely absurd," snapped Richard, instantly getting drawn into it in spite of his resolution not to. "He had nothing to do with your getting the push whatsoever. That was your own silly fault, and you ..."

There was a sharp intake of breath.

"Richard," said Michael in his softest, quietest voice – arguing with him was like getting tangled in parachute silk – "I think you do not understand how important ..."

"Michael," said Susan gently but firmly, holding open the door. Michael Wenton-Weakes nodded faintly and seemed to deflate.

"Your book," Susan added, holding out to him a small and elderly volume on the ecclesiastical architecture of Kent. He took it, murmured some slight thanks, looked about him for a moment as if he'd suddenly realised something rather odd, then gathered himself together, nodded farewell and left.

Richard didn't appreciate quite how tense he had become till Michael left and he was suddenly able to relax. He'd always resented the indulgent soft spot that Susan had for Michael even if she did try to disguise it by being terribly rude to him all the time. Perhaps even because of that.

"Susan, what can I say ...?" he started lamely.

"You could say 'Ouch' for a start. You didn't even give me that satisfaction when I hit you, and I thought I did it rather hard. God, it's freezing in here. What's that window doing wide open?"

She went over to shut it.

"I told you. That's how I got in," said Richard.

He sounded sufficiently as if he meant it to make her look round at him in surprise.

"Really," he said. "Like in the chocolate ads, only I forgot the box of chocolates ..." He shrugged sheepishly.

She stared at him in amazement.

"What on earth possessed you to do that?" she said. She stuck her head out of the window and looked down. "You could have got killed," she said, turning back to him.

"Well, er, yes ..." he said. "It just seemed the only way to ... I don't know." He rallied himself. "You took your key back, remember?"

"Yes. I got fed up with you coming and raiding my larder when you couldn't be bothered to do your own shopping. Richard, you really climbed up this wall?"

"Well, I wanted to be here when you got in."

She shook her head in bewilderment. "It would have been a great deal better if you'd been here when I went out. Is that why you're wearing those filthy old clothes?"

"Yes. You don't think I went to dinner at St Cedd's like this?"

"Well, I no longer know what you consider to be rational behaviour." She sighed and fished about in a small drawer. "Here," she said, "if it's going to save your life," and handed him a couple of keys on a ring. "I'm too tired to be angry anymore. An evening of being lobbied by Michael has taken it out of me."

"Well, I'll never understand why you put up with him," said Richard, going to fetch the coffee.

"I know you don't like him, but he's very sweet and can be charming in his sad kind of way. Usually it's very relaxing to be with someone who's so self-absorbed, because it doesn't make any demands on you. But he's obsessed with the idea that I can do something about his magazine. I can't, of course. Life doesn't work like that. I do feel sorry for him, though."

"I don't. He's had it very, very easy all his life. He still has it very, very easy. He's just had his toy taken away from him, that's all. It's hardly unjust, is it?"

"It's not a matter of whether it's just or not. I feel sorry for him because he's unhappy."

"Well, of course he's unhappy. Al Ross has turned *Fathom* into a really sharp, intelligent magazine that everyone suddenly wants to read. It was just a bumbling shambles before. Its only real function was to let Michael have lunch and toady about with whoever he liked on the pretext that maybe they might like to write a little something. He hardly ever got an actual issue out. The whole thing was a sham. He pampered himself with it. I

really don't find that charming or engaging. I'm sorry, I'm going
on about it and I didn't mean to."

Susan shrugged uneasily.

"I think you overreact," she said, "though I think I will have to
steer clear of him if he's going to keep on at me to do something I
simply can't do. It's too exhausting. Anyway, listen, I'm glad
you had a lousy evening. I want to talk about what we were going
to do this weekend."

"Ah," said Richard, "well ..."

"Oh, I'd better just check the messages first."

She walked past him to the telephone-answering machine,
played the first few seconds of Gordon's message and then
suddenly ejected the cassette.

"I can't be bothered," she said, giving it to him. "Could you
just give this straight to Susan at the office tomorrow? Save her a
trip. If there's anything important on it she can tell me."

Richard blinked, said, "Er, yes," and pocketed the tape,
tingling with the shock of the reprieve.

"Anyway, the weekend –" said Susan, sitting down on the
sofa.

Richard wiped his hand over his brow. "Susan, I ..."

"I'm afraid I've got to work. Nicola's sick and I'm going to
have to dep for her at the Wigmore on Friday week. There's some
Vivaldi and some Mozart I don't know too well, so that means a
lot of extra practice this weekend, I'm afraid. Sorry."

"Well, in fact," said Richard, "I have to work as well." He sat
down by her.

"I know. Gordon keeps on at me to nag you. I wish he
wouldn't. It's none of my business and it puts me in an invidious
position. I'm tired of being pressurised by people, Richard. At
least you don't do that."

She took a sip of her coffee.

"But I'm sure," she added, "that there's some kind of grey area
between being pressurised and being completely forgotten about
that I'd quite like to explore. Give me a hug."

He hugged her, feeling that he was monstrously and

unworthily lucky. An hour later he let himself out and discovered that the Pizza Express was closed.

Meanwhile, Michael Wenton-Weakes made his way back to his home in Chelsea. As he sat in the back of the taxi he watched the streets with a blank stare and tapped his fingers lightly against the window in a slow thoughtful rhythm.

Rap tap tap a rap tap a rap a tap.

He was one of those dangerous people who are soft, squidgy and cowlike provided they have what they want. And because he had always had what he wanted, and had seemed easily pleased with it, it had never occurred to anybody that he was anything other than soft, squidgy and cowlike. You would have to push through a lot of soft squidgy bits in order to find a bit that didn't give when you pushed it. That was the bit that all the soft squidgy bits were there to protect.

Michael Wenton-Weakes was the younger son of Lord Magna, publisher, newspaper owner and over-indulgent father, under whose protective umbrella it had pleased Michael to run his own little magazine at a magnificent loss. Lord Magna had presided over the gradual but dignified and well-respected decline of the publishing empire originally founded by his father, the first Lord Magna.

Michael continued to tap his knuckles lightly on the glass.

A rap tap a rap a tap.

He remembered the appalling, terrible day when his father had electrocuted himself changing a plug, and his mother, his *mother*, took over the business. Not only took it over but started running it with completely unexpected verve and determination. She examined the company with a very sharp eye as to how it was being run, or walked, as she put it, and eventually even got around to looking at the accounts of Michael's magazine.

Tap tap tap.

Now Michael knew just enough about the business side of things to know what the figures ought to be, and he had simply assured his father that that was indeed what they were.

"Can't allow this job just to be a sinecure, you must see that, old fellow, you have to pay your way or how would it look, how would it be?" his father used to say, and Michael would nod seriously, and start thinking up the figures for next month, or whenever it was he would next manage to get an issue out.

His mother, on the other hand, was not so indulgent. Not by a lorryload.

Michael usually referred to his mother as an old battleaxe, but if she was fairly to be compared to a battleaxe it would only be to an exquisitely crafted, beautifully balanced battleaxe, with an elegant minimum of fine engraving which stopped just short of its gleaming razored edge. One swipe from such an instrument and you wouldn't even know you'd been hit until you tried to look at your watch a bit later and discovered that your arm wasn't on.

She had been waiting patiently – or at least with the appearance of patience – in the wings all this time, being the devoted wife, the doting but strict mother. Now someone had taken her – to switch metaphors for a moment – out of her scabbard and everyone was running for cover.

Including Michael.

It was her firm belief that Michael, whom she quietly adored, had been spoiled in the fullest and worst sense of the word, and she was determined, at this late stage, to stop it.

It didn't take her more than a few minutes to see that he had been simply making up the figures every month, and that the magazine was haemorrhaging money as Michael toyed with it, all the time running up huge lunch bills, taxi accounts and staff costs that he would playfully set against fictitious taxes. The whole thing had simply got lost somewhere in the gargantuan accounts of Magna House.

She had then summoned Michael to see her.

Tap tap a rap a tappa.

"How do you want me to treat you," she said, "as my son or as the editor of one of my magazines? I'm happy to do either."

"Your magazines? Well, I am your son, but I don't see ..."

"Right. Michael, I want you to look at these figures," she said briskly, handing over a sheet of computer printout. "The ones on the left show the actual incomings and outgoings of *Fathom*, the ones on the right are your own figures. Does anything strike you about them?"

"Mother, I can explain, I –"

"Good," said Lady Magna sweetly, "I'm very glad of that."

She took the piece of paper back. "Now. Do you have any views on how the magazine should best be run in the future?"

"Yes, absolutely. Very strong ones. I –"

"Good," said Lady Magna, with a bright smile. "Well, that's all perfectly satisfactory, then."

"Don't you want to hear –?"

"No, that's all right, dear. I'm just happy to know that you do have something to say on the matter to clear it all up. I'm sure the new owner of *Fathom* will be glad to listen to whatever it is."

"What?" said a stunned Michael. "You mean you're actually selling *Fathom*?"

"No. I mean I've already sold it. Didn't get much for it, I'm afraid. One pound plus a promise that you would be retained as editor for the next three issues, and after that it's at the new owner's discretion."

Michael stared, pop-eyed.

"Well, come now," said his mother reasonably, "we could hardly continue under the present arrangement, could we? You always agreed with your father that the job should not be a sinecure for you. And since I would have a great deal of difficulty in either believing or resisting your stories, I thought I would hand the problem on to someone with whom you could have a more objective relationship. Now, I have another appointment, Michael."

"Well, but ... who have you sold it to?" spluttered Michael.

"Gordon Way."

"Gordon Way! But for heaven's sake, Mother, he's –"

"He's very anxious to be seen to patronise the arts. And I think I do mean patronise. I'm sure you'll get on splendidly, dear. Now, if you don't mind –"

Michael stood his ground.

"I've never heard of anything so outrageous! I –"

"Do you know, that's exactly what Mr Way said when I showed him these figures and then demanded that you be kept on as editor for three issues."

Michael huffed and puffed and went red and wagged his finger, but could think of nothing more to say. Except, "What difference would it have made to all this if I'd said treat me as the editor of one of your magazines?"

"Why, dear," said Lady Magna with her sweetest smile, "I would have called you Mr Wenton-Weakes, of course. And I wouldn't now be telling you straighten your tie," she added, with a tiny little gesture under her chin.

Rap tap tap rap tap tap.

"Number seventeen, was it, guv?"

"Er ... what?" said Michael, shaking his head.

"It was seventeen you said, was it?" said the cab driver, "'Cause we're 'ere."

"Oh. Oh, yes, thank you," said Michael. He climbed out and fumbled in his pocket for some money.

"Tap tap tap, eh?"

"What?" said Michael handing over the fare.

"Tap tap tap," said the cab driver, "all the bloody way here. Got something on your mind, eh, mate?"

"Mind your own bloody business," snapped Michael savagely.

"If you say so, mate. Just thought you might be going mad or something," said the cabbie and drove off.

Michael let himself into his house and walked through the cold hall to the dining room, turned on the overhead light and poured himself a brandy from the decanter. He took off his coat, threw it across the large mahogany dining table and pulled a chair over to the window where he sat nursing his drink and his grievances.

Tap tap tap, he went on the window.

He had sullenly remained as editor for the stipulated three issues and was then, with little ceremony, let go. A new editor was found, a certain A. K. Ross, who was young, hungry and ambitious, and he quickly turned the magazine into a resounding success. Michael, in the meantime, had been lost and naked. There was nothing else for him.

He tapped on the window again and looked, as he frequently did, at the small table lamp that stood on the sill. It was a rather ugly, ordinary little lamp, and the only thing about it that regularly transfixed his attention was that this was the lamp that had electrocuted his father, and this was where he had been sitting.

The old boy was such a fool with anything technical. Michael could just see him peering with profound concentration through his half moons and sucking his moustache as he tried to unravel the arcane complexities of a thirteen-amp plug. He had, it seemed, plugged it back in the wall without first screwing the cover back on and then tried to change the fuse *in situ*. From this he received the shock which had stilled his already dicky heart.

Such a simple, simple error, thought Michael, such as anyone could have made, anyone, but the consequences of it were catastrophic. Utterly catastrophic. His father's death, his own loss, the rise of the appalling Ross and his disastrously successful magazine and ...

Tap tap tap.

He looked at the window, at his own reflection, and at the dark shadows of the bushes on the other side of it. He looked again at the lamp. This was the very object, this the very place, and the error was such a simple one. Simple to make, simple to prevent.

The only thing that separated him from that simple moment was the invisible barrier of the months that had passed in between.

A sudden, odd calm descended on him as if something inside him had suddenly been resolved.

Tap tap tap.

Fathom was his. It wasn't *meant* to be a success, it was his life. His life had been taken from him, and that demanded a response.

Tap tap tap crack.

He surprised himself by suddenly punching his hand through the window and cutting himself quite badly.

Chapter Fifteen...

Some of the less pleasant aspects of being dead were beginning to creep up on Gordon Way as he stood in front of his "cottage."

It was in fact a rather large house by anybody else's standards, but he had always wanted to have a cottage in the country and so when the time came for him finally to buy one and he discovered that he had rather more money available than he had ever seriously believed he might own, he bought a large old rectory and called it a cottage in spite of its seven bedrooms and its four acres of dank Cambridgeshire land. This did little to endear him to people who only had cottages, but then if Gordon Way had allowed his actions to be governed by what endeared him to people he wouldn't have been Gordon Way.

He wasn't, of course, Gordon Way any longer. He was the ghost of Gordon Way.

In his pocket he had the ghosts of Gordon Way's keys.

It was this realisation that had stopped him for a moment in his invisible tracks. The idea of walking through walls frankly revolted him. It was something he had been trying strenuously to avoid all night. He had instead been fighting to grip and grapple with every object he touched in order to render it, and thereby himself, substantial. To enter his house, his own house, by any means other than that of opening the front door and striding in in a proprietorial manner filled him with a hurtling sense of loss.

He wished, as he stared at it, that the house was not such an extreme example of Victorian Gothic, and that the moonlight didn't play so coldly on its narrow gabled windows and its forbidding turrets. He had joked, stupidly, when he bought it that it looked as if it ought to be haunted, not realising that one day it would be – or by whom.

A chill of the spirit gripped him as he made his way silently up the driveway, lined by the looming shapes of yew trees that were far older than the rectory itself. It was a disturbing thought that anybody else might be scared walking up such a driveway on such a night for fear of meeting something such as him.

Behind a screen of yew trees off to his left stood the gloomy bulk of the old church, decaying now, only used in rotation with others in neighbouring villages and presided over by a vicar who was always breathless from bicycling there and dispirited by the few who were waiting for him when he arrived. Behind the steeple of the church hung the cold eye of the moon.

A glimpse of movement seemed suddenly to catch his eye, as if a figure had moved in the bushes near the house, but it was, he told himself, only his imagination, overwrought by the strain of being dead. What was there here that he could possibly be afraid of?

He continued onwards, around the angle of the wing of the rectory, towards the front door set deep within its gloomy porch wreathed in ivy. He was suddenly startled to realise that there was light coming from within the house. Electric light and also the dim flicker of firelight.

It was a moment or two before he realised that he was, of course, expected that night, though hardly in his present form. Mrs Bennett, the elderly housekeeper, would have been in to make the bed, light the fire and leave out a light supper for him.

The television, too, would be on, especially so that he could turn it off impatiently upon entering.

His footsteps failed to crunch on the gravel as he approached. Though he knew that he must fail at the door, he nevertheless could not but go there first, to try if he could open it, and only then, hidden within the shadows of the porch, would he close his eyes and let himself slip ashamedly through it. He stepped up to the door and stopped.

It was open.

Just half an inch, but it was open. His spirit fluttered in fearful surprise. How could it be open? Mrs Bennett was always so conscientious about such things. He stood uncertainly for a moment and then with difficulty exerted himself against the door. Under the little pressure he could bring to bear on it, it swung slowly and unwillingly open, its hinges groaning in protest. He stepped through and slipped along the stone-flagged hallway. A wide staircase led up into the darkness, but the doors that led off from the hallway all stood closed.

The nearest door led into the drawing room, in which the fire was burning, and from which he could hear the muted car chases of the late movie. He struggled futilely for a minute or two with its shiny brass door knob, but was forced in the end to admit a humiliating defeat, and with a sudden rage flung himself straight at the door – and through it.

The room inside was a picture of pleasant domestic warmth. He staggered violently into it, and was unable to stop himself floating on through a small occasional table set with thick sandwiches and a Thermos flask of hot coffee, through a large overstuffed armchair, into the fire, through the thick hot brickwork and into the cold dark dining room beyond.

The connecting door back into the sitting room was also closed. Gordon fingered it numbly and then, submitting himself to the inevitable, braced himself, and slid back through it, calmly, gently, noticing for the first time the rich internal grain of the wood.

The coziness of the room was almost too much for Gordon, and he wandered distractedly around it, unable to settle, letting the warm liveliness of the firelight play through him. Him it couldn't warm.

What, he wondered, were ghosts supposed to do all night?

He sat, uneasily, and watched the television. Soon, however, the car chases drifted peacefully to a close and there was nothing left but grey snow and white noise, which he was unable to turn off.

He found he'd sunk too far into the chair and confused himself with bits of it as he pushed and pulled himself up. He tried to amuse himself by standing in the middle of a table, but it did little to alleviate a mood that was sliding inexorably from despondency downwards.

Perhaps he would sleep.

Perhaps.

He felt no tiredness or drowsiness, but just a deadly craving for oblivion. He passed back through the closed door and into the dark hallway, from which the wide heavy stairs led to the large gloomy bedrooms above.

Up these, emptily, he trod.

It was for nothing, he knew. If you cannot open the door to a bedroom you cannot sleep in its bed. He slid himself through the door and lifted himself on to the bed which he knew to be cold though he could not feel it. The moon seemed unable to leave him alone and shone full on him as he lay there wide-eyed and empty, unable now to remember what sleep was or how to do it.

The horror of hollowness lay on him, the horror of lying ceaselessly and forever awake at four o'clock in the morning.

He had nowhere to go, nothing to do when he got there, and no one he could go and wake up who wouldn't be utterly horrified to see him.

The worst moment had been when he had seen Richard on the road, Richard's face frozen white in the windscreen. He saw again his face, and that of the pale figure next to him.

That had been the thing which had shaken out of him the lingering shred of warmth at the back of his mind which said that this was just a temporary problem. It seemed terrible in the night hours, but would be all right in the morning when he could see people and sort things out. He fingered the memory of the moment in his mind and could not let it go.

He had seen Richard and Richard, he knew, had seen him.

It was not going to be all right.

Usually when he felt this bad at night he popped downstairs to see what was in the fridge, so he went now. It would be more cheerful than this moonlit bedroom. He would hang around the kitchen going bump in the night.

He slid down – and partially through – the banisters, wafted through the kitchen door without a second thought and then devoted all his concentration and energy for about five minutes to getting the light switch on.

That gave him a real sense of achievement and he determined to celebrate with a beer.

After a minute or two of repeatedly juggling and dropping a can of Fosters he gave it up. He had not the slightest conception of how he could manage to open a ring pull, and besides the stuff was all shaken up by now – and what was he going to do with the stuff even if he did get it open?

He didn't have a body to keep it in. He hurled the can away from him and it scuttled off under a cupboard.

He began to notice something about himself, which was the way in which his ability to grasp things seemed to grow and fade in a slow rhythm, as did his visibility.

There was an irregularity in the rhythm, though, or perhaps it was just that sometimes the effects of it would be much more pronounced than at others. That, too, seemed to vary according to a slower rhythm. Just at that moment it seemed to him that his strength was on the increase.

In a sudden fever of activity he tried to see how many things in the kitchen he could move or use or somehow get to work.

He pulled open cupboards, he yanked out drawers, scattering cutlery on the floor. He got a brief whirr out of the food processor, he knocked over the electric coffee grinder without getting it to work, he turned on the gas on the cooker hob but then couldn't light it, he savaged a loaf of bread with a carving knife. He tried stuffing lumps of bread into his mouth, but they simply fell through his mouth to the floor. A mouse appeared, but scurried from the room, its coat electric with fear.

Eventually he stopped and sat at the kitchen table, emotionally exhausted but physically numb.

How, he wondered, would people react to his death?

Who would be most sorry to know that he had gone?

For a while there would be shock, then sadness, then they would adjust, and he would be a fading memory as people got on with their own lives without him, thinking that he had gone on to wherever people go. That was a thought that filled him with the most icy dread.

He had not gone. He was still here.

He sat facing one cupboard that he hadn't managed to open yet because its handle was too stiff, and that annoyed him. He grappled awkwardly with a tin of tomatoes, then went over again to the large cupboard and attacked the handle with the tin. The door flew open and his own missing bloodstained body fell horribly forward out of it.

Gordon hadn't realised up till this point that it was possible for a ghost to faint.

He realised it now and did it.

He was woken a couple of hours later by the sound of his gas cooker exploding.

Chapter Sixteen...

The following morning Richard woke up twice.

The first time he assumed he had made a mistake and turned over for a fitful few minutes more. The second time he sat up with a jolt as the events of the previous night insisted themselves upon him.

He went downstairs and had a moody and unsettled breakfast, during which nothing went right. He burned the toast, spilled the coffee, and realised that though he'd meant to buy some more marmalade yesterday, he hadn't. He surveyed his feeble attempt at feeding himself and thought that maybe he could at least allow himself the time to take Susan out for an amazing meal tonight, to make up for last night.

If he could persuade her to come.

There was a restaurant that Gordon had been enthusing about at great length and recommending that they try. Gordon was pretty good on restaurants – he certainly seemed to spend enough time in them. He sat and tapped his teeth with a pencil for a couple of minutes, and then went up to his workroom and lugged a telephone directory out from under a pile of computer magazines.

L'Esprit d'Escalier.

He phoned the restaurant and tried to book a table, but when he said when he wanted it for this seemed to cause a little amusement.

"Ah, non, m'sieur," said the maître d', "I regret that it is impossible. At this moment it is necessary to make reservations at least three weeks in advance. Pardon, m'sieur."

Richard marvelled at the idea that there were people who actually knew what they wanted to do three weeks in advance, thanked the maître d' and rang off. Well, maybe a pizza again instead. This thought connected back to the appointment he had failed to keep last night, and after a moment curiosity overcame him and he reached for the phone book again.

Gentleman ...

Gentles ...

Gentry.

There was no Gently at all. Not a single one. He found the other directories, except for the S–Z book which his cleaning lady continually threw away for reasons he had never yet fathomed.

There was certainly no Cjelli, or anything like it. There was no Jently, no Dgently, no Djently, no Dzently, nor anything remotely similar. He wondered about Tjently, Tsentli or Tzentli and tried Directory Enquiries, but they were out. He sat and tapped his teeth with a pencil again and watched his sofa slowly revolving on the screen of his computer.

How very peculiar it had been that it had only been hours earlier that Reg had asked after Dirk with such urgency.

If you really wanted to find someone, how would you set about it, what would you do?

He tried phoning the police, but they were out too. Well, that was that. He had done all he could do for the moment short of hiring a private detective, and he had better ways of wasting his time and money. He would run into Dirk again, as he did every few years or so.

He found it hard to believe there were really such people, anyway, as private detectives.

What sort of people were they? What did they look like, where did they work?

What sort of tie would you wear if you were a private detective? Presumably it would have to be exactly the sort of tie tjat people wouldn't expect private detectives to wear. Imagine having to sort out a problem like that when you'd just got up.

Just out of curiosity as much as anything else, and because the only alternative was settling down to *Anthem* coding, he found himself leafing through the Yellow Pages.

Private Detectives – see Detective Agencies.

The words looked almost odd in such a solid and businesslike context. He flipped back through the book. Dry Cleaners, Dog Breeders, Dental Technicians, Detective Agencies ...

At that moment the phone rang and he answered it, a little curtly. He didn't like being interrupted.

"Something wrong, Richard?"

"Oh, hi, Kate, sorry, no. I was ... my mind was elsewhere."

Kate Anselm was another star programmer at WayForward Technologies. She was working on a long-term Artificial Intelligence project, the sort of thing that sounded like an absurd pipe dream until you heard her talking about it. Gordon needed to hear her talking about it quite regularly, partly because he was nervous about the money it was costing and partly because, well, there was little doubt that Gordon liked to hear Kate talking anyway.

"I didn't want to disturb you," she said. "It's just I was trying to contact Gordon and can't. There's no reply from London or the cottage, or his car or his bleeper. It's just that for someone as obsessively in contact as Gordon it's a bit odd. You heard he's had a phone put in his isolation tank? True."

"I haven't spoken to him since yesterday," said Richard. He suddenly remembered the tape he had taken from Susan's answering machine, and hoped to God there wasn't anything more important in Gordon's message than ravings about rabbits. He said, "I know he was going to the cottage. Er, I don't know where he is. Have you tried –" Richard couldn't think of anywhere else to try – "... er. Good God."

"Richard?"

"How extraordinary..."

"Richard, what's the matter?"

"Nothing, Kate. Er, I've just read the most astounding thing."

"Really, what are you reading?"

"Well, the telephone directory, in fact ..."

"Really? I must rush out and buy one. Have the film rights gone?"

"Look, sorry, Kate, can I get back to you? I don't know where Gordon is at the moment and –"

"Don't worry. I know how it is when you can't wait to turn the next page. They always keep you guessing till the end, don't they? It must have been Zbigniew that did it. Have a good weekend." She hung up.

Richard hung up too, and sat staring at the box advertisement lying open in front of him in the Yellow Pages.

DIRK GENTLY'S
HOLISTIC DETECTIVE AGENCY
We solve the *whole* crime
We find the *whole* person
Phone today for the *whole* solution to your problem
(Missing cats and messy divorces a speciality)
33a Peckender St., London N1 01-354 9112

Peckender Street was only a few minutes' walk away. Richard scribbled down the address, pulled on his coat and trotted downstairs, stopping to make another quick inspection of the sofa. There must, he thought, be something terribly obvious that he was overlooking. The sofa was jammed on a slight turn in the long narrow stairway. At this point the stairs were interrupted for a couple of yards of flat landing, which corresponded with the position of the flat directly beneath Richard's. However, his inspection produced no new insights, and he eventually clambered on over it and out of the front door.

In Islington you can hardly hurl a brick without hitting three antique shops, an estate agent and a bookshop.

Even if you didn't actually hit them you would certainly set off their burglar alarms, which wouldn't be turned off again till after the weekend. A police car played its regular game of dodgems down Upper Street and squealed to a halt just past him. Richard crossed the road behind it.

The day was cold and bright, which he liked. He walked across the top of Islington Green, where winos get beaten up, past the site of the old Collins Music Hall which had got burnt down, and through Camden Passage where American tourists get ripped off. He browsed among the antiques for a while and looked at a pair of earrings that he thought Susan would like, but he wasn't sure. Then he wasn't sure that he liked them, got confused and gave up. He looked in at a bookshop, and on an impulse bought an anthology of Coleridge's poems since it was just lying there.

From here he threaded his way through the winding back streets, over the canal, past the council estates that lined the canal, through a number of smaller and smaller squares, till finally he reached Peckender Street, which had turned out to be a good deal farther than he'd thought.

It was the sort of street where property developers in large Jaguars drive around at the weekend salivating. It was full of end-of-lease shops, Victorian industrial architecture and a short, decaying late-Georgian terrace, all just itching to be pulled down so that sturdy young concrete boxes could sprout in their places. Estate agents roamed the area in hungry packs, eyeing each other warily, their clipboards on a hair trigger.

Number 33, when he eventually found it neatly sandwiched between 37 and 45, was in a poorish state of repair, but no worse than most of the rest.

The ground floor was a dusty travel agent's whose window was cracked and whose faded BOAC posters were probably now quite valuable. The doorway next to the shop had been painted bright red, not well, but at least recently. A push button next to the door said, in neatly pencilled lettering, "Dominique, French lessons, 3me Floor".

The most striking feature of the door, however, was the bold and shiny brass plaque fixed in the dead centre of it, on which was engraved the legend "Dirk Gently's Holistic Detective Agency".

Nothing else. It looked brand new – even the screws that held it in place were still shiny.

The door opened to Richard's push and he peered inside.

He saw a short and musty hallway which contained little but the stairway that led up from it. A door at the back of the hall showed little sign of having been opened in recent years, and had stacks of old metal shelving, a fish tank and the carcass of a bike piled up against it. Everything else, the walls, the floor, the stairs themselves, and as much of the rear door as could be got at, had been painted grey in an attempt to smarten it up cheaply, but it was all now badly scuffed, and little cups of fungus were peeking from a damp stain near the ceiling.

The sounds of angry voices reached him, and as he started up the stairs he was able to disentangle the noises of two entirely separate but heated arguments that were going on somewhere above him.

One ended abruptly – or at least half of it did – as an angry overweight man came clattering down the stairs pulling his raincoat collar straight. The other half of the argument continued in a torrent of aggrieved French from high above them. The man pushed past Richard, said, "Save your money, mate, it's a complete washout," and disappeared out into the chilly morning.

The other argument was more muffled. As Richard reached the first corridor a door slammed somewhere and brought that too to an end. He looked into the nearest open doorway.

It led into a small ante-office. The other, inner door leading from it was firmly closed. A youngish plump-faced girl in a cheap blue coat was pulling sticks of make-up and boxes of Kleenex out of her desk drawer and thrusting them into her bag.

"Is this the detective agency?" Richard asked her tentatively.

The girl nodded, biting her lip and keeping her head down.

"And is Mr Gently in?"

"He may be," she said, throwing back her hair, which was too curly for throwing back properly, "and then again he may not be. I am not in a position to tell. It is not my business to know of his whereabouts. His whereabouts are, as of now, entirely his own business."

She retrieved her last pot of nail varnish and tried to slam the drawer shut. A fat book sitting upright in the drawer prevented it from closing. She tried to slam the drawer again, without success. She picked up the book, ripped out a clump of pages and replaced it. This time she was able to slam the drawer with ease.

"Are you his secretary?" asked Richard.

"I am his ex-secretary and I intend to stay that way," she said, firmly snapping her bag shut. "If he intends to spend his money on stupid expensive brass plaques rather than on paying me, then let him. But I won't stay to stand for it, thank you very much. Good for business, my foot. Answering the phones properly is good for business and I'd like to see his fancy brass plaque do that. If you'll excuse me I'd like to storm out, please."

Richard stood aside, and out she stormed.

"And good riddance!" shouted a voice from the inner office. A phone rang and was picked up immediately.

"Yes?" answered the voice from the inner office, testily. The girl popped back for her scarf, but quietly, so her ex-employer wouldn't hear. Then she was finally gone.

"Yes, Dirk Gently's Holistic Detective Agency. How can we be of help to you?"

The torrent of French from upstairs had ceased. A kind of tense calm descended.

Inside, the voice said, "That's right, Mrs Sunderland, messy divorces are our particular speciality."

There was a pause.

"Yes, thank you, Mrs Sunderland, not quite that messy." Down went the phone again, to be replaced instantly by the ringing of another one.

Richard looked around the grim little office. There was very little in it. A battered chipboard veneer desk, an old grey filing cabinet and a dark green tin wastepaper bin. On the wall was a Duran Duran poster on which someone had scrawled in fat red felt tip, "Take this down please".

Beneath that another hand had scrawled, "No".

Beneath that again the first hand had written, "I insist that you take it down".

Beneath that the second hand had written, "Won't!"

Beneath that – "You're fired".

Beneath that – "Good!"

And there the matter appeared to have rested.

He knocked on the inner door, but was not answered. Instead the voice continued, "I'm very glad you asked me that, Mrs Rawlinson. The term 'holistic' refers to my conviction that what we are concerned with here is the fundamental interconnectedness of all things. I do not concern myself with such petty things as fingerprint powder, telltale pieces of pocket fluff and inane footprints. I see the solution to each problem as being detectable in the pattern and web of the whole. The connections between causes and effects are often much more subtle and complex than we with our rough and ready understanding of the physical world might naturally suppose, Mrs Rawlinson.

"Let me give you an example. If you go to an acupuncturist with toothache he sticks a needle instead into your thigh. Do you know why he does that, Mrs Rawlinson?

"No, neither do I, Mrs Rawlinson, but we intend to find out. A pleasure talking to you, Mrs Rawlinson. Goodbye."

Another phone was ringing as he put this one down.

Richard eased the door open and looked in.

It was the same Svlad, or Dirk, Cjelli. Looking a little rounder about the middle, a little looser and redder about the eyes and the neck, but it was still essentially the same face that he remembered most vividly smiling a grim smile as its owner climbed into the back of one of the Black Marias of the Cambridgeshire constabulary, eight years previously.

He wore a heavy old light brown suit which looked as if it has been worn extensively for bramble hacking expeditions in some distant and better past, a red checked shirt which failed entirely to harmonise with the suit, and a green striped tie which refused to speak to either of them. He also wore thick metal-rimmed spectacles, which probably accounted at least in part for his dress sense.

"Ah, Mrs Bluthall, how thoroughly uplifting to hear from you," he was saying. "I was so distressed to learn that Miss Tiddles has passed over. This is desperate news indeed. And yet, and yet ... Should we allow black despair to hide from us the fairer light in which your blessed moggy now forever dwells?

"I think not. Hark. I think I hear Miss Tiddles miaowing e'en now. She calls to you, Mrs Bluthall. She says she is content, she is at peace. She says she'll be even more at peace when you've paid some bill or other. Does that ring a bell with you at all, Mrs Bluthall? Come to think of it I think I sent you one myself not three months ago. I wonder if it can be that which is disturbing her eternal rest."

Dirk beckoned Richard in with a brisk wave and then motioned him to pass the crumpled pack of French cigarettes that was sitting just out of his reach.

"Sunday night, then, Mrs Bluthall, Sunday night at eight-thirty. You know the address. Yes, I'm sure Miss Tiddles will appear, as I'm sure will your cheque book. Till then, Mrs Bluthall, till then."

Another phone was already ringing as he got rid of Mrs Bluthall. He grabbed at it, lighting his crumpled cigarette at the same time.

"Ah, Mrs Sauskind," he said in answer to the caller, "my oldest and may I say most valued client. Good day to you, Mrs Sauskind, good day. Sadly, no sign as yet of young Roderick, I'm afraid, but the search is intensifying as it moves into what I am confident are its closing stages, and I am sanguine that within mere days from today's date we will have the young rascal permanently restored to your arms and mewing prettily, ah yes the bill, I was wondering if you had received it."

Dirk's crumpled cigarette turned out to be too crumpled to smoke, so he hooked the phone on his shoulder and poked around in the packet for another, but it was empty.

He rummaged on his desk for a piece of paper and a stub of pencil and wrote a note which he passed to Richard.

"Yes, Mrs Sauskind," he assured the telephone, "I am listening with the utmost attention."

The note said "Tell secretary get cigs".

"Yes," continued Dirk into the phone, "but as I have endeavoured to explain to you, Mrs Sauskind, over the seven years of our acquaintance, I incline to the quantum mechanical view in this matter. My theory is that your cat is not lost, but that his waveform has temporarily collapsed and must be restored. Schrödinger. Planck. And so on."

Richard wrote on the note "You haven't got secretary" and pushed it back.

Dirk considered this for a while, then wrote "Damn and blast" on the paper and pushed it to Richard again.

"I grant you, Mrs Sauskind," continued Dirk blithely, "that nineteen years is, shall we say, a distinguished age for a cat to reach, yet can we allow ourselves to believe that a cat such as Roderick has not reached it?

"And should we now in the autumn of his years abandon him to his fate? This surely is the time that he most needs the support of our continuing investigations. This is the time that we should redouble our efforts, and with your permission, Mrs Sauskind, that is what I intend to do. Imagine, Mrs Sauskind, how you would face him if you had not done this simple thing for him."

Richard fidgeted with the note, shrugged to himself, and wrote "I'll get them" on it and passed it back once more.

Dirk shook his head in admonition, then wrote "I couldn't possibly that would be most kind". As soon as Richard had read this, Dirk took the note back and added "Get money from secretary" to it.

Richard looked at the paper thoughtfully, took the pencil and put a tick next to where he had previously written "You haven't got secretary". He pushed the paper back across the table to Dirk, who merely glanced at it and ticked "I couldn't possibly that would be most kind".

"Well, perhaps," continued Dirk to Mrs Sauskind, "you could just run over any of the areas in the bill that cause you difficulty. Just the broader areas."

Richard let himself out.

Running down the stairs, he passed a young hopeful in a denim jacket and close-cropped hair peering anxiously up the stairwell.

"Any good, mate?" he said to Richard.

"Amazing," murmured Richard, "just amazing."

He found a nearby newsagent's and picked up a couple of packets of Disque Bleu for Dirk, and a copy of the new edition of *Personal Computer World*, which had a picture of Gordon Way on the front.

"Pity about him, isn't it?" said the newsagent.

"What? Oh, er ... yes," said Richard. He often thought the same himself, but was surprised to find his feelings so widely echoed. He picked up a *Guardian* as well, paid and left.

Dirk was still on the phone with his feet on the table when Richard returned, and it was clear that he was relaxing into his negotiations.

"Yes, expenses were, well, expensive in the Bahamas, Mrs Sauskind, it is in the nature of expenses to be so. Hence the name." He took the proffered packets of cigarettes, seemed disappointed there were only two, but briefly raised his eyebrows to Richard in acknowledgment of the favour he had done him, and then waved him to a chair.

The sounds of an argument conducted partly in French drifted down from the floor above.

"Of course I will explain to you again why the trip to the Bahamas was so vitally necessary," said Dirk Gently soothingly. "Nothing could give me greater pleasure. I believe, as you know, Mrs Sauskind, in the fundamental interconnectedness of all things. Furthermore I have plotted and triangulated the vectors of the interconnectedness of all things and traced them to a beach in Bermuda which it is therefore necessary for me to visit from time to time in the course of my investigations. I wish it were not the case, since, sadly, I am allergic to both the sun and rum punches, but then we all have our crosses to bear, do we not, Mrs Sauskind?"

A babble seemed to break out from the telephone.

"You sadden me, Mrs Sauskind. I wish I could find it in my heart to tell you that I find your scepticism rewarding and invigorating, but with the best will in the world I cannot. I am drained by it, Mrs Sauskind, drained. I think you will find an item in the bill to that effect. Let me see."

He picked up a flimsy carbon copy lying near him.

"'Detecting and triangulating the vectors of interconnectedness of all things, one hundred and fifty pounds.' We've dealt with that.

"'Tracing same to beach on Bahamas, fare and accommodation'. A mere fifteen hundred. The accommodation was, of course, distressingly modest.

"Ah yes, here we are, 'Struggling on in the face of draining scepticism from client, drinks – three hundred and twenty-seven pounds fifty.'

"Would that I did not have to make such charges, my dear Mrs Sauskind, would that the occasion did not continually arise. Not believing in my methods only makes my job more difficult, Mrs Sauskind, and hence, regrettably, more expensive."

Upstairs, the sounds of argument were becoming more heated by the moment. The French voice seemed to be verging on hysteria.

"I do appreciate, Mrs Sauskind," continued Dirk, "that the cost of the investigation has strayed somewhat from the original estimate, but I am sure that you will in your turn appreciate that a job which takes seven years to do must clearly be more difficult than one that can be pulled off in an afternoon and must therefore be charged at a higher rate. I have continually to revise my estimate of how difficult the task is in the light of how difficult it has so far proved to be."

The babble from the phone became more frantic.

"My dear Mrs Sauskind – or may I call you Joyce? Very well then. My dear Mrs Sauskind, let me say this. Do not worry yourself about this bill, do not let it alarm or discomfit you. Do not, I beg you, let it become a source of anxiety to you. Just grit your teeth and pay it."

He pulled his feet down off the table and leaned forward over the desk, inching the telephone receiver inexorably back towards its cradle.

"As always, the very greatest pleasure to speak with you, Mrs Sauskind. For now, goodbye."

He at last put down the receiver, picked it up again, and dropped it for the moment into the waste basket.

"My dear Richard MacDuff," he said, producing a large flat box from under his desk and pushing it across the table at him, "your pizza."

Richard started back in astonishment.

"Er, no thanks," he said, "I had breakfast. Please. You have it."

Dirk shrugged. "I told them you'd pop in and settle up over the weekend," he said. "Welcome, by the way, to my offices."

He waved a vague hand around the tatty surroundings.

"The light works," he said, indicating the window, "the gravity works," he said, dropping a pencil on the floor. "Anything else we have to take our chances with."

Richard cleared his throat. "What," he said, "is this?"

"What is what?"

"This," exclaimed Richard, "all this. You appear to have a Holistic Detective Agency and I don't even know what one is."

"I provide a service that is unique in this world," said Dirk. "The term 'holistic' refers to my conviction that what we are concerned with here is the fundamental interconnectedness of all –"

"Yes, I got that bit earlier," said Richard. "I have to say that it sounded a bit like an excuse for exploiting gullible old ladies."

"Exploiting?" asked Dirk. "Well, I suppose it would be if anybody ever paid me, but I do assure you, my dear Richard, that there never seems to be the remotest danger of that. I live in what are known as hopes. I hope for fascinating and remunerative cases, my secretary hopes that I will pay her, her landlord hopes that she will produce some rent, the Electricity Board hopes that he will settle their bill, and so on. I find it a wonderfully optimistic way of life.

"Meanwhile I give a lot of charming and silly old ladies something to be happily cross about and virtually guarantee the freedom of their cats. Is there, you ask – and I put the question for you because I know you know I hate to be interrupted – is there a single case that exercises the tiniest part of my intellect, which, as you hardly need me to tell you, is prodigious? No. But do I despair? Am I downcast? Yes. Until," he added, "today."

"Oh, well, I'm glad of that," said Richard, "but what was all that rubbish about cats and quantum mechanics?"

With a sigh Dirk flipped up the lid of the pizza with a single flick of practised fingers. He surveyed the cold round thing with a kind of sadness and then tore off a hunk of it. Pieces of pepperoni and anchovy scattered over his desk.

"I am sure, Richard," he said, "that you are familiar with the notion of Schrödinger's Cat," and he stuffed the larger part of the hunk into his mouth.

"Of course," said Richard. "Well, reasonably familiar."

"What is it?" said Dirk through a mouthful.

Richard shifted irritably in his seat. "It's an illustration," he said, "of the principle that at a quantum level all events are governed by probabilities ..."

"At a quantum level, and therefore at all levels," interrupted Dirk. "Though at any level higher than the subatomic the cumulative effect of those probabilities is, in the normal course of events, indistinguishable from the effect of hard and fast physical laws. Continue."

He put some more cold pizza into his face.

Richard reflected that Dirk's was a face into which too much had already been put. What with that and the amount he talked, the traffic through his mouth was almost incessant. His ears, on the other hand, remained almost totally unused in normal conversation.

It occurred to Richard that if Lamarck had been right and you were to take a line through this behaviour for several generations, the chances were that some radical replumbing of the interior of the skull would eventually take place.

Richard continued, "Not only are quantum level events governed by probabilities, but those probabilities aren't even resolved into actual events until they are measured. Or to use a phrase that I just heard you use in a rather bizarre context, the act of measurement collapses the probability waveform. Up until that point all the possible courses of action open to, say, an electron, coexist as probability waveforms. Nothing is decided. Until it's measured."

Dirk nodded. "More or less," he said, taking another mouthful. "But what of the cat?"

Richard decided that there was only one way to avoid having to watch Dirk eat his way through all the rest of the pizza, and that was to eat the rest himself. He rolled it up and took a token nibble off the end. It was rather good. He took another bite.

Dirk watched this with startled dismay.

"So," said Richard, "the idea behind Schrödinger's Cat was to try and imagine a way in which the effects of probabilistic behaviour at a quantum level could be considered at a macroscopic level. Or let's say an everyday level."

"Yes, let's," said Dirk, regarding the rest of the pizza with a stricken look. Richard took another bite and continued cheerfully.

"So you imagine that you take a cat and put it in a box that you can seal completely. Also in the box you put a small lump of radioactive material, and a phial of poison gas. You arrange it so that within a given period of time there is an exactly fifty-fifty chance that an atom in the radioactive lump will decay and emit an electron. If it does decay then it triggers the release of the gas and kills the cat. If it doesn't, the cat lives. Fifty-fifty. Depending on the fifty-fifty chance that a single atom does or does not decay.

"The point as I understand it is this: since the decay of a single atom is a quantum level event that wouldn't be resolved either way until it was observed, and since you don't make the observation until you open the box and see whether the cat is alive or dead, then there's a rather extraordinary consequence.

"Until you do open the box the cat itself exists in an indeterminate state. The possibility that it is alive, and the possibility that it is dead, are two different waveforms superimposed on each other inside the box. Schrödinger put forward this idea to illustrate what he thought was absurd about quantum theory."

Dirk got up and padded over to the window, probably not so much for the meagre view it afforded over an old warehouse on which an alternative comedian was lavishing his vast lager commercial fees developing into luxury apartments, as for the lack of view it afforded of the last piece of pizza disappearing.

"Exactly," said Dirk, "bravo!"

"But what's all that got to do with this – this Detective Agency?"

"Oh, that. Well, some researchers were once conducting such an experiment, but when they opened up the box, the cat was neither alive nor dead but was in fact completely missing, and they called me in to investigate. I was able to deduce that nothing very dramatic had happened. The cat had merely got fed up with being repeatedly locked up in a box and occasionally gassed and had taken the first opportunity to hoof it through the window. It was for me the work of a moment to set a saucer of milk by the window and call 'Bernice' in an enticing voice – the cat's name was Bernice, you understand –"

"Now, wait a minute – " said Richard.

" – and the cat was soon restored. A simple enough matter, but it seemed to create quite an impression in certain circles, and soon one thing led to another as they do and it all culminated in the thriving career you see before you."

"Wait a minute, wait a minute," insisted Richard, slapping the table.

"Yes?" enquired Dirk innocently.

"Now, what are you talking about, Dirk?"

"You have a problem with what I have told you?"

"Well, I hardly know where to begin," protested Richard. "All right. You said that some people were performing the experiment.

That's nonsense. Schrödinger's Cat isn't a real experiment. It's just an illustration for arguing about the idea. It's not something you'd actually do."

Dirk was watching him with odd attention.

"Oh, really?" he said at last. "And why not?"

"Well, there's nothing you can test. The whole point of the idea is to think about what happens before you make your observation. You can't know what's going on inside the box without looking, and the very instant you look the wave packet collapses and the probabilities resolve. It's self-defeating. It's completely purposeless."

"You are, of course, perfectly correct as far as you go," replied Dirk, returning to his seat. He drew a cigarette out of the packet, tapped it several times on the desk, and leant across the desk and pointed the filter at Richard.

"But think about this," he continued. "Supposing you were to introduce a psychic, someone with clairvoyant powers, into the experiment – someone who is able to divine what state of health the cat is in without opening the box. Someone who has, perhaps, a certain eerie sympathy with cats. What then? Might that furnish us with an additional insight into the problem of quantum physics?"

"Is that what they wanted to do?"

"It's what they did."

"Dirk, this is *complete nonsense*."

Dirk raised his eyebrows challengingly.

"All right, all right," said Richard, holding up his palms, "let's just follow it through. Even if I accepted – which I don't for one second – that there was any basis at all for clairvoyance, it wouldn't alter the fundamental undoableness of the experiment. As I said, the whole thing turns on what happens inside the box before it's observed. It doesn't matter how you observe it, whether you look into the box with your eyes or – well, with your mind, if you insist. If clairvoyance works, then it's just another way of looking into the box, and if it doesn't then of course it's irrelevant."

"It might depend, of course, on the view you take of clairvoyance ..."

"Oh yes? And what view do you take of clairvoyance? I should be very interested to know, given your history."

Dirk tapped the cigarette on the desk again and looked narrowly at Richard.

There was a deep and prolonged silence, disturbed only by the sound of distant crying in French.

"I take the view I have always taken," said Dirk eventually.

"Which is?"

"That I am not clairvoyant."

"Really," said Richard. "Then what about the exam papers?"

The eyes of Dirk Gently darkened at the mention of this subject.

"A coincidence," he said, in a low, savage voice, "a strange and chilling coincidence, but none the less a coincidence. One, I might add, which caused me to spend a considerable time in prison. Coincidences can be frightening and dangerous things."

Dirk gave Richard another of his long appraising looks.

"I have been watching you carefully," he said. "You seem to be extremely relaxed for a man in your position."

This seemed to Richard to be an odd remark, and he tried to make sense of it for a moment. Then the light dawned, and it was an aggravating light.

"Good heavens," he said, "he hasn't got to you as well, has he?"

This remark seemed to puzzle Dirk in return.

"Who hasn't got to me?" he said.

"Gordon. No, obviously not. Gordon Way. He has this habit of trying to get other people to bring pressure on me to get on with what he sees as important work. I thought for a moment – oh, never mind. What did you mean, then?"

"Ah. Gordon Way *has* this habit, has he?"

"Yes. I don't like it. Why?"

Dirk looked long and hard at Richard, tapping a pencil lightly on the desk.

Then he leaned back in his chair and said as follows: "The body of Gordon Way was discovered before dawn this morning. He had been shot, strangled, and then his house was set on fire. Police are working on the theory that he was not actually shot in the house because no shotgun pellets were discovered there other than those in the body.

"However, pellets were found near to Mr Way's Mercedes 500 SEC, which was found abandoned about three miles from his house. This suggests that the body was moved after the murder. Furthermore the doctor who examined the body is of the opinion that Mr Way was in fact strangled after he was shot, which seems to suggest a certain confusion in the mind of the killer.

"By a startling coincidence it appears that the police last night had occasion to interview a very confused-seeming gentleman who said that he was suffering from some kind of guilt complex about having just run over his employer.

"That man was a Mr Richard MacDuff, and his employer was the deceased, Mr Gordon Way. It has further been suggested that Mr Richard MacDuff is one of the two people most likely to benefit from Mr Way's death, since WayForward Technologies would almost certainly pass at least partly into his hands. The other person is his only living relative, Miss Susan Way, into whose flat Mr Richard MacDuff was observed to break last night. The police don't know that bit, of course. Nor, if we can help it, will they. However, any relationship between the two of them will naturally come under close scrutiny. The news reports on the radio say that they are urgently seeking Mr MacDuff, who they believe will be able to help them with their enquiries, but the tone of voice says that he's clearly guilty as hell.

"My scale of charges is as follows: two hundred pounds a day, plus expenses. Expenses are not negotiable and will sometimes strike those who do not understand these matters as somewhat tangential. They are all necessary and are, as I say, not negotiable. Am I hired?"

"Sorry," said Richard, nodding slightly. "Would you start that again?"

Chapter Seventeen...

The Electric Monk hardly knew what to believe any more.

He had been through a bewildering number of belief systems in the previous few hours, most of which had failed to provide him with the long-term spiritual solace that it was his bounden programming eternally to seek.

He was fed up. Frankly. And tired. And dispirited.

And furthermore, which caught him by surprise, he rather missed his horse. A dull and menial creature, to be sure, and as such hardly worthy of the preoccupation of one whose mind was destined forever to concern itself with higher things beyond the understanding of a simple horse, but nevertheless he missed it.

He wanted to sit on it. He wanted to pat it. He wanted to feel that it didn't understand.

He wondered where it was.

He dangled his feet disconsolately from the branch of the tree in which he had spent the night. He had climbed it in pursuit of some wild fantastic dream and then had got stuck and had to stay there till the morning.

Even now, by daylight, he wasn't certain how he was going to get down. He came for a moment perilously close to believing that he could fly, but a quick-thinking error-checking protocol cut in and told him not to be so silly.

It was a problem though.

Whatever burning fire of faith had borne him, inspired on wings of hope, upwards through the branches of the tree in the magic hours of night, had not also provided him with instructions on how to get back down again when, like altogether too many of these burning fiery night-time faiths, it had deserted him in the morning.

And speaking – or rather thinking – of burning fiery things, there had been a major burning fiery thing a little distance from here in the early pre-dawn hours.

It lay, he thought, in the direction from which he himself had come when he had been drawn by a deep spiritual compulsion towards this inconveniently high but otherwise embarrassingly ordinary tree. He had longed to go and worship at the fire, to pledge himself eternally to its holy glare, but while he had been struggling hopelessly to find a way downwards through the branches, fire engines had arrived and put the divine radiance out, and that had been another creed out of the window.

The sun had been up for some hours now, and though he had occupied the time as best as he could, believing in clouds, believing in twigs, believing in a peculiar form of flying beetle, he believed now that he was fed up, and was utterly convinced, furthermore, that he was getting hungry.

He wished he'd taken the precaution of providing himself with some food from the dwelling place he had visited in the night, to which he had carried his sacred burden for entombment in the holy broom cupboard, but he had left in the grip of a white passion, believing that such mundane matters as food were of no consequence, that the tree would provide.

Well, it had provided.

It had provided twigs.

Monks did not eat twigs.

In fact, now he came to think of it, he felt a little uncomfortable about some of the things he had believed last night and had found some of the results a little confusing. He had been quite clearly instructed to "shoot off" and had felt strangely compelled to obey, but perhaps he had made a mistake in acting so precipitately on an instruction given in a language he had learned only two minutes before. Certainly the reaction of the person he had shot off at had seemed a little extreme.

In his own world when people were shot at like that they came back next week for another episode, but he didn't think this person would be doing that.

A gust of wind blew through the tree, making it sway giddily. He climbed down a little way. The first part was reasonably easy, since the branches were all fairly close together. It was the last bit that appeared to be an insuperable obstacle – a sheer drop which could cause him severe internal damage or rupture and might in turn cause him to start believing things that were seriously strange.

The sound of voices over in a distant corner of the field suddenly caught his attention. A lorry had pulled up by the side of the road. He watched carefully for a moment, but couldn't see anything particular to believe in and so returned to his introspection.

There was, he remembered, an odd function call he had had last night, which he hadn't encountered before, but he had a feeling that it might be something he'd heard of called remorse. He hadn't felt at all comfortable about the way the person he had shot at had just lain there, and after initially walking away the Monk had returned to have another look. There was definitely an expression on the person's face which seemed to suggest that something was up, that this didn't fit in with the scheme of things. The Monk worried that he might have badly spoiled his evening.

Still, he reflected, so long as you did what you believed to be right, that was the main thing.

The next thing he had believed to be right was that having spoiled this person's evening he should at least convey him to his home, and a quick search of his pockets had produced an address, some maps and some keys. The trip had been an arduous one, but he had been sustained on the way by his faith.

The word "bathroom" floated unexpectedly across the field.

He looked up again at the lorry in the distant corner. There was a man in a dark blue uniform explaining something to a man in rough working clothes, who seemed a little disgruntled about whatever it was. The words "until we trace the owner" and "completely batty, of course" were gusted over on the wind. The man in the working clothes clearly agreed to accept the situation, but with bad grace.

A few moments later, a horse was led out of the back of the lorry and into the field. The Monk blinked. His circuits thrilled and surged with astonishment. Now here at last was something he could believe in, a truly miraculous event, a reward at last for his unstinting if rather promiscuous devotion.

The horse walked with a patient, uncomplaining gait. It had long grown used to being wherever it was put, but for once it felt it didn't mind this. Here, it thought, was a pleasant field. Here was grass. Here was a hedge it could look at. There was enough space that it could go for a trot later on if it felt the urge. The humans drove off and left it to its own devices, to which it was quite content to be left. It went for a little amble, and then, just for the hell of it, stopped ambling. It could do what it liked.

What pleasure.

What very great and unaccustomed pleasure.

It slowly surveyed the whole field, and then decided to plan out a nice relaxed day for itself. A little trot later on, it thought, maybe around threeish. After that a bit of a lie down over on the east side of the field where the grass was thicker. It looked like a suitable spot to think about supper in.

Lunch, it rather fancied, could be taken at the south end of the field where a small stream ran. Lunch by a stream, for heaven's sake. This was bliss.

It also quite liked the notion of spending half an hour walking alternately a little bit to the left and then a little bit to the right, for no apparent reason. It didn't know whether the time between two and three would be best spent swishing its tail or mulling things over.

Of course, it could always do both, if it so wished, and go for its trot a little later. And it had just spotted what looked like a fine piece of hedge for watching things over, and that would easily while away a pleasant pre-prandial hour or two.

Good.

An excellent plan.

And the best thing about it was that having made it the horse could now completely and utterly ignore it. It went instead for a leisurely stand under the only tree in the field.

From out of its branches the Electric Monk dropped on to the horse's back, with a cry which sounded suspiciously like "Geronimo".

Chapter Eighteen...

Dirk Gently briefly ran over the salient facts once more while Richard MacDuff's world crashed slowly and silently into a dark, freezing sea which he hadn't even known was there, waiting, inches beneath his feet. When Dirk had finished for the second time the room fell quiet while Richard stared fixedly at his face.

"Where did you hear this?" said Richard at last.

"The radio," said Dirk, with a slight shrug, "at least the main points. It's all over the news of course. The details? Well, discreet enquiries among contacts here and there. There are one or two people I got to know at Cambridge police station, for reasons which may occur to you."

"I don't even know whether to believe you," said Richard quietly. "May I use the phone?"

Dirk courteously picked a telephone receiver out of the wastepaper bin and handed it to him. Richard dialled Susan's number.

The phone was answered almost immediately and a frightened voice said, "Hello?"

"Susan, it's Ri —"

"*Richard!* Where are you? For God's sake, where are you? Are you all right?"

"Don't tell her where you are," said Dirk.

"Susan, what's happened?"

"Don't you —?"

"Somebody told me that something's happened to Gordon, but ..."

"Something's *happened* –? He's *dead*, Richard, he's been *murdered* –"

"Hang up," said Dirk.

"Susan, listen. I – "

"Hang up," repeated Dirk, and then leaned forward to the phone and cut him off.

"The police will probably have a trace on the line," he explained. He took the receiver and chucked it back in the bin.

"But I have to go to the police," Richard exclaimed.

"*Go* to the police?"

"What else can I do? I have to go to the police and tell them that it wasn't me."

"Tell them that it wasn't you?" said Dirk incredulously. "Well, I expect that will probably make it all right, then. Pity Dr Crippen didn't think of that. Would have saved him a lot of bother."

"Yes, but he was guilty!"

"Yes, so it would appear. And so it would appear, at the moment, are you."

"But I didn't do it, for God's sake!"

"You are talking to someone who has spent time in prison for something he didn't do, remember. I told you that coincidences are strange and dangerous things. Believe me, it is a great deal better to find cast-iron proof that you're innocent, than to languish in a cell hoping that the police – who already think you're guilty – will find it for you."

"I can't think straight," said Richard, with his hand to his forehead. "Just stop for a moment and let me think this out – "

"If I may – "

"Let me think – !"

Dirk shrugged and turned his attention back to his cigarette, which seemed to be bothering him.

"It's no good," said Richard shaking his head after a few moments, "I can't take it in. It's like trying to do trigonometry when someone's kicking your head. OK, tell me what you think I should do."

"Hypnotism."

"What?"

"It is hardly surprising in the circumstances that you should be unable to gather your thoughts clearly. However, it is vital that somebody gathers them. It will be much simpler for both of us if you will allow me to hypnotise you. I strongly suspect that there is a very great deal of information jumbled up in your head that will not emerge while you are shaking it up so – that might not emerge at all because you do not realise its significance. With your permission we can short-cut all that."

"Well, that's decided then," said Richard, standing up, "I'm going to the police."

"Very well," said Dirk, leaning back and spreading his palms on the desk, "I wish you the very best of luck. Perhaps on your way out you would be kind enough to ask my secretary to get me some matches."

"You haven't got a secretary," said Richard, and left.

Dirk sat and brooded for a few seconds, made a valiant but vain attempt to fold the sadly empty pizza box into the wastepaper bin, and then went to look in the cupboard for a metronome.

Richard emerged blinking into the daylight. He stood on the top step rocking slightly, then plunged off down the street with an odd kind of dancing walk which reflected the whirling dance of his mind. On the one hand he simply couldn't believe that the evidence wouldn't show perfectly clearly that he couldn't have committed the murder; on the other hand he had to admit that it all looked remarkably odd.

He found it impossible to think clearly or rationally about it. The idea that Gordon had been murdered kept blowing up in his mind and throwing all other thoughts into total confusion and disruption.

It occurred to him for a moment that whoever did it must have been a damn fast shot to get the trigger pulled before being totally overwhelmed by waves of guilt, but instantly he regretted the thought. In fact he was a little appalled by the general quality of the thoughts that sprang into his mind. They seemed inappropriate and unworthy and mostly had to do with how it would affect his projects in the company.

He looked about inside himself for any feeling of great sorrow or regret, and assumed that it must be there somewhere, probably hiding behind the huge wall of shock.

He arrived back within sight of Islington Green, hardly noticing the distance he had walked. The sudden sight of the police squad car parked outside his house hit him like a hammer and he swung on his heel and stared with furious concentration at the menu displayed in the window of a Greek restaurant.

"Dolmades," he thought, frantically.

"Souvlaki," he thought.

"A small spicy Greek sausage," passed hectically through his mind. He tried to reconstruct the scene in his mind's eye without turning round. There had been a policeman standing watching the street, and as far as he could recall from the brief glance he had, it looked as if the side door of the building which led up to his flat was standing open.

The police were in his flat. *In* his flat. Fassolia Plaki! A filling bowl of haricot beans cooked in a tomato and vegetable sauce!

He tried to shift his eyes sideways and back over his shoulder. The policeman was looking at him. He yanked his eyes back to the menu and tried to fill his mind with finely ground meat mixed with potato, breadcrumbs, onions and herbs rolled into small balls and fried. The policeman must have recognised him and was at that very moment dashing across the road to grab him and lug him off in a Black Maria just as they had done to Dirk all those years ago in Cambridge.

He braced his shoulders against the shock, but no hand came to grab him. He glanced back again, but the policeman was looking unconcernedly in another direction. Stifado.

It was very apparent to him that his behaviour was not that of one who was about to go and hand himself in to the police.

So what else was he to do?

Trying in a stiff, awkward way to walk naturally, he yanked himself away from the window, strolled tensely down the road a few yards, and then ducked back down Camden Passage again, walking fast and breathing hard. Where could he go? To Susan? No – the police would be there or watching. To the WFT offices in Primrose Hill? No – same reason. What on earth, he screamed silently at himself, was he doing suddenly as a fugitive?

He insisted to himself, as he had insisted to Dirk, that he should not be running away from the police. The police, he told himself, as he had been taught when he was a boy, were there to help and protect the innocent. This thought caused him instantly to break into a run and he nearly collided with the proud new owner of an ugly Edwardian floor lamp.

"Sorry," he said, "sorry." He was startled that anyone should want such a thing, and slowed his pace to a walk, glancing with sharp hunted looks around him. The very familiar shop fronts full of old polished brass, old polished wood and pictures of Japanese fish suddenly seemed very threatening and aggressive.

Who could possibly have wanted to kill Gordon? This was the thought that suddenly hammered at him as he turned down Charlton Place. All that had concerned him so far was that he hadn't.

But who had?

This was a new thought.

Plenty of people didn't care for him much, but there is a huge difference between disliking somebody – maybe even disliking them a lot – and actually shooting them, strangling them, dragging them through the fields and setting their house on fire. It was a difference which kept the vast majority of the population alive from day to day.

Was it just theft? Dirk hadn't mentioned anything being missing but then he hadn't asked him.

Dirk. The image of his absurd but oddly commanding figure sitting like a large toad, brooding in his shabby office, kept insisting itself upon Richard's mind. He realised that he was retracing the way he had come, and deliberately made himself turn right instead of left.

That way madness lay.

He just needed a space, a bit of time to think and collect his thoughts together.

All right – so where was he going? He stopped for a moment, turned around and then stopped again. The idea of dolmades suddenly seemed very attractive and it occurred to him that the cool, calm and collected course of action would have been simply to walk in and have some. That would shown Fate who was boss.

Instead, Fate was engaged on exactly the same course of action. It wasn't actually sitting in a Greek restaurant eating dolmades, but it might as well have been, because it was clearly in charge. Richard's footsteps drew him inexorably back through the winding streets, over the canal.

He stopped, briefly, at a corner shop, and then hurried on past the council estates, and into developer territory again until he was standing once more outside 33 Peckender Street. At about the same time as Fate would have been pouring itself the last of the retsina, wiping its mouth and wondering if it had any room left for baklavas, Richard gazed up at the tall ruddy Victorian building with its soot-darkened brickwork and its heavy, forbidding windows. A gust of wind whipped along the street and a small boy bounded up to him.

"Fuck off," chirped the little boy, then paused and looked at him again.

"'Ere, mister," he added, "can I have your jacket?"

"No," said Richard.

"Why not?" said the boy.

"Er, because I like it," said Richard.

"Can't see why," muttered the boy. "Fuck off." He slouched off moodily down the street, kicking a stone at a cat.

Richard entered the building once more, mounted the stairs uneasily and looked again into the office.

Dirk's secretary was sitting at her desk, head down, arms folded.

"I'm not here," she said.

"I see," said Richard.

"I only came back," she said, without looking up from the spot on her desk at which she was staring angrily, "to make sure he notices that I've gone. Otherwise he might just forget."

"Is he in?" asked Richard.

"Who knows? Who cares? Better ask someone who works for him, because I don't."

"Show him in!" boomed Dirk's voice.

She glowered for a moment, stood up, went to the inner door, wrenched it open, said "Show him in yourself," slammed the door once more and returned to her seat.

"Er, why don't I just show myself in?" said Richard.

"I can't even hear you," said Dirk's ex-secretary, staring resolutely at her desk. "How do you expect me to hear you if I'm not even here?"

Richard made a placatory gesture, which was ignored, and walked through and opened the door to Dirk's office himself. He was startled to find the room in semi-darkness. A blind was drawn down over the window, and Dirk was lounging back in his seat, his face bizarrely lit by the strange arrangement of objects sitting on the desk. At the forward edge of the desk sat an old grey bicycle lamp, facing backwards and shining a feeble light on a metronome which was ticking softly back and forth, with a highly polished silver teaspoon strapped to its metal rod.

Richard tossed a couple of boxes of matches on to the desk.

"Sit down, relax, and keep looking at the spoon," said Dirk, "you are already feeling sleepy ..."

Another police car pulled itself up to a screeching halt outside Richard's flat, and a grim-faced man climbed out and strode over to one of the constables on duty outside, flashing an identity card.

"Detective Inspector Mason, Cambridgeshire CID," he said. "This the MacDuff place?"

The constable nodded and showed him to the side-door entrance which opened on to the long narrow staircase leading up to the top flat. Mason bustled in and then bustled straight out again.

"There's a sofa halfway up the stairs," he told the constable. "Get it moved."

"Some of the lads have already tried, sir," the constable replied anxiously. "It seems to be stuck. Everyone's having to climb over it for the moment, sir. Sorry, sir."

Mason gave him another grim look from a vast repertoire he had developed which ranged from very, very blackly grim indeed at the bottom of the scale, all the way up to tiredly resigned and only faintly grim, which he reserved for his children's birthdays.

"Get it moved," he repeated grimly, and bustled grimly back through the door grimly hauling up his trousers and coat in preparation for the grim ascent ahead.

"No sign of him yet?" asked the driver of the car, coming over himself. "Sergeant Gilks," he introduced himself. He looked tired.

"Not as far as I know," said the constable, "but no one tells me anything."

"Know how you feel," agreed Gilks. "Once the CID gets involved you just get relegated to driving them about. And I'm the only one who knows what he looked like. Stopped him in the road last night. We just came from Way's house. Right mess."

"Bad night, eh?"

"Varied. Everything from murder to hauling horses out of bathrooms. No, don't even ask. Do you have the same cars as these?" he added, pointing at his own. "This one's been driving me crazy all the way up. Cold even with the heater on full blast, and the radio keeps turning itself on and off."

Chapter Nineteen...

The same morning found Michael Wenton-Weakes in something of an odd mood.

You would need to know him fairly well to know that it was an especially odd mood, because most people regarded him as being a little odd to start with. Few people knew him that well. His mother, perhaps, but there existed between them a state of cold war and neither had spoken to the other now in weeks.

He also had an elder brother, Peter, who was now tremendously senior in the Marines. Apart from at their father's funeral, Michael had not seen Peter since he came back from the Falklands, covered in glory, promotion, and contempt for his younger brother.

Peter had been delighted that their mother had taken over Magna, and had sent Michael a regimental Christmas card to that effect. His own greatest satisfaction still remained that of throwing himself into a muddy ditch and firing a machine gun for at least a minute, and he didn't think that the British newspaper and publishing industry, even in its current state of unrest, was likely to afford him that pleasure, at least until some more Australians moved into it.

Michael had risen very late after a night of cold savagery and then of troubled dreams which still disturbed him now in the late morning daylight.

His dreams had been filled with the familiar sensations of loss, isolation, guilt and so forth, but had also been inexplicably involved with large quantities of mud. By the telescopic power of the night, the nightmare of mud and loneliness had seemed to stretch on for terrifying, unimaginable lengths of time, and had only concluded with the appearance of slimy things with legs that had crawled on the slimy sea. This had been altogether too much and he had woken with a start in a cold sweat.

Though all the business with the mud had seemed strange to him, the sense of loss, of isolation, and above all the aggrievement, the need to undo what had been done, these had all found an easy home in his spirit.

Even the slimy things with legs seemed oddly familiar and ticked away irritably at the back of his mind while he made himself a late breakfast, a piece of grapefruit and some China tea, allowed his eyes to rest lightly on the arts pages of the *Daily Telegraph* for a while, and then rather clumsily changed the dressing on the cuts on his hand.

These small tasks accomplished, he was then in two minds as to what to do next.

He was able to view the events of the previous night with a cool detachment that he would not have expected. It had been right, it had been proper, it had been correctly done. But it resolved nothing. All that mattered was yet to be done.

All what? He frowned at the odd way his thoughts ebbed and flowed.

Normally he would pop along to his club at about this time. It used to be that he would do this with a luxurious sense of the fact that there were many other things that he should be doing. Now there was nothing else to do, which made time spent there, as anywhere else, hang somewhat heavy on his hands.

When he went he would do as he always did – indulge in a gin and tonic and a little light conversation, and then allow his eyes to rest gently on the pages of the *Times Literary Supplement*, *Opera*, *The New Yorker* or whatever else fell easily to hand, but there was no doubt that he did it these days with less verve and relish than previously.

Then there would be lunch. Today, he had no lunch date planned – again – and would probably therefore have stayed at his club, and eaten a lightly grilled Dover sole, with potatoes garnished with parsley and boiled to bits, followed by a large heap of trifle. A glass or two of Sancerre. And coffee. And then the afternoon, with whatever that might bring.

But today he felt oddly impelled not to do that. He flexed the muscles in his cut hand, poured himself another cup of tea, looked with curious dispassion at the large kitchen knife that still lay by the fine bone china teapot, and waited for a moment to see what he would do next. What he did next, in fact, was to walk upstairs.

His house was rather chill in its formal perfection, and looked much as people who buy reproduction furniture would like their houses to look. Except of course that everything here was genuine – crystal, mahogany and Wilton – and only looked as if it might be fake because there was no life to any of it.

He walked up into his workroom, which was the only room in the house that was not sterile with order, but here the disorder of books and papers was instead sterile with neglect. A thin film of dust had settled over everything. Michael had not been into it in weeks, and the cleaner was under strict instructions to leave it well alone. He had not worked here since he edited the last edition of *Fathom*. Not, of course, the actual last edition, but the last proper edition. The last edition as far as *he* was concerned.

He set his china cup down in the fine dust and went to inspect his elderly record player. On it he found an elderly recording of some Vivaldi wind concertos, set it to play and sat down.

He waited again to see what he would do next and suddenly found to his surprise that he was already doing it, and it was this: he was *listening* to the music.

A bewildered look crept slowly across his face as he realised that he had never done this before. He had *heard* it many, many times and thought that it made a very pleasant noise. Indeed, he found that it made a pleasant background against which to discuss the concert season, but it had never before occurred to him that there was anything actually to *listen* to.

He sat thunderstruck by the interplay of melody and

counterpoint which suddenly stood revealed to him with a clarity that owed nothing to the dust-ridden surface of the record or the fourteen-year-old stylus.

But with this revelation came an almost immediate sense of disappointment, which confused him all the more. The music suddenly revealed to him was oddly unfulfilling. It was as if his capacity to understand the music had suddenly increased up to and far beyond the music's ability to satisfy it, all in one dramatic moment.

He strained to listen for what was missing, and felt that the music was like a flightless bird that didn't even know what capacity it had lost. It walked very well, but it walked where it should soar, it walked where it should swoop, it walked where it should climb and bank and dive, it walked where it should thrill with the giddiness of flight. It never even looked up.

He looked up.

After a while he became aware that all he was doing was simply staring stupidly at the ceiling. He shook his head, and discovered that the perception had faded, leaving him feeling slightly sick and dizzy. It had not vanished entirely, but had dropped deep inside him, deeper than he could reach.

The music continued. It was an agreeable enough assortment of pleasant sounds in the background, but it no longer stirred him.

He needed some clues as to what it was he had just experienced, and a thought flicked momentarily at the back of his mind as to where he might find them. He let go of the thought in anger, but it flicked at him again, and kept on flicking at him until at last he acted upon it.

From under his desk he pulled out the large tin wastepaper bin. Since he had barred his cleaning lady from even coming in here for the moment, the bin had remained unemptied and he found in it the tattered shreds of what he was looking for with the contents of an ashtray emptied over them.

He overcame his distaste with grim determination and slowly jiggled around the bits of the hated object on his desk, clumsily sticking them together with bits of sticky tape that curled around

and stuck the wrong bit to the wrong bit and stuck the right bit to
his pudgy fingers and then to the desk, until at last there lay
before him, crudely reassembled, a copy of *Fathom*. As edited
by the execrable creature A. K. Ross.

Appalling.

He turned the sticky lumpish pages as if he was picking over
chicken giblets. Not a single line drawing of Joan Sutherland or
Marilyn Horne anywhere. No profiles of any of the major Cork
Street art dealers, not a one.

His series on the Rossettis: discontinued.

"Green Room Gossip": discontinued.

He shook his head in incredulity and then he found the article
he was after.

"Music and Fractal Landscapes" by Richard MacDuff.

He skipped over the first couple of paragraphs of introduction
and picked it up further on:

> Mathematical analysis and computer modelling are
> revealing to us that the shapes and processes we
> encounter in nature – the way that plants grow, the way
> that mountains erode or rivers flow, the way that
> snowflakes or islands achieve their shapes, the way that
> light plays on a surface, the way the milk folds and
> spins into your coffee as you stir it, the way that
> laughter sweeps through a crowd of people – all these
> things in their seemingly magical complexity can be
> described by the interaction of mathematical processes
> that are, if anything, even more magical in their
> simplicity.
>
> Shapes that we think of as random are in fact the
> products of complex shifting webs of numbers obeying
> simple rules. The very word "natural" that we have
> often taken to mean "unstructured" in fact describes
> shapes and processes that appear so unfathomably
> complex that we cannot consciously perceive the simple
> natural laws at work.
>
> They can all be described by numbers.

Oddly, this idea seemed less revolting now to Michael than it had done on his first, scant reading.

He read on with increasing concentration.

We know, however, that the mind is capable of understanding these matters in all their complexity and in all their simplicity. A ball flying through the air is responding to the force and direction with which it was thrown, the action of gravity, the friction of the air which it must expend its energy on overcoming, the turbulence of the air around its surface, and the rate and direction of the ball's spin.

And yet, someone who might have difficulty consciously trying to work out what $3 \times 4 \times 5$ comes to would have no trouble in doing differential calculus and a whole host of related calculations so astoundingly fast that they can *actually catch a flying ball*.

People who call this "instinct" are merely giving the phenomenon a name, not explaining anything.

I think that the closest that human beings come to expressing our understanding of these natural complexities is in music. It is the most abstract of the arts – it has no meaning or purpose other than to be itself.

Every single aspect of a piece of music can be represented by numbers. From the organisation of movements in a whole symphony, down through the patterns of pitch and rhythm that make up the melodies and harmonies, the dynamics that shape the performance, all the way down to the timbres of the notes themselves, their harmonics, the way they change over time, in short, all the elements of a noise that distinguish between the sound of one person piping on a piccolo and another one thumping a drum – all of these things can be expressed by patterns and hierarchies of numbers.

And in my experience the more internal relationships there are between the patterns of numbers at different levels of the hierarchy, however complex and subtle those relationships may be, the more satisfying and, well, whole, the music will seem to be.

In fact the more subtle and complex those relationships, and the further they are beyond the grasp of the conscious mind, the more the instinctive part of your mind – by which I mean that part of your mind that can do differential calculus so astoundingly fast that it will put your hand in the right place to catch a flying ball – the more that part of your brain revels in it.

Music of any complexity (and even "Three Blind Mice" is complex in its way by the time someone has actually performed it on an instrument with its own individual timbre and articulation) passes beyond your conscious mind into the arms of your own private mathematical genius who dwells in your unconscious responding to all the inner complexities and relationships and proportions that we think we know nothing about.

Some people object to such a view of music, saying that if you reduce music to mathematics, where does the emotion come into it? I would say that it's never been out of it.

The things by which our emotions can be moved – the shape of a flower or a Grecian urn, the way a baby grows, the way the wind brushes across your face, the way clouds move, their shapes, the way light dances on the water, or daffodils flutter in the breeze, the way in which the person you love moves their head, the way their hair follows that movement, the curve described by the dying fall of the last chord of a piece of music – all these things can be described by the complex flow of numbers.

That's not a reduction of it, that's the beauty of it.

Ask Newton.

Ask Einstein.

Ask the poet (Keats) who said that what the imagination seizes as beauty must be truth.

He might also have said that what the hand seizes as a ball must be truth, but he didn't, because he was a poet and preferred loafing about under trees with a bottle of laudanum and a notebook to playing cricket, but it would have been equally true.

This jogged a thought at the back of Michael's memory, but he couldn't immediately place it.

> Because that is at the heart of the relationship between on the one hand our "instinctive" understanding of shape, form, movement, light, and on the other hand our emotional responses to them.
> And that is why I believe that there must be a form of music inherent in nature, in natural objects, in the patterns of natural processes. A music that would be as deeply satisfying as any naturally occurring beauty – and our own deepest emotions are, after all, a form of naturally occurring beauty ...

Michael stopped reading and let his gaze gradually drift from the page.

He wondered if he knew what such a music would be and tried to grope in the dark recesses of his mind for it. Each part of his mind that he visited seemed as if that music had been playing there only seconds before and all that was left was the last dying echo of something he was unable to catch at and hear. He laid the magazine limply aside.

Then he remembered what it was that the mention of Keats had jogged in his memory.

The slimy things with legs from his dream.

A cold calm came over him as he felt himself coming very close to something.

Coleridge. That man.

> Yea, slimy things did crawl with legs
> Upon the slimy sea.

"The Rime of the Ancient Mariner."

Dazed, Michael walked over to the bookshelf and pulled down his Coleridge anthology. He took it back to his seat and with a

certain apprehension he riffled through the pages until he found
the opening lines.

> It is an ancient Mariner,
> And he stoppeth one of three.

The words were very familiar to him, and yet as he read on
through them they awoke in him strange sensations and fearful
memories that he knew were not his. There reared up inside him a
sense of loss and desolation of terrifying intensity which, while
he knew it was not his own, resonated so perfectly now with his
own aggrievements that he could not but surrender to it
absolutely.

> And a thousand thousand slimy things
> Lived on; and so did I.

Chapter Twenty...

The blind rolled up with a sharp rattle and Richard blinked.

"A fascinating evening you appear to have spent," said Dirk Gently, "even though the most interesting aspects of it seem to have escaped your curiosity entirely."

He returned to his seat and lounged back in it pressing his fingertips together.

"Please," he said, "do not disappoint me by saying 'where am I?' A glance will suffice."

Richard looked around him in slow puzzlement and felt as if he were returning unexpectedly from a long sojourn on another planet where all was peace and light and music that went on for ever and ever. He felt so relaxed he could hardly be bothered to breathe.

The wooden toggle on the end of the blind cord knocked a few times against the window, but otherwise all was now silent. The metronome was still. He glanced at his watch. It was just after one o'clock.

"You have been under hypnosis for a little less than an hour," said Dirk, "during which I have learned many interesting things and been puzzled by some others which I would now like to discuss with you. A little fresh air will probably help revive you and I suggest a bracing stroll along the canal. No one will be looking for you there. Janice!"

Silence.

A lot of things were still not clear to Richard, and he frowned to himself. When his immediate memory returned a moment later, it was like an elephant suddenly barging through the door and he sat up with a startled jolt.

"Janice!" shouted Dirk again. "Miss Pearce! Damn the girl."

He yanked the telephone receivers out of the wastepaper basket and replaced them. An old and battered leather briefcase stood by the desk, and he picked this up, retrieved his hat from the floor and stood up, screwing his hat absurdly on his head.

"Come," he said, sweeping through the door to where Miss Janice Pearce sat glaring at a pencil, "let us go. Let us leave this festering hellhole. Let us think the unthinkable, let us do the undoable. Let us prepare to grapple with the ineffable itself, and see if we may not eff it after all. Now, Janice –"

"Shut up."

Dirk shrugged, and then picked off her desk the book which earlier she had mutilated when trying to slam her drawer. He leafed through it, frowning, and then replaced it with a sigh. Janice returned to what she had clearly been doing a moment or two earlier, which was writing a long note with the pencil.

Richard regarded all this in silence, still feeling only semi-present. He shook his head.

Dirk said to him, "Events may seem to you to be a tangled mass of confusion at the moment. And yet we have some interesting threads to pull on. For of all the things you have told me that have happened, only two are actually physically impossible."

Richard spoke at last. "Impossible?" he said with a frown.

"Yes," said Dirk, "completely and utterly impossible."

He smiled.

"Luckily," he went on, "you have come to exactly the right place with your interesting problem, for there is no such word as 'impossible' in my dictionary. In fact," he added, brandishing the abused book, "everything between 'herring' and 'marmalade' appears to be missing. Thank you, Miss Pearce, you have once again rendered me sterling service, for which I thank you and will, in the event of a successful outcome to this endeavour, even attempt to pay you. In the meantime we have much to think on, and I leave the office in your very capable hands."

The phone rang and Janice answered it.

"Good afternoon," she said, "Wainwright's Fruit Emporium. Mr Wainwright is not able to take calls at this time since he is not right in the head and thinks he is a cucumber. Thank you for calling."

She slammed the phone down. She looked up again to see the door closing softly behind her ex-employer and his befuddled client.

"Impossible?" said Richard again, in surprise.

"Everything about it," insisted Dirk, "completely and utterly – well, let us say inexplicable. There is no point in using the word 'impossible' to describe something that has clearly happened. But it cannot be explained by anything we know."

The briskness of the air along the Grand Union Canal got in among Richard's senses and sharpened them up again. He was restored to his normal faculties, and though the fact of Gordon's death kept jumping at him all over again every few seconds, he was at least now able to think more clearly about it. Oddly enough, though, that seemed for the moment to be the last thing on Dirk's mind. Dirk was instead picking on the most trivial of the night's sequence of bizarre incidents on which to cross-examine him.

A jogger going one way and a cyclist going the other both shouted at each other to get out of the way, and narrowly avoided hurling each other into the murky, slow-moving waters of the canal. They were watched carefully by a very slow-moving old lady who was dragging an even slower-moving old dog.

On the other bank large empty warehouses stood startled, every window shattered and glinting. A burned-out barge lolled brokenly in the water. Within it a couple of detergent bottles floated on the brackish water. Over the nearest bridge heavy-goods lorries thundered, shaking the foundations of the houses, belching petrol fumes into the air and frightening a mother trying to cross the road with her pram.

Dirk and Richard were walking along from the fringes of South Hackney, a mile from Dirk's office, back towards the heart of Islington, where Dirk knew the nearest lifebelts were positioned.

"But it was only a conjuring trick, for heaven's sake," said Richard. "He does them all the time. It's just sleight of hand. Looks impossible but I'm sure if you asked any conjurer he'd say it's easy once you know how these things are done. I once saw a man on the street in New York doing –"

"I know how these things are done," said Dirk, pulling two lighted cigarettes and a large glazed fig out of his nose. He tossed the fig up in to the air, but it somehow failed to land anywhere. "Dexterity, misdirection, suggestion. All things you can learn if you have a little time to waste. Excuse me, dear lady," he said to the elderly, slow-moving dog-owner as they passed her. He bent down to the dog and pulled a long string of brightly coloured flags from its bottom. "I think he will move more comfortably now," he said, tipped his hat courteously to her and moved on.

"These things, you see," he said to a flummoxed Richard, "are easy. Sawing a lady in half is easy. Sawing a lady in half and then joining her up together again is less easy, but can be done with practice. The trick you described to me with the two-hundred-year-old vase and the college salt cellar is –" he paused for emphasis – "completely and utterly inexplicable."

"Well there was probably some detail of it I missed, but …"

"Oh, without question. But the benefit of questioning somebody under hypnosis is that it allows the questioner to see the scene in much greater detail than the subject was even aware of at the time. The girl Sarah, for instance. Do you recall what she was wearing?"

"Er, no," said Richard, vaguely, "a dress of some kind, I suppose –"

"Colour? Fabric?"

"Well, I can't remember, it was dark. She was sitting several places away from me. I hardly glimpsed her."

"She was wearing a dark blue cotton velvet dress gathered to a dropped waist. It had raglan sleeves gathered to the cuffs, a white

Peter Pan collar and six small pearl buttons down the front – the third one down had a small thread hanging off it. She had long dark hair pulled back with a red butterfly hairgrip."

"If you're going to tell me you know all that from looking at a scuff mark on my shoes, like Sherlock Holmes, then I'm afraid I don't believe you."

"No, no," said Dirk, "it's much simpler than that. You told me yourself under hypnosis."

Richard shook his head.

"Not true," he said, "I don't even know what a Peter Pan collar is."

"But I do and you described it to me perfectly accurately. As you did the conjuring trick. And that trick was not possible in the form in which it occurred. Believe me. I know whereof I speak. There are some other things I would like to discover about the Professor, like for instance who wrote the note you discovered on the table and how many questions George III actually asked, but –"

"What?"

"– but I think I would do better to question the fellow directly. Except ..." He frowned deeply in concentration. "Except," he added, "that being rather vain in these matters I would prefer to know the answers before I asked the questions. And I do not. I absolutely do not." He gazed abstractedly into the distance, and made a rough calculation of the remaining distance to the nearest lifebelt.

"And the second impossible thing," he added, just as Richard was about to get a word in edgeways, "or at least, the next completely inexplicable thing, is of course the matter of your sofa."

"Dirk," exclaimed Richard in exasperation, "may I remind you that Gordon Way is dead, and that I appear to be under suspicion of his murder! None of these things have the remotest connection with that, and I –"

"But I am extremely inclined to believe that they are connected."

"That's absurd!"

"I believe in the fundamental inter–"

"Oh, yeah, yeah," said Richard, "the fundamental interconnectedness of all things. Listen, Dirk, I am not a gullible old lady and you won't be getting any trips to Bermuda out of me. If you're going to help me then let's stick to the point."

Dirk bridled at this. "I believe that all things are fundamentally interconnected, as anyone who follows the principles of quantum mechanics to their logical extremes cannot, if they are honest, help but accept. But I also believe that some things are a great deal more interconnected than others. And when two apparently impossible events and a sequence of highly peculiar ones all occur to the same person, and when that person suddenly becomes the suspect of a highly peculiar murder, then it seems to me that we should look for the solution in the connection between these events. You are the connection, and you yourself have been behaving in a highly peculiar and eccentric way."

"I have not," said Richard. "Yes, some odd things have happened to me, but I –"

"You were last night observed, by me, to climb the outside of a building and break into the flat of your girlfriend, Susan Way."

"It may have been unusual," said Richard, "it may not even have been wise. But it was perfectly logical and rational. I just wanted to undo something I had done before it caused any damage."

Dirk thought for a moment, and slightly quickened his pace.

"And what you did was a perfectly reasonable and normal response to the problem of the message you had left on the tape – yes, you told me all about that in our little session – it's what anyone would have done?"

Richard frowned as if to say that he couldn't see what all the fuss was about. "I don't say anyone would have done it," he said, "I probably have a slightly more logical and literal turn of mind than many people, which is why I can write computer software. It was a logical and literal solution to the problem."

"Not a little disproportionate, perhaps?"

"It was very important to me not to disappoint Susan yet again."

"So you are absolutely satisfied with your own reasons for doing what you did?"

"Yes," insisted Richard angrily.

"Do you know," said Dirk, "what my old maiden aunt who lived in Winnipeg used to tell me?"

"No," said Richard. He quickly took off all his clothes and dived into the canal. Dirk leapt for the lifebelt, with which they had just drawn level, yanked it out of its holder and flung it to Richard, who was floundering in the middle of the canal looking completely lost and disoriented.

"Grab hold of this," shouted Dirk, "and I'll haul you in."

"It's all right," spluttered Richard, "I can swim –"

"No, you can't," yelled Dirk, "now grab it."

Richard tried to strike out for the bank, but quickly gave up in consternation and grabbed hold of the lifebelt. Dirk pulled on the rope till Richard reached the edge, and then bent down to give him a hand out. Richard came up out of the water puffing and spitting, then turned and sat shivering on the edge with his hands in his lap.

"God, it's foul in there!" he exclaimed and spat again. "It's absolutely disgusting. Yeuchh. Whew. God. I'm usually a pretty good swimmer. Must have got some kind of cramp. Lucky coincidence we were so close to the lifebelt. Oh thanks." This last he said in response to the large towel which Dirk handed him.

He rubbed himself down briskly, almost scraping himself with the towel to get the filthy canal water off him. He stood up and looked about. "Can you find my pants?"

"Young man," said the old lady with the dog, who had just reached them. She stood looking at them sternly, and was about to rebuke them when Dirk interrupted.

"A thousand apologies, dear lady," he said, "for any offence my friend may inadvertently have caused you. Please," he added, drawing a slim bunch of anemones from Richard's bottom, "accept these with my compliments."

The lady dashed them out of Dirk's hand with her stick, and hurried off, horror-struck, yanking her dog after her.

"That wasn't very nice of you," said Richard, pulling on his clothes underneath the towel that was now draped strategically around him.

"I don't think she's a very nice woman," replied Dirk, "she's always down here, yanking her poor dog around and telling people off. Enjoy your swim?"

"Not much, no," said Richard, giving his hair a quick rub. "I hadn't realised how filthy it would be in there. And cold. Here," he said, handing the towel back to Dirk, "thanks. Do you always carry a towel around in your briefcase?"

"Do you always go swimming in the afternoons?"

"No, I usually go in the mornings, to the swimming pool on Highbury Fields, just to wake myself up, get the brain going. It just occurred to me I hadn't been this morning."

"And, er – that was why you just dived into the canal?"

"Well, yes. I just thought that getting a bit of exercise would probably help me deal with all this."

"Not a little disproportionate, then, to strip off and jump into the canal."

"No," he said, "it may not have been wise given the state of the water, but it was perfectly –"

"You were perfectly satisfied with your own reasons for doing what you did."

"Yes –"

"And it was nothing to do with my aunt, then?"

Richard's eyes narrowed suspiciously. "What on earth are you talking about?" he said.

"I'll tell you," said Dirk. He went and sat on a nearby bench and opened his case again. He folded the towel away into it and took out instead a small Sony tape recorder. He beckoned Richard over and then pushed the Play button. Dirk's own voice floated from the tiny speaker in a lilting sing-song voice. It said, "In a minute I will click my fingers and you will wake and forget all of this except for the instructions I shall now give you.

"In a little while we will go for a walk along the canal, and when you hear me say the words 'my old maiden aunt who lived in Winnipeg' –"

Dirk suddenly grabbed Richard's arm to restrain him.

The tape continued, "You will take off all your clothes and dive into the canal. You will find that you are unable to swim, but you will not panic or sink, you will simply tread water until I throw you the lifebelt ..."

Dirk stopped the tape and looked round at Richard's face, which for the second time that day was pale with shock.

"I would be interested to know exactly what it was that possessed you to climb into Miss Way's flat last night," said Dirk, "and why."

Richard didn't respond – he was continuing to stare at the tape recorder in some confusion. Then he said in a shaking voice,"There was a message from Gordon on Susan's tape. He phoned from the car. The tape's in my flat. Dirk, I'm suddenly very frightened by all this."

Chapter Twenty-one...

Dirk watched the police officer on duty outside Richard's house from behind a van parked a few yards away. He had been stopping and questioning everyone who tried to enter the small side alley down which Richard's door was situated, including, Dirk was pleased to note, other policemen if he didn't immediately recognise them. Another police car pulled up and Dirk started to move.

A police officer climbed out of the car carrying a saw and walked towards the doorway. Dirk briskly matched his pace with him, a step or two behind, striding authoritatively.

"It's all right, he's with me," said Dirk, sweeping past at the exact moment that the one police officer stopped the other.

And he was inside and climbing the stairs.

The officer with the saw followed him in.

"Er, excuse me, sir," he called up after Dirk.

Dirk had just reached the point where the sofa obstructed the stairway. He stopped and twisted round.

"Stay here," he said, "guard this sofa. Do not let anyone touch it, and I mean anyone. Understood?"

The officer seemed flummoxed for a moment.

"I've had orders to saw it up," he said.

"Countermanded," barked Dirk. "Watch it like a hawk. I shall want a full report."

He turned back and climbed up over the thing. A moment or two later he emerged into a large open area. This was the lower of the two floors that comprised Richard's flat.

"Have you searched that?" snapped Dirk at another officer, who was sitting at Richard's dining table looking through some notes. The officer looked up in surprise and started to stand up. Dirk was pointing at the wastepaper basket.

"Er, yes –"

"Search it again. Keep searching it. Who's here?"

"Er, well –"

"I haven't got all day."

"Detective Inspector Mason just left, with –"

"Good, I'm having him pulled off. I'll be upstairs if I'm needed, but I don't want any interruptions unless it's very important. Understood?"

"Er, who –"

"I don't see you searching the wastepaper basket."

"Er, right, sir. I'll –"

"I want it deep-searched. You understand?"

"Er –"

"Get cracking." Dirk swept on upstairs and into Richard's workroom.

The tape was lying exactly where Richard had told him it would be, on the long desk on which the six Macintoshes sat. Dirk was about to pocket it when his curiosity was caught by the image of Richard's sofa slowly twisting and turning on the big Macintosh screen, and he sat down at the keyboard.

He explored the program Richard had written for a short while, but quickly realised that in its present form it was less than self-explanatory and he learned little. He managed at last to get the sofa unstuck and move it back down the stairs, but he realised that he had had to turn part of the wall off in order to do it. With a grunt of irritation he gave up.

Another computer he looked at was displaying a steady sine wave. Around the edges of the screen were the small images of other waveforms which could be selected and added to the main one or used to modify it in other ways. He quickly discovered that this enabled you to build up very complex waveforms from simple ones and he played with this for a while. He added a

simple sine wave to itself, which had the effect of doubling the
height of the peaks and troughs of the wave. Then he slid one of
the waves half a step back with respect to the other, and the peaks
and troughs of one simply cancelled out the peaks and troughs of
the other, leaving a completely flat line. Then he changed the
frequency of one of the sine waves by a small extent.

The result of this was that at some positions along the
combined waveform the two waves reinforced each other, and at
others they cancelled each other out. Adding a third simple wave
of yet another frequency resulted in a combined wave in which it
was hard to see any pattern at all. The line danced up and down
seemingly at random, staying quite low for some periods and then
suddenly building into very large peaks and troughs as all three
waves came briefly into phase with each other.

Dirk assumed that there must be amongst this array of
equipment a means for translating the waveform dancing on the
Macintosh screen into an actual musical tone and hunted among
the menus available in the program. He found one menu item
which invited him to transfer the wave sample into an Emu.

This puzzled him. He glanced around the room in search of a
large flightless bird, but was unable to locate any such thing. He
activated the process anyway, and then traced the cable which led
from the back of the Macintosh, down behind the desk, along the
floor, behind a cupboard, under a rug until it fetched up plugged
into the back of a large grey keyboard called an Emulator II.

This, he assumed, was where his experimental waveform had
just arrived. Tentatively he pushed a key.

The nasty farting noise that surged instantly out of the speakers
was so loud that for a moment he didn't hear the words "Svlad
Cjelli!" that were barked simultaneously from the doorway.

Richard sat in Dirk's office and threw tiny screwed-up balls of
paper at the wastepaper bin which was already full of telephones.
He broke pencils. He played major extracts from an old Ginger
Baker solo on his knees.

In a word, he fretted.

He had been trying to write down on a piece of Dirk's notepaper all that he could remember of the events of the previous evening and, as far as he could pinpoint them, the times at which each had occurred. He was astonished at how difficult it was, and how feeble his conscious memory seemed to be in comparison with his unconscious memory, as Dirk had demonstrated it to him.

"Damn Dirk," he thought. He wanted to talk to Susan.

Dirk had told him he must not do so on any account as there would be a trace on the phone lines.

"Damn Dirk," he said suddenly, and sprang to his feet.

"Have you got any ten-pence pieces?" he said to the resolutely glum Janice.

Dirk turned.

Framed in the doorway stood a tall dark figure.

The tall dark figure appeared to be not at all happy with what it saw, to be rather cross about it, in fact. To be more than cross. It appeared to be a tall dark figure who could very easily yank the heads off half a dozen chickens and still be cross at the end of it.

It stepped forward into the light and revealed itself to be Sergeant Gilks of the Cambridgeshire Constabulary.

"Do you know," said Sergeant Gilks of the Cambridgeshire Constabulary, blinking with suppressed emotion, "that when I arrive back here to discover one police officer guarding a sofa with a saw and another dismembering an innocent wastepaper basket I have to ask myself certain questions? And I have to ask them with the disquieting sense that I am not going to like the answers when I find them.

"I then find myself mounting the stairs with a horrible premonition, Svlad Cjelli, a very horrible premonition indeed. A premonition, I might add, that I now find horribly justified. I suppose you can't shed any light on a horse discovered in a bathroom as well? That seemed to have an air of you about it."

"I cannot," said Dirk, "as yet. Though it interests me strangely."

"I should think it bloody did. It would have interested you strangely if you'd had to get the bloody thing down a bloody winding staircase at one o'clock in the morning as well. What the hell are you doing here?" said Sergeant Gilks, wearily.

"I am here," said Dirk, "in pursuit of justice."

"Well, I wouldn't mix with me then," said Gilks, "and I certainly wouldn't mix with the Met. What do you know of MacDuff and Way?"

"Of Way? Nothing beyond what is common knowledge. MacDuff I knew at Cambridge."

"Oh, you did, did you? Describe him."

"Tall. Tall and absurdly thin. And good-natured. A bit like a preying mantis that doesn't prey – a non-preying mantis if you like. A sort of pleasant genial mantis that's given up preying and taken up tennis instead."

"Hmm," said Gilks gruffly, turning away and looking about the room. Dirk pocketed the tape.

"Sounds like the same one," said Gilks.

"And of course," said Dirk, "completely incapable of murder."

"That's for us to decide."

"And of course a jury."

"Tchah! Juries!"

"Though, of course, it will not come to that, since the facts will speak for themselves long before it comes to a court of law for my client."

"Your bleeding client, eh? All right, Cjelli, where is he?"

"I haven't the faintest idea."

"I'll bet you've got a billing address."

Dirk shrugged.

"Look, Cjelli, this is a perfectly normal, harmless murder enquiry, and I don't want you mucking it up. So consider yourself warned off as of now. If I see a single piece of evidence being levitated I'll hit you so hard you won't know if it's tomorrow or Thursday. Now get out, and give me that tape on the way." He held out his hand.

Dirk blinked, genuinely surprised. "What tape?"

Gilks sighed. "You're a clever man, Cjelli, I grant you that," he said, "but you make the same mistake a lot of clever people do of thinking everyone else is stupid. If I turn away it's for a reason, and the reason was to see what you picked up. I didn't need to see you pick it up, I just had to see what was missing afterwards. We are trained you know. We used to get half an hour Observation Training on Tuesday afternoons. Just as a break after four hours solid of Senseless Brutality."

Dirk hid his anger with himself behind a light smile. He fished in the pocket of his leather overcoat and handed over the tape.

"Play it," said Gilks, "let's see what you didn't want us to hear."

"It wasn't that I didn't want you to hear it," said Dirk, with a shrug. "I just wanted to hear it first." He went over to the shelf which carried Richard's hi-fi equipment and slipped the tape into the cassette player.

"So do you want to give me a little introduction?"

"It's a tape," said Dirk, "from Susan Way's telephone-answering machine. Way apparently had this habit of leaving long ..."

"Yeah, I know about that. And his secretary goes round picking up his prattlings in the morning, poor devil."

"Well, I believe there may be a message on the tape from Gordon Way's car last night."

"I see. OK. Play it."

With a gracious bow Dirk pressed the Play button.

"Oh, Susan, hi, it's Gordon," said the tape once again. "Just on my way to the cottage –"

"Cottage!" exclaimed Gilks, satirically.

"It's, er, Thursday night, and it's, er ... 8.47. Bit misty on the roads. Listen, I have those people from the States coming over this weekend ..."

Gilks raised his eyebrows, looked at his watch, and made a note on his pad.

Both Dirk and the police sergeant experienced a chill as the dead man's voice filled the room.

"– it's a wonder I don't end up dead in the ditch, that would be something wouldn't it, leaving your famous last words on somebody's answering machine, there's no reason –"

They listened in a tense silence as the tape played on through the entire message.

"That's the problem with crunch-heads – they have one great idea that actually works and then they expect you to carry on funding them for years while they sit and calculate the topographies of their navels. I'm sorry, I'm going to have to stop and close the boot properly. Won't be a moment."

Next came the muffled bump of the telephone receiver being dropped on the passenger seat, and a few seconds later the sound of the car door being opened. In the meantime, the music from the car's sound system could be heard burbling away in the background.

A few seconds later still came the distant, muffled, but unmistakable double blam of a shotgun.

"Stop the tape," said Gilks sharply and glanced at his watch. "Three minutes and twenty-five seconds since he said it was 8.47." He glanced up at Dirk again. "Stay here. Don't move. Don't touch anything. I've made a note of the position of every particle of air in this room, so I shall know if you've been breathing."

He turned smartly and left. Dirk heard him saying as he went down the stairs, "Tuckett, get on to WayForward's office, get the details of Way's carphone, what number, which network ..."

The voice faded away downstairs.

Quickly Dirk twisted down the volume control on the hi-fi, and resumed playing the tape.

The music continued for a while. Dirk drummed his fingers in frustration. Still the music continued.

He flicked the Fast Forward button for just a moment. Still music. It occurred to him that he was looking for something, but that he didn't know what. That thought stopped him in his tracks.

He was very definitely looking for something.

He very definitely didn't know what.

The realisation that he didn't know exactly why he was doing what he was doing suddenly chilled and electrified him. He turned slowly like a fridge door opening.

There was no one there, at least no one that he could see. But he knew the chill prickling through his skin and detested it above all things.

He said in a low savage whisper, "If anyone can hear me, hear this. My mind is my centre and everything that happens there is my responsibility. Other people may believe what it pleases them to believe, but I will do nothing without I know the reason why and know it clearly. If you want something then let me know, but do not you dare touch my mind."

He was trembling with a deep and old rage. The chill dropped slowly and almost pathetically from him and seemed to move off into the room. He tried to follow it with his senses, but was instantly distracted by a sudden voice that seemed to come at him on the edge of his hearing, on a distant howl of wind.

It was a hollow, terrified, bewildered voice, no more than an insubstantial whisper, but it was there, audible, on the telephone-answering machine tape.

It said, "Susan! Susan, help me! Help me for God's sake. Susan, I'm dead –"

Dirk whirled round and stopped the tape.

"I'm sorry," he said under his breath, "but I have the welfare of my client to consider."

He wound the tape back a very short distance, to just before where the voice began, twisted the Record Level knob to zero and pressed Record. He left the tape to run, wiping off the voice and anything that might follow it. If the tape was going to establish the time of Gordon Way's death, then Dirk didn't want any embarrassing examples of Gordon speaking to turn up on the tape after that point, even if it was only to confirm that he was, in fact, dead.

There seemed to be a great eruption of emotion in the air near to him. A wave of something surged through the room, causing the furniture to flutter in its wake. Dirk watched where it seemed to go, towards a shelf near the door on which, he suddenly realised, stood Richard's own telephone-answering machine. The machine started to jiggle fitfully where it sat, but then sat still as Dirk approached it. Dirk reached out slowly and calmly and pushed the button which set the machine to Answer.

The disturbance in the air then passed back through the room to Richard's long desk where two old-fashioned rotary-dial telephones nestled among the piles of paper and micro floppy disks. Dirk guessed what would happen, but elected to watch rather than to intervene.

One of the telephone receivers toppled off its cradle. Dirk could hear the dialling tone. Then, slowly and with obvious difficulty, the dial began to turn. It moved unevenly round, further round, slower and slower, and then suddenly slipped back.

There was a moment's pause. Then the receiver rests went down and up again to get a new dialling tone. The dial began to turn again, but creaking even more fitfully than the last time.

Again it slipped back.

There was a longer pause this time, and then the entire process was repeated once more.

When the dial slipped back a third time there was a sudden explosion of fury – the whole phone leapt into the air and hurtled across the room. The receiver cord wrapped itself round an Anglepoise lamp on the way and brought it crashing down in a tangle of cables, coffee cups and floppy disks. A pile of books erupted off the desk and on to the floor.

The figure of Sergeant Gilks stood stony-faced in the doorway.

"I'm going to come in again," he said, "and when I do, I don't want to see anything of that kind going on whatsoever. Is that understood?" He turned and disappeared.

Dirk leapt for the cassette player and hit the Rewind button. Then he turned and hissed at the empty air, "I don't know who you are, but I can guess. If you want my help, don't you ever embarrass me like that again!"

A few moments later, Gilks walked in again. "Ah, there you are," he said.

He surveyed the wreckage with an even gaze. "I'll pretend I can't see any of this, so that I won't have to ask any questions the answers to which would, I know, only irritate me."

Dirk glowered.

In the moment or two of silence that followed, a slight ticking whirr could be heard which caused the sergeant to look sharply at the cassette player.

"What's that tape doing?"

"Rewinding."

"Give it to me."

The tape reached the beginning and stopped as Dirk reached it. He took it out and handed it to Gilks.

"Irritatingly, this seems to put your client completely in the clear," said the sergeant. "Cellnet have confirmed that the last call made from the car was at 8.46 pm last night, at which point your client was lightly dozing in front of several hundred witnesses. I say witnesses, in fact they were mostly students, but we will probably be forced to assume that they can't all be lying."

"Good," said Dirk, "well, I'm glad that's all cleared up."

"We never thought he had actually done it, of course. Simply didn't fit. But you know us – we like to get results. Tell him we still want to ask him some questions, though."

"I shall be sure to mention it if I happen to run into him."

"You just do that little thing."

"Well, I shan't detain you any longer, Sergeant," said Dirk, airily waving at the door.

"No, but I shall bloody detain you if you're not out of here in thirty seconds, Cjelli. I don't know what you're up to, but if I can possibly avoid finding out I shall sleep easier in my office. Out."

"Then I shall bid you good day, Sergeant. I won't say it's been a pleasure because it hasn't."

Dirk swept out of the room, and made his way out of the flat, noting with sorrow that where there had been a large chesterfield sofa wedged magnificently in the staircase, there was now just a small, sad pile of sawdust.

With a jerk Michael Wenton-Weakes looked up from his book.

His mind suddenly was alive with purpose. Thoughts, images, memories, intentions, all crowded in upon him, and the more they seemed to contradict each other the more they seemed to fit together, to pair and settle.

The match at last was perfect, the teeth of one slowly aligned with the teeth of another.

A pull and they were zipped.

Though the waiting had seemed an eternity of eternities when it was filled with failure, with fading waves of weakness, with feeble groping and lonely impotence, the match once made cancelled it all. Would cancel it all. Would undo what had been so disastrously done.

Who thought that? It did not matter, the match was made, the match was perfect.

Michael gazed out of the window across the well-manicured Chelsea street and did not care whether what he saw were slimy things with legs or whether they were all Mr A. K. Ross. What mattered was what they had stolen and what they would be compelled to return. Ross now lay in the past. What he was now concerned with lay still further in it.

His large soft cowlike eyes returned to the last few lines of "Kubla Khan", which he had just been reading. The match was made, the zip was pulled.

He closed the book and put it in his pocket.

His path back now was clear. He knew what he must do. It only remained to do a little shopping and then do it.

Chapter Twenty-two...

"You? Wanted for murder? Richard what are you talking about?"

The telephone wavered in Richard's hand. He was holding it about half an inch away from his ear anyway because it seemed that somebody had dipped the earpiece in some chow mein recently, but that wasn't so bad. This was a public telephone so it was clearly an oversight that it was working at all. But Richard was beginning to feel as if the whole world had shifted about half an inch away from him, like someone in a deodorant commercial.

"Gordon," said Richard, hesitantly, "Gordon's been murdered – hasn't he?"

Susan paused before she answered.

"Yes, Richard" she said in a distressed voice, "but no one thinks you did it. They want to question you of course, but –"

"So there are no police with you now?"

"No, Richard," insisted Susan, "Look, why don't you come here?"

"And they're not out searching for me?"

"No! Where on earth did you get the idea that you were wanted for – that they thought you had done it?"

"Er – well, this friend of mine told me."

"Who?"

"Well, his name is Dirk Gently."

"You've never mentioned him. Who is he? Did he say anything else?"

"He hypnotised me and, er, made me jump in the canal, and, er, well, that was it really –"

There was a terribly long pause at the other end.

"Richard," said Susan at last with the sort of calmness that comes over people when they realise that however bad things may seem to be, there is absolutely no reason why they shouldn't simply get worse and worse, "come over here. I was going to say I need to see you, but I think you need to see me."

"I should probably go to the police."

"Go to the police later. Richard, please. A few hours won't make any difference. I ... I can hardly even think. Richard, it's so awful. It would just help if you were here. Where are you?"

"OK," said Richard, "I'll be with you in about twenty minutes."

"Shall I leave the window open or would you like to try the door?" she said with a sniff.

Chapter Twenty-three...

"No, please," said Dirk, restraining Miss Pearce's hand from opening a letter from the Inland Revenue, "there are wilder skies than these."

He had emerged from a spell of tense brooding in his darkened office, and there was an air of excited concentration about him. It had taken his actual signature on an actual salary cheque to persuade Miss Pearce to forgive him for the latest unwarrantable extravagance with which he had returned to the office and he felt that just to sit there blatantly opening letters from the taxman was to take his magnanimous gesture in entirely the wrong spirit.

She put the envelope aside.

"Come!" he said. "I have something I wish you to see. I shall observe your reactions with the very greatest of interest."

He bustled back into his own office and sat at his desk.

She followed him in patiently and sat opposite, pointedly ignoring the new unwarrantable extravagance sitting on the desk.

The flashy brass plaque for the door had stirred her up pretty badly but the silly phone with big red push buttons she regarded as being beneath contempt. And she certainly wasn't going to do anything rash like smile until she knew for certain that the cheque wouldn't bounce. The last time he signed a cheque for her he cancelled it before the end of the day, to prevent it, as he explained, "falling into the wrong hands". The wrong hands, presumably, being those of her bank manager.

He thrust a piece of paper across the desk.

She picked it up and looked at it. Then she turned it round and looked at it again. She looked at the other side and then she put it down.

"Well?" demanded Dirk. "What do you make of it? Tell me!"

Miss Pearce sighed.

"It's a lot of meaningless squiggles done in blue felt tip on a piece of typing paper," she said. "It looks like you did them yourself."

"No!" barked Dirk, "Well, yes," he admitted, "but only because I believe that it is the answer to the problem!"

"What problem?"

"The problem," insisted Dirk, slapping the table, "of the conjuring trick! I told you!"

"Yes, Mr Gently, several times. I think it was just a conjuring trick. You see them on the telly."

"With this difference – that this one was completely impossible!"

"Couldn't have been impossible or he wouldn't have done it. Stands to reason."

"Exactly!" said Dirk excitedly. "Exactly! Miss Pearce, you are a lady of rare perception and insight."

"Thank you, sir, can I go now?"

"Wait! I haven't finished yet! Not by a long way, not by a bucketful! You have demonstrated to me the depth of your perception and insight, allow me to demonstrate mine!"

Miss Pearce slumped patiently in her seat.

"I think," said Dirk, "you will be impressed. Consider this. An intractable problem. In trying to find the solution to it I was going round and round in little circles in my mind, over and over the same maddening things. Clearly I wasn't going to be able to think of anything else until I had the answer, but equally clearly I would have to think of something else if I was ever going to *get* the answer. How to break this circle? Ask me how."

"How?" said Miss Pearce obediently, but without enthusiasm.

"By writing down what the answer is!" exclaimed Dirk. "And here it is!" He slapped the piece of paper triumphantly and sat back with a satisfied smile.

Miss Pearce looked at it dumbly.

"With the result," continued Dirk, "that I am now able to turn my mind to fresh and intriguing problems, like, for instance ..."

He took the piece of paper, covered with its aimless squiggles and doodlings, and held it up to her.

"What language," he said in a low, dark voice, "is this written in?"

Miss Pearce continued to look at it dumbly.

Dirk flung the piece of paper down, put his feet up on the table, and threw his head back with his hands behind it.

"You see what I have done?" he asked the ceiling, which seemed to flinch slightly at being yanked so suddenly into the conversation. "I have transformed the problem from an intractably difficult and possibly quite insoluble conundrum into a mere linguistic puzzle. Albeit," he muttered, after a long moment of silent pondering, "an intractably difficult and possibly insoluble one."

He swung back to gaze intently at Janice Pearce.

"Go on," he urged, "say that it's insane – but it might just work!"

Janice Pearce cleared her throat.

"It's insane," she said, "trust me."

Dirk turned away and sagged sideways off his chair, much as the sitter for The Thinker probably did when Rodin went off to be excused.

He suddenly looked profoundly tired and depressed.

"I know," he said in a low, dispirited voice, "that there is something profoundly wrong somewhere. And I know that I must go to Cambridge to put it right. But I would feel less fearful if I knew what it was ..."

"Can I get on now, please, then?" said Miss Pearce.

Dirk looked up at her glumly.

"Yes," he said with a sigh, "but just – just tell me –" he flicked at the piece of paper with his fingertips – "what do you think of this, then?"

"Well, I think it's childish," said Janice Pearce, frankly.

"But – but – but!" said Dirk thumping the table in frustration. "Don't you understand that we need to be childish in order to understand? Only a child sees things with perfect clarity, because it hasn't developed all those filters which prevent us from seeing things that we don't expect to see?"

"Then why don't you go and ask one?"

"Thank you, Miss Pearce," said Dirk reaching for his hat, "once again you have rendered me an inestimable service for which I am profoundly grateful."

He swept out.

Chapter Twenty-four...

The weather began to bleaken as Richard made his way to Susan's flat. The sky which had started out with such verve and spirit in the morning was beginning to lose its concentration and slip back into its normal English condition, that of a damp and rancid dish cloth. Richard took a taxi, which got him there in a few minutes.

"They should all be deported," said the taxi driver as they drew to a halt.

"Er, who should?" said Richard, who realised he hadn't been listening to a word the driver said.

"Er –" said the driver, who suddenly realised he hadn't been listening either, "er, the whole lot of them. Get rid of the whole bloody lot, that's what I say. And their bloody newts," he added for good measure.

"Expect you're right," said Richard, and hurried into the house.

Arriving at the front door of her flat he could hear from within the sounds of Susan's cello playing a slow, stately melody. He was glad of that, that she was playing. She had an amazing emotional self-sufficiency and control provided she could play her cello. He had noticed an odd and extraordinary thing about her relationship with the music she played. If ever she was feeling emotional or upset she could sit and play some music with utter concentration and emerge seeming fresh and calm.

The next time she played the same music, however, it would all burst from her and she would go completely to pieces.

He let himself in as quietly as possible so as not to disturb her concentration.

He tiptoed past the small room she practised in, but the door was open so he paused and looked at her, with the slightest of signals that she shouldn't stop. She was looking pale and drawn, but gave him a flicker of a smile and continued bowing with a sudden intensity.

With an impeccable timing of which it is very rarely capable the sun chose that moment to burst briefly through the gathering rainclouds, and as she played her cello a stormy light played on her and on the deep old brown of the wood of the instrument. Richard stood transfixed. The turmoil of the day stood still for a moment and kept a respectful distance.

He didn't know the music, but it sounded like Mozart and he remembered her saying she had some Mozart to learn. He walked quietly on and sat down to wait and listen.

Eventually she finished the piece, and there was about a minute of silence before she came through. She blinked and smiled and gave him a long, trembling hug, then released herself and put the phone back on the hook. It usually got taken off when she was practising.

"Sorry," she said, "I didn't want to stop." She briskly brushed away a tear as if it was a slight irritation. "How are you, Richard?"

He shrugged and gave her a bewildered look. That seemed about to cover it.

"And I'm going to have to carry on, I'm afraid," said Susan with a sigh "I'm sorry. I've just been ..." She shook her head. "Who would do it?"

"I don't know. Some madman. I'm not sure that it matters who."

"No," she said. "Look, er, have you had any lunch?"

"No. Susan, you keep playing and I'll see what's in the fridge. We can talk about it all over some lunch."

Susan nodded.

"All right," she said, "except ..."

"Yes?"

"Well, just for the moment I don't really want to talk about Gordon. Just till it sinks in. I feel sort of caught out. It would be easier if I'd been closer to him, but I wasn't and I'm sort of embarrassed by not having a reaction ready. Talking about it would be all right except that you have to use the past tense and that's what's ..."

She clung to him for a moment and then quieted herself with a sigh.

"There's not much in the fridge at the moment," she said, "some yoghurt, I think, and a jar of roll-mop herrings you could open. I'm sure you'll be able to muck it up if you try, but it's actually quite straightforward. The main trick is not to throw them all over the floor or get jam on them."

She gave him a hug, a kiss and a glum smile and then retreated back to her music room.

The phone rang and Richard answered it.

"Hello?" he said. There was nothing, just a faint sort of windy noise on the line.

"Hello?" he said again, waited, shrugged and put the phone back down.

"Was there anybody there?" called Susan.

"No, no one," said Richard.

"That's happened a couple of times," said Susan. "I think it's a sort of minimalist heavy breather." She resumed playing.

Richard went into the kitchen and opened the fridge. He was less of a health-conscious eater than Susan and was therefore less than thrilled by what he found there, but he managed to put some roll-mop herrings, some yoghurt, some rice and some oranges on a tray without difficulty and tried not to think that a couple of fat hamburgers and fries would round it off nicely.

He found a bottle of white wine and carried it all through to the small dining table.

After a minute or two Susan joined him there. She was at her most calm and composed, and after a few mouthsful she asked him about the canal.

Richard shook his head in bemusement and tried to explain about it, and about Dirk.

"*What* did you say his name was?" said Susan with a frown when he had come, rather lamely, to a conclusion.

"It's, er, Dirk Gently," said Richard, "in a way."

"In a way?"

"Er, yes," said Richard with a difficult sigh. He reflected that just about anything you could say about Dirk was subject to these kind of vague and shifty qualifications. There was even, on his letter heading, a string of vague and shifty-looking qualifications after his name. He pulled out the piece of paper on which he had vainly been trying to organise his thoughts earlier in the day.

"I ...," he started, but the doorbell rang. They looked at each other.

"If it's the police," said Richard, "I'd better see them. Let's get it over with."

Susan pushed back her chair, went to the front door and picked up the Entryphone.

"Hello?" she said.

"Who?" she said after a moment. She frowned as she listened, then swung round and frowned at Richard.

"You'd better come up," she said in a less than friendly tone of voice and then pressed the button. She came back and sat down.

"Your friend," she said evenly, "Mr Gently."

The Electric Monk's day was going tremendously well and he broke into an excited gallop. That is to say that, excitedly, he spurred his horse to a gallop and, unexcitedly, his horse broke into it.

This world, the Monk thought, was a good one. He loved it. He didn't know whose it was or where it had come from, but it was certainly a deeply fulfilling place for someone with his unique and extraordinary gifts.

He was appreciated. All day he had gone up to people, fallen into conversation with them, listened to their troubles, and then quietly uttered those three magic words, "I believe you."

The effect had invariably been electrifying. It wasn't that people on this world didn't occasionally say it to each other, but they rarely, it seemed, managed to achieve that deep timbre of sincerity which the Monk had been so superbly programmed to reproduce.

On his own world, after all, he was taken for granted. People would just expect him to get on and believe things for them without bothering them. Someone would come to the door with some great new idea or proposal or even a new religion, and the answer would be "Oh, go and tell that to the Monk." And the Monk would sit and listen and patiently believe it all, but no one would take any further interest.

Only one problem seemed to arise on this otherwise excellent world. Often, after he had uttered the magic words, the subject would rapidly change to that of money, and the Monk of course didn't have any – a shortcoming that had quickly blighted a number of otherwise very promising encounters.

Perhaps he should acquire some – but where?

He reined his horse in for a moment, and the horse jerked gratefully to a halt and started in on the grass on the roadside verge. The horse had no idea what all this galloping up and down was in aid of, and didn't care. All it did care about was that it was being made to gallop up and down past a seemingly perpetual roadside buffet. It made the best of its moment while it had it.

The Monk peered keenly up and down the road. It seemed vaguely familiar. He trotted a little further up it for another look. The horse resumed its meal a few yards further along.

Yes. The Monk had been here last night.

He remembered it clearly, well, sort of clearly. He believed that he remembered it clearly, and that, after all, was the main thing. Here was where he had walked to in a more than usually confused state of mind, and just around the very next corner, if he was not very much mistaken, again, lay the small roadside establishment at which he had jumped into the back of that nice man's car – the nice man who had subsequently reacted so oddly to being shot at.

Perhaps they would have some money there and would let him have it. He wondered. Well, he would find out. He yanked the horse from its feast once again and galloped towards it.

As he approached the petrol station he noticed a car parked there at an arrogant angle. The angle made it quite clear that the car was not there for anything so mundane as to have petrol put into it, and was much too important to park itself neatly out of the way. Any other car that arrived for petrol would just have to manoeuvre around it as best it could. The car was white with stripes and badges and important looking lights.

Arriving at the forecourt the Monk dismounted and tethered his horse to a pump. He walked towards the small shop building and saw that inside it there was a man with his back to him wearing a dark blue uniform and a peaked cap. The man was dancing up and down and twisting his fingers in his ears, and this was clearly making a deep impression on the man behind the till.

The Monk watched in transfixed awe. The man, he believed with an instant effortlessness which would have impressed even a Scientologist, must be a God of some kind to arouse such fervour. He waited with bated breath to worship him. In a moment the man turned around and walked out of the shop, saw the Monk and stopped dead.

The Monk realised that the God must be waiting for him to make an act of worship, so he reverently danced up and down twisting his fingers in his ears.

His God stared at him for a moment, caught hold of him, twisted him round, slammed him forward spreadeagled over the car and frisked him for weapons.

Dirk burst into the flat like a small podgy tornado.

"Miss Way," he said, grasping her slightly unwilling hand and doffing his absurd hat, "it is the most inexpressible pleasure to meet you, but also the matter of the deepest regret that the occasion of our meeting should be one of such great sorrow and one which bids me extend to you my most profound sympathy and commiseration. I ask you to believe me that I would not intrude upon your private grief for all the world if it were not on a matter of the gravest moment and magnitude. Richard – I have solved the problem of the conjuring trick and it's extraordinary."

He swept through the room and deposited himself on a spare chair at the small dining table, on which he put his hat.

"You will have to excuse us, Dirk –" said Richard, coldly.

"No, I am afraid you will have to excuse me," returned Dirk. "The puzzle is solved, and the solution is so astounding that it took a seven-year-old child on the street to give it to me. But it is undoubtedly the correct one, absolutely undoubtedly. 'What, then, is the solution?' you ask me, or rather would ask me if you could get a word in edgeways, which you can't, so I will save you the bother and ask the question for you, and answer it as well by saying that I will not tell you, because you won't believe me. I shall instead show you, this very afternoon.

"Rest assured, however, that it explains everything. It explains the trick. It explains the note you found – that should have made it perfectly clear to me but I was a fool. And it explains what the missing third question was, or rather – and this is the significant point – it explains what the missing *first* question was!"

"What missing question?" exclaimed Richard, confused by the sudden pause, and leaping in with the first phrase he could grab.

Dirk blinked as if at an idiot. "The missing question that George III asked, of course," he said.

"Asked who?"

"Well, the Professor," said Dirk impatiently. "Don't you listen to anything you say? The whole thing was obvious!" he exclaimed, thumping the table, "So obvious that the only thing which prevented me from seeing the solution was the trifling fact that it was *completely impossible*. Sherlock Holmes observed that once you have eliminated the impossible, then whatever remains, however improbable, must be the answer. I, however, do not like to eliminate the impossible. Now. Let us go."

"No."

"What?" Dirk glanced up at Susan, from whom this unexpected – or at least, unexpected to him – opposition had come.

"Mr Gently," said Susan in a voice you could notch a stick with, "why did you deliberately mislead Richard into thinking that he was wanted by the police?"

Dirk frowned.

"But he was wanted by the police," he said, "and still is."

"Yes, but just to answer questions! Not because he's a suspected murderer."

Dirk looked down.

"Miss Way," he said, "the police are interested in knowing who murdered your brother. I, with the very greatest respect, am not. It may, I concede, turn out to have a bearing on the case, but it may just as likely turn out to be a casual madman. I wanted to know, still need desperately to know, *why Richard climbed into this flat last night.*"

"I told you," protested Richard.

"What you told me is immaterial – it only reveals the crucial fact that you do not know the reason yourself! For heaven's sake, I thought I had demonstrated that to you clearly enough at the canal!"

Richard simmered.

"It was perfectly clear to me watching you," pursued Dirk, "that you had very little idea what you were doing, and had absolutely no concern about the physical danger you were in. At first I thought, watching, that it was just a brainless thug out on his first and quite possibly last burgle. But then the figure looked back and I realised it was you – and I know you to be an intelligent, rational, and moderate man. Richard MacDuff? Risking his neck carelessly climbing up drainpipes at night? It seemed to me that you would only behave in such a reckless and extreme way if you were desperately worried about something of terrible importance. Is that not true, Miss Way?"

He looked sharply up at Susan, who slowly sat down, looking at him with an alarm in her eyes which said that he had struck home.

"And yet, when you came to see me this morning you seemed perfectly calm and collected. You argued with me perfectly rationally when I talked a lot of nonsense about Schrödinger's Cat. This was not the behaviour of someone who had the previous night been driven to extremes by some desperate purpose. I confess that it was at that moment that I stooped to, well, exaggerating your predicament, simply in order to keep hold of you."

"You didn't. I left."

"With certain ideas in your head. I knew you would be back. I apologise most humbly for having misled you, er, somewhat, but I knew that what *I* had to find out lay far beyond what the police would concern themselves with. And it was this – if you were not quite yourself when you climbed the wall last night ... then *who were you, – and why*?"

Richard shivered. A silence lengthened.

"What has it got to do with conjuring tricks?" he said at last.

"That is what we must go to Cambridge to find out."

"But what makes you so sure –?"

"It disturbs me," said Dirk, and a dark and heavy look came into his face.

For one so garrulous he seemed suddenly oddly reluctant to speak.

He continued, "It disturbs me very greatly when I find that I know things and do not know why I know them. Maybe it is the same instinctive processing of data that allows you to catch a ball almost before you've seen it. Maybe it is the deeper and less explicable instinct that tells you when someone is watching you. It is a very great offence to my intellect that the very things that I despise other people for being credulous of actually occur to me. You will remember the ... unhappiness surrounding certain exam questions."

He seemed suddenly distressed and haggard. He had to dig deep inside himself to continue speaking.

He said, "The ability to put two and two together and come up instantly with four is one thing. The ability to put the square root of five hundred and thirty-nine point seven together with the cosine of twenty-six point four three two and come up with ...

with whatever the answer to that is, is quite another. And I ...
well, let me give you an example."

He leant forward intently. "Last night I saw you climbing into
this flat. I *knew* that something was wrong. Today I got you to
tell me every last detail you knew about what happened last night,
and already, as a result, using my intellect alone, I have
uncovered possibly the greatest secret lying hidden on this planet.
I swear to you that this is true and that I can prove it. Now you
must believe me when I tell you that I know, I *know* that there is
something terribly, desperately, appallingly wrong and that we
must find it. Will you go with me now, to Cambridge?"

Richard nodded dumbly.

"Good," said Dirk. "What is this?" he added, pointing at
Richard's plate.

"A pickled herring. Do you want one?"

"Thank you, no," said Dirk, rising and buckling his coat.
"There is," he added as he headed towards the door, steering
Richard with him, "no such word as 'herring' in my dictionary.
Good afternoon, Miss Way, wish us God speed."

Chapter Twenty-five...

There was a rumble of thunder, and the onset of that interminable light drizzle from the north-east by which so many of the world's most momentous events seem to be accompanied.

Dirk turned up the collar of his leather overcoat against the weather, but nothing could dampen his demonic exuberance as he and Richard approached the great twelfth-century gates.

"St Cedd's College, Cambridge," he exclaimed, looking at them for the first time in eight years. "Founded in the year something or other, by someone I forget in honour of someone whose name for the moment escapes me."

"St Cedd?" suggested Richard.

"Do you know, I think it very probably was? One of the duller Northumbrian saints. His brother Chad was even duller. Has a cathedral in Birmingham if that gives you some idea. Ah, Bill, how good to see you again," he added, accosting the porter who was just walking into the college as well. The porter looked round.

"Mr Cjelli, nice to see you back, sir. Sorry you had a spot of bother, hope that's all behind you now."

"Indeed, Bill, it is. You find me thriving. And Mrs Roberts? How is she? Foot still troubling her?"

"Not since she had it off, thanks for asking, sir. Between you and me, sir, I would've been just as happy to have had her amputated and kept the foot. I had a little spot reserved on the mantelpiece, but there we are, we have to take things as we find them.

"Mr MacDuff, sir," he added, nodding curtly at Richard. "Oh, that horse you mentioned, sir, when you were here last night, I'm afraid we had to have it removed. It was bothering Professor Chronotis."

"I was only curious, er, Bill," said Richard. "I hope it didn't disturb you."

"Nothing ever disturbs me, sir, so long as it isn't wearing a dress. Can't abide it when the young fellers wear dresses, sir."

"If the horse bothers you again, Bill," interrupted Dirk, patting him on the shoulder, "send it up to me and I shall speak with it. Now, you mention the good Professor Chronotis. Is he in at the moment? We've come on an errand."

"Far as I know, sir. Can't check for you because his phone's out of order. Suggest you go and look yourself. Far left corner of Second Court."

"I know it well, Bill, thank you, and my best to what remains of Mrs Roberts."

They swept on through into First Court, or at least Dirk swept, and Richard walked in his normal heron-like gait, wrinkling up his face against the measly drizzle.

Dirk had obviously mistaken himself for a tour guide.

"St Cedd's," he pronounced, "the college of Coleridge, and the college of Sir Isaac Newton, renowned inventor of the milled-edge coin and the catflap!"

"The what?" said Richard.

"The catflap! A device of the utmost cunning, perspicuity and invention. It is a door within a door, you see, a ..."

"Yes," said Richard, "there was also the small matter of gravity."

"Gravity," said Dirk with a slightly dismissive shrug, "yes, there was that as well, I suppose. Though that, of course, was merely a discovery. It was there to be discovered."

He took a penny out of his pocket and tossed it casually on to the pebbles that ran alongside the paved pathway.

"You see?" he said, "They even keep it on at weekends. Someone was bound to notice sooner or later. But the catflap ...

ah, there is a very different matter. Invention, pure creative invention."

"I would have thought it was quite obvious. Anyone could have thought of it."

"Ah," said Dirk, "it is a rare mind indeed that can render the hitherto non-existent blindingly obvious. The cry 'I could have thought of that' is a very popular and misleading one, for the fact is that they didn't, and a very significant and revealing fact it is too. This if I am not mistaken is the staircase we seek. Shall we ascend?"

Without waiting for an answer he plunged on up the stairs. Richard, following uncertainly, found him already knocking on the inner door. The outer one stood open.

"Come in!" called a voice from within. Dirk pushed the door open, and they were just in time to see the back of Reg's white head as he disappeared into the kitchen.

"Just making some tea," he called out. "Like some? Sit down, sit down, whoever you are."

"That would be most kind," returned Dirk. "We are two." Dirk sat, and Richard followed his lead.

"Indian or China?" called Reg.

"Indian, please."

There was a rattle of cups and saucers.

Richard looked around the room. It seemed suddenly humdrum. The fire was burning quietly away to itself, but the light was that of the grey afternoon. Though everything about it was the same, the old sofa, the table burdened with books, there seemed nothing to connect it with the hectic strangeness of the previous night. The room seemed to sit there with raised eyebrows, innocently saying "Yes?"

"Milk?" called out Reg from the kitchen.

"Please," replied Dirk. He gave Richard a smile which seemed to him to be half-mad with suppressed excitement.

"One lump or two?" called Reg again.

"One, please," said Dirk, "… and two spoons of sugar if you would."

There was a suspension of activity in the kitchen. A moment or two passed and Reg stuck his head round the door.

"Svlad Cjelli!" he exclaimed. "Good heavens! Well, that was quick work, young MacDuff, well done. My dear fellow, how very excellent to see you, how good of you to come."

He wiped his hands on a tea towel he was carrying and hurried over to shake hands.

"My dear Svlad."

"Dirk, please, if you would," said Dirk, grasping his hand warmly, "I prefer it. It has more of a sort of Scottish dagger feel to it, I think. Dirk Gently is the name under which I now trade. There are certain events in the past, I'm afraid, from which I would wish to disassociate myself."

"Absolutely, I know how you feel. Most of the fourteenth century, for instance, was pretty grim," agreed Reg earnestly.

Dirk was about to correct the misapprehension, but thought that it might be somewhat of a long trek and left it.

"So how have you been, then, my dear Professor?" he said instead, decorously placing his hat and scarf upon the arm of the sofa.

"Well," said Reg, "it's been an interesting time recently, or rather, a dull time. But dull for interesting reasons. Now, sit down again, warm yourselves by the fire, and I will get the tea and endeavour to explain." He bustled out again, humming busily, and left them to settle themselves in front of the fire.

Richard leant over to Dirk. "I had no idea you knew him so well," he said with a nod in the direction of the kitchen.

"I don't," said Dirk instantly. "We met once by chance at some dinner, but there was an immediate sympathy and rapport."

"So how come you never met again?"

"He studiously avoided me, of course. Close rapports with people are dangerous if you have a secret to hide. And as secrets go, I fancy that this is somewhat of a biggie. If there is a bigger secret anywhere in the world I would very much care," he said quietly, "to know what it is."

He gave Richard a significant look and held his hands out to the fire. Since Richard had tried before without success to draw him out on exactly what the secret was, he refused to rise to the bait on this occasion, but sat back in his armchair and looked about him.

"Did I ask you," said Reg, returning at that moment, "if you wanted any tea?"

"Er, yes," said Richard, "we spoke about it at length. I think we agreed in the end that we would, didn't we?"

"Good," said Reg, vaguely, "by a happy chance there seems to be some ready in the kitchen. You'll have to forgive me. I have a memory like a … like a … what are those things you drain rice in? What am I talking about?"

With a puzzled look he turned smartly round and disappeared once more into the kitchen.

"Very interesting," said Dirk quietly, "I wondered if his memory might be poor."

He stood, suddenly, and prowled around the room. His eyes fell on the abacus which stood on the only clear space on the large mahogany table.

"Is this the table," he asked Richard in a low voice, "where you found the note about the salt cellar?"

"Yes," said Richard, standing, and coming over, "tucked into this book." He picked up the guide to the Greek islands and flipped through it.

"Yes, yes, of course," said Dirk, impatiently. "We know about all that. I'm just interested that this was the table." He ran his fingers along its edge, curiously.

"If you think it was some sort of prior collaboration between Reg and the girl," Richard said, "then I must say that I don't think it possibly can have been."

"Of course it wasn't," said Dirk testily, "I would have thought that was perfectly clear."

Richard shrugged in an effort not to get angry and put the book back down again.

"Well, it's an odd coincidence that the book should have been …"

"Odd coincidence!" snorted Dirk. "Ha! We shall see how much of a coincidence. We shall see exactly how odd it was. I would like you, Richard, to ask our friend how he performed the trick."

"I thought you said you knew already."

"I do," said Dirk airily. "I would like to hear it confirmed."

"Oh, I see," said Richard, "yes, that's rather easy, isn't it? Get him to explain it, and then say, 'Yes, that's exactly what I thought it was!' Very good, Dirk. Have we come all the way up here in order to have him explain how he did a conjuring trick? I think I must be mad."

Dirk bridled at this.

"Please do as I ask," he snapped angrily. "You saw him do the trick, you must ask how he did it. Believe me, there is an astounding secret hidden within it. I know it, but I want you to hear it from him."

He spun round as Reg re-entered, bearing a tray, which he carried round the sofa and put on to the low coffee table that sat in front of the fire.

"Professor Chronotis ..." said Dirk.

"Reg," said Reg, "please."

"Very, well," said Dirk, "Reg ..."

"Sieve!" exclaimed Reg.

"What?"

"Thing you drain rice in. A sieve. I was trying to remember the word, though I forget now the reason why. No matter. Dirk, dear fellow, you look as if you are about to explode about something. Why don't you sit down and make yourself comfortable?"

"Thank you, no, I would rather feel free to pace up and down fretfully if I may. Reg ..."

He turned to face him square on, and raised a single finger.

"I must tell you," he said, "that I know your secret."

"Ah, yes, er – do you indeed?" mumbled Reg, looking down awkwardly and fiddling with the cups and teapot. "I see."

The cups rattled violently as he moved them. "Yes, I was afraid of that."

"And there are some questions that we would like to ask you. I must tell you that I await the answers with the very greatest apprehension."

"Indeed, indeed," Reg muttered. "Well, perhaps it is at last time. I hardly know myself what to make of recent events and am ... fearful myself. Very well. Ask what you will." He looked up sharply, his eyes glittering.

Dirk nodded curtly at Richard, turned, and started to pace, glaring at the floor.

"Er," said Richard, "well, I'd be ... interested to know how you did the conjuring trick with the salt cellar last night."

Reg seemed surprised and rather confused by the question. "The *conjuring* trick?" he said.

"Er, yes," said Richard, "the conjuring trick."

"Oh," said Reg, taken aback, "well, the conjuring part of it, I'm not sure I should – Magic Circle rules, you know, very strict about revealing these secrets. Very strict. Impressive trick, though, don't you think?" he added slyly.

"Well, yes," said Richard, "it seemed very natural at the time, but now that I ... think about it, I have to admit that it was a bit dumbfounding."

"Ah, well," said Reg, "it's skill, you see. Practice. Make it look natural."

"It did look very natural," continued Richard, feeling his way, "I was quite taken in."

"You liked it?"

"It was very impressive."

Dirk was getting a little impatient. He shot a look to that effect at Richard.

"And I can quite see," said Richard firmly, "why it's impossible for you to tell me. I was just interested, that's all. Sorry I asked."

"Well," said Reg in a sudden seizure of doubt, "I suppose ... well, so long as you absolutely promise not to tell anyone else," he carried on, "I suppose you can probably work out for yourself that I used two of the salt cellars on the table. No one was going to notice the difference between one and another. The quickness of the hand, you know, deceives the eye, particularly some of the eyes around that table. While I was fiddling with my woolly hat, giving, though I say so myself, a very cunning simulation of clumsiness and muddle, I simply slipped the salt cellar down my sleeve. You see?"

His earlier agitation had been swept away completely by his pleasure in showing off his craft.

"It's the oldest trick in the world, in fact," he continued, "but nevertheless takes a great deal of skill and deftness. Then a little later, of course, I returned it to the table with the appearance of simply passing it to someone else. Takes years of practice, of course, to make it look natural, but I much prefer it to simply slipping the thing down to the floor. Amateur stuff that. You can't pick it up, and the cleaners never notice it for at least a fortnight. I once had a dead thrush under my seat for a month. No trick involved there, of course. Cat killed it."

Reg beamed.

Richard felt he had done his bit, but hadn't the faintest idea where it was supposed to have got them. He glanced at Dirk, who gave him no help whatsoever, so he plunged on blindly.

"Yes," he said, "yes, I understand that that can be done by sleight of hand. What I don't understand is how the salt cellar got embedded in the pot."

Reg looked puzzled once again, as if they were all talking at cross purposes. He looked at Dirk, who stopped pacing and stared at him with bright, expectant eyes.

"Well, that's ... perfectly straightforward," said Reg, "didn't take any conjuring skill at all. I nipped out for my hat, you remember?"

"Yes," said Richard, doubtfully.

"Well," said Reg, "while I was out of the room I went to find the man who made the pot. Took some time, of course. About three weeks of detective work to track him down and another couple of days to sober him up, and then with a little difficulty I persuaded him to bake the salt cellar into the pot for me. After that I briefly stopped off somewhere to find some, er, powder to disguise the suntan, and of course I had to time the return a little carefully so as to make it all look natural. I bumped into myself in the ante-room, which I always find embarrassing, I never know where to look, but, er ... well, there you have it."

He smiled a rather bleak and nervous smile.

Richard tried to nod, but eventually gave up.

"What on earth are you talking about?" he said.

Reg looked at him in surprise.

"I thought you said you knew my secret," he said.

"I do," said Dirk, with a beam of triumph. "He, as yet, does not, though he furnished all the information I needed to discover it. Let me," he added, "fill in a couple of little blanks. In order to help disguise the fact that you had in fact been away for weeks when as far as anyone sitting at the table was concerned you had only popped out of the door for a couple of seconds, you had to write down for your own reference the last thing you said, in order that you could pick up the thread of conversation again as naturally as possible. An important detail if your memory is not what it once was. Yes?"

"What it once was," said Reg, slowly shaking his white head, "I can hardly remember what it once was. But yes, you are very sharp to pick up such a detail."

"And then there is the little matter," continued Dirk, "of the questions that George III asked. Asked you."

This seemed to catch Reg quite by surprise.

"He asked you," continued Dirk, consulting a small notebook he had pulled from his pocket, "if there was any particular reason why one thing happened after another and if there was any way of stopping it. Did he not also ask you, and ask you *first*, if it was possible to move backwards in time, or something of that kind?"

Reg gave Dirk a long and appraising look.

"I was right about you," he said, "you have a very remarkable mind, young man." He walked slowly over to the window that looked out on to Second Court. He watched the odd figures scuttling through it hugging themselves in the drizzle or pointing at things.

"Yes," said Reg at last in a subdued voice, "that is precisely what he said."

"Good," said Dirk, snapping shut his notebook with a tight little smile which said that he lived for such praise, "then that explains why the answers were 'yes, no and maybe – in that order. Now. Where is it?"

"Where is what?"

"The time machine."

"You're standing in it," said Reg.

Chapter Twenty-six...

A party of noisy people spilled into the train at Bishop's Stortford. Some were wearing morning suits with carnations looking a little battered by a day's festivity. The women of the party were in smart dresses and hats, chattering excitedly about how pretty Julia had looked in all that silk taffeta, how Ralph still looked like a smug oaf even done up in all his finery, and generally giving the whole thing about two weeks.

One of the men stuck his head out of the window and hailed a passing railway employee just to check that this was the right train and was stopping at Cambridge. The porter confirmed that of course it bloody was. The young man said that they didn't all want to find they were going off in the wrong direction, did they, and made a sound a little like that of a fish barking, as if to indicate that this was a pricelessly funny remark, and then pulled his head back in, banging it on the way.

The alcohol content of the atmosphere in the carriage rose sharply.

There seemed to be a general feeling in the air that the best way of getting themselves in the right mood for the post-wedding reception party that evening was to make a foray to the bar so that any members of the party who were not already completely drunk could finish the task. Rowdy shouts of acclamation greeted this notion, the train restarted with a jolt and a lot of those still standing fell over.

Three young men dropped into the three empty seats round one table, of which the fourth was already taken by a sleekly overweight man in an old-fashioned suit. He had a lugubrious face and his large, wet, cowlike eyes gazed into some unknown distance.

Very slowly his eyes began to refocus all the way from infinity and gradually to home in on his more immediate surroundings, his new and intrusive companions. There was a need he felt, as he had felt before.

The three men were discussing loudly whether they would all go to the bar, whether some of them would go to the bar and bring back drinks for the others, whether the ones who went to the bar would get so excited by all the drinks there that they would stay put and forget to bring any back for the others who would be sitting here anxiously awaiting their return, and whether even if they did remember to come back immediately with the drinks they would actually be capable of carrying them and wouldn't simply throw them all over the carriage on the way back, incommoding other passengers.

Some sort of consensus seemed to be reached, but almost immediately none of them could remember what it was. Two of them got up, then sat down again as the third one got up. Then he sat down. The two other ones stood up again, expressing the idea that it might be simpler if they just bought the entire bar.

The third was about to get up again and follow them, when slowly, but with unstoppable purpose, the cow-eyed man sitting opposite him leant across, and gripped him firmly by the forearm.

The young man in his morning suit looked up as sharply as his somewhat bubbly brain would allow and, startled, said, "What do you want?"

Michael Wenton-Weakes gazed into his eyes with terrible intensity, and said, in a low voice, "I was on a ship ..."

"What?"

"A ship ..." said Michael.

"What ship, what are you talking about? Get off me. Let go!"

"We came," continued Michael, in a quiet, almost inaudible, but compelling voice, "a monstrous distance. We came to build a paradise. A paradise. Here."

His eyes swam briefly round the carriage, and then gazed briefly out through the spattered windows at the gathering gloom of a drizzly East Anglian evening. He gazed with evident loathing. His grip on the other's forearm tightened.

"Look, I'm going for a drink," said the wedding guest, though feebly, because he clearly wasn't.

"We left behind those who would destroy themselves with war," murmured Michael. "Ours was to be a world of peace, of music, of art, of enlightenment. All that was petty, all that was mundane, all that was contemptible would have no place in our world ..."

The stilled reveller looked at Michael wonderingly. He didn't look like an old hippy. Of course, you never could tell. His own elder brother had once spent a couple of years living in a Druidic commune, eating LSD doughnuts and thinking he was a tree, since when he had gone on to become a director of a merchant bank. The difference, of course, was that he hardly ever still thought he was a tree, except just occasionally, and he had long ago learnt to avoid the particular claret which sometimes triggered off that flashback.

"There were those who said we would fail," continued Michael in his low tone that carried clearly under the boisterous noise that filled the carriage, "who prophesied that we too carried in us the seed of war, but it was our high resolve and purpose that only art and beauty should flourish, the highest art, the highest beauty – music. We took with us only those who believed, who wished it to be true."

"But what are you talking about?" asked the wedding guest, though not challengingly, for he had fallen under Michael's mesmeric spell. "When was this? Where was this?"

Michael breathed hard. "Before you were born –" he said at last, "be still, and I will tell you."

Chapter Twenty-seven...

There was a long startled silence during which the evening gloom outside seemed to darken appreciably and gather the room into its grip. A trick of the light wreathed Reg in shadows.

Dirk was, for one of the few times in a life of exuberantly prolific loquacity, wordless. His eyes shone with a child's wonder as they passed anew over the dull and shabby furniture of the room, the panelled walls, the threadbare carpets. His hands were trembling.

Richard frowned faintly to himself for a moment as if he was trying to work out the square root of something in his head, and then looked back directly at Reg.

"Who are you?" he asked.

"I have absolutely no idea," said Reg brightly, "much of my memory's gone completely. I am very old, you see. Startlingly old. Yes, I think if I were to tell you how old I was it would be fair to say that you would be startled. Odds are that so would I, because I can't remember. I've seen an awful lot, you know. Forgotten most of it, thank God. Trouble is, when you start getting to my age, which, as I think I mentioned earlier, is a somewhat startling one – did I say that?"

"Yes, you did mention it."

"Good. I'd forgotten whether I had or not. The thing is that your memory doesn't actually get any bigger, and a lot of stuff just falls out. So you see, the major difference between someone of my age and someone of yours is not how much I know, but how much I've forgotten. And after a while you even forget what it is you've forgotten, and after that you even forget that there was something to remember. Then you tend to forget, er, what it was you were talking about."

He stared helplessly at the teapot.

"Things you remember ..." prompted Richard gently.

"Smells and earrings."

"I beg your pardon?"

"Those are things that linger for some reason," said Reg, shaking his head in a puzzled way. He sat down suddenly. "The earrings that Queen Victoria wore on her Silver Jubilee. Quite startling objects. Toned down in the pictures of the period, of course. The smell of the streets before there were cars in them. Hard to say which was worse. That's why Cleopatra remains so vividly in the memory, of course. A quite devastating combination of earrings and smell. I think that will probably be the last thing that remains when all else has finally fled. I shall sit alone in a darkened room, *sans* teeth, *sans* eyes, *sans* taste, *sans* everything but a little grey old head, and in that little grey old head a peculiar vision of hideous blue and gold dangling things flashing in the light, and the smell of sweat, catfood and death. I wonder what I shall make of it ..."

Dirk was scarcely breathing as he began to move slowly round the room, gently brushing his fingertips over the walls, the sofa, the table.

"How long," he said, "has this been –"

"Here?" said Reg. "Just about two hundred years. Ever since I retired."

"Retired from what?"

"Search me. Must have been something pretty good, though, what do you think?"

"You mean you've been in this same set of rooms here for ... two hundred years?" murmured Richard. "You'd think someone would notice, or think it was odd."

"Oh, that's one of the delights of the older Cambridge colleges," said Reg, "everyone is so discreet. If we all went around mentioning what was odd about each other we'd be here till Christmas. Svlad, er – Dirk, my dear fellow, please don't touch that just at the moment."

Dirk's hand was reaching out to touch the abacus standing on its own on the only clear spot on the big table.

"What is it?" said Dirk sharply.

"It's just what it looks like, an old wooden abacus," said Reg. "I'll show you in a moment, but first I must congratulate you on your powers of perception. May I ask how you arrived at the solution?"

"I have to admit," said Dirk with rare humility, "that I did not. In the end I asked a child. I told him the story of the trick and asked him how he thought it had been done, and he said, and I quote, 'It's bleedin' obvious, innit, he must've 'ad a bleedin' time machine.' I thanked the little fellow and gave him a shilling for his trouble. He kicked me rather sharply on the shin and went about his business. But he was the one who solved it. My only contribution to the matter was to see that he *must* be right. He had even saved me the bother of kicking myself."

"But you had the perception to think of asking a child," said Reg. "Well then, I congratulate you on that instead."

Dirk was still eyeing the abacus suspiciously.

"How ... does it work?" he said, trying to make it sound like a casual enquiry.

"Well, it's really terribly simple," said Reg, "it works any way you want it to. You see, the computer that runs it is a rather advanced one. In fact it is more powerful than the sum total of all the computers on this planet including – and this is the tricky part – including itself. Never really understood that bit myself, to be honest with you. But over ninety-five per cent of that power is used in simply understanding what it is you want it to do. I simply plonk my abacus down there and it understands the way I use it. I think I must have been brought up to use an abacus when I was a ... well, a child, I suppose.

"Richard, for instance, would probably want to use his own personal computer. If you put it down there, where the abacus is, the machine's computer would simply take charge of it and offer you lots of nice user-friendly time-travel applications complete with pull-down menus and desk accessories if you like. Except that you point to 1066 on the screen and you've got the Battle of Hastings going on outside your door, er, if that's the sort of thing you're interested in."

Reg's tone of voice suggested that his own interests lay in other areas.

"It's, er, really quite fun in its way," he concluded. "Certainly better than television and a great deal easier to use than a video recorder. If I miss a programme I just pop back in time and watch it. I'm hopeless fiddling with all those buttons."

Dirk reacted to this revelation with horror.

"You have a time machine and you use it for ... watching television?"

"Well, I wouldn't use it at all if I could get the hang of the video recorder. It's a very delicate business, time travel, you know. Full of appalling traps and dangers, if you should change the wrong thing in the past, you could entirely disrupt the course of history.

"Plus, of course, it mucks up the telephone. I'm sorry," he said to Richard a little sheepishly, "that you were unable to phone your young lady last night. There seems to be something fundamentally inexplicable about the British telephone system, and my time machine doesn't like it. There's never any problem with the plumbing, the electricity, or even the gas. The connection interfaces are taken care of at some quantum level I don't entirely understand, and it's never been a problem.

"The phone on the other hand is definitely a problem. Every time I use the time machine, which is, of course, hardly at all, partly because of this very problem with the phone, the phone goes haywire and I have to get some lout from the phone company to come and fix it, and he starts asking stupid questions the answers to which he has no hope of understanding.

"Anyway, the point is that I have a very strict rule that I must not change anything in the past at all –" Reg sighed – "whatever the temptation."

"What temptation?" said Dirk, sharply.

"Oh, it's just a little, er, thing I'm interested in," said Reg, vaguely, "it is perfectly harmless because I stick very strictly to the rule. It makes me sad, though."

"But you broke your own rule!" insisted Dirk. "Last night! You changed something in the past –"

"Well, yes," said Reg, a little uncomfortably, "but that was different. Very different. If you had seen the look on the poor child's face. So miserable. She thought the world should be a marvellous place, and all those appalling old dons were pouring their withering scorn on her just because it wasn't marvellous for them anymore.

"I mean," he added, appealing to Richard, "remember Cawley. What a bloodless old goat. Someone should get some humanity into him even if they have to knock it in with a brick. No, that was perfectly justifiable. Otherwise, I make it a very strict rule –"

Richard looked at him with dawning recognition of something.

"Reg," he said politely, "may I give you a little advice?"

"Of course you may, my dear fellow, I should adore you to," said Reg.

"If our mutual friend here offers to take you for a stroll along the banks of the River Cam, *don't go.*"

"What on earth do you mean?"

"He means," said Dirk earnestly, "that he thinks there may be something a little disproportionate between what you actually did, and your stated reasons for doing it."

"Oh. Well, odd way of saying it –"

"Well, he's a very odd fellow. But you see, there sometimes may be other reasons for things you do which you are not necessarily aware of. As in the case of post-hypnotic suggestion – or possession."

Reg turned very pale.

"Possession –" he said.

"Professor – Reg – I believe there was some reason you wanted to see me. What exactly was it?"

"Cambridge! this is ... Cambridge!" came the lilting squawk of the station public address system.

Crowds of noisy revellers spewed out on to the platform barking and honking at each other.

"Where's Rodney?" said one, who had clambered with difficulty from the carriage in which the bar was situated. He and his companion looked up and down the platform, totteringly. The large figure of Michael Wenton-Weakes loomed silently past them and out to the exit.

They jostled their way down the side of the train, looking in through the dirty carriage windows. They suddenly saw their missing companion still sitting, trance-like, in his seat in the now almost empty compartment. They banged on the window and hooted at him. For a moment or two he didn't react, and when he did he woke suddenly in a puzzled way as if seeming not to know where he was.

"He's pie-eyed!" his companions bawled happily, bundling themselves on to the train again and bundling Rodney back off.

He stood woozily on the platform and shook his head. Then glancing up he saw through the railings the large bulk of Michael Wenton-Weakes heaving himself and a large heavy bag into a taxi-cab, and he stood for a moment transfixed.

"'Straordinary thing," he said, "that man. Telling me a long story about some kind of shipwreck."

"Har har," gurgled one of his two companions, "get any money off you?"

"What?" said Rodney, puzzled. "No. No, I don't think so. Except it wasn't a shipwreck, more an accident, an explosion –? He seems to think he caused it in some way. Or rather there was an accident, and he caused an explosion trying to put it right and killed everybody. Then he said there was an awful lot of rotting mud for years and years, and then slimy things with legs. It was all a bit peculiar."

"Trust Rodney! Trust Rodney to pick a madman!"

"I think he must have been mad. He suddenly went off on a

tangent about some bird. He said the bit about the bird was all nonsense. He wished he could get rid of the bit about the bird. But then he said it would be put right. It would all be put right. For some reason I didn't like it when he said that."

"Should have come along to the bar with us. Terribly funny, we –"

"I also didn't like the way he said goodbye. I didn't like that at all."

Chapter Twenty-eight...

"You remember," said Reg, "when you arrived this afternoon I said that times recently had been dull, but for ... interesting reasons?"

"I remember it vividly," said Dirk, "it happened a mere ten minutes ago. You were standing exactly there as I recall. Indeed you were wearing the very clothes with which you are currently apparelled, and –"

"Shut up, Dirk," said Richard, "let the poor man talk, will you?"

Dirk made a slight, apologetic bow.

"Quite so," said Reg. "Well, the truth is that for many weeks, months even, I have not used the time machine at all, because I had the oddest feeling that someone or something was trying to make me do it. It started as the very faintest urge, and then it seemed to come at me in stronger and stronger waves. It was extremely disturbing. I had to fight it very hard indeed because it was trying to make me do something I actually wanted to do. I don't think I would have realised that it was something outside of me creating this pressure and not just my own wishes asserting themselves if it wasn't for the fact that I was so wary of allowing myself to do any such thing. As soon as I began to realise that it was something else trying to invade me things got really bad and the furniture began to fly about. Quite damaged my little Georgian writing desk. Look at the marks on the –"

"Is that what you were afraid of last night, upstairs?" asked Richard.

"Oh yes," said Reg in a hushed voice, "most terribly afraid. But it was only that rather nice horse, so that was all right. I expect it just wandered in when I was out getting some powder to cover up my suntan."

"Oh?" said Dirk, "And where did you go for that?" he asked. "I can't think of many chemists that a horse would be likely to visit."

"Oh, there's a planet off in what's known here as the Pleiades where the dust is exactly the right –"

"You went," said Dirk in a whisper, "to another planet? To get face powder?"

"Oh, it's no distance," said Reg cheerfully. "You see, the actual distance between two points in the whole of the space/time continuum is almost infinitely smaller than the apparent distance between adjacent orbits of an electron. Really, it's a lot less far than the chemist, and there's no waiting about at the till. I never have the right change, do you? Go for the quantum jump is always my preference. Except of course that you then get all the trouble with the telephone. Nothing's ever that easy, is it?"

He looked bothered for a moment.

"I think you may be right in what I think you're thinking, though," he added quietly.

"Which is?"

"That I went through a rather elaborate bit of business to achieve a very small result. Cheering up a little girl, charming, delightful and sad though she was, doesn't seem to be enough explanation for – well, it was a fairly major operation in time-engineering, now that I come to face up to it. There's no doubt that it would have been simpler to compliment her on her dress. Maybe the ... ghost – we are talking of a ghost here, aren't we?"

"I think we are, yes," said Dirk slowly.

"A ghost?" said Richard, "Now come on –"

"Wait!" said Dirk, abruptly. "Please continue," he said to Reg.

"It's possible that the ... ghost caught me off my guard. I was fighting so strenuously against doing one thing that it easily tripped me into another –"

"And now?"

"Oh, it's gone completely. The ghost left me last night."

"And where, we wonder," said Dirk, turning his gaze on Richard, "did it go?"

"No, please," said Richard, "not this. I'm not even sure I've agreed we're talking about time machines yet, and now suddenly it's ghosts?"

"So what was it," hissed Dirk, "that got into you to make you climb the wall?"

"Well, you suggested that I was under post-hypnotic suggestion from someone –"

"I did not! I demonstrated the power of post-hypnotic suggestion to you. But I believe that hypnosis and possession work in very, very similar ways. You can be made to do all kinds of absurd things, and will then cheerfully invent the most transparent rationalisations to explain them to yourself. But – you cannot be made to do something that runs against the fundamental grain of your character. You will fight. You will resist!"

Richard remembered then the sense of relief with which he had impulsively replaced the tape in Susan's machine last night. It had been the end of a struggle which he had suddenly won. With the sense of another struggle that he was now losing he sighed and related this to the others.

"Exactly!" exclaimed Dirk. "You wouldn't do it! Now we're getting somewhere! You see, hypnosis works best when the subject has some fundamental sympathy with what he or she is being asked to do. Find the right subject for your task and the hypnosis can take a very, very deep hold indeed. And I believe the same to be true of possession. So. What do we have?

"We have a ghost that wants something done and is looking for the right person to take possession of to do that for him. Professor –"

"Reg –" said Reg.

"Reg – may I ask you something that may be terribly personal? I will understand perfectly if you don't want to answer, but I will just keep pestering you until you do. Just my methods, you see.

You said there was something that you found to be a terrible temptation to you. That you wanted to do but would not allow yourself, and that the ghost was trying to make you do? Please. This may be difficult for you, but I think it would be very helpful if you would tell us what it is."

"I will not tell you."

"You must understand how important –"

"I'll show you instead," said Reg.

Silhouetted in the gates of St Cedd's stood a large figure carrying a large heavy black nylon bag. The figure was that of Michael Wenton-Weakes, the voice that asked the porter if Professor Chronotis was currently in his room was that of Michael Wenton-Weakes, the ears that heard the porter say he was buggered if he knew because the phone seemed to be on the blink again was that of Michael Wenton-Weakes, but the spirit that gazed out of his eyes was his no longer.

He had surrendered himself completely. All doubt, disparity and confusion had ceased.

A new mind had him in full possession.

The spirit that was not Michael Wenton-Weakes surveyed the college which lay before it, to which it had grown accustomed in the last few frustrating, infuriating weeks.

Weeks! Mere microsecond blinks.

Although the spirit – the ghost – that now inhabited Michael Wenton-Weakes' body had known long periods of near oblivion, sometimes even for centuries at a stretch, the time for which it had wandered the earth was such that it seemed only minutes ago that the creatures which had erected these walls had arrived. Most of his personal eternity – not really eternity, but a few billion years could easily seem like it – had been spent wandering across interminable mud, wading through ceaseless seas, watching with stunned horror when the slimy things with legs suddenly had begun to crawl from those rotting seas – and here they were, suddenly walking around as if they owned the place and complaining about the phones.

Deep in a dark and silent part of himself he knew that he was now mad, had been driven mad almost immediately after the accident by the knowledge of what he had done and of the existence he faced, by the memories of his fellows who had died and who for a while had haunted him even as he had haunted the Earth.

He knew that what he now had been driven to would have revolted the self he only infinitesimally remembered, but that it was the only way for him to end the ceaseless nightmare in which each second of billions of years had been worse than the previous one.

He hefted the bag and started to walk.

Chapter   Twenty-nine...

Deep in the rain forest it was doing what it usually does in rain forests, which was raining: hence the name.

It was a gentle, persistent rain, not the heavy slashing which would come later in the year, in the hot season. It formed a fine dripping mist through which the occasional shaft of sunlight would break, be softened and pass through on its way towards the wet bark of a calvaria tree on which it would settle and glisten. Sometimes it would do this next to a butterfly or a tiny motionless sparkling lizard, and then the effect would be almost unbearable.

Away up. in the high canopy of the trees an utterly extraordinary thought would suddenly strike a bird, and it would go flapping wildly through the branches and settle at last in a different and altogether better tree where it would sit and consider things again more calmly until the same thought came along and struck it again, or it was time to eat.

The air was full of scents – the light fragrance of flowers, and the heavy odour of the sodden mulch with which the floor of the forest was carpeted.

Confusions of roots tangled through the mulch, moss grew on them, insects crawled.

In a space in the forest, on an empty patch of wet ground between a circle of craning trees, appeared quietly and without fuss a plain white door. After a few seconds it opened a little way with a slight squeak. A tall thin man looked out, looked around, blinked in surprise, and quietly pulled the door closed again.

A few seconds later the door opened again and Reg looked out.

"It's real," he said, "I promise you. Come out and see for yourself." Walking out into the forest, he turned and beckoned the other two to follow him.

Dirk stepped boldly through, seemed disconcerted for about the length of time it takes to blink twice, and then announced that he saw exactly how it worked, that it was obviously to do with the unreal numbers that lay between minimum quantum distances and defined the fractal contours of the enfolded Universe and he was only astonished at himself for not having thought of it himself.

"Like the catflap," said Richard from the doorway behind him.

"Er, yes, quite so," said Dirk, taking off his spectacles and leaning against a tree wiping them, "you spotted of course that I was lying. A perfectly natural reflex in the circumstances as I think you'll agree. Perfectly natural." He squinted slightly and put his spectacles back on. They began to mist up again almost immediately.

"Astounding," he admitted.

Richard stepped through more hesitantly and stood rocking for a moment with one foot still on the floor in Reg's room and the other on the wet earth of the forest. Then he stepped forward and committed himself fully.

His lungs instantly filled with the heady vapours and his mind with the wonder of the place. He turned and looked at the doorway through which he had walked. It was still a perfectly ordinary door frame with a perfectly ordinary little white door swinging open in it, but it was standing free in the open forest, and through it could clearly be seen the room he had just stepped out of.

He walked wonderingly round the back of the door, testing each foot on the muddy ground, not so much for fear of slipping as for fear that it might simply not be there. From behind it was just a perfectly ordinary open door frame, such as you might fail to find in any perfectly ordinary rain forest. He walked through the door from behind, and looking back again could once more see, as if he had just stepped out of them again, the college rooms of Professor Urban Chronotis of St Cedd's College, Cambridge, which must be thousands of miles away. Thousands? Where were they?

He peered off through the trees and thought he caught a slight shimmer in the distance, between the trees.

"Is that the sea?" he asked.

"You can see it a little more clearly from up here," called Reg, who had walked on a little way up a slippery incline and was now leaning, puffing, against a tree. He pointed.

The other two followed him up, pulling themselves noisily through the branches and causing a lot of cawing and complaining from unseen birds high above.

"The Pacific?" asked Dirk.

"The Indian Ocean," said Reg.

Dirk wiped his glasses again and had another look.

"Ah, yes, of course," he said.

"Not Madagascar?" said Richard. "I've been there –"

"Have you?" said Reg. "One of the most beautiful and astonishing places on Earth, and one that is also full of the most appalling ... temptations for me. No."

His voice trembled slightly, and he cleared his throat.

"No," he continued, "Madagascar is – let me see, which direction are we – where's the sun? Yes. That way. Westish. Madagascar is about five hundred miles roughly west of here. The island of Réunion lies roughly in-between."

"Er, what's the place called?" said Dirk suddenly, rapping his knuckles on the tree and frightening a lizard. "Place where that stamp comes from, er – Mauritius."

"Stamp?" said Reg.

"Yes, you must know," said Dirk, "very famous stamp. Can't remember anything about it, but it comes from here. Mauritius. Famous for its very remarkable stamp, all brown and smudged and you could buy Blenheim Palace with it. Or am I thinking of British Guiana?"

"Only you," said Richard, "know what you are thinking of."

"Is it Mauritius?"

"It is," said Reg, "it is Mauritius."

"But you don't collect stamps?"

"No."

"What on *earth's* that?" said Richard suddenly, but Dirk carried on with his thought to Reg, "Pity, you could get some nice first-day covers, couldn't you?"

Reg shrugged. "Not really interested," he said.

Richard slithered back down the slope behind them.

"So what's the great attraction here?" said Dirk. "It's not, I have to confess, what I was expecting. Very nice in its way, of course, all this nature, but I'm a city boy myself, I'm afraid." He cleaned his glasses once again and pushed them back up his nose.

He started backwards at what he saw, and heard a strange little chuckle from Reg. Just in front of the door back into Reg's room, the most extraordinary confrontation was taking place.

A large cross bird was looking at Richard and Richard was looking at a large cross bird. Richard was looking at the bird as if it was the most extraordinary thing he had ever seen in his life, and the bird was looking at Richard as if defying him to find its beak even remotely funny.

Once it had satisfied itself that Richard did not intend to laugh, the bird regarded him instead with a sort of grim irritable tolerance and wondered if he was just going to stand there or actually do something useful and feed it. It padded a couple of steps back and a couple of steps to the side and then just a single step forward again, on great waddling yellow feet. It then looked at him again, impatiently, and squarked an impatient squark.

The bird then bent forward and scraped its great absurd red beak across the ground as if to give Richard the idea that this might be a good area to look for things to give it to eat.

"It eats the nuts of the calvaria tree," called out Reg to Richard.

The big bird looked sharply up at Reg in annoyance, as if to say that it was perfectly clear to any idiot what it ate. It then looked back at Richard once more and stuck its head on one side as if it had suddenly been struck by the thought that perhaps it was an idiot it had to deal with, and that it might need to reconsider its strategy accordingly.

"There are one or two on the ground behind you," called Reg softly.

In a trance of astonishment Richard turned awkwardly and saw one or two large nuts lying on the ground. He bent and picked one up, glancing up at Reg, who gave him a reassuring nod.

Tentatively Richard held the thing out to the bird, which leant forward and pecked it sharply from between his fingers. Then, because Richard's hand was still stretched out, the bird knocked it irritably aside with its beak.

Once Richard had withdrawn to a respectful distance, it stretched its neck up, closed its large yellow eyes and seemed to gargle gracelessly as it shook the nut down its neck into its maw.

It appeared then to be at least partially satisfied. Whereas before it had been a cross dodo, it was at least now a cross, fed dodo, which was probably about as much as it could hope for in this life.

It made a slow, waddling, on-the-spot turn and padded back into the forest whence it had come, as if defying Richard to find the little tuft of curly feathers stuck up on top of its backside even remotely funny.

"I only come to look," said Reg in a small voice, and glancing at him Dirk was discomfited to see that the old man's eyes were brimming with tears which he quickly brushed away. "Really, it is not for me to interfere –"

Richard came scurrying breathlessly up to them.

"Was that a *dodo*?" he exclaimed.

"Yes," said Reg, "one of only three left at this time. The year is 1676. They will all be dead within four years, and after that no one will ever see them again. Come," he said, "let us go."

Behind the stoutly locked outer door in the corner staircase in the Second Court of St Cedd's College, where only a millisecond earlier there had been a slight flicker as the inner door departed, there was another slight flicker as the inner door now returned.

Walking through the dark evening towards it the large figure of Michael Wenton-Weakes looked up at the corner windows. If any slight flicker had been visible, it would have gone unnoticed in the dim dancing firelight that spilled from the window.

The figure then looked up into the darkness of the sky, looking for what it knew to be there though there was not the slightest chance of seeing it, even on a clear night which this was not. The orbits of Earth were now so cluttered with pieces of junk and debris that one more item among them – even such a large one as this was – would pass perpetually unnoticed. Indeed, it had done so, though its influence had from time to time exerted itself. From time to time. When the waves had been strong. Not for nearly two hundred years had they been so strong as now they were again.

And all at last was now in place. The perfect carrier had been found.

The perfect carrier moved his footsteps onwards through the court.

The Professor himself had seemed the perfect choice at first, but that attempt had ended in frustration, fury, and then – inspiration! Bring a Monk to Earth! They were designed to believe anything, to be completely malleable. It could be suborned to undertake the task with the greatest of ease.

Unfortunately, however, this one had proved to be completely hopeless. Getting it to believe something was very easy. Getting it to continue to believe the same thing for more than five minutes at a time had proved to be an even more impossible task than that of getting the Professor to do what he fundamentally wanted to do but wouldn't allow himself.

Then another failure and then, miraculously, the perfect carrier had come at last.

The perfect carrier had already proved that it would have no compunction in doing what would have to be done.

Damply, clogged in mist, the moon struggled in a corner of the sky to rise. At the window, a shadow moved.

Chapter Thirty...

From the window overlooking Second Court Dirk watched the moon. "We shall not," he said, "have long to wait."

"To wait for what?" said Richard.

Dirk turned.

"For the ghost," he said, "to return to us. Professor –," he added to Reg, who was sitting anxiously by the fire, "do you have any brandy, French cigarettes or worry beads in your rooms?"

"No," said Reg.

"Then I shall have to fret unaided," said Dirk and returned to staring out of the window.

"I have yet to be convinced," said Richard, "that there is not some other explanation than that of ... ghosts to –"

"Just as you required actually to see a time machine in operation before you could accept it," returned Dirk. "Richard, I commend you on your scepticism, but even the sceptical mind must be prepared to accept the unacceptable when there is no alternative. If it looks like a duck, and quacks like a duck, we have at least to consider the possibility that we have a small aquatic bird of the family *Anatidae* on our hands."

"Then what *is* a ghost?"

"I think that a ghost ..." said Dirk, "is someone who died either violently or unexpectedly with unfinished business on his, her – or its – hands. Who cannot rest until it has been finished, or put right."

He turned to face them again.

"Which is why," he said, "a time machine would have such a fascination for a ghost once it knew of its existence. A time machine provides the means to put right what, in the ghost's opinion, went wrong in the past. To free it.

"Which is why it will be back. It tried first to take possession of Reg himself, but he resisted. Then came the incident with the conjuring trick, the face powder and the horse in the bathroom which I –" he paused – "which even I do not understand, though I intend to if it kills me. And then you, Richard, appear on the scene. The ghost deserts Reg and concentrates instead on you. Almost immediately there occurs an odd but significant incident. You do something that you then wish you hadn't done.

"I refer, of course, to the phone call you made to Susan and left on her answering machine.

"The ghost seizes its chance and tries to induce you to undo it. To, as it were, go back into the past and erase that message – to change the mistake you had made. Just to see if you would do it. Just to see if it was in your character.

"If it had been, you would now be totally under its control. But at the very last second your nature rebelled and you would not do it. And so the ghost gives you up as a bad job and deserts you in turn. It must find someone else.

"How long has it been doing this? I do not know. Does this now make sense to you? Do you recognise the truth of what I am saying?"

Richard turned cold.

"Yes," he said, "I think you must be absolutely right."

"And at what moment, then," said Dirk, "did the ghost leave you?"

Richard swallowed.

"When Michael Wenton-Weakes walked out of the room," he said.

"So I wonder," said Dirk quietly, "what possibilities the ghost saw in him. I wonder whether this time it found what it wanted. I believe we shall not have long to wait."

There was a knock on the door.

When it opened, there stood Michael Wenton-Weakes.

He said simply, "Please, I need your help."

Reg and Richard stared at Dirk, and then at Michael.

"Do you mind if I put this down somewhere?" said Michael. "It's rather heavy. Full of scuba-diving equipment."

"Oh, I see," said Susan, "oh well, thanks, Nicola, I'll try that fingering. I'm sure he only put the E flat in there just to annoy people. Yes, I've been at it solidly all afternoon. Some of those semiquaver runs in the second movement are absolute bastards. Well, yes, it helped take my mind off it all. No, no news. It's all just mystifying and absolutely horrible. I don't want even to – look, maybe I'll give you a call again later and see how you're feeling. I know, yes, you never know which is worse, do you, the illness, the antibiotics, or the doctor's bedside manner. Look after yourself, or at least, make sure Simon does. Tell him to bring you gallons of hot lemon. OK. Well, I'll talk to you later. Keep warm. Bye now."

She put the phone down and returned to her cello. She had hardly started to reconsider the problem of the irritating E flat when the phone went again. She had simply left it off the hook for the afternoon, but had forgotten to do so again after making her own call.

With a sigh she propped up the cello, put down the bow, and went to the phone again.

"Hello?" she demanded.

Again, there was nothing, just a distant cry of wind. Irritably, she slammed the receiver back down once more.

She waited a few seconds for the line to clear, and then was about to take the phone off the hook once more when she realised that perhaps Richard might need her.

She hesitated.

She admitted to herself that she hadn't been using the answering machine, because she usually just put it on for Gordon's convenience, and that was something of which she did not currently wish to be reminded.

Still, she put the answering machine on, turned the volume right down, and returned again to the E flat that Mozart had put in only to annoy cellists.

In the darkness of the offices of Dirk Gently's Holistic Detective Agency, Gordon Way clumsily fumbled the telephone receiver back on to its rest and sat slumped in the deepest dejection. He didn't even stop himself slumping all the way through the seat until he rested lightly on the floor.

Miss Pearce had fled the office the first time the telephone had started actually using itself, her patience with all this sort of thing finally exhausted again, since which time Gordon had had the office to himself. However, his attempts to contact anybody had failed completely.

Or rather, his attempts to contact Susan, which was all he cared about. It was Susan he had been speaking to when he died and he knew he had somehow to speak to her again. But she had left her phone off the hook most of the afternoon and even when she had answered she could not hear him.

He gave up. He roused himself from the floor, stood up, and slipped out and down into the darkening streets. He drifted aimlessly for a while, went for a walk on the canal, which was a trick that palled very quickly, and then wandered back up to the street again.

The houses with light and life streaming from them upset him most particularly since the welcome they seemed to extend would not be extended to him. He wondered if anyone would mind if he simply slipped into their house and watched television for the evening. He wouldn't be any trouble.

Or a cinema.

That would be better, he could go to the cinema.

He turned with more positive, if still insubstantial, footsteps into Noel Road and started to walk up it.

Noel Road, he thought. It rang a vague bell. He had a feeling that he had recently had some dealings with someone in Noel Road. Who was it?

His thoughts were interrupted by a terrible scream of horror that rang through the street. He stood stock still. A few seconds later a door flew open a few yards from him and a woman ran out of it, wild-eyed and howling.

Chapter Thirty-one...

Richard had never liked Michael Wenton-Weakes and he liked him even less with a ghost in him. He couldn't say why, he had nothing against ghosts personally, didn't think a person should be judged adversely simply for being dead, but – he didn't like it.

Nevertheless, it was hard not to feel a little sorry for him.

Michael sat forlornly on a stool with his elbow resting on the large table and his head resting on his fingers. He looked ill and haggard. He looked deeply tired. He looked pathetic. His story had been a harrowing one, and concluded with his attempts to possess first Reg and then Richard.

"You were," he concluded, "right. Entirely."

He said this last to Dirk, and Dirk grimaced as if trying not to beam with triumph too many times in a day.

The voice was Michael's and yet it was not Michael's. Whatever timbre a voice acquires through a billion or so years of dread and isolation, this voice had acquired it, and it filled those who heard it with a dizzying chill akin to that which clutches the mind and stomach when standing on a cliff at night.

He turned his eyes on Reg and on Richard, and the effect of the eyes, too, was one that provoked pity and terror. Richard had to look away.

"I owe you both an apology," said the ghost within Michael, "which I offer you from the depths of my heart, and only hope that as you come to understand the desperation of my predicament, and the hope which this machine offers me, you will understand why I have acted as I have, and that you will find it within yourselves to forgive me. And to help me. I beg you."

"Give the man a whisky," said Dirk gruffly.

"Haven't got any whisky," said Reg. "Er, port? There's a bottle or so of Margaux I could open. Very fine one. Should be chambréd for an hour, but I can do that of course, it's very easy, I –"

"Will you help me?" interrupted the ghost.

Reg bustled to fetch some port and some glasses.

"Why have you taken over the body of this man?" said Dirk.

"I need to have a voice with which to speak and a body with which to act. No harm will come to him, no harm –"

"Let me ask the question again. Why have you taken over the body of this man?" insisted Dirk.

The ghost made Michael's body shrug.

"He was willing. Both of these two gentlemen quite understandably resisted being ... well, hypnotised – your analogy is fair. This one? Well, I think his sense of self is at a low ebb, and he has acquiesced. I am very grateful to him and will not do him any harm."

"His sense of self," repeated Dirk thoughtfully, "is at a low ebb."

"I suppose that is probably true," said Richard quietly to Dirk. "He seemed very depressed last night. The one thing that was important to him had been taken away because he, well, he wasn't really very good at it. Although he's proud I expect he was probably quite receptive to the idea of actually being wanted for something."

"Hmmm," said Dirk, and said it again. He said it a third time with feeling. Then he whirled round and barked at the figure on the stool.

"Michael Wenton-Weakes!"

Michael's head jolted back and he blinked.

"Yes?" he said, in his normal lugubrious voice. His eyes followed Dirk as he moved.

"You can hear me," said Dirk, "and you can answer for yourself?"

"Oh, yes," said Michael, "most certainly I can."

"This … being, this spirit. You know he is in you? You accept his presence? You are a willing party to what he wishes to do?"

"That is correct. I was much moved by his account of himself, and am very willing to help him. In fact I think it is right for me to do so."

"All right," said Dirk with a snap of his fingers, "you can go."

Michael's head slumped forward suddenly, and then after a second or so it slowly rose again, as if being pumped up from inside like a tyre.

The ghost was back in possession.

Dirk took hold of a chair, spun it round and sat astride it facing the ghost in Michael, peering intently into its eyes.

"Again," he said, "tell me again. A quick snap account."

Michael's body tensed slightly. It reached out to Dirk's arm.

"Don't – touch me!" snapped Dirk. "Just tell me the facts. The first time you try and make me feel sorry for you I'll poke you in the eye. Or at least, the one you've borrowed. So leave out all the stuff that sounded like … er –"

"Coleridge," said Richard suddenly, "it sounded exactly like Coleridge. It was like 'The Rime of the Ancient Mariner'. Well, bits of it were."

Dirk frowned. "Coleridge?" he said.

"I tried to tell him my story," admitted the ghost, "I –"

"Sorry," said Dirk, "you'll have to excuse me – I've never cross-examined a four-billion-year-old ghost before. Are we talking Samuel Taylor here? Are you saying you told your story to Samuel Taylor Coleridge?"

"I was able to enter his mind at … certain times. When he was in an impressionable state."

"You mean when he was on laudanum?" said Richard.

"That is correct. He was more relaxed then."

"I'll say," snorted Reg, "I sometimes encountered him when he was quite astoundingly relaxed. Look, I'll make some coffee." He disappeared into the kitchen, where he could be heard laughing to himself.

"It's another world," muttered Richard to himself, sitting down and shaking his head.

"But unfortunately when he was fully in possession of himself I, so to speak, was not," said the ghost, "and so that failed. And what he wrote was very garbled."

"Discuss," said Richard, to himself, raising his eyebrows.

"Professor," called out Dirk, "this may sound absurd. Did – Coleridge ever try to ... er ... use your time machine? Feel free to discuss the question in any way which appeals to you."

"Well, do you know," said Reg, looking round the door, "he did come in prying around on one occasion, but I think he was in a great deal too relaxed a state to do anything."

"I see," said Dirk. "But why," he added turning back to the strange figure of Michael slumped on its stool, "why has it taken you so long to find someone?"

"For long, long periods I am very weak, almost totally non-existent, and unable to influence anything at all. And then, of course, before that time there was no time machine here, and ... no hope for me at all –"

"Perhaps ghosts exist like wave patterns," suggested Richard, "like interference patterns between the actual with the possible. There would be irregular peaks and troughs, like in a musical waveform."

The ghost snapped Michael's eyes around to Richard.

"You ..." he said, "you wrote that article ..."

"Er, yes –"

"It moved me very greatly," said the ghost, with a sudden remorseful longing in his voice which seemed to catch itself almost as much by surprise as it did its listeners.

"Oh. I see," said Richard, "Well, thank you. You didn't like it so much last time you mentioned it. Well, I know that wasn't you as such –"

Richard sat back frowning to himself.

"So," said Dirk, "to return to the beginning –"

The ghost gathered Michael's breath for him and started again. "We were on a ship –" it said.

"A spaceship."

"Yes. Out from Salaxala, a world in ... well, very far from here. A violent and troubled place. We – a party of some nine dozen of us – set out, as people frequently did, to find a new world for ourselves. All the planets in this system were completely unsuitable for our purpose, but we stopped on this world to replenish some necessary mineral supplies.

"Unfortunately our landing ship was damaged on its way into the atmosphere. Damaged quite badly, but still quite reparable.

"I was the engineer on board and it fell to me to supervise the task of repairing the ship and preparing it to return to our main ship. Now, in order to understand what happened next you must know something of the nature of a highly-automated society. There is no task that cannot be done more easily with the aid of advanced computerisation. And there were some very specific problems associated with a trip with an aim such as ours –"

"Which was?" said Dirk sharply.

The ghost in Michael blinked as if the answer was obvious.

"Well, to find a new and better world on which we could all live in freedom, peace and harmony forever, of course," he said.

Dirk raised his eyebrows.

"Oh, that," he said. "You'd thought this all out carefully, I assume."

"We'd had it thought out for us. We had with us some very specialised devices for helping us to continue to believe in the purpose of the trip even when things got difficult. They generally worked very well, but I think we probably came to rely on them too much."

"What on earth were they?" said Dirk.

"It's probably hard for you to understand how reassuring they were. And that was why I made my fatal mistake. When I wanted to know whether or not it was safe to take off, I didn't want to know that it might *not* be safe. I just wanted to be reassured that it *was*. So instead of checking it myself, you see, I sent out one of the Electric Monks."

Chapter Thirty-two...

The brass plaque on the red door in Peckender Street glittered as it reflected the yellow light of a street lamp. It glared for a moment as it reflected the violent flashing light of a passing police car sweeping by.

It dimmed slightly as a pale, pale wraith slipped silently through it. It glimmered as it dimmed, because the wraith was trembling with such terrible agitation.

In the dark hallway the ghost of Gordon Way paused. He needed something to lean on for support, and of course there was nothing. He tried to get a grip on himself, but there was nothing to get a grip on. He retched at the horror of what he had seen, but there was, of course, nothing in his stomach. He half stumbled, half swam up the stairs, like a drowning man trying to grapple for a grip on the water.

He staggered through the wall, through the desk, through the door, and tried to compose and settle himself in front of the desk in Dirk's office.

If anyone had happened into the office a few minutes later – a night cleaner perhaps, if Dirk Gently had ever employed one, which he didn't on the grounds that they wished to be paid and he did not wish to pay them, or a burglar, perhaps, if there had been anything in the office worth burgling, which there wasn't – they would have seen the following sight and been amazed by it.

The receiver of the large red telephone on the desk suddenly rocked and tumbled off its rest on to the desk top.

A dialling tone started to burr. Then, one by one, seven of the large, easily pushed buttons depressed themselves, and after the very long pause which the British telephone system allows you within which to gather your thoughts and forget who it is you're phoning, the sound of a phone ringing at the other end of the line could be heard.

After a couple of rings there was a click, a whirr, and a sound as of a machine drawing breath. Then a voice started to say, "Hello, this is Susan. I can't come to the phone right at the moment because I'm trying to get an E flat right, but if you'd like to leave your name ..."

"So then, on the say so of an – I can hardly bring myself to utter the words – Electric Monk," said Dirk in a voice ringing with derision, "you attempt to launch the ship and to your utter astonishment it explodes. Since when –?"

"Since when," said the ghost, abjectly, "I have been alone on this planet. Alone with the knowledge of what I had done to my fellows on the ship. All, all alone ..."

"Yes, skip that, I said," snapped Dirk angrily. "What about the main ship? That presumably went on and continued its search for –"

"No."

"Then what happened to it?"

"Nothing. It's still there."

"Still *there*?"

Dirk leapt to his feet and whirled off to pace the room, his brow furiously furrowed.

"Yes." Michael's head drooped a little, but he looked up piteously at Reg and at Richard. "All of us were aboard the landing craft. At first I felt myself to be haunted by the ghosts of the rest, but it was only in my imagination. For millions of years, and then billions, I stalked the mud utterly alone. It is impossible for you to conceive of even the tiniest part of the torment of such eternity. Then," he added, "just recently life arose on the planet. Life. Vegetation, things in the sea, then, at last, you. Intelligent life. I turn to you to release me from the torment I have endured."

Michael's head sank abjectly on to his chest for some few seconds. Then slowly, wobblingly, it rose and stared at them again, with yet darker fires in his eyes.

"Take me back," he said, "I beg you, take me back to the landing craft. Let me undo what was done. A word from me, and it can be undone, the repairs properly made, the landing craft can then return to the main ship, we can be on our way, my torment will be extinguished, and I will cease to be a burden to you. I beg you."

There was a short silence while his plea hung in the air.

"But that can't work, can it?" said Richard. "If we do that, then this won't have happened. Don't we generate all sorts of paradoxes?"

Reg stirred himself from thought. "No worse than many that exist already," he said. "If the Universe came to an end every time there was some uncertainty about what had happened in it, it would never have got beyond the first picosecond. And many of course don't. It's like a human body, you see. A few cuts and bruises here and there don't hurt it. Not even major surgery if it's done properly. Paradoxes are just the scar tissue. Time and space heal themselves up around them and people simply remember a version of events which makes as much sense as they require it to make.

"That isn't to say that if you get involved in a paradox a few things won't strike you as being very odd, but if you've got through life without that already happening to you, then I don't know which Universe you've been living in, but it isn't this one."

"Well, if that's the case," said Richard, "why were you so fierce about not doing anything to save the dodo?"

Reg sighed. "You don't understand at all. The dodo wouldn't have died if I hadn't worked so hard to save the coelacanth."

"The coelacanth? The prehistoric fish? But how could one possibly affect the other?"

"Ah. Now there you're asking. The complexities of cause and effect defy analysis. Not only is the continuum like a human body, it is also very like a piece of badly put up wallpaper. Push down a bubble somewhere, another one pops up somewhere else. There are no more dodos because of my interference. In the end I imposed the rule on myself because I simply couldn't bear it any more. The only thing that really gets hurt when you try and change time is yourself." He smiled bleakly, and looked away.

Then he added, after a long moment's reflection, "No, it can be done. I'm just cynical because it's gone wrong so many times. This poor fellow's story is a very pathetic one, and it can do no harm to put an end to his misery. It happened so very, very long ago on a dead planet. If we do this we will each remember whatever it is that has happened to us individually. Too bad if the rest of the world doesn't quite agree. It will hardly be the first time."

Michael's head bowed.

"You're very silent, Dirk," said Richard.

Dirk glared angrily at him. "I want to see this ship," he demanded.

In the darkness, the red telephone receiver slipped and slid fitfully back across the desk. If anybody had been there to see it they might just have discerned a shape that moved it.

It shone only very faintly, less than would the hands of a luminous watch. It seemed more as if the darkness around it was just that much darker and the ghostly shape sat within it like thickened scar tissue beneath the surface of the night.

Gordon grappled one last time with the recalcitrant receiver. At length he got a final grip and slipped it up on to the top of the instrument.

From there it fell back on to its rest and disconnected the call. At the same moment the ghost of Gordon Way, his last call finally completed, fell back to his own rest and vanished.

Chapter Thirty-three...

Swinging slowly round in the shadow of the Earth, just one more piece of debris among that which floated now forever in high orbit, was one dark shape that was larger and more regularly formed than the rest. And far, far older.

For four billion years it had continued to absorb data from the world below it, scanning, analysing, processing. Occasionally it sent pieces back if it thought they would help, if it thought they might be received. But otherwise, it watched, it listened, it recorded. Not the lapping of a wave nor the beating of a heart escaped its attention.

Otherwise, nothing inside it had moved for four billion years, except for the air which circulated still, and the motes of dust within the air that danced and danced and danced and danced ... and danced.

It was only a very slight disturbance that occurred now. Quietly, without fuss, like a dew drop precipitating from the air on to a leaf, there appeared in a wall which had stood blank and grey for four billion years, a door. A plain, ordinary white-panelled door with a small dented brass handle.

This quiet event, too, was recorded and incorporated in the continual stream of data processing that the ship ceaselessly performed. Not only the arrival of the door, but the arrival of those behind the door, the way they looked, the way they moved, the way they felt about being there. All processed, all recorded, all transformed.

After a moment or two had passed, the door opened.

Within it could be seen a room unlike any on the ship. A room of wooden floors, of shabby upholstery, a room in which a fire danced. And as the fire danced, its data danced within the ship's computers, and the motes of dust in the air also danced with it.

A figure stood in the doorway – a large lugubrious figure with a strange light that danced now in its eyes. It stepped forward across the threshold into the ship, and its face was suddenly suffused with a calm for which it had longed but had thought never again to experience.

Following him stepped out a smaller, older man with hair that was white and wayward. He stopped and blinked with wonder as he passed from out of the realm of his room and into the realm of the ship. Following him came a third man, impatient and tense, with a large leather overcoat that flapped about him. He, too, stopped and was momentarily bewildered by something he didn't understand. With a look of deepest puzzlement on his face he walked forward and looked around at the grey and dusty walls of the ancient ship.

At last came a fourth man, tall and thin. He stooped as he walked out of the door, and then instantly stopped as if he had walked into a wall.

He had walked into a wall, of a kind.

He stood transfixed. If anyone had been looking at his face at that moment, it would have been abundantly clear to them that the single most astonishing event of this man's entire existence was currently happening to him.

When slowly he began to move it was with a curious gait, as if he was swimming very slowly. Each tiniest movement of his head seemed to bring fresh floods of awe and astonishment into his face. Tears welled in his eyes, and he became breathless with gasping wonder.

Dirk turned to look at him, to hurry him along.

"What's the matter?" he called above the noise.

"The ... music ..." whispered Richard.

The air was full of music. So full it seemed there was room for nothing else. And each particle of air seemed to have its own music, so that as Richard moved his head he heard a new and different music, though the new and different music fitted quite perfectly with the music that lay beside it in the air.

The modulations from one to another were perfectly accomplished – astonishing leaps to distant keys made effortlessly in the mere shifting of the head. New themes, new strands of melody, all perfectly and astoundingly proportioned, constantly involved themselves into the continuing web. Huge slow waves of movement, faster dances that thrilled through them, tiny scintillating scampers that danced on the dances, long tangled tunes whose ends were so like their beginnings that they twisted around upon themselves, turned inside out, upside down, and then rushed off again on the back of yet another dancing melody in a distant part of the ship.

Richard staggered against the wall.

Dirk hurried to grab him.

"Come on," he said, brusquely, "what's the matter? Can't you stand the music? It's a bit loud, isn't it? For God's sake, pull yourself together. There's something here I still don't understand. It's not right. Come on –"

He tugged Richard after him, and then had to support him as Richard's mind sank further and further under the overwhelming weight of music. The visions that were woven in his mind by the million thrilling threads of music as they were pulled through it, were increasingly a welter of chaos, but the more the chaos burgeoned the more it fitted with the other chaos, and the next greater chaos, until it all became a vast exploding ball of harmony expanding in his mind faster than any mind could deal with.

And then it was all much simpler.

A single tune danced through his mind and all his attention rested upon it. It was a tune that seethed through the magical flood, shaped it, formed it, lived through it hugely, lived through it minutely, was its very essence. It bounced and trilled along, at first a little tripping tune, then it slowed, then it danced again but with more difficulty, seemed to founder in eddies of doubt and confusion, and then suddenly revealed that the eddies were just the first ripples of a huge new wave of energy surging up joyfully from beneath.

Richard began very, very slowly to faint.

He lay very still.

He felt he was an old sponge steeped in paraffin and left in the sun to dry.

He felt like the body of an old horse burning hazily in the sun. He dreamed of oil, thin and fragrant, of dark heaving seas. He was on a white beach, drunk with fish, stupefied with sand, bleached, drowsing, pummelled with light, sinking, estimating the density of vapour clouds in distant nebulae, spinning with dead delight. He was a pump spouting fresh water in the springtime, gushing into a mound of reeking newmown grass. Sounds, almost unheard, burned away like distant sleep.

He ran and was falling. The lights of a harbour spun into night. The sea like a dark spirit slapped infinitesimally at the sand, glimmering, unconscious. Out where it was deeper and colder he sank easily with the heavy sea swelling like oil around his ears, and was disturbed only by a distant burr burr as of the phone ringing.

He knew he had been listening to the music of life itself. The music of light dancing on water that rippled with the wind and the tides, of the life that moved through the water, of the life that moved on the land, warmed by the light.

He continued to lie very still. He continued to be disturbed by a distant burr burr as of a phone ringing.

Gradually he became aware that the distant burr burr as of a phone ringing was a phone ringing.

He sat up sharply.

He was lying on a small crumpled bed in a small untidy panelled room that he knew he recognised but couldn't place. It was cluttered with books and shoes. He blinked at it and was blank.

The phone by the bed was ringing. He picked it up.

"Hello?" he said.

"Richard!" It was Susan's voice, utterly distraught. He shook his head and had no recollection of anything useful.

"Hello?" he said again.

"Richard, is that you? *Where are you?*"

"Er, hold on, I'll go and look."

He put the receiver down on the crumpled sheets, where it lay squawking, climbed shakily off the bed, staggered to the door and opened it.

Here was a bathroom. He peered at it suspiciously. Again, he recognised it but felt that there was something missing. Oh yes. There should be a horse in it. Or at least, there had been a horse in it the last time he had seen it. He crossed the bathroom floor and went out of the other door. He found his way shakily down the stairs and into Reg's main room.

He was surprised by what he saw when he got there.

Chapter Thirty-four...

The storms of the day before, and of the day before that, and the floods of the previous week, had now abated. The skies still bulged with rain, but all that actually fell in the gathering evening gloom was a dreary kind of prickle.

Some wind whipped across the darkening plain, blundered through the low hills and gusted across a shallow valley where stood a structure, a kind of tower, alone in a nightmare of mud, and leaning.

It was a blackened stump of a tower. It stood like an extrusion of magma from one of the more pestilential pits of hell, and it leaned at a peculiar angle, as if oppressed by something altogether more terrible than its own considerable weight. It seemed a dead thing, long ages dead.

The only movement was that of a river of mud that moved sluggishly along the bottom of the valley past the tower. A mile or so further on, the river ran down a ravine and disappeared underground.

But as the evening darkened it became apparent that the tower was not entirely without life. There was a single dim red light guttering deep within it.

It was this scene that Richard was surprised to see from a small white doorway set in the side of the valley wall, a few hundred yards from the tower.

"Don't step out!" said Dirk, putting up an arm, "The atmosphere is poisonous. I'm not sure what's in it but it would certainly get your carpets nice and clean."

Dirk was standing in the doorway watching the valley with deep mistrust.

"Where are we?" asked Richard.

"Bermuda," said Dirk. "It's a bit complicated."

"Thank you," said Richard and walked groggily back across the room.

"Excuse me," he said to Reg, who was busy fussing round Michael Wenton-Weakes, making sure that the scuba diving suit he was wearing fitted snuggly everywhere, that the mask was secure and that the regulator for the air supply was working properly.

"Sorry, can I just get past?" said Richard. "Thanks."

He climbed back up the stairs, went back into Reg's bedroom, sat shakily on the edge of the bed and picked up the phone again.

"Bermuda -" he said, "it's a bit complicated."

Downstairs, Reg finished smearing Vaseline on all the joins of the suit and the few pieces of exposed skin around the mask, and then announced that all was ready.

Dirk swung himself away from the door and stood aside with the utmost bad grace.

"Well then," he said, "be off with you. Good riddance. I wash my hands of the whole affair. I suppose we will have to wait here for you to send back the empty, for what it's worth." He stalked round the sofa with an angry gesture. He didn't like this. He didn't like any of it. He particularly didn't like Reg knowing more about space/time than he did. It made him angry that he didn't know why he didn't like it.

"My dear fellow," said Reg in a conciliatory tone, "consider what a very small effort it is for us to help the poor soul. I'm sorry if it seems to you an anti-climax after all your extraordinary feats of deduction. I know you feel that a mere errand of mercy seems not enough for you, but you should be more charitable."

"Charitable, ha!" said Dirk. "I pay my taxes, what more do you want?"

He threw himself on to the sofa, ran his hands through his hair and sulked.

The possessed figure of Michael shook hands with Reg and said a few words of thanks. Then he walked stiffly to the door, turned and bowed to them both.

Dirk flung his head round and glared at him, his eyes flashing behind their spectacles and his hair flying wildly. The ghost looked at Dirk, and for a moment shivered inside with apprehension. A superstitious instinct suddenly made the ghost wave. He waved Michael's hand round in a circle, three times, and then said a single word.

"Goodbye," he said.

With that he turned again, gripped the sides of the doorway and stepped resolutely out into the mud, and into the foul and poisonous wind.

He paused for a moment to be sure that his footing was solid, that he had his balance, and then without another look back he walked away from them, out of the reach of the slimy things with legs, towards his ship.

"Now, what on earth did *that* mean?" said Dirk, irritably mimicking the odd triple wave.

Richard came thundering down the stairs, threw open the door and plunged into the room, wild-eyed.

"Ross has been murdered!" he shouted.

"Who the hell's Ross?" shouted Dirk back at him.

"Whatsisname Ross, for God's sake," exclaimed Richard, "the new editor of *Fathom*."

"What's *Fathom*?" shouted Dirk again.

"Michael's bloody magazine, Dirk! Remember? Gordon chucked Michael off the magazine and gave it to this Ross guy to run instead. Michael hated him for that. Well, last night Michael went and bloody murdered him!"

He paused, panting. "At least," he said, "he was murdered. And Michael was the only one with any reason to."

He ran to the door, looked out at the retreating figure disappearing into the gloom, and spun round again.

"Is he coming back?" said Richard.

Dirk leapt to his feet and stood blinking for a moment.

"That's it ..." he said, "*that's* why Michael was the perfect subject. *That's* what I should have been looking for. The thing the ghost made him do in order to establish his hold, the thing he had to be fundamentally *willing* to do, the thing that would match the ghost's own purpose. Oh my dear God. He thinks we've supplanted them and that's what he wants to reverse.

"He thinks this is their world not ours. *This* was where they were going to settle and build their blasted paradise. It matches every step of the way.

"You see," he said, turning on Reg, "what we have done? I would not be surprised to discover that the accident your poor tormented soul out there is trying to reverse is the very thing which started life on this planet!"

He turned his eyes suddenly from Reg, who was white and trembling, back to Richard.

"When did you hear this?" he said, puzzled.

"Er, just now," said Richard, "on ... on the phone. Upstairs."

"What?"

"It was Susan, I don't know how – said she had a message on her answering machine telling her about it. She said the message ... was from – she said it was from Gordon, but I think she was hysterical. Dirk, what the hell is happening? Where are we?"

"We are four billion years in the past," said Reg in a shaking voice, "please don't ask me why it is that the phone works when we are anywhere in the Universe other than where it's actually connected, that's a matter you will have to take up with British Telecom, but –"

"Damn and blast British Telecom," shouted Dirk, the words coming easily from force of habit. He ran to the door and peered again at the dim shadowy figure trudging through the mud towards the Salaxalan ship, completely beyond their reach.

"How long," said Dirk, quite calmly, "would you guess that it's going to take that fat self-deluding bastard to reach his ship? Because that is how long we have.

"Come. Let us sit down. Let us think. We have two minutes in which to decide what we are going to do. After that, I very much suspect that the three of us, and everything we have ever known, including the coelacanth and the dodo, dear Professor, will cease ever to have existed."

He sat heavily on the sofa, then stood up again and removed Michael's discarded jacket from under him. As he did so, a book fell out of the pocket.

Chapter Thirty-five...

"I think it's an appalling act of desecration," said Richard to Reg, as they sat hiding behind a hedge.

The night was full of summer smells from the cottage garden, and the occasional whiff of sea air which came in on the light breezes that were entertaining themselves on the coast of the Bristol Channel.

There was a bright moon playing over the sea off in the distance, and by its light it was also possible to see some distance over Exmoor stretching away to the south of them.

Reg sighed.

"Yes, maybe," he said, "but I'm afraid he's right, you know, it must be done. It was the only sure way. All the instructions were clearly contained in the piece once you knew what you were looking for. It has to be suppressed. The ghost will always be around. In fact two of him now. That is, assuming this works. Poor devil. Still, I suppose he brought it on himself."

Richard fretfully pulled up some blades of grass and twisted them between his fingers.

He held them up to the moonlight, turned them to different angles, and watched the way light played on them.

"Such music," he said. "I'm not religious, but if I were I would say it was like a glimpse into the mind of God. Perhaps it was and I ought to be religious. I have to keep reminding myself that they didn't create the music, they only created the instrument which could read the score. And the score was life itself. And it's all up there."

He glanced into the sky. Unconsciously he started to quote:

> "Could I revive within me
> Her symphony and song
> To such a deep delight 'twould win me
> That with music loud and long
> I would build that dome in air,
> That sunny dome, those caves of ice!"

"Hmmm," said Reg to himself, "I wonder if he arrived early enough."

"What did you say?"

"Oh, nothing. Just a thought."

"Good God, he can talk, can't he?" Richard exclaimed suddenly. "He's been in there over an hour now. I wonder what's going on."

He got up and looked over the hedge at the small farm cottage basking in the moonlight behind them. About an hour earlier Dirk had walked boldly up to the front door and rapped on it.

When the door had opened, somewhat reluctantly, and a slightly dazed face had looked out, Dirk had doffed his absurd hat and said in a loud voice, "Mr Samuel Coleridge?

"I was just passing by, on my way from Porlock, you understand, and I was wondering if I might trouble you to vouchsafe me an interview? It's just for a little parish broadsheet I edit. Won't take much of your time I promise, I know you must be busy, famous poet like you, but I do so admire your work, and ..."

The rest was lost, because by that time Dirk had effected his entry and closed the door behind him.

"Would you excuse me a moment?" said Reg.

"What? Oh sure," said Richard, "I'm just going to have a look and see what's happening."

While Reg wandered off behind a tree Richard pushed open the little gate and was just about to make his way up the path when he heard the sound of voices approaching the front door from within.

He hurriedly darted back, as the front door started to open.

"Well, thank you very much indeed, Mr Coleridge," said Dirk, as he emerged, fiddling with his hat and bowing, "you have been most kind and generous with your time, and I do appreciate it very much, as I'm sure will my readers. I'm sure it will work up into a very nice little article, a copy of which you may rest assured I will send you for you to peruse at your leisure. I will most certainly welcome your comments if you have any, any points of style, you know, hints, tips, things of that nature. Well, thank you again, so much, for your time, I do hope I haven't kept you from anything important –"

The door slammed violently behind him.

Dirk turned with another in a long succession of triumphant beams and hurried down the path to Richard.

"Well, that's put a stop to that," he said, patting his hands together, "I think he'd made a start on writing it down, but he won't remember another word, that's for certain. Where's the egregious Professor? Ah, there you are. Good heavens, I'd no idea I'd been that long. A most fascinating and entertaining fellow, our Mr Coleridge, or at least I'm sure he would have been if I'd given him the chance, but I was rather too busy being fascinating myself.

"Oh, but I did do as you asked, Richard, I asked him at the end about the albatross and he said what albatross? So I said, oh it wasn't important, the albatross did not signify. He said what albatross didn't signify, and I said never mind the albatross, it didn't matter, and he said it did matter – someone comes to his house in the middle of the night raving about albatrosses, he wanted to know why. I said blast the bloody albatross and he said he had a good mind to and he wasn't certain that that didn't give him an idea for a poem he was working on. Much better, he said, than being hit by an asteroid, which he thought was stretching credulity a bit. And so I came away.

"Now. Having saved the entire human race from extinction I could do with a pizza. What say you to such a proposal?"

Richard didn't offer an opinion. He was staring instead with some puzzlement at Reg.

"Something troubling you?" said Reg, taken aback.

"That's a good trick," said Richard, "I could have sworn you didn't have a beard before you went behind the tree."

"Oh –" Reg fingered the luxuriant three-inch growth – "yes," he said, "just carelessness," he said, "carelessness."

"What have you been up to?"

"Oh, just a few adjustments. A little surgery, you understand. Nothing drastic."

A few minutes later as he ushered them into the extra door that a nearby cowshed had mysteriously acquired, he looked back up into the sky behind them, just in time to see a small light flare up and disappear.

"Sorry, Richard," he muttered, and followed them in.

Chapter Thirty Six...

"Thank you, no," said Richard firmly, "much as I would love the opportunity to buy you a pizza and watch you eat it, Dirk, I want to go straight home. I have to see Susan. Is that possible, Reg? Just straight to my flat? I'll come up to Cambridge next week and collect my car."

"We are already there," said Reg, "simply step out of the door, and you are home in your own flat. It is early on Friday evening and the weekend lies before you."

"Thanks. Er, look, Dirk, I'll see you around, OK? Do I owe you something? I don't know."

Dirk waved the matter aside airily. "You will hear from my Miss Pearce in due course," he said.

"Fine, OK, well I'll see you when I've had some rest. It's been, well, unexpected."

He walked to the door and opened it. Stepping outside he found himself halfway up his own staircase, in the wall of which the door had materialised.

He was about to start up the stairs when he turned again as a thought struck him. He stepped back in, closing the door behind him.

"Reg, could we make one tiny detour?" he said. "I think it would be a good move if I took Susan out for a meal tonight, only the place I have in mind you have to book in advance. Could you manage three weeks for me?"

"Nothing could be easier," said Reg, and made a subtle adjustment to the disposition of the beads on the abacus. "There," he said, "We have travelled backwards in time three weeks. You know where the phone is."

Richard hurried up the internal staircase to Reg's bedroom and phoned L'Esprit d'Escalier. The maître d' was charmed and delighted to take his reservation, and looked forward to seeing him in three weeks' time. Richard went back downstairs shaking his head in wonder.

"I need a weekend of solid reality," he said. "Who was that just going out of the door?"

"That," said Dirk, "was your sofa being delivered. The man asked if we minded him opening the door so they could manoeuvre it round and I said we would be delighted."

It was only a few minutes later that Richard found himself hurrying up the stairs to Susan's flat. As he arrived at her front door he was pleased, as he always was, to hear the deep tones of her cello coming faintly from within. He quietly let himself in and then as he walked to the door of her music room he suddenly froze in astonishment. The tune she was playing was one he had heard before. A little tripping tune, that slowed, then danced again but with more difficulty...

His face was so amazed that she stopped playing the instant she saw him.

"What's wrong?" she said, alarmed.

"Where did you get that music?" said Richard in a whisper.

She shrugged. "Well, from the music shop," she said, puzzled. She wasn't being facetious, she simply didn't understand the question.

"What is it?"

"It's from a cantata I'm playing in in a couple of weeks," she said, "Bach, number six."

"Who wrote it?"

"Well, Bach I expect. If you think about it."

"Who?"

"Watch my lips. Bach. B-A-C-H. Johannes Sebastian. Remember?"

"No, never heard of him. Who is he? Did he write anything else?"

Susan put down her bow, propped up her cello, stood up and came over to him.

"Are you all right?" she said.

"Er, it's rather hard to tell. What's…"

He caught sight of a pile of music books sitting in a corner of the room with the same name on the top one. BACH. He threw himself at the pile and started to scrabble through it. Book after book – J. S. BACH. Cello sonatas. Brandenburg Concertos. A Mass in B Minor.

He looked up at her in blank incomprehension.

"I've never seen any of this before," he said.

"Richard my darling," she said, putting her hand to his cheek, "what on earth's the matter? It's just Bach sheet music."

"But don't you understand?" he said, shaking a handful of the stuff. "I've never, ever seen any of this before!"

"Well," she said with mock gravity, "perhaps if you didn't spend all your time playing with computer music…"

He looked at her with wild surprise, then slowly he sat back against the wall and began to laugh hysterically.

On Monday afternoon Richard phoned Reg.

"Reg!" he said. "Your phone is working. Congratulations."

"Oh yes, my dear fellow," said Reg, "how delightful to hear from you. Yes. A very capable young man arrived and fixed the phone a little earlier. I don't think it will go wrong again now. Good news, don't you think?"

"Very good. You got back safely then."

"Oh yes, thank you. Oh, we had high excitement here when we returned from dropping you off. Remember the horse? Well he turned up again with his owner. They'd had some unfortunate encounter with the constabulary and wished to be taken home. Just as well. Dangerous sort of chap to have on the loose I think. So. How are you then?

"Reg… The music –"

"Ah, yes, I thought you'd be pleased. Took a bit of work, I can tell you. I saved only the tiniest tiniest scrap, of course, but even so I cheated. It was rather more than one man could actually do in a lifetime, but I don't suppose anybody will look at that too seriously."

"Reg, can't we get some more of it?"

"Well, no. The ship has gone, and besides –"

"We could go back in time –"

"No, well, I told you. They've fixed the phone so it won't go wrong again."

"So?"

"Well, the time machine won't work now. Burnt out. Dead as a dodo. I think that's it I'm afraid. Probably just as well, though, don't you think?"

On Monday, Mrs Sauskind phoned Dirk Gently's Holistic Detective Agency to complain about her bill.

"I don't understand what all this is about," she said, "it's complete nonsense. What's the meaning of it?"

"My dear Mrs Sauskind," he said, "I can hardly tell you how much I have been looking forward to having this exact same conversation with you yet again. Where shall we begin today? Which particular item is it that you would like to discuss?"

"None of them, thank you very much, Mr Gently. I do not know who you are or why you should think my cat is missing. Dear Roderick passed away in my arms two years ago and I have not wished to replace him."

"Ah, well Mrs Sauskind," said Dirk, "what you probably fail to appreciate is that it is as a direct result of my efforts that – If I might explain about the interconnectedness of all –" He stopped. It was pointless. He slowly dropped the telephone back on its cradle.

"Miss Pearce!" he called out, "Kindly send out a revised bill would you to our dear Mrs Sauskind. The new bill reads 'To: saving human race from total extinction – no charge.'"

He put on his hat and left for the day.

The Long Dark Tea-Time of the Soul

For Jane

Author's Note

This book was written and typeset on an Apple Macintosh II and an Apple LaserWriter II NTX. The word processing software was FullWrite Professional from Ashton Tate. The final proofing and photosetting was done by The Last Word, London SW6.

I would like to say an enormous thank you to my amazing and wonderful editor, Sue Freestone.

Her help, support, criticism, encouragement, enthusiasm and sandwiches have been beyond measure. I also owe thanks and apologies to Sophie, James and Vivian who saw so little of her during the final weeks of work.

Chapter 1

It can hardly be a coincidence that no language on Earth has ever produced the expression "as pretty as an airport".

Airports are ugly. Some are very ugly. Some attain a degree of ugliness that can only be the result of a special effort. This ugliness arises because airports are full of people who are tired, cross, and have just discovered that their luggage has landed in Murmansk (Murmansk airport is the only known exception to this otherwise infallible rule), and architects have on the whole tried to reflect this in their designs.

They have sought to highlight the tiredness and crossness motif with brutal shapes and nerve-jangling colours, to make effortless the business of separating the traveller for ever from his or her luggage or loved ones, to confuse the traveller with arrows that appear to point at the windows, distant tie racks, or the current position of Ursa Minor in the night sky, and wherever possible to expose the plumbing on the grounds that it is functional, and conceal the location of the departure gates, presumably on the grounds that they are not.

Caught in the middle of a sea of hazy light and a sea of hazy noise, Kate Schechter stood and doubted.

All the way out of London to Heathrow she had suffered from doubt. She was not a superstitious person, or even a religious person, she was simply someone who was not at all sure she should be flying to Norway. But she was finding it increasingly easy to believe that God, if there was a God, and if it was remotely possible that any godlike being who could order the disposition of particles at the creation of the Universe would also be interested in directing traffic on the M4, did not want her to fly to Norway either. All the trouble with the tickets, finding a next-door neighbour to look after the cat, then finding the cat so it could be looked after by the next-door neighbour, the sudden leak in the roof, the missing wallet, the weather, the unexpected death of the next-door neighbour, the pregnancy of the cat – it all had the semblance of an orchestrated campaign of obstruction which had begun to assume godlike proportions.

Even the taxi-driver – when she had eventually found a taxi – had said, "Norway? What you want to go there for?" And when she hadn't instantly said, "The aurora borealis!" or "Fjords!" but had looked doubtful for a moment and bitten her lip, he had said, "I know, I bet it's some bloke dragging you out there. Tell you what, tell him to stuff it. Go to Tenerife."

There was an idea.

Tenerife.

Or even, she dared to think for a fleeting second, home.

She had stared dumbly out of the taxi window at the angry tangles of traffic and thought that however cold and miserable the weather was here, that was nothing to what it would be like in Norway.

Or, indeed, at home. Home would be about as icebound as Norway right now. Icebound, and punctuated with geysers of steam bursting out of the ground, catching in the frigid air and dissipating between the glacial cliff faces of Sixth Avenue.

A quick glance at the itinerary Kate had pursued in the course of her thirty years would reveal her without any doubt to be a New Yorker. For though she had lived in the city very little, most of her life had been spent at a constant distance from it. Los Angeles, San Francisco, Europe, and a period of distracted wandering around South America five years ago following the loss of her newly married husband, Luke, in a New York taxi-hailing accident.

She enjoyed the notion that New York was home, and that she missed it, but in fact the only thing she really missed was pizza. And not just any old pizza, but the sort of pizza they brought to your door if you phoned them up and asked them to. That was the only real pizza. Pizza that you had to go out and sit at a table staring at red paper napkins for wasn't real pizza however much extra pepperoni and anchovy they put on it.

London was the place she liked living in most, apart, of course, from the pizza problem, which drove her crazy. Why would no one deliver pizza? Why did no one understand that it was fundamental to the whole nature of pizza that it arrived at your front door in a hot cardboard box? That you slithered it out of greaseproof paper and ate it in folded slices in front of the TV? What was the fundamental flaw in the stupid, stuck-up, sluggardly English that they couldn't grasp this simple principle? For some odd reason it was the one frustration she could never learn simply to live with and accept, and about once a month or so she would get very depressed, phone a pizza restaurant, order the biggest, most lavish pizza she could describe – pizza with an extra pizza on it, essentially – and then, sweetly, ask them to deliver it.

"To what?"

"Deliver. Let me give you the address – "

"I don't understand. Aren't you going to come and pick it up?"

"No. Aren't you going to deliver? My address – "

"Er, we don't do that, miss."

"Don't do what?"

"Er, deliver…"

"You *don't deliver*? Am I *hearing* you correctly…?"

The exchange would quickly degenerate into an ugly slanging match which would leave her feeling drained and shaky, but much, much better the following morning. In all other respects she was one of the most sweet-natured people you could hope to meet.

But today was testing her to the limit.

There had been terrible traffic jams on the motorway, and when the distant flash of blue lights made it clear that the cause was an accident somewhere ahead of them Kate had become more tense and had stared fixedly out of the other window as eventually they had crawled past it.

The taxi-driver had been bad-tempered when at last he had dropped her off because she didn't have the right money, and there was a lot of disgruntled hunting through tight trouser pockets before he was eventually able to find change for her. The atmosphere was heavy and thundery and now, standing in the middle of the main check-in concourse at Terminal Two, Heathrow Airport, she could not find the check-in desk for her flight to Oslo.

She stood very still for a moment, breathing calmly and deeply and trying not to think of Jean-Philippe.

Jean-Philippe was, as the taxi-driver had correctly guessed, the reason why she was going to Norway, but was also the reason why she was convinced that Norway was not at all a good place for her to go. Thinking of him therefore made her head oscillate and it seemed best not to think about him at all but simply to go to Norway as if that was where she happened to be going anyway. She would then be terribly surprised to bump into him at whatever hotel it was he had written on the card that was tucked into the side pocket of her handbag.

In fact she would be surprised to find him there anyway. What she would be much more likely to find was a message from him saying that he had been unexpectedly called away to

Guatemala, Seoul or Tenerife and that he would call her from there. Jean-Philippe was the most continually absent person she had ever met. In this he was the culmination of a series. Since she had lost Luke to the great yellow Chevrolet she had been oddly dependent on the rather vacant emotions that a succession of self-absorbed men had inspired in her.

She tried to shut all this out of her mind, and even shut her eyes for a second. She wished that when she opened them again there would be a sign in front of her saying "This way for Norway" which she could simply follow without needing to think about it or anything else ever again. This, she reflected, in a continuation of her earlier train of thought, was presumably how religions got started, and must be the reason why so many sects hang around airports looking for converts. They know that people there are at their most vulnerable and perplexed, and ready to accept any kind of guidance.

Kate opened her eyes again and was, of course, disappointed. But then a second or two later there was a momentary parting in a long surging wave of cross Germans in inexplicable yellow polo shirts and through it she had a brief glimpse of the check-in desk for Oslo. Lugging her garment bag on to her shoulder, she made her way towards it.

There was just one other person before her in the line at the desk and he, it turned out, was having trouble or perhaps making it.

He was a large man, impressively large and well-built – even expertly built – but he was also definitely odd-looking in a way that Kate couldn't quite deal with. She couldn't even say what it was that was odd about him, only that she was immediately inclined not to include him on her list of things to think about at the moment. She remembered reading an article which had explained that the central processing unit of the human brain only had seven memory registers, which meant that if you had seven things in your mind at the same time and then thought of something else, one of the other seven would instantly drop out.

In quick succession she thought about whether or not she was likely to catch the plane, about whether it was just her imagination that the day was a particularly bloody one, about airline staff who smile charmingly and are breathtakingly rude, about Duty Free shops which are able to charge much lower prices than ordinary shops but – mysteriously – don't, about whether or not she felt a magazine article about airports coming on which might help pay for the trip, about whether her garment bag would hurt less on her other shoulder and finally, in spite of all her intentions to the contrary, about Jean-Philippe, who was another set of at least seven subtopics all to himself.

The man standing arguing in front of her popped right out of her mind.

It was only the announcement on the airport Tannoy of the last call for her flight to Oslo which forced her attention back to the situation in front of her.

The large man was making trouble about the fact that he hadn't been given a first class seat reservation. It had just transpired that the reason for this was that he didn't in fact have a first class ticket.

Kate's spirits sank to the very bottom of her being and began to prowl around there making a low growling noise.

It now transpired that the man in front of her didn't actually have a ticket at all, and the argument then began to range freely and angrily over such topics as the physical appearance of the airline check-in girl, her qualities as a person, theories about her ancestors, speculations as to what surprises the future might have in store for her and the airline for which she worked, and finally lit by chance on the happy subject of the man's credit card.

He didn't have one.

Further discussions ensued, and had to do with cheques, and why the airline did not accept them.

Kate took a long, slow, murderous look at her watch.

"Excuse me," she said, interrupting the transactions. "Is this going to take long? I have to catch the Oslo flight."

"I'm just dealing with this gentleman," said the girl, "I'll be with you in just one second."

Kate nodded, and politely allowed just one second to go by.

"It's just that the flight's about to leave," she said then. "I have one bag, I have my ticket, I have a reservation. It'll take about thirty seconds. I hate to interrupt, but I'd hate even more to miss my flight for the sake of thirty seconds. That's thirty actual seconds, not thirty 'just one' seconds, which could keep us here all night."

The check-in girl turned the full glare of her lipgloss on to Kate, but before she could speak the large blond man looked round, and the effect of his face was a little disconcerting.

"I, too," he said in a slow, angry Nordic voice, "wish to fly to Oslo."

Kate stared at him. He looked thoroughly out of place in an airport, or rather, the airport looked thoroughly out of place around him.

"Well," she said, "the way we're stacked up at the moment it looks like neither of us is going to make it. Can we just sort this one out? What's the hold-up?"

The check-in girl smiled her charming, dead smile and said, "The airline does not accept cheques, as a matter of company policy."

"Well I do," said Kate, slapping down her own credit card. "Charge the gentleman's ticket to this, and I'll take a cheque from him.

"OK?" she added to the big man, who was looking at her with slow surprise. His eyes were large and blue and conveyed the impression that they had looked at a lot of glaciers in their time. They were extraordinarily arrogant and also muddled.

"OK?" she repeated briskly. "My name is Kate Schechter. Two 'c's, two 'h's, two 'e's and also a 't', an 'r' and an 's'. Provided they're all there the bank won't be fussy about the order they come in. They never seem to know themselves."

The man very slowly inclined his head a little towards her in a rough bow of acknowledgement. He thanked her for her kindness, courtesy and some Norwegian word that was lost on her, said that it was a long while since he had encountered anything of the kind, that she was a woman of spirit and some other Norwegian word, and that he was indebted to her. He also added, as an afterthought, that he had no cheque-book.

"Right!" said Kate, determined not to be deflected from her course. She fished in her handbag for a piece of paper, took a pen from the check-in counter, scribbled on the paper and thrust it at him.

"That's my address," she said, "send me the money. Hock your fur coat if you have to. Just send it me. OK? I'm taking a flyer on trusting you."

The big man took the scrap of paper, read the few words on it with immense slowness, then folded it with elaborate care and put it into the pocket of his coat. Again he bowed to her very slightly.

Kate suddenly realised that the check-in girl was silently waiting for her pen back to fill in the credit card form. She pushed it back at her in annoyance, handed over her own ticket and imposed on herself an icy calm.

The airport Tannoy announced the departure of their flight.

"May I see your passports, please?" said the girl unhurriedly.

Kate handed hers over, but the big man didn't have one.

"You *what*?" exclaimed Kate. The airline girl simply stopped moving at all and stared quietly at a random point on her desk waiting for someone else to make a move. It wasn't her problem.

The man repeated angrily that he didn't have a passport. He shouted it and banged his fist on the counter so hard that it was slightly dented by the force of the blow.

Kate picked up her ticket, her passport and her credit card and hoisted her garment bag back up on to her shoulder.

"This is where I get off," she said, and simply walked away.

She felt that she had made every effort a human being could possibly be expected to make to catch her plane, but that it was not to be. She would send a message to Jean-Philippe saying that she could not be there, and it would probably sit in a slot next to his message to her saying why he could not be there either. For once they would be equally absent.

For the time being she would go and cool off. She set off in search of first a newspaper and then some coffee, and by dint of following the appropriate signs was unable to locate either. She was then unable to find a working phone from which to send a message, and decided to give up on the airport altogether. Just get out, she told herself, find a taxi, and go back home.

She threaded her way back across the check-in concourse, and had almost made it to the exit when she happened to glance back at the check-in desk that had defeated her, and was just in time to see it shoot up through the roof engulfed in a ball of orange flame.

As she lay beneath a pile of rubble, in pain, darkness, and choking dust, trying to find sensation in her limbs, she was at least relieved to be able to think that she hadn't merely been imagining that this was a bad day. So thinking, she passed out.

Chapter 2

The usual people tried to claim responsibility.

First the IRA, then the PLO and the Gas Board. Even British Nuclear Fuels rushed out a statement to the effect that the situation was completely under control, that it was a one in a million chance, that there was hardly any radioactive leakage at all, and that the site of the explosion would make a nice location for a day out with the kids and a picnic, before finally having to admit that it wasn't actually anything to do with them at all.

No cause could be found for the explosion.

It seemed to have happened spontaneously and of its own free will. Explanations were advanced, but most of these were simply phrases which restated the problem in different words, along the same principles which had given the world "metal fatigue". In fact, a very similar phrase was invented to account for the sudden transition of wood, metal, plastic and concrete into an explosive condition, which was "non-linear catastrophic structural exasperation", or to put it another way – as a junior cabinet minister did on television the following night in a phrase which was to haunt the rest of his career – the check-in desk had just got "fundamentally fed up with being where it was".

As in all such disastrous events, estimates of the casualties varied wildly. They started at forty-seven dead, eighty-nine seriously injured, went up to sixty-three dead, a hundred and thirty injured, and rose as high as one hundred and seventeen dead before the figures started to be revised downwards once more. The final figures revealed that once all the people who could be accounted for had been accounted for, in fact no one had been killed at all. A small number of people were in hospital suffering from cuts and bruises and varying degrees of traumatised shock, but that, unless anyone had any information about anybody actually being missing, was that.

This was yet another inexplicable aspect to the whole affair. The force of the explosion had been enough to reduce a large part of the front of Terminal Two to rubble, and yet everyone inside the building had somehow either fallen very luckily, or been shielded from one piece of falling masonry by another, or had the shock of the explosion absorbed by their luggage. All in all, very little luggage had survived at all. There were questions asked in Parliament about this, but not very interesting ones.

It was a couple of days before Kate Schechter became aware of any of these things, or indeed of anything at all in the outside world.

She passed the time quietly in a world of her own in which she was surrounded as far as the eye could see with old cabin trunks full of past memories in which she rummaged with great curiosity, and sometimes bewilderment. Or, at least, about a tenth of the cabin trunks were full of vivid, and often painful or uncomfortable memories of her past life; the other nine-tenths were full of penguins, which surprised her. Insofar as she recognised at all that she was dreaming, she realised that she must be exploring her own subconscious mind. She had heard it said that humans are supposed only to use about a tenth of their brains, and that no one was very clear what the other nine-tenths were for, but she had certainly never heard it suggested that they were used for storing penguins.

Gradually the trunks, the memories and the penguins began to grow indistinct, to become all white and swimmy, then to become like walls that were all white and swimmy, and finally to become walls that were merely white, or rather a yellowish, greenish kind of off-white, and to enclose her in a small room.

The room was in semi-darkness. A bedside light was on but turned down low, and the light from a street lamp found its way between the grey curtains and threw sodium patterns on the opposite wall. She became dimly aware of the shadowed shape of her own body lying under the white, turned-down sheet and the pale, neat blankets. She stared at it for a nervous while, checking that it looked right before she tried, tentatively, to move any part of it. She tried her right hand, and that seemed to be fine. A little stiff and aching, but the fingers all responded, and all seemed to be of the right length and thickness, and to bend in the right places and in the right directions.

She panicked briefly when she couldn't immediately locate her left hand, but then she found it lying across her stomach and nagging at her in some odd way. It took her a second or two of concentration to put together a number of rather disturbing feelings and realise that there was a needle bandaged into her arm. This shook her quite badly. From the needle there snaked a long thin transparent pipe that glistened yellowly in the light from the street lamp and hung in a gentle curl from a thick plastic bag suspended from a tall metal stand. An array of horrors briefly assailed her in respect of this apparatus, but she peered dimly at the bag and saw the words "Dextro-Saline". She made herself calm down again and lay quietly for a few moments before continuing her exploration.

Her ribcage seemed undamaged. Bruised and tender, but there was no sharper pain anywhere to suggest that anything was broken. Her hips and thighs ached and were stiff, but revealed no serious hurt. She flexed the muscles down her right leg and then her left. She rather fancied that her left ankle was sprained.

In other words, she told herself, she was perfectly all right. So what was she doing here in what she could tell from the septic colour of the paint was clearly a hospital?

She sat up impatiently, and immediately rejoined the penguins for an entertaining few minutes.

The next time she came round she treated herself with a little more care, and lay quietly, feeling gently nauseous.

She poked gingerly at her memory of what had happened. It was dark and blotchy and came at her in sick, greasy waves like the North Sea. Lumpy things jumbled themselves out of it and slowly arranged themselves into a heaving airport. The airport was sour and ached in her head, and in the middle of it, pulsing like a migraine, was the memory of a moment's whirling splurge of light.

It became suddenly very clear to her that the check-in concourse of Terminal Two at Heathrow Airport had been hit by a meteorite. Silhouetted in the flare was the fur-coated figure of a big man who must have caught the full force of it and been reduced instantly to a cloud of atoms that were free to go as they pleased. The thought caused a deep and horrid shudder to go through her. He had been infuriating and arrogant, but she had liked him in an odd way. There had been something oddly noble in his perverse bloody-mindedness. Or maybe, she realised, she liked to think that such perverse bloody-mindedness was noble because it reminded her of herself trying to order pizza to be delivered in an alien, hostile and non-pizza-delivering world. Nobleness was one word for making a fuss about the trivial inevitabilities of life, but there were others.

She felt a sudden surge of fear and loneliness, but it quickly ebbed away and left her feeling much more composed, relaxed, and wanting to go to the lavatory.

According to her watch it was shortly after three o'clock, and according to everything else it was night-time. She should probably call a nurse and let the world know she had come round. There was a window in the side wall of the room through which she could see a dim corridor in which stood a stretcher trolley and a tall black oxygen bottle, but which was otherwise empty. Things were very quiet out there.

Peering around her in the small room she saw a white-painted plywood cupboard, a couple of tubular steel and vinyl chairs lurking quietly in the shadows, and a white-painted plywood bedside cabinet which supported a small bowl with a single banana in it. On the other side of the bed stood her drip stand. Set into the wall on that side of the bed was a metal plate with a couple of black knobs and a set of old bakelite headphones hanging from it, and wound around the tubular side pillar of the bedhead was a cable with a bell push attached to it, which she fingered, and then decided not to push.

She was fine. She could find her own way about.

Slowly, a little woozily, she pushed herself up on to her elbows, and slid her legs out from under the sheets and on to the floor, which was cold to her feet. She could tell almost immediately that she shouldn't be doing this because every part of her feet was sending back streams of messages telling her exactly what every tiniest bit of the floor that they touched felt like, as if it was a strange and worrying thing the like of which they had never encountered before. Nevertheless she sat on the edge of the bed and made her feet accept the floor as something they were just going to have to get used to.

The hospital had put her into a large, baggy, striped thing. It wasn't merely baggy, she decided on examining it more closely, it actually was a bag. A bag of loose blue and white striped cotton. It opened up the back and let in chilly night draughts. Perfunctory sleeves flopped half-way down her arms. She moved her arms around in the light, examining the skin, rubbing it and pinching it, especially around the bandage which held her drip needle in place. Normally her arms were lithe and the skin was firm and supple. Tonight, however, they looked like bits of chickens. Briefly she smoothed each forearm with her other hand, and then looked up again, purposefully.

She reached out and gripped the drip stand and, because it wobbled slightly less than she did, she was able to use it to pull herself slowly to her feet. She stood there, her tall slim figure trembling, and after a few seconds she held the drip stand away at a bent arm's length, like a shepherd holding a crook.

She had not made it to Norway, but she was at least standing up.

The drip stand rolled on four small and independently perverse wheels which behaved like four screaming children in a supermarket, but nevertheless Kate was able to propel it to the door ahead of her. Walking increased her sense of wooziness, but also increased her resolve not to give in to it. She reached the door, opened it, and pushing the drip stand out ahead of her, looked out into the corridor.

To her left the corridor ended in a couple of swing-doors with circular porthole windows, which seemed to lead into a larger area, an open ward perhaps. To her right a number of smaller doors opened off the corridor as it continued on for a short distance before turning a sharp corner. One of those doors would probably be the lavatory. The others? Well, she would find out as she looked for the lavatory.

The first two were cupboards. The third was slightly bigger and had a chair in it and therefore probably counted as a room since most people don't like to sit in cupboards, even nurses, who have to do a lot of things that most people wouldn't like to. It also had a stack of styro beakers, a lot of semi-congealed coffee creamer and an elderly coffee maker, all sitting on top of a small table together and seeping grimly over a copy of the *Evening Standard*.

Kate picked up the dark, damp paper and tried to reconstruct some of her missing days from it. However, what with her own wobbly condition making it difficult to read, and the droopily stuck-together condition of the newspaper, she was able to glean little more than the fact that no one could really say for certain

what had happened. It seemed that no one had been seriously
hurt, but that an employee of one of the airlines was still
unaccounted for. The incident had now been officially classified
as an "Act of God".

"Nice one, God," thought Kate. She put down the remains of
the paper and closed the door behind her.

The next door she tried was another small side ward like her
own. There was a bedside table and a single banana in the fruit
bowl.

The bed was clearly occupied. She pulled the door to quickly,
but she did not pull it quickly enough. Unfortunately something
odd had caught her attention, but although she had noticed it,
she could not immediately say what it was. She stood there with
the door half closed, staring at the floor, knowing that she should
not look again, and knowing that she would.

Carefully she eased the door back open again.

The room was darkly shadowed and chilly. The chilliness did
not give her a good feeling about the occupant of the bed. She
listened. The silence didn't sound too good either. It wasn't the
silence of healthy deep sleep, it was the silence of nothing but a
little distant traffic noise.

She hesitated for a long while, silhouetted in the doorway,
looking and listening. She wondered about the sheer bulk of the
occupant of the bed and how cold he was with just a thin blanket
pulled over him. Next to the bed was a small tubular-legged
vinyl bucket chair which was rather overwhelmed by the huge
and heavy fur coat draped over it, and Kate thought that the coat
should more properly be draped over the bed and its cold
occupant.

At last, walking as softly and cautiously as she could, she
moved into the room and over to the bed. She stood looking
down at the face of the big, Nordic man. Though cold, and
though his eyes were shut, his face was frowning slightly as if
he was still rather worried about something. This struck Kate as
being almost infinitely sad. In life the man had had the air of

someone who was beset by huge, if somewhat puzzling, difficulties, and the appearance that he had almost immediately found things beyond this life that were a bother to him as well was miserable to contemplate.

She was astonished that he appeared to be so unscathed. His skin was totally unmarked. It was rugged and healthy – or rather had been healthy until very recently. Closer inspection showed a network of fine lines which suggested that he was older than the mid-thirties she had originally assumed. He could even have been a very fit and healthy man in his late forties.

Standing against the wall, by the door, was something unexpected. It was a large Coca-Cola vending machine. It didn't look as if it had been installed there: it wasn't plugged in and it had a small neat sticker on it explaining that it was temporarily out of order. It looked as if it had simply been left there inadvertently by someone who was probably even now walking around wondering which room he had left it in. Its large red and white wavy panel stared glassily into the room and did not explain itself. The only thing the machine communicated to the outside world was that there was a slot into which coins of a variety of denominations might be inserted, and an aperture to which a variety of different cans would be delivered if the machine was working, which it was not. There was also an old sledge-hammer leaning against it which was, in its own way, odd.

Faintness began to creep over Kate, the room began to develop a slight spin, and there was some restless rustling in the cabin trunks of her mind.

Then she realised that the rustling wasn't simply her imagination. There was a distinct noise in the room – a heavy, beating, scratching noise, a muffled fluttering. The noise rose and fell like the wind, but in her dazed and woozy state, Kate could not at first tell where the noise was coming from. At last her gaze fell on the curtains. She stared at them with the worried frown of a drunk trying to work out why the door is dancing.

The sound was coming from the curtains. She walked uncertainly towards them and pulled them apart. A huge eagle with circles tattooed on its wings was clattering and beating against the window, staring in with great yellow eyes and pecking wildly at the glass.

Kate staggered back, turned and tried to heave herself out of the room. At the end of the corridor the porthole doors swung open and two figures came through them. Hands rushed towards her as she became hopelessly entangled in the drip stand and began slowly to spin towards the floor.

She was unconscious as they carefully laid her back in her bed. She was unconscious half an hour later when a disturbingly short figure in a worryingly long white doctor's coat arrived, wheeled the big man away on a stretcher trolley and then returned after a few minutes for the Coca-Cola machine.

She woke a few hours later with a wintry sun seeping through the window. The day looked very quiet and ordinary, but Kate was still shaking.

Chapter 3

The same sun later broke in through the upper windows of a house in North London and struck the peacefully sleeping figure of a man.

The room in which he slept was large and bedraggled and did not much benefit from the sudden intrusion of light. The sun crept slowly across the bedclothes, as if nervous of what it might find amongst them, slunk down the side of the bed, moved in a rather startled way across some objects it encountered on the floor, toyed nervously with a couple of motes of dust, lit briefly on a stuffed fruitbat hanging in the corner, and fled.

This was about as big an appearance as the sun ever put in here, and it lasted for about an hour or so, during which time the sleeping figure scarcely stirred.

At eleven o'clock the phone rang, and still the figure did not respond, any more than it had responded when the phone had rung at twenty-five to seven in the morning, again at twenty to seven, again at ten to seven, and again for ten minutes continuously starting at five to seven, after which it had settled into a long and significant silence, disturbed only by the braying of police sirens in a nearby street at around nine o'clock, the delivery of a large eighteenth-century dual manual harpsichord at around nine-fifteen, and the collection of same by bailiffs at a little after ten. This was a not uncommon sort of occurrence – the people concerned were accustomed to finding the key under the doormat, and the man in the bed was accustomed to sleeping through it. You would probably not say that he was sleeping the sleep of the just, unless you meant the just asleep, but it was certainly the sleep of someone who was not fooling about when he climbed into bed of a night and turned off the light.

The room was not a room to elevate the soul. Louis XIV, to pick a name at random, would not have liked it, would have found it not sunny enough, and insufficiently full of mirrors. He would have desired someone to pick up the socks, put the records away, and maybe burn the place down. Michelangelo would have been distressed by its proportions, which were neither lofty nor shaped by any noticeable inner harmony or symmetry, other than that all parts of the room were pretty much equally full of old coffee mugs, shoes and brimming ashtrays, most of which were now sharing their tasks with each other. The walls were painted in almost precisely that shade of green which Raffaello Sanzio would have bitten off his own right hand at the wrist rather than use, and Hercules, on seeing the room, would probably have returned half an hour later armed with a navigable river. It was, in short, a dump, and was likely to remain so for as long as it remained in the custody of Mr Svlad, or "Dirk", Gently, né Cjelli.

At last Gently stirred.

The sheets and blankets were pulled up tightly around his head, but from somewhere half-way down the length of the bed a hand slowly emerged from under the bedclothes and its fingers felt their way in little tapping movements along the floor. Working from experience, they neatly circumvented a bowl of something very nasty that had been sitting there since

Michaelmas, and eventually happened upon a half-empty pack of untipped Gauloises and a box of matches. The fingers shook a crumpled white tube free of the pack, seized it and the box of matches, and then started to poke a way through the sheets tangled together at the top of the bed, like a magician prodding at a handkerchief from which he intends to release a flock of doves.

The cigarette was at last inserted into the hole. The cigarette was lit. For a while the bed itself appeared to be smoking the cigarette in great heaving drags. It coughed long, loud and shudderingly and then began at last to breathe in a more measured rhythm. In this way, Dirk Gently achieved consciousness.

He lay there for a while feeling a terrible sense of worry and guilt about something weighing on his shoulders. He wished he could forget about it, and promptly did. He levered himself out of bed and a few minutes later padded downstairs.

The mail on the doormat consisted of the usual things: a rude letter threatening to take away his American Express card, an invitation to apply for an American Express card, and a few bills of the more hysterical and unrealistic type. He couldn't understand why they kept sending them. The cost of the postage seemed merely to be good money thrown after bad. He shook his head in wonderment at the malevolent incompetence of the world, threw the mail away, entered the kitchen and approached the fridge with caution.

It stood in the corner.

The kitchen was large and shrouded in a deep gloom that was not relieved, only turned yellow, by the action of switching on the light. Dirk squatted down in front of the fridge and carefully examined the edge of the door. He found what he was looking for. In fact he found more than he was looking for.

Near the bottom of the door, across the narrow gap which separated the door from the main body of the fridge, which held the strip of grey insulating rubber, lay a single human hair. It was stuck there with dried saliva. That he had expected. He had stuck it there himself three days earlier and had checked it on several occasions since then. What he had not expected to find was a second hair.

He frowned at it in alarm. A *second* hair?

It was stuck across the gap in the same way as the first one, only this hair was near the top of the fridge door, and he had not put it there. He peered at it closely, and even went so far as to go and open the old shutters on the kitchen windows to let some extra light in upon the scene.

The daylight shouldered its way in like a squad of policemen, and did a lot of *what's-all-this*ing around the room which, like the bedroom, would have presented anyone of an aesthetic disposition with difficulties. Like most of the rooms in Dirk's house it was large, looming and utterly dishevelled. It simply sneered at anyone's attempts to tidy it, sneered at them and brushed them aside like one of the small pile of dead and disheartened flies that lay beneath the window, on top of a pile of old pizza boxes.

The light revealed the second hair for what it was – a grey hair at root, dyed a vivid metallic orange. Dirk pursed his lips and thought very deeply. He didn't need to think hard in order to realise who the hair belonged to – there was only one person who regularly entered the kitchen looking as if her head had been used for extracting metal oxides from industrial waste – but he did have seriously to consider the implications of the discovery that she had been plastering her hair across the door of his fridge.

It meant that the silently waged conflict between himself and his cleaning lady had escalated to a new and more frightening level. It was now, Dirk reckoned, fully three months since this fridge door had been opened, and each of them was grimly determined not to be the one to open it first. The fridge no longer merely stood there in the corner of the kitchen, it actually lurked. Dirk could quite clearly remember the day on which the thing had started lurking. It was about a week ago, when Dirk had tried a simple subterfuge to trick Elena – the old bat's name was Elena, pronounced to rhyme with cleaner, which was an irony that Dirk now no longer relished – into opening the fridge door. The subterfuge had been deftly deflected and had nearly rebounded horribly on Dirk.

He had resorted to the strategy of going to the local mini-market to buy a few simple groceries. Nothing contentious – a little milk, some eggs, some bacon, a carton or two of chocolate custard and a simple half-pound of butter. He had left them, innocently, on top of the fridge as if to say, "Oh, when you have a moment, perhaps you could pop these inside..."

When he had returned that evening his heart bounded to see that they were no longer on top of the fridge. They were gone! They had not been merely moved aside or put on a shelf, they were nowhere to be seen. She must finally have capitulated and put them away. In the fridge. And she would surely have cleaned it out once it was actually open. For the first and only time his heart swelled with warmth and gratitude towards her, and he was about to fling open the door of the thing in relief and triumph when an eighth sense (at the last count, Dirk reckoned he had eleven) warned him to be very, very careful, and to consider first where Elena might have put the cleared out contents of the fridge.

A nameless doubt gnawed at his mind as he moved noiselessly towards the garbage bin beneath the sink. Holding his breath, he opened the lid and looked.

There, nestling in the folds of the fresh black bin liner, were his eggs, his bacon, his chocolate custard and his simple half-pound of butter. Two milk bottles stood rinsed and neatly lined up by the sink into which their contents had presumably been poured.

She had thrown it away.

Rather than open the fridge door, she had thrown his food away. He looked round slowly at the grimy, squat, white monolith, and that was the exact moment at which he realised without a shadow of a doubt that his fridge had now begun seriously to lurk.

He made himself a stiff black coffee and sat, slightly trembling. He had not even looked directly at the sink, but he knew that he must unconsciously have noticed the two clean milk bottles there, and some busy part of his mind had been alarmed by them.

The next day he had explained all this away to himself. He was becoming needlessly paranoiac. It had surely been an innocent or careless mistake on Elena's part. She had probably been brooding distractedly on her son's attack of bronchitis, peevishness or homosexuality or whatever it was that regularly prevented her from either turning up, or from having noticeable effect when she did. She was Italian and probably had absent-mindedly mistaken his food for garbage.

But the business with the hair changed all that. It established beyond all possible doubt that she knew exactly what she was doing. She was under no circumstances going to open the fridge door until he had opened it first, and he was under no circumstances going to open the fridge until she had.

Obviously she had not noticed his hair, otherwise it would have been her most effective course simply to pull it off, thus tricking him into thinking she had opened the fridge. He should presumably now remove her hair in the hope of pulling that same trick on her, but even as he sat there he knew that somehow that wouldn't work, and that they were locked into a tightening spiral of non-fridge-opening that would lead them both to madness or perdition.

He wondered if he could hire someone to come and open the fridge.

No. He was not in a position to hire anybody to do anything. He was not even in a position to pay Elena for the last three weeks. The only reason he didn't ask her to leave was that sacking somebody inevitably involved paying them off, and this he was in no position to do. His secretary had finally left him on her own initiative and gone off to do something reprehensible in the travel business. Dirk had attempted to cast scorn on her preferring monotony of pay over –

"*Regularity* of pay," she had calmly corrected him.

– over job satisfaction.

She had nearly said, "Over *what?*", but at that moment she realised that if she said that she would have to listen to his reply, which would be bound to infuriate her into arguing back. It occurred to her for the first time that the only way of escaping was just not to get drawn into these arguments. If she simply did not respond this time, then she was free to leave. She tried it. She felt a sudden freedom. She left. A week later, in much the same mood, she married an airline cabin steward called Smith.

Dirk had kicked her desk over, and then had to pick it up himself later when she didn't come back.

The detective business was currently as brisk as the tomb. Nobody, it seemed, wished to have anything detected. He had recently, to make ends meet, taken up doing palmistry in drag on Thursday evenings, but he wasn't comfortable with it. He could have withstood it – the hateful, abject humiliation of it all was something to which he had, in different ways, now become accustomed, and he was quite anonymous in his little tent in the back garden of the pub – he could have withstood it all if he hadn't been so horribly, excruciatingly good at it. It made him break out in a sweat of self-loathing. He tried by every means to cheat, to fake, to be deliberately and cynically bad, but whatever fakery he tried to introduce always failed and he invariably ended up being right.

His worst moment had come about as a result of the poor woman from Oxfordshire who had come in to see him one evening. Being in something of a waggish mood, he had suggested that she should keep an eye on her husband, who, judging by her marriage line, looked to be a bit of a flighty type. It transpired that her husband was in fact a fighter pilot, and that his plane had been lost in an exercise over the North Sea only a fortnight earlier.

Dirk had been flustered by this and had soothed meaninglessly at her. He was certain, he said, that her husband would be restored to her in the fullness of time, that all would be well, and that all manner of things would be well and so on. The woman said that she thought this was not very likely seeing as the world record for staying alive in the North Sea was rather less than an hour, and since no trace of her husband had been found in two weeks it seemed fanciful to imagine that he was anything other than stone dead, and she was trying to get used to the idea, thank you very much. She said it rather tartly.

Dirk had lost all control at this point and started to babble.

He said that it was very clear from reading her hands that the great sum of money she had coming to her would be no consolation to her for the loss of her dear, dear husband, but that at least it might comfort her to know that he had gone on to that great something or other in the sky, that he was floating on the fleeciest of white clouds, looking very handsome in his new set of wings, and that he was terribly sorry to be talking such appalling drivel but she had caught him rather by surprise. Would she care for some tea, or some vodka, or some soup?

The woman demurred. She said she had only wandered into the tent by accident, she had been looking for the lavatories, and what was that about the money?

"Complete gibberish," Dirk had explained. He was in great difficulties, what with having the falsetto to keep up. "I was making it up as I went along," he said. "Please allow me to tender my most profound apologies for intruding so clumsily on your private grief, and to escort you to, er, or rather, direct you to the, well, what I can only in the circumstances call the lavatory, which is out of the tent and on the left."

Dirk had been cast down by this encounter, but was then utterly horrified a few days later when he discovered that the very following morning the unfortunate woman had learnt that she had won £250,000 on the Premium Bonds. He spent several hours that night standing on the roof of his house, shaking his fist at the dark sky and shouting, "Stop it!" until a neighbour complained to the police that he couldn't sleep. The police had come round in a screaming squad car and woken up the rest of the neighbourhood as well.

Today, this morning, Dirk sat in his kitchen and stared dejectedly at his fridge. The bloody-minded ebullience which he usually relied on to carry him through the day had been knocked out of him in its very opening moments by the business with the fridge. His will sat imprisoned in it, locked up by a single hair.

What he needed, he thought, was a client. Please, God, he thought, if there is a god, any god, bring me a client. Just a simple client, the simpler the better. Credulous and rich. Someone like that chap yesterday. He tapped his fingers on the table.

The problem was that the more credulous the client, the more Dirk fell foul at the end of his own better nature, which was constantly rearing up and embarrassing him at the most inopportune moments. Dirk frequently threatened to hurl his better nature to the ground and kneel on its windpipe, but it usually managed to get the better of him by dressing itself up as guilt and self-loathing, in which guise it could throw him right out of the ring.

Credulous and rich. Just so that he could pay off some, perhaps even just one, of the more prominent and sensational bills. He lit a cigarette. The smoke curled upwards in the morning light and attached itself to the ceiling.

Like that chap yesterday...

He paused.

The chap yesterday...

The world held its breath.

Quietly and gently there settled on him the knowledge that something, somewhere, was ghastly. Something was terribly wrong.

There was a disaster hanging silently in the air around him waiting for him to notice it. His knees tingled.

What he needed, he had been thinking, was a client. He had been thinking that as a matter of habit. It was what he always thought at this time of the morning. What he had forgotten was that he had one.

He stared wildly at his watch. Nearly eleven-thirty. He shook his head to try and clear the silent ringing between his ears, then made a hysterical lunge for his hat and his great leather coat that hung behind the door.

Fifteen seconds later he left the house, five hours late but moving fast.

Chapter 4

A minute or two later Dirk paused to consider his best strategy. Rather than arrive five hours late and flustered it would be better all round if he were to arrive five hours and a few extra minutes late, but triumphantly in command.

"Pray God I am not too soon!" would be a good opening line as he swept in, but it needed a good follow-through as well, and he wasn't sure what it should be.

Perhaps it would save time if he went back to get his car, but then again it was only a short distance, and he had a tremendous propensity for getting lost when driving. This was largely because of his method of "Zen" navigation, which was simply to find any car that looked as if it knew where it was going and follow it. The results were more often surprising than successful, but he felt it was worth it for the sake of the few occasions when it was both.

Furthermore he was not at all certain that his car was working.

It was an elderly Jaguar, built at that very special time in the company's history when they were making cars which had to stop for repairs more often than they needed to stop for petrol, and frequently needed to rest for months between outings. He was, however, certain, now that he came to think about it, that the car didn't have any petrol and furthermore he did not have any cash or valid plastic to enable him to fill it up.

He abandoned that line of thought as wholly fruitless.

He stopped to buy a newspaper while he thought things over. The clock in the newsagent's said eleven thirty-five. Damn, damn, damn. He toyed with the idea of simply dropping the case. Just walking away and forgetting about it. Having some lunch. The whole thing was fraught with difficulties in any event. Or rather it was fraught with one particular difficulty which was that of keeping a straight face. The whole thing was complete and utter nonsense. The client was clearly loopy and Dirk would not have considered taking the case except for one very important thing.

Three hundred pounds a day plus expenses.

The client had agreed to it just like that. And when Dirk had started his usual speech to the effect that his methods, involving as they did the fundamental interconnectedness of all things, often led to expenses that might appear to the untutored eye to be somewhat tangential to the matter in hand, the client had simply waved the matter aside as trifling. Dirk liked that in a client.

The only thing the client had insisted upon in the midst of this almost superhuman fit of reasonableness was that Dirk had to be there, absolutely had, had, had to be there ready, functioning and alert, without fail, without even the merest smidgen of an inkling of failure, at six-thirty in the morning. Absolute.

Well, he was just going to have to see reason about that as well. Six-thirty was clearly a preposterous time and he, the client, obviously hadn't meant it seriously. A civilised six-thirty for twelve noon was almost certainly what he had in mind, and if he wanted to cut up rough about it, Dirk would have no option but to start handing out some serious statistics. Nobody got murdered before lunch. But nobody. People weren't up to it. You needed a good lunch to get both the blood-sugar and blood-lust levels up. Dirk had the figures to prove it.

Did he, Anstey (the client's name was Anstey, an odd, intense man in his mid-thirties with staring eyes, a narrow yellow tie and one of the big houses in Lupton Road; Dirk hadn't actually liked him very much and thought he looked as if he was trying to swallow a fish), did he know that 67 per cent of all known murderers, who expressed a preference, had had liver and bacon for lunch? And that another 22 per cent had been torn between either a prawn biryani or an omelette? That dispensed with 89 per cent of the threat at a stroke, and by the time you had further discounted the salad eaters and the turkey and ham sandwich munchers and started to look at the number of people who would contemplate such a course of action without any lunch at all, then you were well into the realms of negligibility and bordering on fantasy.

After two-thirty, but nearer to three o'clock, was when you had to start being on your guard. Seriously. Even on good days. Even when you weren't receiving death threats from strange gigantic men with green eyes, you had to watch people like a hawk after the lunching hour. The really dangerous time was after four o'clockish, when the streets began to fill up with marauding packs of publishers and agents, maddened with fettucine and kir and baying for cabs. Those were the times that tested men's souls. Six-thirty in the morning? Forget it. Dirk had.

With his resolve well stiffened Dirk stepped back out of the newsagent's into the nippy air of the street and strode off.

"Ah, I expect you'll be wanting to pay for that paper, then, won't you, Mr Dirk, sir?" said the newsagent, trotting gently after him.

"Ah, Bates," said Dirk loftily, "you and your expectations. Always expecting this and expecting that. May I recommend serenity to you? A life that is burdened with expectations is a heavy life. Its fruit is sorrow and disappointment. Learn to be one with the joy of the moment."

"I think it's twenty pence that one, sir," said Bates, tranquilly.

"Tell you what I'll do, Bates, seeing as it's you. Do you have a pen on you at all? A simple ball-point will suffice."

Bates produced one from an inner pocket and handed it to Dirk, who then tore off the corner of the paper on which the price was printed and scribbled "IOU" above it. He handed the scrap of paper to the newsagent.

"Shall I put this with the others, then, sir?"

"Put it wherever it will give you the greatest joy, dear Bates, I would want you to put it nowhere less. For now, dear man, farewell."

"I expect you'll be wanting to give me back my pen as well, Mr Dirk."

"When the times are propitious for such a transaction, my dear Bates," said Dirk, "you may depend upon it. For the moment, higher purposes call it. Joy, Bates, great joy. Bates, please let go of it."

After one last listless tug, the little man shrugged and padded back towards his shop.

"I expect I'll be seeing you later, then, Mr Dirk," he called out over his shoulder, without enthusiasm.

Dirk gave a gracious bow of his head to the man's retreating back, and then hurried on, opening the newspaper at the horoscope page as he did so.

"Virtually everything you decide today will be wrong," it said bluntly.

Dirk slapped the paper shut with a grunt. He did not for a second hold with the notion that great whirling lumps of rock light years away knew something about your day that you didn't. It just so happened that "The Great Zaganza" was an old friend of his who knew when Dirk's birthday was, and always wrote his column deliberately to wind him up. The paper's circulation had dropped by nearly a twelfth since he had taken over doing the horoscope, and only Dirk and The Great Zaganza knew why.

He hurried on, flapping his way quickly through the rest of the paper. As usual, there was nothing interesting. A lot of stuff about the search for Janice Smith, the missing airline girl from Heathrow, and how she could possibly have disappeared just like that. They printed the latest picture of her, which was on a swing with pigtails, aged six. Her father, a Mr Jim Pearce, was quoted as saying it was quite a good likeness, but she had grown up a lot now and was usually in better focus. Impatiently, Dirk tucked the paper under his arm and strode onwards, his thoughts on a much more interesting topic.

Three hundred pounds a day. Plus expenses.

He wondered how long he could reasonably expect to sustain in Mr Anstey his strange delusions that he was about to be murdered by a seven foot tall, shaggy-haired creature with huge green eyes and horns, who habitually waved things at him: a contract written in some incomprehensible language and signed with a splash of blood, and also a kind of scythe. The other notable feature of this creature was that no one other than his client had been able to see it, which Mr Anstey dismissed as a trick of the light.

Three days? Four? Dirk didn't think he'd be able to manage a whole week with a straight face, but he was already looking at something like a grand for his trouble. And he would stick a new fridge down on the list of tangential but non-negotiable expenses. That would be a good one. Getting the old fridge thrown out was definitely part of the interconnectedness of all things.

He began to whistle at the thought of simply getting someone to come round and cart the thing away, turned into Lupton Road and was surprised at all the police cars there. And the ambulance. He didn't like them being there. It didn't feel right. It didn't sit comfortably in his mind alongside his visions of a new fridge.

Chapter 5

Dirk knew Lupton Road. It was a wide tree-lined affair, with large late-Victorian terraces which stood tall and sturdily and resented police cars. Resented them if they turned up in numbers, that is, and if their lights were flashing. The inhabitants of Lupton Road liked to see a nice, well-turned-out single police car patrolling up and down the street in a cheerful and robust manner – it kept property values cheerful and robust too. But the moment the lights started flashing in that knuckle-whitening blue, they cast their pallor not only on the neatly pointed bricks that they flashed across, but also on the very values those bricks represented.

Anxious faces peered from behind the glass of neighbouring windows, and were irradiated by the blue strobes.

There were three of them, three police cars left askew across the road in a way that transcended mere parking. It sent out a massive signal to the world saying that the law was here now taking charge of things, and that anyone who just had normal, good and cheerful business to conduct in Lupton Road could just fuck off.

Dirk hurried up the road, sweat pricking at him beneath his heavy leather coat. A police constable loomed up ahead of him with his arms spread out, playing at being a stop barrier, but Dirk swept him aside in a torrent of words to which the constable was unable to come up with a good response off the top of his head. Dirk sped on to the house.

At the door another policeman stopped him, and Dirk was about to wave an expired Marks and Spencer charge card at him with a deft little flick of the wrist that he had practised for hours in front of a mirror on those long evenings when nothing much else was on, when the officer suddenly said, "Hey, is your name Gently?"

Dirk blinked at him warily. He made a slight grunting noise that could be either "yes" or "no" depending on the circumstances.

"Because the Chief has been looking for you."

"Has he?" said Dirk.

"I recognised you from his description," said the officer, looking him up and down with a slight smirk.

"In fact," continued the officer, "he's been using your name in a manner that some might find highly offensive. He even sent Big Bob the Finder off in a car to find you. I can tell that he didn't find you from the fact that you're looking reasonably well. Lot of people get found by Big Bob the Finder, they come in a bit wobbly. Just about able to help us with our enquiries but that's about all. You'd better go in. Rather you than me," he added quietly.

Dirk glanced at the house. The stripped-pine shutters were closed across all the windows. Though in all other respects the house seemed well cared for, groomed into a state of clean, well-pointed affluence, the closed shutters seemed to convey an air of sudden devastation.

Oddly, there seemed to be music coming from the basement,

or rather, just a single disjointed phrase of thumping music
being repeated over and over again. It sounded as if the stylus
had got stuck in the groove of a record, and Dirk wondered why
no one had turned it off, or at least nudged the stylus along so
that the record could continue. The song seemed very vaguely
familiar and Dirk guessed that he had probably heard it on the
radio recently, though he couldn't place it. The fragment of lyric
seemed to be something like:

"Don't pick it up, pick it up, pick i –
"Don't pick it up, pick it up, pick i –
"Don't pick it up, pick it up, pick i – " and so on.

"You'll be wanting to go down to the basement," said the
officer impassively, as if that was the last thing that anyone in
their right mind would be wanting to do.

Dirk nodded to him curtly and hurried up the steps to the
front door, which was standing slightly ajar. He shook his head
and clenched his shoulders to try and stop his brain fluttering.

He went in.

The hallway spoke of prosperity imposed on a taste that had
originally been formed by student living. The floors were
stripped boards heavily polyurethaned, the walls white with
Greek rugs hung on them, but expensive Greek rugs. Dirk would
be prepared to bet (though probably not to pay up) that a
thorough search of the house would reveal, amongst who knew
what other dark secrets, five hundred British Telecom shares and
a set of Dylan albums that was complete up to *Blood on the
Tracks*.

Another policeman was standing in the hall. He looked
terribly young, and he was leaning very slightly back against the
wall, staring at the floor and holding his helmet against his
stomach. His face was pale and shiny. He looked at Dirk
blankly, and nodded faintly in the direction of the stairs leading
down.

Up the stairs came the repeated sound:

"Don't pick it up, pick it up, pick i –

"Don't pick it up, pick it up, pick i – "

Dirk was trembling with a rage that was barging around inside him looking for something to hit or throttle. He wished that he could hotly deny that any of this was his fault, but until anybody tried to assert that it was, he couldn't.

"How long have you been here?" he said curtly.

The young policeman had to gather himself together to answer.

"We arrived about half-hour ago," he replied in a thick voice. "Hell of a morning. Rushing around."

"Don't tell me about rushing around," said Dirk, completely meaninglessly. He launched himself down the stairs.

"Don't pick it up, pick it up, pick i –

"Don't pick it up, pick it up, pick i – "

At the bottom there was a narrow corridor. The main door off it was heavily cracked and hanging off its hinges. It opened into a large double room. Dirk was about to enter when a figure emerged from it and stood barring his way.

"I hate the fact that this case has got you mixed up in it," said the figure, "I hate it very much. Tell me what you've got to do with it so I know exactly what it is I'm hating."

Dirk stared at the neat, thin face in astonishment.

"Gilks?" he said.

"Don't stand there looking like a startled whatsisname, what are those things that aren't seals? Much worse than seals. Big, blubbery things. Dugongs. Don't stand there looking like a startled dugong. Why has that..." Gilks pointed into the room behind him, "why has that...man in there got your name and telephone number on an envelope full of money?"

"How m..." started Dirk. "How, may I ask, do you come to be here, Gilks? What are you doing so far from the Fens? Surprised you find it dank enough for you here."

"Three hundred pounds," said Gilks. "Why?"

"Perhaps you would allow me to speak to my client," said Dirk.

"Your client, eh?" said Gilks grimly. "Yes. All right. Why don't you speak to him? I'd be interested to hear what you have to say." He stood back stiffly, and waved Dirk into the room.

Dirk gathered his thoughts and entered the room in a state of controlled composure which lasted for just over a second.

Most of his client was sitting quietly in a comfortable chair in front of the hi-fi. The chair was placed in the optimal listening position – about twice as far back from the speakers as the distance between them, which is generally considered to be ideal for stereo imaging.

He seemed generally to be casual and relaxed with his legs crossed and a half-finished cup of coffee on the small table beside him. Distressingly, though, his head was sitting neatly on the middle of the record which was revolving on the hi-fi turntable, with the tone arm snuggling up against the neck and constantly being deflected back into the same groove. As the head revolved it seemed once every 1.8 seconds or so to shoot Dirk a reproachful glance, as if to say, "See what happens when you don't turn up on time like I asked you to," then it would sweep on round to the wall, round, round, and back to the front again with more reproach.

"Don't pick it up, pick it up, pick i –

"Don't pick it up, pick it up, pick i – "

The room swayed a little around Dirk, and he put his hand out against the wall to steady it.

"Was there any particular service you were engaged to provide for your client?" said Gilks behind him, very quietly.

"Oh, er, just a small matter," said Dirk weakly. "Nothing connected with all this. No, he, er, didn't mention any of this kind of thing at all. Well, look, I can see you're busy, I think I'd better just collect my fee and leave. You say he left it out for me?"

Having said this, Dirk sat heavily on a small bentwood chair standing behind him, and broke it.

Gilks hauled him back to his feet again, and propped him

against the wall. Briefly he left the room, then came back with a small jug of water and a glass on a tray. He poured some water into the glass, took it to Dirk and threw it at him.

"Better?"

"No," spluttered Dirk, "can't you at least turn the record off?"

"That's forensic's job. Can't touch anything till the clever dicks have been. Maybe that's them now. Go out on to the patio and get some air. Chain yourself to the railing and beat yourself up a little, I'm pushed for time myself. And try to look less green, will you? It's not your colour."

"Don't pick it up, pick it up, pick i –

"Don't pick it up, pick it up, pick i – "

Gilks turned round, looking tired and cross, and was about to go out and up the stairs to meet the newcomers whose voices could be heard up on the ground floor, when he paused and watched the head revolving patiently on its heavy platter for a few seconds.

"You know," he said at last, "these smart-alec show-off suicides really make me tired. They only do it to annoy."

"Suicide?" said Dirk.

Gilks glanced round at him.

"Windows secured with iron bars half an inch thick," he said. "Door locked from the inside with the key still in the lock. Furniture piled against the inside of the door. French windows to the patio locked with mortice door bolts. No signs of a tunnel. If it was murder then the murderer must have stopped to do a damn fine job of glazing on the way out. Except that all the putty's old and painted over.

"No. Nobody's left this room, and nobody's broken into it except for us, and I'm pretty sure we didn't do it.

"I haven't time to fiddle around on this one. Obviously suicide, and just done to be difficult. I've half a mind to do the deceased for wasting police time. Tell you what," he said, glancing at his watch, "you've got ten minutes. If you come up with a plausible explanation of how he did it that I can put in my

report, I'll let you keep the evidence in the envelope minus 20
per cent compensation to me for the emotional wear and tear
involved in not punching you in the mouth."

Dirk wondered for a moment whether or not to mention the
visits his client claimed to have received from a strange and
violent green-eyed, fur-clad giant who regularly emerged out of
nowhere bellowing about contracts and obligations and waving a
three foot glittering-edged scythe, but decided, on balance, no.

"Don't pick it up, pick it up, pick i –
"Don't pick it up, pick it up, pick i – "

He was seething at himself at last. He had not been able to
seethe at himself properly over the death of his client because it
was too huge and horrific a burden to bear. But now he had been
humiliated by Gilks, and found himself in too wobbly and
disturbed a state to fight back, so he was able to seethe at
himself about that.

He turned sharply away from his tormentor and let himself
out into the patio garden to be alone with his seethings.

The patio was a small, paved, west-facing area at the rear
which was largely deprived of light, cut off as it was by the high
back wall of the house and by the high wall of some industrial
building that backed on to the rear. In the middle of it stood, for
who knew what possible reason, a stone sundial. If any light at
all fell on the sundial you would know that it was pretty close to
noon, GMT. Other than that, birds perched on it. A few plants
sulked in pots.

Dirk jabbed a cigarette in his mouth and burnt a lot of the end
of it fiercely.

"Don't pick it up, pick it up, pick i –
"Don't pick it up, pick it up, pick i – " still nagged from
inside the house.

· Neat garden walls separated the patio on either side from the
gardens of neighbouring houses. The one to the left was the
same size as this one, the one to the right extended a little
further, benefiting from the fact that the industrial building

finished flush with the intervening garden wall. There was an air of well-kemptness. Nothing grand, nothing flashy, just a sense that all was well and that upkeep on the houses was no problem. The house to the right, in particular, looked as if it had had its brickwork repointed quite recently, and its windows reglossed.

Dirk took a large gulp of air and stood for a second staring up into what could be seen of the sky, which was grey and hazy. A single dark speck was wheeling against the underside of the clouds. Dirk watched this for a while, glad of any focus for his thoughts other than the horrors of the room he had just left. He was vaguely aware of comings and goings within the room, of a certain amount of tape-measuring happening, of a feeling that photographs were being taken, and that severed-head-removal activities were taking place.

"Don't pick it up, pick it up, pick i –
"Don't pick it up, pick it up, pick i –
"Don't pi – "

Somebody at last picked it up, the nagging repetition was at last hushed, and now the gentle sound of a distant television floated peacefully on the noontime air.

Dirk, however, was having a great deal of difficulty in taking it all in. He was much more aware of taking a succession of huge swimmy whacks to the head, which were the assaults of guilt. It was not the normal background-noise type of guilt that comes from just being alive this far into the twentieth century, and which Dirk was usually fairly adept at dealing with. It was an actual stunning sense of, "this specific terrible thing is specifically and terribly my fault". All the normal mental moves wouldn't let him get out of the path of the huge pendulum. *Wham* it came again, *whizz, wham*, again and again, *wham, wham, wham.*

He tried to remember any of the details of what his late client (*wham, wham*) had said (*wham*) to him (*wham*), but it was (*wham*) virtually impossible (*wham*) with all this whamming taking place (*wham*). The man had said (*wham*) that (Dirk took a deep breath) (*wham*) he was being pursued (*wham*) by (*wham*) a large, hairy, green-eyed monster armed with a scythe.

Wham!

Dirk had secretly smiled to himself about this.

Whim, wham, whim, wham, whim, wham!

And had thought, "What a silly man."

Whim, whim, whim, whim, wham!

A scythe (*wham*), and a contract (*wham*).

He hadn't known, or even had the faintest idea as to what the contract was for.

"Of course," Dirk had thought (*wham*).

But he had a vague feeling that it might have something to do with a potato. There was a bit of a complicated story attached to that (*whim, whim, whim*).

Dirk had nodded seriously at this point (*wham*), and made a reassuring tick (*wham*) on a pad which he kept on his desk (*wham*) for the express purpose of making reassuring ticks on (*wham, wham, wham*). He had prided himself at that moment on having managed to convey the impression that he had made a tick in a small box marked "Potatoes".

Wham, wham, wham, wham!

Mr Anstey had said he would explain further about the potatoes when Dirk arrived to carry out his task.

And Dirk had promised (*wham*), easily (*wham*), casually (*wham*), with an airy wave of his hand (*wham, wham, wham*), to be there at six-thirty in the morning (*wham*), because the contract (*wham*) fell due at seven o'clock.

Dirk remembered having made another tick in a notional "Potato contract falls due at 7.00 a.m." box. (*Wh...*)

He couldn't handle all this whamming any more. He couldn't blame himself for what had happened. Well, he could. Of course he could. He did. It was, in fact, his fault (*wham*). The point was that he couldn't continue to blame himself for what had happened and think clearly about it, which he was going to have to do. He would have to dig this horrible thing (*wham*) up by the roots, and if he was going to be fit to do that he had somehow to divest himself (*wham*) of this whamming.

A huge wave of anger surged over him as he contemplated his predicament and the tangled distress of his life. He hated this neat patio. He hated all this sundial stuff, and all these neatly painted windows, all these hideously trim roofs. He wanted to blame it all on the paintwork rather than on himself, on the revoltingly tidy patio paving-stones, on the sheer disgusting abomination of the neatly repointed brickwork.

"Excuse me…"

"What?" He whirled round, caught unawares by this intrusion into his private raging of a quiet polite voice.

"Are you connected with…?" The woman indicated all the unpleasantness and the lower-ground-floorness and the horrible sort of policeness of things next door to her with a little floating movement of her wrist. Her wrist wore a red bracelet which matched the frames of her glasses. She was looking over the garden wall from the house on the right, with an air of slightly anxious distaste.

Dirk glared at her speechlessly. She looked about forty-somethingish and neat, with an instant and unmistakable quality of advertising about her.

She gave a troubled sigh.

"I know it's probably all very terrible and everything," she said, "but do you think it will take long? We only called in the police because the noise of that ghastly record was driving us up the wall. It's all a bit…"

She gave him a look of silent appeal, and Dirk decided that it could all be her fault. She could, as far as he was concerned, take the blame for everything while he sorted it out. She deserved it, if only for wearing a bracelet like that.

Without a word, he turned his back on her, and took his fury back inside the house where it began rapidly to freeze into something hard and efficient.

"Gilks!" he said. "Your smart-alec suicide theory. I like it. It works for me. And I think I see how the clever bastard pulled it off. Bring me pen. Bring me paper."

He sat down with a flourish at the cherrywood farmhouse table which occupied the centre of the rear portion of the room and deftly sketched out a scheme of events which involved a number of household or kitchen implements, a swinging, weighted light fitting, some very precise timing, and hinged on the vital fact that the record turntable was Japanese.

"That should keep your forensic chaps happy," said Dirk briskly to Gilks. The forensic chaps glanced at it, took in its salient points and liked them. They were simple, implausible, and of exactly that nature which a coroner who liked the same sort of holidays in Marbella which they did would be sure to relish.

"Unless," said Dirk casually, "you are interested in the notion that the deceased had entered into some kind of diabolical contract with a supernatural agency for which payment was now being exacted?"

The forensic chaps glanced at each other and shook their heads. There was a strong sense from them that the morning was wearing on and that this kind of talk was only introducing unnecessary complications into a case which otherwise could be well behind them before lunch.

Dirk made a satisfied shrug, peeled off his share of the evidence and, with a final nod to the constabulary, made his way back upstairs.

As he reached the hallway, it suddenly became apparent to him that the gentle sounds of day-time television which he had heard from out in the garden had previously been masked from inside by the insistent sound of the record stuck in its groove.

He was surprised now to realise that they were in fact coming from somewhere upstairs in this house. With a quick look round to see that he was not observed he stood on the bottom step of the staircase leading to the upstairs floors of the house and glanced up them in surprise.

Chapter 6

The stairs were carpeted with a tastefully austere matting type of substance. Dirk quietly made his way up them, past some tastefully dried large things in a pot that stood on the first landing, and looked into the rooms on the first floor. They, too, were tasteful and dried.

The larger of the two bedrooms was the only one that showed any signs of current use. It had clearly been designed to allow the morning light to play on delicately arranged flowers and duvets stuffed with something like hay, but there was a feeling that socks and used shaving heads were instead beginning to gather the room into their grip. There was a distinct absence of anything female in the room – the same sort of absence that a missing picture leaves behind it on a wall. There was an air of tension and of sadness and of things needing to be cleaned out from under the bed.

The bathroom, which opened out from it, had a gold disc hung on the wall in front of the lavatory, for sales of five hundred thousand copies of a record called *Hot Potato* by a band called Pugilism and the Third Autistic Cuckoo. Dirk had a vague recollection of having read part of an interview with the leader of the band (there were only two of them, and one of them was the leader) in a Sunday paper. He had been asked about their name, and he had said that there was an interesting story about it, though it turned out not to be. "It can mean whatever people want it to mean," he had added with a shrug from the sofa of his manager's office somewhere off Oxford Street.

Dirk remembered visualising the journalist nodding politely and writing this down. A vile knot had formed in Dirk's stomach which he had eventually softened with gin.

"*Hot Potato...*" thought Dirk. It suddenly occurred to him, looking at the gold disc hanging in its red frame, that the record on which the late Mr Anstey's head had been perched was obviously this one. Hot Potato. Don't pick it up.

What could that mean?

Whatever people wanted it to mean, Dirk thought with bad grace.

The other thing that he remembered now about the interview was that Pain (the leader of Pugilism and the Third Autistic Cuckoo was called Pain) claimed to have written the lyrics down more or less verbatim from a conversation which he or somebody had overheard in a café or a sauna or an aeroplane or something like that. Dirk wondered how the originators of the conversation would feel to hear their words being repeated in the circumstances in which he had just heard them.

He peered more closely at the label in the centre of the gold record. At the top of the label it said simply, "ARRGH!", while underneath the actual title were the writers' credits – "Paignton, Mulville, Anstey".

Mulville was presumably the member of Pugilism and the Third Autistic Cuckoo who wasn't the leader. And Geoff Anstey's inclusion on the writing credits of a major-selling single was probably what had paid for this house. When Anstey had talked about the contract having something to do with

Potato he had assumed that Dirk knew what he meant. And he, Dirk, had as easily assumed that Anstey was blithering. It was very easy to assume that someone who was talking about green-eyed monsters with scythes was also blithering when he talked about potatoes.

Dirk sighed to himself with deep uneasiness. He took a dislike to the neat way the trophy was hanging on the wall and adjusted it a little so that it hung at a more humane and untidy angle. Doing this caused an envelope to fall out from behind the frame and flutter towards the floor. Dirk tried unsuccessfully to catch it. With an unfit grunt he bent over and picked the thing up.

It was a largish, cream envelope of rich, heavy paper, roughly slit open at one end, and resealed with Sellotape. In fact it looked as if it had been opened and resealed with fresh layers of tape many times, an impression which was borne out by the number of names to which the envelope had in its time been addressed – each successively crossed out and replaced by another.

The last name on it was that of Geoff Anstey. At least Dirk assumed it was the last name because it was the only one that had not been crossed out, and crossed out heavily. Dirk peered at some of the other names, trying to make them out.

Some memory was stirred by a couple of the names which he could just about discern, but he needed to examine the envelope much more closely. He had been meaning to buy himself a magnifying glass ever since he had become a detective, but had never got around to it. He also did not possess a penknife, so reluctantly he decided that the most prudent course was to tuck the envelope away for the moment in one of the deeper recesses of his coat and examine it later in privacy.

He glanced quickly behind the frame of the gold disc to see if any other goodies might emerge but was disappointed, and so he quit the bathroom and resumed his exploration of the house.

The other bedroom was neat and soulless. Unused. A pine

bed, a duvet and an old battered chest of drawers that had been revived by being plunged into a vat of acid were its main features. Dirk pulled the door of it closed behind him, and started to ascend the small, wobbly, white-painted stairway that led up to an attic from which the sounds of Bugs Bunny could be heard.

At the top of the stairs was a minute landing which opened on one side into a bathroom so small that it would best be used by standing outside and sticking into it whichever limb you wanted to wash. The door to it was kept ajar by a length of green hosepipe which trailed from the cold tap of the wash-basin, out of the bathroom, across the landing and into the only other room here at the top of the house.

It was an attic room with a severely pitched roof which offered only a few spots where a person of anything approaching average height could stand up.

Dirk stood hunched in the doorway and surveyed its contents, nervous of what he might find amongst them. There was a general grunginess about the place. The curtains were closed and little light made it past them into the room, which was otherwise illuminated only by the flickering glow of an animated rabbit. An unmade bed with dank, screwed-up sheets was pushed under a particularly low angle of the ceiling. Part of the walls and the more nearly vertical surfaces of the ceiling were covered with pictures crudely cut out of magazines.

There didn't seem to be any common theme or purpose behind the cuttings. As well as a couple of pictures of flashy German cars and the odd bra advertisement, there were also a badly torn picture of a fruit flan, part of an advertisement for life insurance and other random fragments which suggested they had been selected and arranged with a dull, bovine indifference to any meaning that any of them might have or effect they might achieve.

The hosepipe curled across the floor and led around the side of an elderly armchair pulled up in front of the television set.

The rabbit rampaged. The glow of his rampagings played on the frayed edges of the armchair. Bugs was wrestling with the controls of an aeroplane which was plunging to the ground. Suddenly he saw a button marked "Autopilot" and pressed it. A cupboard opened and a robot pilot clambered out, took one look at the situation and baled out. The plane hurtled on towards the ground but, luckily, ran out of fuel just before reaching it and so the rabbit was saved.

Dirk could also see the top of a head.

The hair on this head was dark, matted and greasy. Dirk watched it for a long, uneasy moment before advancing slowly into the room to see what, if anything, it was attached to. His relief at discovering, as he rounded the armchair, that the head was, after all, attached to a living body was a little marred by the sight of the living body to which it was attached.

Slumped in the armchair was a boy.

He was probably about thirteen or fourteen, and although he didn't look ill in any specific physical way, he was definitely not a well person. His hair sagged on his head, his head sagged on his shoulders, and he lay in the armchair in a sort of limp, crumpled way, as if he'd been hurled there from a passing train. He was dressed merely in a cheap leather jacket and sleeping-bag.

Dirk stared at him.

Who was he? What was a boy doing here watching television in a house where someone had just been decapitated? Did he know what had happened? Did Gilks know about him? Had Gilks even bothered to come up here? It was, after all, several flights of stairs for a busy policeman with a tricky suicide on his hands.

After Dirk had been standing there for twenty seconds or so, the boy's eyes climbed up towards him, failed utterly to acknowledge him in any way at all, and then dropped again and locked back on to the rabbit.

Dirk was unused to making quite such a minuscule impact on

anybody. He checked to be sure that he did have his huge leather coat and his absurd red hat on and that he was properly and dramatically silhouetted by the light of the doorway.

He felt momentarily deflated and said, "Er..." by way of self-introduction, but it didn't get the boy's attention. He didn't like this. The kid was deliberately and maliciously watching television at him. He frowned. There was a kind of steamy tension building in the room it seemed to Dirk, a kind of difficult, hissing quality to the whole air of the place which he did not know how to respond to. It rose in intensity and then suddenly ended with an abrupt click which made Dirk start.

The boy unwound himself like a slow, fat snake, leaned sideways over the far side of the armchair and made some elaborate unseen preparations which clearly involved, as Dirk now realised, an electric kettle. When he resumed his earlier splayed posture it was with the addition of a plastic pot clutched in his right hand, from which he forked rubbery strands of steaming gunk into his mouth.

The rabbit brought his affairs to a conclusion and gave way to a jeering comedian who wished the viewers to buy a certain brand of lager on the basis of nothing better than his own hardly disinterested say-so.

Dirk felt that it was time to make a slightly greater impression on the proceedings than he had so far managed to do. He stepped forward directly into the boy's line of sight.

"Kid," Dirk said in a tone that he hoped would sound firm but gentle and not in any way at all patronising or affected or gauche, "I need to know who – "

He was distracted at that moment by the sight which met him from the new position in which he was standing. On the other side of the armchair there was a large, half-full catering-size box of Pot Noodles, a large, half-full catering-size box of Mars Bars, a half demolished pyramid of cans of soft drink, and the end of the hosepipe. The hosepipe ended in a plastic tap nozzle, and was obviously used for refilling the kettle.

Dirk had simply been going to ask the boy who he was, but seen from this angle the family resemblance was unmistakable. He was clearly the son of the lately decapitated Geoffrey Anstey. Perhaps this behaviour was just his way of dealing with shock. Or perhaps he really didn't know what had happened. Or perhaps he...

Dirk hardly liked to think.

In fact he was finding it hard to think clearly while the television beside him was, on behalf of a toothpaste manufacturing company, trying to worry him deeply about some of the things which might be going on in his mouth.

"OK," he said, "I don't like to disturb you at what I know must be a difficult and distressing time for you, but I need to know first of all if you actually realise that this is a difficult and distressing time for you."

Nothing.

All right, thought Dirk, time for a little judicious toughness. He leant back against the wall, stuck his hands in his pockets in an OK-if-that's-the-way-you-want-to-play-it manner, stared moodily at the floor for a few seconds, then swung his head up and let the boy have a hard look right between the eyes.

"I have to tell you, kid," he said tersely, "your father's dead."

This might have worked if it hadn't been for a very popular and long-running commercial which started at that moment. It seemed to Dirk to be a particularly astounding example of the genre.

The opening sequence showed the angel Lucifer being hurled from heaven into the pit of hell where he then lay on a burning lake until a passing demon arrived and gave him a can of a fizzy soft drink called *s*Hades. Lucifer took it and tried it. He greedily guzzled the whole contents of the can and then turned to camera, slipped on some Porsche design sunglasses, said, "Now we're *really* cookin'!" and lay back basking in the glow of the burning coals being heaped around him.

At that point an impossibly deep and growly American voice,

which sounded as if it had itself crawled from the pit of hell, or at least from a Soho basement drinking club to which it was keen to return as soon as possible to marinade itself into shape for the next voice-over, said, "*s*Hades. The Drink from Hell…" and the can revolved a little to obscure the initial "*s*", and thus spell "Hades".

The theology of this seemed a little confused, reflected Dirk, but what was one tiny extra droplet of misinformation in such a raging torrent?

Lucifer then mugged at the camera again and said, "I could really *fall* for this stuff…" and just in case the viewer had been rendered completely insensate by all these goings-on, the opening shot of Lucifer being hurled from heaven was briefly replayed in order to emphasise the word "fall".

The boy's attention was entirely captivated by this.

Dirk squatted down in between the boy and the screen.

"Listen to me," he began.

The boy craned his neck round to look past Dirk at the screen. He had to redistribute his limbs in the chair in order to be able to do this and continue to fork Pot Noodle into himself

"Listen," insisted Dirk again.

Dirk felt he was beginning to be in serious danger of losing the upper hand in the situation. It wasn't merely that the boy's attention was on the television, it was that nothing else seemed to have any meaning or independent existence for him at all. Dirk was merely a featureless object in the way of the television. The boy seemed to bear him no malice, he merely wished to see past him.

"Look, can we turn this off for a moment?" Dirk said, and he tried not to make it sound testy.

The boy did not respond. Maybe there was a slight stiffening of the shoulders, maybe it was a shrug. Dirk turned around and was at a loss to find which button to push to turn the television off. The whole control panel seemed to be dedicated to the single purpose of keeping itself turned on – there was no single button marked "on" or "off". Eventually Dirk simply disconnected the set from the power socket on the wall and turned back to the boy, who broke his nose.

Dirk felt his septum crunching from the terrific impact of the boy's forehead as they both toppled heavily backwards against the set, but the noise of the bone breaking, and the noise of his own cry of pain as it broke was completely obliterated by the howling screams of rage that erupted from the boy's throat. Dirk flailed helplessly to try and protect himself from the fury of the onslaught, but the boy was on top with his elbow in Dirk's eye, his knees pounding first on Dirk's ribcage, then his jaw and then on Dirk's already traumatised nose, as he scrambled over him to reconnect the power to the television. He then settled back comfortably into the armchair and watched with a moody and unsettled eye as the picture reassembled itself.

"You could at least have waited for the news," he said in a dull voice.

Dirk gaped at him. He sat huddled on the floor, coddling his bleeding nose in his hands, and gaped at the monstrously uninterested creature.

"Whhfff...fffmmm...nnggh!" he protested, and then gave up for the time being, while he probed his nose for the damage.

There was definitely a wobbly bit that clicked nastily between his fingers, and the whole thing seemed suddenly to be a horribly unfamiliar shape. He fished a handkerchief out of his pocket and held it up to his face. Blood spread easily through it. He staggered to his feet, brushed aside non-existent offers of help, stomped out of the room and into the tiny bathroom. There, he yanked the hosepipe angrily off the tap, found a towel, soaked it in cold water and held it to his face for a minute or two until the flow of blood gradually slowed to a trickle and stopped. He stared at himself in the mirror. His nose was quite definitely leaning at a slightly rakish angle. He tried bravely to shift it, but not bravely enough. It hurt abominably, so he contented himself with dabbing at it a little more with the wet towel and swearing quietly.

Then he stood there for a second or two longer, leaning against the basin, breathing heavily, and practising saying "All right!" fiercely into the mirror. It came out as "Aww-bwigh!" and lacked any real authority. When he felt sufficiently braced, or at least as braced as he was likely to feel in the immediate future, he turned and stalked grimly back into the den of the beast.

The beast was sitting quietly absorbing news of some of the exciting and stimulating game shows that the evening held in store for the determined viewer, and did not look up as Dirk re-entered.

Dirk walked briskly over to the window and drew the curtains sharply back, half hoping that the beast might shrivel up shrieking if exposed to daylight, but other than wrinkling up its nose, it did not react. A dark shadow flapped briefly across the window, but the angle was such that Dirk could not see what caused it.

He turned and faced the boy-beast. The midday news bulletin was starting on television, and the boy seemed somehow a little more open, a little more receptive to the world outside the flickering coloured rectangle. He glanced up at Dirk with a sour, tired look.

"Whaddayawananyway?" he said.

"I ted you whad I wad," said Dirk, fiercely but hopelessly, "I wad…hag od a bobed…I gnow thad faith!"

Dirk's attention had switched suddenly to the television screen, where a rather more up-to-date photograph of the missing airline check-in girl was being shown.

"Whadayadoingere?" said the boy.

"Jjchhhhh!" said Dirk, and perched himself down on the arm of the chair, peering intently at the face on the screen. It had been taken about a year ago, before the girl had learnt about corporate lipgloss. She had frizzy hair and a frumpy, put-upon look.

"Whoareyou? Wassgoinon?" insisted the boy.

"Loog, chuddub," snapped Dirk, "I'b tryid to wodge dthith!"

The newscaster said that the police professed themselves to be mystified by the fact that there was no trace of Janice Smith at the scene of the incident. They explained that there was a limit to the number of times they could search the same buildings, and appealed for anyone who might have a clue as to her whereabouts to come forward.

"Thadth by segradry! Thadth Mith Pearth!" exclaimed Dirk in astonishment.

The boy was not interested in Dirk's ex-secretary, and gave up trying to attract Dirk's attention. He wriggled out of the sleeping-bag and sloped off to the bathroom.

Dirk sat staring at the television, bewildered that he hadn't realised before who the missing girl was. Still, there was no reason why he should have done, he realised. Marriage had changed her name, and this was the first time they had shown a photograph that actually identified her. So far he had taken no real interest in the strange incident at the airport, but now it demanded his attention.

The explosion was now officially designated an "Act of God".

But, thought Dirk, what god? And why?

What god would be hanging around Terminal Two of Heathrow Airport trying to catch the 15.37 flight to Oslo?

After the miserable lassitude of the last few weeks, he suddenly had a great deal that required his immediate attention. He frowned in deep thought for a few moments, and hardly noticed when the beast-boy snuck back in and snuggled back into his sleeping-bag just in time for the advertisements to start. The first one showed how a perfectly ordinary stock cube could form the natural focus of a normal, happy family life.

Dirk leapt to his feet, but even as he was about to start questioning the boy again his heart sank as he looked at him. The beast was far away, sunk back in his dark, flickering lair, and Dirk did not feel inclined to disturb him again at the moment.

He contented himself with barking at the unresponding child that he would be back, and bustled heavily down the stairs, his big leather coat flapping madly behind him.

In the hallway he encountered the loathed Gilks once more.

"What happened to you?" said the policeman sharply, catching sight of Dirk's bruised and bulging nose.

"Ondly whad you dold me," said Dirk, innocently. "I bead bythelf ub."

Gilks demanded to know what he had been doing, and Dirk generously explained that there was a witness upstairs with some interesting information to impart. He suggested that Gilks go and have a word with him, but that it would be best if he turned off the television first.

Gilks nodded curtly. He started to go up the stairs, but Dirk stopped him.

"Doedth eddydthig dthrike you adth dthraydge aboud dthidth houdth?" he said.

"What did you say?" said Gilks in irritation.

"Subbthig dthraydge," said Dirk.

"Something *what*?"

"Dthraydge!" insisted Dirk.

"Strange?"

"Dthadth right, dthraydge."

Gilks shrugged. "Like what?" he said.

"Id dtheemdth to be cobbleedly dthouledth."

"Completely what?"

"Dthouledth!" He tried again. "Thoul-leth! I dthigg dthadth dverry idderedthigg!"

With that he doffed his hat politely, and swept on out of the house and up the street, where an eagle swooped out of the sky at him and came within a whisker of causing him to fall under a 73 bus on its way south.

For the next twenty minutes, hideous yells and screams emanated from the top floor of the house in Lupton Road, and caused much tension among the neighbours. The ambulance took away the upper and lower remains of Mr Anstey and also a policeman with a bleeding face. For a short while after this, there was quietness.

Then another police car drew up outside the house. A lot of "Bob's here" type of remarks floated from the house, as an extremely large and burly policeman heaved himself out of the car and bustled up the steps. A few minutes and a great deal of screaming and yelling later he re-emerged also clutching his face, and drove off in deep dudgeon, squealing his tyres in a violent and unnecessary manner.

Twenty minutes later a van arrived from which emerged another policeman carrying a tiny pocket television set. He entered the house, and re-emerged a short while later leading a docile thirteen-year-old boy, who was content with his new toy.

Once all policemen had departed, save for the single squad car which remained parked outside to keep watch on the house, a large, hairy, green-eyed figure emerged from its hiding place behind one of the molecules in the large basement room.

It propped its scythe against one of the hi-fi speakers, dipped a long, gnarled finger in the almost congealed pool of blood that had collected on the deck of the turntable, smeared the finger across the bottom of a sheet of thick, yellowing paper, and then disappeared off into a dark and hidden otherworld whistling a strange and vicious tune and returning only briefly to collect its scythe.

Chapter 7

A little earlier in the morning, at a comfortable distance from all
these events, set at a comfortable distance from a well-
proportioned window through which cool mid-morning light
was streaming, lay an elderly one-eyed man in a white bed. A
newspaper sat like a half-collapsed tent on the floor, where it
had been hurled two minutes before, at shortly after ten o'clock
by the clock on the bedside table.

The room was not large, but was furnished in excessively
bland good taste, as if it were a room in an expensive private
hospital or clinic, which is exactly what it was – the Woodshead
Hospital, set in its own small but well-kempt grounds on the
outskirts of a small but well-kempt village in the Cotswolds.

The man was awake but not glad to be.

His skin was very delicately old, like finely stretched,
translucent parchment, delicately freckled. His exquisitely frail
hands lay slightly curled on the pure white linen sheets and
quivered very faintly.

His name was variously given as Mr Odwin, or Wodin, or

Odin. He was – is – a god, and furthermore he was that least good of all gods to be alongside, a cross god. His one eye glinted.

He was cross because of what he had been reading in the newspapers, which was that another god had been cutting loose and making a nuisance of himself. It didn't say that in the papers, of course. It didn't say, "God cuts loose, makes nuisance of himself in airport," it merely described the resulting devastation and was at a loss to draw any meaningful conclusions from it.

The story had been deeply unsatisfactory in all sorts of ways, on account of its perplexing inconclusiveness, its going-nowhereness and the irritating (from the newspapers' point of view) lack of any good solid carnage. There was of course a mystery attached to the lack of carnage, but a newspaper preferred a good whack of carnage to a mere mystery any day of the week.

Odin, however, had no such difficulty in knowing what was going on. The accounts had "Thor" written all over them in letters much too big for anyone other than another god to see. He had thrown this morning's paper aside in irritation, and was now trying to concentrate on his relaxation exercises in order to avoid getting too disturbed about all this. These involved breathing in in a certain way and breathing out in a certain other way and were good for his blood pressure and so on. It was not as if he was about to die or anything – ha! – but there was no doubt that at his time of life – ha! – he preferred to take things easy and look after himself.

Best of all he liked to sleep.

Sleeping was a very important activity for him. He liked to sleep for longish periods, great swathes of time. Merely sleeping overnight was not taking the business seriously. He enjoyed a good night's sleep and wouldn't miss one for the world, but he didn't regard it as anything even half approaching enough. He liked to be asleep by half-past eleven in the morning if possible, and if that could come directly after a nice leisurely lie-in then so much the better. A little light breakfast and a quick trip to the bathroom while fresh linen was applied to his bed is really all the activity he liked to undertake, and he took care that it didn't jangle the sleepiness out of him and thus disturb his afternoon of napping. Sometimes he was able to spend an entire week asleep, and this he regarded as a good snooze. He had also slept through the whole of 1986 and hadn't missed it.

But he knew to his deep disgruntlement that he would shortly have to arise and undertake a sacred and irritating trust. Sacred, because it was godlike, or at least involved gods, and irritating because of the particular god that it involved.

Sneakily, he twitched the curtains at a distance, using nothing but his divine will. He sighed heavily. He needed to think and, what was more, it was time for his morning visit to the bathroom.

He rang for the orderly.

The orderly arrived promptly in his well-pressed loose green tunic, good-morninged cheerfully, and bustled around locating bedroom slippers and dressing-gown. He helped Odin out of bed, which was a little like rolling a stuffed crow out of a box, and escorted him slowly to the bathroom. Odin walked stiffly, like a head hung between two heavy stilts draped in striped Viyella and white towelling. The orderly knew Odin as Mr Odwin, and didn't realise that he was a god, which was something that Odin tended to keep quiet about, and wished that Thor would too.

Thor was the God of Thunder and, frankly, acted like it. It was inappropriate. He seemed unwilling, or unable, or maybe just too stupid to understand or accept...Odin stopped himself. He sensed that he was beginning mentally to rant. He would have to consider calmly what next to do about Thor, and he was on his way to the right place for a good think.

As soon as Odin had completed his stately hobble to the bathroom door, two nurses hurried in and stripped and remade the bed with immense precision, patting down the fresh linen, pulling it taut, turning it and tucking it. One of the nurses, clearly the senior, was plump and matronly, the other younger, darker and more generally bird-like. The newspaper was whisked off the floor and neatly refolded, the floor was briskly Hoovered, the curtains hooked back, the flowers and the untouched fruit replaced with fresh flowers and fresh fruit that would, like every piece of fruit before them, remain untouched.

When after a little while the old god's morning ablutions had been completed and the bathroom door reopened, the room had been transformed. The actual differences were tiny, of course, but the effect was of a subtle but magical transformation into something cool and fresh. Odin nodded in quiet satisfaction to see it. He made a little show of inspecting the bed, like a monarch inspecting a line of soldiers.

"Is it well tucked?" he asked in his old and whispery voice.

"It is very well tucked, Mr Odwin," said the senior nurse with an obsequious beam.

"Is it neatly turned?" It clearly was. This was merely a ritual.

"Turned very neatly indeed, Mr Odwin," said the nurse, "I supervised the turning down of the sheets myself."

"I'm glad of that, Sister Bailey, very glad," said Odin. "You have a fine eye for a trimly turned fold. It alarms me to know what I shall do without you."

"Well, I'm not about to go anywhere, Mr Odwin," said Sister Bailey, oozing happy reassurance.

"But you won't last for ever, Sister Bailey," said Odin. It was a remark that puzzled Sister Bailey on the times she had heard it, because of its apparent extreme callousness.

"Sure, and none of us lasts for ever, Mr Odwin," she said gently as she and the other nurse between them managed the difficult task of lifting Odin back into bed while keeping his dignity intact.

"You're Irish aren't you, Sister Bailey?" he asked, once he was properly settled.

"I am indeed so, Mr Odwin."

"Knew an Irishman once. Finn something. Told me a lot of stuff I didn't need to know. Never told me about the linen. Still, I know now."

He nodded curtly at this memory and lowered his head stiffly back on to the firmly plumped up pillows and ran the back of his finely freckled hand over the folded-back linen sheet. Quite simply he was in love with linen. Clean, lightly starched, white Irish linen, pressed, folded, tucked – the words themselves were almost a litany of desire for him. In centuries nothing had obsessed him or moved him so much as linen now did. He could not for the life of him understand how he could ever have cared for anything else.

Linen.

And sleep. Sleep and linen. Sleep in linen. Sleep.

Sister Bailey regarded him with a sort of proprietary fondness. She did not know that he was a god as such, in fact she thought he was probably an old film producer or Nazi war criminal. Certainly he had an accent she couldn't quite place, and his careless civility, his natural selfishness and his obsession with personal hygiene spoke of a past that was rich with horrors.

If she could have been transported to where she might see her secretive patient enthroned, warrior father of the warrior Gods of Asgard, she would not have been surprised. That is not quite true, in fact. She would have been startled quite out of her wits. But she would at least have recognised that it was consistent with the qualities she perceived in him, once she had recovered from the shock of discovering that virtually everything the human race had ever chosen to believe in was true. Or that it continued to be true long after the human race particularly needed it to be true any more.

Odin dismissed his medical attendants with a gesture, having first asked for his personal assistant to be found and sent to him once more.

This caused Sister Bailey to tighten her lips just a very little.

She did not like Mr Odwin's personal assistant, general factotum, manservant, call him what you will. His eyes were malevolent, he made her jump, and she strongly suspected him of making unspeakable suggestions to her nurses during their tea breaks.

He had what Sister Bailey supposed was what people meant by an olive complexion, in that it was extraordinarily close to being green. Sister Bailey was convinced that it was not right at all.

She was of course the last person to judge somebody by the colour of their skin – or if not absolutely the last, she had at least done it as recently as yesterday afternoon when an African diplomat had been brought in to have some gallstones removed and she had conceived an instant resentment of him. She didn't like him. She couldn't say exactly what it was she didn't like about him, because she was a nurse, not a taxi-driver, and she wouldn't let her personal feelings show for an instant. She was much too professional, much too good at her job, and treated everyone with a more or less equal efficient and cheerful courtesy, even, she thought – and a profound iciness settled on her at this point – even Mr Rag.

"Mr Rag" was the name of Mr Odwin's personal assistant. There was nothing she could do about it. It was not her place to criticise Mr Odwin's personal arrangements. But if it had been her business, which it wasn't, then she would greatly have preferred it, and not just for herself, but for Mr Odwin's own well-being as well, which was the important thing, if he could have employed someone who didn't give her the absolute heebie-jeebies, that was all.

She thought no more about it, merely went to look for him. She had been relieved to discover when she came on duty this morning that Mr Rag had left the premises the previous night, but had then, with a keen sense of disappointment, spotted him returning about an hour or so ago.

She found him exactly where he was not supposed to be. He

was squatting on one of the seats in the visitors' waiting-room
wearing what looked horribly like a soiled and discarded
doctor's gown that was much too big for him. Not only that, but
he was playing a thinly unmusical tune on a sort of pipe that he
had obviously carved out of a large disposable hypodermic
syringe which he absolutely should not have had.

He glanced up at her with his quick, dancing eyes, grinned
and continued to tootle and squeak, only significantly louder.

Sister Bailey ran through in her mind all the things that it was
completely pointless to say about either the coat or the syringe,
or about him being in the visitors' room frightening, or
preparing to frighten, the visitors. She knew she wouldn't be
able to stand the air of injured innocence with which he would
reply, or the preposterous absurdity of his answers. Her only
course was simply to let it pass and just get him away from the
room and out of the way as quickly as possible.

"Mr Odwin would like to see you," she said. She tried to jam
some of her normal lilting quality into her voice, but it just
wouldn't go. She wished his eyes would stop dancing like that.
Apart from finding it highly disturbing from both a medical and
aesthetic point of view she also could not help but be piqued by
the impression it conveyed that there were at least thirty-seven
things in the room more interesting than her.

He gazed at her in this disconcerting manner for a few
seconds then, muttering that there was no peace for the wicked,
not even the extremely wicked, he pushed past Sister Bailey and
skedaddled up the corridor to receive instructions from his lord
and master, quickly, before his lord and master fell asleep.

Chapter 8

By the end of the morning Kate had discharged herself from hospital. There were some initial difficulties involved in this because first the ward sister and then the doctor in charge of Kate's case were adamant that she was in no fit state to leave. She had only just emerged from a minor coma and she needed care, she needed –

"Pizza – " insisted Kate.

– rest, she needed –

"– my own home, and fresh air. The air in here is *horrible*. It smells like a vacuum cleaner's armpit."

– further medication, and should definitely remain under observation for another day or so until they were satisfied that she had made a full recovery.

At least, they were fairly adamant. During the course of the morning Kate demanded and got a telephone and started trying to order pizza to be delivered to her ward. She phoned around all of the least co-operative pizza restaurants she knew in London, harangued them, then made some noisily unsuccessful attempts

to muster a motorbike to roam around the West End and try and
pick up for her an American Hot with a list of additional peppers
and mushrooms and cheeses which the controller of the courier
service refused even to attempt to remember, and after an hour
or so of this sort of behaviour the objections to Kate discharging
herself from the hospital gradually fell away like petals from an
autumn rose.

And so, a little after lunchtime, she was standing on a bleak
West London street feeling weak and shaky but in charge of
herself. She had with her the empty, tattered remains of the
garment bag which she had refused to relinquish, and also a
small scrap of paper in her purse, which had a single name
scribbled on it.

She hailed a taxi and sat in the back with her eyes closed
most of the way back to her home in Primrose Hill. She climbed
up the stairs and let herself into her top-floor flat. There were ten
messages on her answering machine, which she simply erased
without listening to.

She threw open the window in her bedroom and for a moment
or two leaned out of it at the rather dangerous and awkward
angle which allowed her to see a patch of the park. It was a
small corner patch, with just a couple of plane trees standing in
it. The backs of some of the intervening houses framed it, or
rather, just failed totally to obscure it, and made it very personal
and private to Kate in a way which a vast, sweeping vista would
not have been.

On one occasion she had gone to this corner of the park and
walked around the invisible perimeter that marked out the limits
of what she could see, and had come very close to feeling that
this was her own domain. She had even patted the plane trees in
a proprietorial sort of way, and had then sat beneath them
watching the sun going down over London – over its badly
spoiled skyline and its non-delivering pizza restaurants – and
had come away with a profound sense of something or other,
though she wasn't quite certain what. Still, she had told herself,

these days she should feel grateful for a profound sense of anything at all, however unspecific.

She hauled herself in from the window, left it wide open in spite of the chill of the outside air, padded through into the small bathroom and ran the bath. It was a bath of the sprawling Edwardian type which took up a wonderfully disproportionate amount of the space available, and encompassed most of the rest of the room with cream-painted pipes. The taps seethed. As soon as the room was sufficiently full of steam to be warm, Kate undressed and then went and opened the large bathroom cupboard.

She felt faintly embarrassed by the sheer profusion of things she had for putting in baths, but she was for some reason incapable of passing any chemist or herb shop without going in to be seduced by some glass-stoppered bottle of something blue or green or orange and oily that was supposed to restore the natural balance of some vague substance she didn't even know she was supposed to have in her pores.

She paused, trying to choose.

Something pink? Something with extra Vitamin B? Vitamin B12? B13? Just the number of things with different types of Vitamin B in them was an embarrassment of choice in itself. There were powders as well as oils, tubes of gel, even packets of some kind of pungent smelling seed that was meant to be good for some obscure part of you in some arcane way.

How about some of the green crystals? One day, she had told herself in the past, she would not even bother trying to choose, but would simply put a bit of everything in. When she really felt in need of it. She rather thought that today was the day, and with a sudden reviving rush of pleasure she set about putting a drop or two of everything in the cupboard into the seething bath until it was confused with mingling, muddying colours and verging on the glutinous to touch.

She turned off the taps, went to her handbag for a moment, then returned and lowered herself into the bath, where she lay with her eyes closed, breathing slowly for fully three minutes before at last turning her attention to the scrap of paper she had brought with her from the hospital.

It had one word on it, and it was a word she had dragged out of an oddly reluctant young nurse who had taken her temperature that morning.

Kate had questioned her about the big man. The big man whom she had encountered at the airport, whose body she had seen in a nearby side ward in the early hours of the night.

"Oh no," the nurse had said, "he wasn't dead. He was just in some sort of coma."

Could she see him? Kate had asked. What was his name?

She had tried to ask idly, in passing as it were, which was a difficult trick to pull off with a thermometer in her mouth, and she wasn't at all certain she had succeeded. The nurse had said that she couldn't really say, she wasn't really meant to talk about other patients. And anyway, the man wasn't there any more, he had been taken somewhere else. They had sent an ambulance to collect him and take him somewhere else.

This had taken Kate considerably by surprise.

Where had they taken him? What was this special place? But the nurse had been unwilling to say anything much more, and a second or two later had been summoned away by the Sister. The only word the nurse had said was the one that Kate had then scribbled down on the piece of paper she was now looking at.

The word was "Woodshead".

Now that she was more relaxed she had a feeling that the name was familiar to her in some way, though she could not remember where she had heard it.

The instant she remembered, she could not stay in the bath any longer, but got out and made straight for the telephone, pausing only briefly to shower all the gunk off her.

Chapter 9

The big man awoke and tried to look up, but could hardly raise his head. He tried to sit up but couldn't do that either. He felt as if he'd been stuck to the floor with superglue and after a few seconds he discovered the most astounding reason for this.

He jerked his head up violently, yanking out great tufts of yellow hair which stayed painfully stuck to the floor, and looked around him. He was in what appeared to be a derelict warehouse, probably an upper floor judging by the wintry sky he could see creeping past the grimy, shattered windows.

The ceilings were high and hung with cobwebs built by spiders who did not seem to mind that most of what they caught was crumbling plaster and dust. They were supported by pillars made from upright steel joists on which the dirty old cream paint was bubbled and flaking, and these in turn stood on a floor of battered old oak on to which he had clearly been glued. Extending out for a foot or two in a rough oval all around his naked body the floor glistened darkly and dully. Thin, nostril-cleaning fumes rose from it. He could not believe it. He roared with rage, tried to wriggle and shake himself but succeeded only in tugging painfully at his skin where it was stuck fast to the oak planks.

This had to be the old man's doing.

He threw his head back hard against the floor in a blow that cracked the boards and made his ears sing. He roared again and took some furious satisfaction in making as much hopeless, stupid noise as he could. He roared until the steel pillars rang and the cracked remains of the windows shattered into finer shards. Then, as he threw his head angrily from one side to the other he caught sight of his sledge-hammer leaning against the wall a few feet from him, heaved it up into the air with a word, and sent it hurtling round the great space, beating and clanging on every pillar until the whole building reverberated like a mad gong.

Another word and the hammer flew back at him, missed his head by a hand's-width and punched straight down through the floor, shattering the wood and the plaster below.

In the darker space beneath him the hammer spun, and swung round in a slow heavy parabola as bits of plaster fell about it and rattled on the concrete floor below. Then it gathered a violent momentum and hurtled back up through the ceiling, smacking up a stack of startled splinters as it punched through another oak floorboard a hand's-width from the soles of the big man's feet.

It soared up into the air, hung there for a moment as if its weight had suddenly vanished, then, deftly flicking its short handle up above its head, it drove hard back down through the floor again – then up again, then down again, punching holes in a splintered ring around its master until, with a long heavy groan, the whole oval section of punctured floor gave way and plunged, twisting, through the air. It shattered itself against the floor below amidst a rain of plaster debris, from which the figure of the big man then emerged, staggering, flapping at the dusty air and coughing. His back, his arms and his legs were still covered with great splintered hunks of oak flooring, but at least he was able to move. He leant the flat of his hands against the wall and violently coughed some of the dust from his lungs.

As he turned back, his hammer danced out of the air towards him, then suddenly evaded his grasp and skidded joyfully off across the floor striking sparks from the concrete with its great head, flipped up and parked itself against a nearby pillar at a jaunty angle.

In front of him the shape of a large Coca-Cola vending machine loomed through the settling cloud of dust. He regarded it with the gravest suspicion and worry. It stood there with a sort of glazed, blank look to it, and had a note from his father stuck on the front panel saying whatever he was doing, stop it. It was signed "You-know-who", but this had been crossed out and first the word "Odin" and then in larger letters "Your Father" had been substituted. Odin never ceased to make absolutely clear his view of his son's intellectual accomplishments. The big man tore the note off and stared at it in anger. A postscript added darkly "Remember Wales. You don't want to go through all that again." He screwed the note up and hurled it out of the nearest window, where the wind whipped it up and away. For a moment he thought he heard an odd squeaking noise, but it was probably just the blustering of the wind as it whistled between the nearby derelict buildings.

He turned and walked to the window and stared out of it in a belligerent sulk. Glued to the floor. At his age. What the devil was that supposed to mean? "Keep your head down," was what he guessed. "If you don't keep it down, I'll have to keep it down for you." That was what it meant. "Stick to the ground."

He remembered now the old man saying exactly that to him at the time of all the unpleasantness with the Phantom fighter jet. "Why can't you just stick to the ground?" he had said. He could imagine the old man in his soft-headed benign malice thinking it very funny to make the lesson so literal.

Rage began to rumble menacingly inside him but he pushed it down hard. Very worrying things had recently begun happening when he got angry and he had a bad feeling, looking back at the Coca-Cola vending machine, that another of those very worrying things must have just happened. He stared at it and fretted.

He felt ill.

He had felt ill a lot of late, and he found it impossible to discharge what were left of his godly duties when he felt he was suffering from a sort of continual low-grade flu. He experienced headaches, dizzy spells, guilt and all the sorts of ailments that were featured so often in television advertisements. He even suffered terrifying blackouts whenever the great rage gripped him.

He always used to have such a wonderful time getting angry. Great gusts of marvellous anger would hurl him through life. He felt huge. He felt flooded with power and light and energy. He had always been provided with such wonderful things to get angry about – immense acts of provocation or betrayal, people hiding the Atlantic ocean in his helmet, dropping continents on him or getting drunk and pretending to be trees. Stuff you could really work up a rage about and hit things. In short he had felt good about being a Thunder God. Now suddenly it was headaches, nervous tension, nameless anxieties and guilt. These were new experiences for a god, and not pleasant ones.

"You look ridiculous!"

The voice screeched out and affected Thor like fingernails scratched across a blackboard lodged in the back of his brain. It was a mean voice, a spiteful, jeering voice, a cheap white nylon shirt of a voice, a shiny-trousered pencil moustache of a voice, a voice, in short, which Thor did not like. He reacted very badly to it at the best of times, and was particularly provoked to have to hear it while standing naked in the middle of a decrepit warehouse with large sections of an oak floor still stuck to his back.

He spun round angrily. He wanted to be able to turn round calmly and with crushing dignity, but no such strategy ever worked with this creature, and since he, Thor, would only end up feeling humiliated and ridiculous whatever posture he adopted, he might as well go with one he felt comfortable with.

"Toe Rag!" he roared, yanked his hammer spinning into the air and hurled it with immense, stunning force at the small creature who was squatting complacently in the shadows on top of a small heap of rubble, leaning forward a little.

Toe Rag caught the hammer and placed it neatly on top of the pile of Thor's clothes that lay next to him. He grinned, and allowed a stray shaft of sunlight to glitter on one of his teeth. These things don't happen by accident. Toe Rag had spent some time while Thor was unconscious working out how long it would take him to recover, then industriously moving the pile of rubble to exactly this spot, checking the height and then calculating the exact angle at which to lean. As a provocateur he regarded himself as a professional.

"Did you do this to me?" roared Thor. "Did you – "

Thor searched for any way of saying "glue me to the floor" that didn't sound like "glue me to floor", but eventually the pause got too long and he had to give up.

"– glue me to the floor?" he demanded at last. He wished he hadn't asked such a stupid question.

"Don't even answer that!" he added angrily and wished he hadn't said that either. He stamped his foot and shook the foundations of the building a little just to make the point. He wasn't certain what the point was, but he felt that it had to be made. Some dust settled gently around him.

Toe Rag watched him with his dancing, glittering eyes.

"I merely carry out the instructions given to me by your father," he said in a grotesque parody of obsequiousness.

"It seems to me," said Thor, "that the instructions my father has been giving since you entered his service have been very odd. I think you have some kind of evil grip on him. I don't know what kind of evil grip it is, but it's definitely a grip, and it's definitely..." synonyms failed him "...evil," he concluded.

Toe Rag reacted like an iguana to whom someone had just complained about the wine.

"Me?" he protested. "How can I possibly have a grip on your father? Odin is the greatest of the Gods of Asgard, and I am his devoted servant in all things. Odin says, 'Do this,' and I do it. Odin says, 'Go there,' and I go there. Odin says, 'Go and get my big stupid son out of hospital before he causes any more trouble, and then, I don't know, glue him to the floor or something,' and I do exactly as he asks. I am merely the most humble of functionaries. However small or menial the task, Odin's bidding is what I am there to perform."

Thor was not sufficiently subtle a student of human nature or, for that matter, divine or goblin nature, to be able to argue that this was in fact a very powerful grip to hold over anybody, particularly a fallible and pampered old god. He just knew that it was all wrong.

"Well then," he shouted, "take this message back to my father, Odin. Tell him that I, Thor, the God of Thunder, demand to meet him. And not in his damned hospital either! I'm not going to hang about reading magazines and looking at fruit while he has his bed changed! Tell him that Thor, the God of Thunder, will meet Odin, the Father of the Gods of Asgard, to-night, at the Challenging Hour in the Halls of Asgard!"

"Again?" said Toe Rag, with a sly glance sideways at the Coca-Cola vending machine.

"Er, yes," said Thor. "Yes!" he repeated in a rage. "Again!"

Toe Rag made a tiny sigh, such as one who felt resigned to carrying out the bidding of a temperamental simpleton might make, and said, "Well, I'll tell him. I don't suppose he will be best pleased."

"It is no matter of yours whether he is pleased or not!" shouted Thor, disturbing the foundations of the building once more. "This is between my father and myself! You may think yourself very clever, Toe Rag, and you may think that I am not – "

Toe Rag arched an eyebrow. He had prepared for this moment. He stayed silent and merely let the stray beam of sunlight glint on his dancing eyes. It was a silence of the most profound eloquence.

"I may not know what you're up to, Toe Rag, I may not know a lot of things, but I do know one thing. I know that I am Thor, the God of Thunder, and that I will not be made a fool of by a goblin!"

"Well," said Toe Rag with a light grin, "when you know two things I expect you'll be twice as clever. Remember to put your clothes on before you go out." He gestured casually at the pile beside him and departed.

Chapter 10

The trouble with the sort of shop that sells things like magnifying glasses and penknives is that they tend also to sell all kinds of other fascinating things, like the quite extraordinary device with which Dirk eventually emerged after having been hopelessly unable to decide between the knife with the built-in Philips screwdriver, toothpick and ball-point pen and the one with the 13-tooth gristle saw and the tig-welded rivets.

The magnifying glasses had held him in thrall for a short while, particularly the 25-diopter, high-index, vacuum-deposited, gold-coated glass model with the integral handle and mount and the notchless seal glazing, but then Dirk had happened to catch sight of a small electronic I Ching calculator and he was lost.

He had never before even guessed at the existence of such a thing. And to be able to move from total ignorance of something to total desire for it, and then actually to own the thing all within the space of about forty seconds was, for Dirk, something of an epiphany.

The electronic I Ching calculator was badly made. It had probably been manufactured in whichever of the South-East Asian countries was busy tooling up to do to South Korea what South Korea was busy doing to Japan. Glue technology had obviously not progressed in that country to the point where things could be successfully held together with it. Already the back had half fallen off and needed to be stuck back on with Sellotape.

It was much like an ordinary pocket calculator, except that the LCD screen was a little larger than usual, in order to accommodate the abridged judgements of King Wen on each of the sixty-four hexagrams, and also the commentaries of his son, the Duke of Chou, on each of the lines of each hexagram. These were unusual texts to see marching across the display of a pocket calculator, particularly as they had been translated from the Chinese via the Japanese and seemed to have enjoyed many adventures on the way.

The device also functioned as an ordinary calculator, but only to a limited degree. It could handle any calculation which returned an answer of anything up to "4".

"1 + 1" it could manage ("2"), and "1 + 2" ("3") and "2 + 2" ("4") or "tan 74" ("3.4874145"), but anything above "4" it represented merely as "A Suffusion of Yellow". Dirk was not certain if this was a programming error or an insight beyond his ability to fathom, but he was crazy about it anyway, enough to hand over £20 of ready cash for the thing.

"Thank you, sir," said the proprietor. "It's a nice piece that. I think you'll be happy with it."

"I ab," said Dirk.

"Glad to hear it, sir," replied the proprietor. "Do you know you've broken your nose?"

Dirk looked up from fawning on his new possession.

"Yedth," he said testily, "obf courth I dknow."

The man nodded, satisfied.

"Just that a lot of my customers wouldn't always know about

a thing like that," he explained.

Dirk thanked him tersely and hurried out with his purchase. A few minutes later he took up residence at the small corner table of an Islington café, ordered a small but incredibly strong cup of coffee, and attempted to take stock of his day. A moment's reflection told him that he was almost certainly going to need a small but incredibly strong beer as well, and he attempted to add this to his order.

"A wha?" said the waiter. His hair was very black and filled with brilliantine. He was tall, incredibly fit and too cool to listen to customers or say consonants.

Dirk repeated his order, but what with having the café's music system, a broken nose, and the waiter's insuperable cool to contend with, he eventually found it simpler to write out the order on a napkin with a stub of pencil. The waiter peered at it in an offended manner, and left.

Dirk exchanged a friendly nod with the girl sitting half-reading a book at the next table, who had watched this exchange with sympathy. Then he set about laying out his morning's acquisitions on the table in front of him – the newspaper, the electronic I Ching calculator and the envelope which he had retrieved from behind the gold disc on Geoffrey Anstey's bathroom wall. He then spent a minute or two dabbing at his nose with a handkerchief, and prodding it tenderly to see how much it hurt, which turned out to be quite a lot. He sighed and stuffed the handkerchief back in his pocket.

A few seconds later the waiter returned bearing a herb omelette and a single breadstick. Dirk explained that this wasn't what he had ordered. The waiter shrugged and said that it wasn't his fault.

Dirk had no idea what to say to this, and said so. He was still having a great deal of difficulty speaking. The waiter asked Dirk if he knew that he had broken his nose and Dirk said that yedth, dthagg you berry budge, he did. The waiter said that his friend Neil had once broken his nose and Dirk said that he hobed it hurd like hell, which seemed to draw the conversation to a close. The waiter took the omelette and left, vowing never to return.

When the girl sitting at the next table looked away for a moment, Dirk leaned over and took her coffee. He knew that he was perfectly safe doing this because she would simply not be able to believe that this had happened. He sat sipping at the lukewarm cup and casting his mind back over the day.

He knew that before consulting the I Ching, even an electronic one, he should try and compose his thoughts and allow them to settle calmly.

This was a tough one.

However much he tried to clear his mind and think in a calm and collected way, he was unable to stop Geoffrey Anstey's head revolving incessantly in his mind. It revolved disapprovingly, as if pointing an accusing finger at Dirk. The fact that it did not have an accusing finger with which to point only served to drive the point it was trying to make home all the harder.

Dirk screwed up his eyes and attempted to concentrate instead on the problem of the mysteriously vanished Miss Pearce, but was unable to get much of a grip on it. When she had used to work for him she would often disappear mysteriously for two or three days at a time, but the papers didn't make any kind of fuss about it then. Admittedly, there weren't things exploding around her at the time, at least, not that he was aware of. She had never mentioned anything exploding particularly.

Furthermore, whenever he thought of her face, which he had last seen on the television set in Geoffrey Anstey's house, his thoughts tended instantly to sink towards the head which was busy revolving thirty-three and a third times a minute three floors beneath it. This was not conducive to the calm and contemplative mood he was seeking. Nor was the very loud music on the café's music system.

He sighed, and stared at the electronic I Ching calculator.

If he wanted to get his thoughts into some kind of order then

maybe chronological order would be as good a one as any. He
decided to cast his mind back to the beginning of the day, before
any of these appalling things had happened, or at least, before
they'd happened to him.

First there had been the fridge.

It seemed to him that by comparison with everything else, the
problem of what to do about his fridge had now shrunk to fairly
manageable proportions. It still provoked a discernible twinge of
fear and guilt, but here, he thought, was a problem which he
could face up to with relative calm.

The little book of instructions suggested that he should
simply concentrate "soulfully" on the question which was
"besieging" him, write it down, ponder on it, enjoy the silence,
and then once he had achieved inner harmony and tranquillity he
should push the red button.

There wasn't a red button, but there was a blue button
marked "Red", and this Dirk took to be the one.

He concentrated for a while on the question, then looked
through his pockets for a piece of paper, but was unable to find
one. In the end he wrote his question, "Should I buy a new
fridge?" on a corner of his napkin. Then he took the view that if
he was going to wait until he had achieved inner harmony and
tranquillity he could be there all night, so he went ahead and
pushed the blue button marked "Red" anyway. A symbol flashed
up in a corner of the screen, a hexagram which looked like this:

3 : CHUN

The I Ching calculator then scrolled this text across its tiny

LCD display:

> *"THE JUDGEMENT OF KING WEN:*
> *"Chun Signifies Difficulties At Outset, As Of Blade Of*
> *Grass Pushing Up Against Stone. The Time Is Full Of*
> *Irregularities And Obscurities: Superior Man Will Adjust*
> *His Measures As In Sorting The Threads Of The Warp*
> *And Woof. Firm Correctness Will Bring At Last Success.*
> *Early Advances Should Only Be Made With Caution.*
> *There Will Be Advantage In Appointing Feudal Princes.*
> *"LINE 6 CHANGES:*
> *"THE COMMENTARY OF THE DUKE OF CHOU:*
> *"The Horses And The Chariot Obliged To Retreat.*
> *Streams Of Bloody Tears Will Flow."*

Dirk considered this for a few moments, and then decided
that on balance it appeared to be a vote in favour of getting the
new fridge, which, by a staggering coincidence, was the course
of action which he himself favoured.

There was a pay phone in one of the dark corners where
waiters slouched moodily at one another. Dirk threaded his way
through them, wondering whom it was they reminded him of,
and eventually deciding that it was the small crowd of naked
men standing around behind the Holy Family in Michelangelo's
picture of the same name, for no more apparent reason than that
Michelangelo rather liked them.

He telephoned an acquaintance of his called Nobby Paxton,
or so he claimed, who worked the darker side of the domestic
appliance supply business. Dirk came straight to the point.

"Dobby, I deed a fridge."

"Dirk, I been saving one against the day you'd ask me."

Dirk found this highly unlikely.

"Only I wand a good fridge you thee, Dobby."

"This is the best, Dirk. Japanese. Microprocessor controlled."

"What would a microprothethor be doing id a fridge,
Dobby?"

"Keeping itself cool, Dirk. I'll get the lads to bring it round right away. I need to get it off the premises pretty sharpish for reasons which I won't trouble you with."

"I apprethiade thid, Dobby," said Dirk. "Problem id, I'm not at home at preddent."

"Gaining access to houses in the absence of their owners is only one of the panoply of skills with which my lads are blessed. Let me know if you find anything missing afterwards, by the way."

"I'd be happy to, Dobby. Id fact if your ladth are in a mood for carting thtuff off I'd be glad if they would thtart with my old fridge. It badly needth throwing away."

"I shall see that it's done, Dirk. There's usually a skip or two on your street these days. Now, do you expect to be paying for this or shall I just get you kneecapped straight off, save everybody time and aggravation all round?"

It was never one hundred per cent clear to Dirk exactly when Nobby was joking and he was not keen to put it to the test. He assured him that he would pay him, as soon as next they met.

"See you very soon then, Dirk," said Nobby. "By the way, do you know you sound exactly as if someone's broken your nose?"

There was a pause.

"You there, Dirk?" said Nobby.

"Yed," said Dirk. "I wad judd liddening to a reggord."

"Hot Potato!" roared the hi-fi in the café.

"Don't pick it up, pick it up, pick it up,

"Quick, pass it on, pass it on, pass it on."

"I said, do you know you sound exactly as if someone's broken your nose?" repeated Nobby.

Dirk said that he did know this, thanked Nobby for pointing it out, said goodbye, stood thoughtfully for a moment, made another quick couple of phone calls, and then threaded his way back through the huddle of posing waiters to find the girl whose coffee he had appropriated sitting at his table.

"Hello," she said, meaningfully.

Dirk was as gracious as he knew how.

He bowed to her very politely, doffed his hat, since all this gave him a second or so to recover himself, and requested her permission to sit down.

"Go ahead," she said, "it's your table." She gestured magnanimously.

She was small, her hair was neat and dark, she was in her mid-twenties, and was looking quizzically at the half-empty cup of coffee in the middle of the table.

Dirk sat down opposite her and leant forward conspiratorially. "I expeg," he said in a low voice, "you are enquirigg after your coffee."

"You betcha," said the girl.

"Id very bad for you, you dow."

"Is it?"

"Id id. Caffeide. Cholethderog in the milgg."

"I see, so it was just my health you were thinking of."

"I was thiggigg of meddy thiggs," said Dirk airily.

"You saw me sitting at the next table and you thought, 'There's a nice-looking girl with her health in ruins. Let me save her from herself.'"

"In a nudthell."

"Do you know you've broken your nose?"

"Yeth, of courth I do," said Dirk crossly. "Everybody keepth – "

"How long ago did you break it?" the girl asked.

"Id wad broked for me," said Dirk, "aboud tweddy middidd ago."

"I thought so," said the girl. "Close your eyes for a moment."

Dirk looked at her suspiciously.

"Why?"

"It's all right," she said with a smile, "I'm not going to hurt you. Now close them."

With a puzzled frown, Dirk closed his eyes just for a moment. In that moment the girl reached over and gripped him firmly by the nose, giving it a sharp twist. Dirk nearly exploded with pain and howled so loudly that he almost attracted the attention of a waiter.

"You widge!" he yelled, staggering wildly back from the table clutching his face. "You double-dabbed widge!"

"Oh, be quiet and sit down," she said. "All right, I lied about it not going to hurt you, but at least it should be straight now, which will save you a lot worse later on. You should get straight round to a hospital to have some splints and padding put on. I'm a nurse, I know what I'm doing. Or at least, I think I do. Let's have a look at you."

Panting and spluttering, Dirk sat down once more, his hands cupped round his nose. After a few long seconds he began to prod it tenderly again and then let the girl examine it.

She said, "My name's Sally Mills, by the way. I usually try to introduce myself properly before physical intimacy takes place, but sometimes," she sighed, "there just isn't time."

Dirk ran his fingers up either side of his nose again.

"I thigg id id trader," Dirk said at last.

"Straighter," Sally said. "Say 'straighter' properly. It'll help you feel better. "

"Straighter," said Dirk. "Yed. I thee wad you mead."

"What?"

"I see what you mead."

"Good," she said with a sigh of relief, "I'm glad that worked. My horoscope this morning said that virtually everything I decided today would be wrong."

"Yes, well you don't want to believe all that rubbish," said Dirk sharply.

"I don't," said Sally.

"Particularly not The Great Zaganza."

"Oh, you read it too, did you?"

"No. That is, well, not for the same reason."

"My reason was that a patient asked me to read his horoscope to him this morning just before he died. What was yours?"

"Er, a very complicated one."

"I see," said Sally, sceptically. "What's this?"

"It's a calculator," said Dirk. "Well, look, I mustn't keep you. I am indebted to you, my dear lady, for the tenderness of your ministrations and the loan of your coffee, but lo! the day wears on, and I am sure you have a heavy schedule of grievous bodily harm to attend to."

"Not at all. I came off night duty at nine o'clock this morning, and all I have to do all day is keep awake so that I can sleep normally tonight. I have nothing better to do than to sit around talking to strangers in cafés. You, on the other hand, should get yourself to a casualty department as soon as possible. As soon as you've paid my bill, in fact."

She leant over to the table she had originally been sitting at and picked up the running-total lying by her plate. She looked at it, shaking her head disapprovingly.

"Five cups of coffee, I'm afraid. It was a long night on the wards. All sorts of comings and goings in the middle of it. One patient in a coma who had to be moved to a private hospital in the early hours. God knows why it had to be done at that time of night. Just creates unnecessary trouble. I wouldn't pay for the second croissant if I were you. I ordered it but it never came."

She pushed the bill across to Dirk who picked it up with a reluctant sigh.

"Inordinate," he said, "larcenously inordinate. And, in the circumstances, adding a 15 per cent service charge is tantamount to jeering at you. I bet they won't even bring me a knife."

He turned and tried, without any real hope of success, to summon any of the gaggle of waiters lounging among the sugar bowls at the back.

Sally Mills took her bill and Dirk's and attempted to add them up on Dirk's calculator.

"The total seems to come to 'A Suffusion of Yellow'," she said.

"Thank you, I'll take that," said Dirk turning back crossly

and relieving her of the electronic I Ching set which he put into his pocket. He resumed his hapless waving at the tableau of waiters.

"What do you want a knife for, anyway?" asked Sally.

"To open this," said Dirk, waggling the large, heavily Sellotaped envelope at her.

"I'll get you one," she said. A young man sitting on his own at another nearby table was looking away at that moment, so Sally quickly leaned across and nabbed his knife.

"I am indebted to you," said Dirk and put out his hand to take the knife from her.

She held it away from him.

"What's in the envelope?" she said.

"You are an extremely inquisitive and presumptuous young lady," exclaimed Dirk.

"And you," said Sally Mills, "are very strange."

"Only," said Dirk, "as strange as I need to be."

"Humph," said Sally. "What's in the envelope?" She still wouldn't give him the knife.

"The envelope is not yours," proclaimed Dirk, "and its contents are not your concern."

"It looks very interesting though. What's in it?"

"Well, I won't know till I've opened it!"

She looked at him suspiciously, then snatched the envelope from him.

"I insist that you – " expostulated Dirk, incompletely.

"What's your name?" demanded Sally.

"My name is Gently. Mr Dirk Gently."

"And not Geoffrey Anstey, or any of these other names that have been crossed out?" She frowned, briefly, looking at them.

"No," said Dirk. "Certainly not."

"So you mean the envelope is not yours either?"

"I – that is – "

"Aha! So you are also being extremely…what was it?"

"Inquisitive and presumptuous. I do not deny it. But I am a

private detective. I am paid to be inquisitive and presumptuous. Not as often or copiously as I would wish, but I am nevertheless inquisitive and presumptuous on a professional basis."

"How sad. I think it's much more fun being inquisitive and presumptuous as a hobby. So you are a professional while I am merely an amateur of Olympic standard. You don't look like a private detective."

"No private detective looks like a private detective. That's one of the first rules of private detection."

"But if no private detective looks like a private detective, how does a private detective know what it is he's supposed not to look like? Seems to me there's a problem there."

"Yes, but it's not one that keeps me awake at nights," said Dirk in exasperation. "Anyway, I am not as other private detectives. My methods are holistic and, in a very proper sense of the word, chaotic. I operate by investigating the fundamental interconnectedness of all things."

Sally Mills merely blinked at him.

"Every particle in the universe," continued Dirk, warming to his subject and beginning to stare a bit, "affects every other particle, however faintly or obliquely. Everything interconnects with everything. The beating of a butterfly's wings in China can affect the course of an Atlantic hurricane. If I could interrogate this table-leg in a way that made sense to me, or to the table-leg, then it could provide me with the answer to any question about the universe. I could ask anybody I liked, chosen entirely by chance, any random question I cared to think of, and their answer, or lack of it, would in some way bear upon the problem to which I am seeking a solution. It is only a question of knowing how to interpret it. Even you, whom I have met entirely by chance, probably know things that are vital to my investigation, if only I knew what to ask you, which I don't, and if only I could be bothered to, which I can't."

He paused, and said, "Please will you let me have the envelope and the knife?"

"You make it sound as if someone's life depends on it."

Dirk dropped his eyes for a moment.

"I rather think somebody's life did depend on it," he said. He said it in such a way that a cloud seemed to pass briefly over them.

Sally Mills relented and passed the envelope and the knife over to Dirk. A spark seemed to go out of her.

The knife was too blunt and the Sellotape too thickly applied. Dirk struggled with it for a few seconds but was unable to slice through it. He sat back in his seat feeling tired and irritable.

He said, "I'll go and ask them if they've got anything sharper," and stood up, clutching the envelope.

"You should go and get your nose fixed," said Sally Mills quietly.

"Thank you," said Dirk and bowed very slightly to her.

He picked up the bills and set out to visit the exhibition of waiters mounted at the rear of the café. He encountered a certain coolness when he was disinclined to augment the mandatory 15 per cent service charge with any voluntary additional token of his personal appreciation, and was told that no, that was the only type of knife they had and that's all there was to it.

Dirk thanked them and walked back through the café.

Sitting in his seat talking to Sally Mills was the young man whose knife she had purloined. He nodded to her, but she was deeply engrossed in conversation with her new friend and did not notice.

"...in a coma," she was saying, "who had to be moved to a private hospital in the early hours. God knows why it had to be done at that time of night. Just creates unnecessary trouble. Excuse me rabbiting on, but the patient had his own personal Coca-Cola machine and sledge-hammer with him, and that sort of thing is all very well in a private hospital, but on a short-staffed NHS ward it just makes me tired, and I talk too much when I'm tired. If I suddenly fall insensible to the floor, would you let me know?"

Dirk walked on, and then noticed that Sally Mills had left the book she had been reading on her original table, and something about it caught his attention.

It was a large book, called *Run Like the Devil*. In fact it was extremely large and a little dog-eared, looking more like a puff pastry cliff than a book. The bottom half of the cover featured the normal woman-in-cocktail-dress-framed-in-the-sights-of-a-gun, while the top half was entirely taken up with the author's name, Howard Bell, embossed in silver.

Dirk couldn't immediately work out what it was about the book that had caught his eye, but he knew that some detail of the cover had struck a chord with him somewhere. He gave a circumspect glance at the girl whose coffee he had purloined, and whose five coffees and two croissants, one undelivered and uneaten, he had subsequently paid for. She wasn't looking, so he purloined her book as well and slipped it into the pocket of his leather coat.

He stepped out on to the street, where a passing eagle swooped out of the sky at him, nearly forcing him into the path of a cyclist, who cursed and swore at him from a moral high ground that cyclists alone seem able to inhabit.

Chapter 11

Into the well-kempt grounds that lay just on the outskirts of a well-kempt village on the fringes of the well-kempt Cotswolds turned a less than well-kempt car.

It was a battered yellow Citroën 2CV which had had one careful owner but also three suicidally reckless ones. It made its way up the driveway with a reluctant air as if all it asked for from life was to be tipped into a restful ditch in one of the adjoining meadows and there allowed to settle in graceful abandonment, instead of which here it was being asked to drag itself all the way up this long gravelled drive which it would no doubt soon be called upon to drag itself all the way back down again, to what possible purpose it was beyond its wit to imagine.

It drew to a halt in front of the elegant stone entrance to the main building, and then began to trundle slowly backwards again until its occupant yanked on the handbrake, which evoked from the car a sort of strangled "eek".

A door flopped open, wobbling perilously on its one remaining hinge, and there emerged from the car a pair of the sort of legs which soundtrack editors are unable to see without needing to slap a smoky saxophone solo all over, for reasons which no one besides soundtrack editors has ever been able to understand. In this particular case, however, the saxophone would have been silenced by the proximity of the kazoo which the same soundtrack editor would almost certainly have slapped all over the progress of the vehicle.

The owner of the legs followed them in the usual manner, closed the car door tenderly, and then made her way into the building.

The car remained parked in front of it.

After a few minutes a porter came out and examined it, adopted a disapproving manner and then, for lack of anything more positive to do, went back in.

A short time later, Kate was shown into the office of Mr Ralph Standish, the Chief Consultant Psychologist and one of the directors of the Woodshead Hospital, who was just completing a telephone conversation.

"Yes, it is true," he was saying, "that sometimes unusually intelligent and sensitive children can appear to be stupid. But, Mrs Benson, stupid children can sometimes appear to be stupid as well. I think that's something you might have to consider. I know it's very painful, yes. Good day, Mrs Benson."

He put the phone away into a desk drawer and spent a couple of seconds collecting his thoughts before looking up.

"This is very short notice, Miss, er, Schechter," he said to her at last.

In fact what he had said was, "This is very short notice, Miss, er –" and then he had paused and peered into another of his desk drawers before saying "Schechter".

It seemed to Kate that it was very odd to keep your visitors' names in a drawer, but then he clearly disliked having things cluttering up his fine, but severely designed, black ash desk because there was nothing on it at all. It was completely blank, as was every other surface in his office. There was nothing on the small neat steel and glass coffee table which sat squarely between two Barcelona chairs. There was nothing on top of the two expensive-looking filing cabinets which stood at the back of the room.

There were no bookshelves – if there were any books they were presumably hidden away behind the white doors of the large blank built-in cupboards – and although there was one plain black picture frame hanging on the wall, this was presumably a temporary aberration because there was no picture in it.

Kate looked around her with a bemused air.

"Do you have no ornaments in here at all, Mr Standish?" she asked.

He was, for a moment, somewhat taken aback by her transatlantic directness, but then answered her.

"Indeed I have ornaments," he said, and pulled open another drawer. He pulled out from this a small china model of a kitten playing with a ball of wool and put it firmly on the desk in front of him.

"As a psychologist I am aware of the important role that ornamentation plays in nourishing the human spirit," he pronounced.

He put the china kitten back in the drawer and slid it closed with a smooth click.

"Now."

He clasped his hands together on the desk in front of him, and looked at her enquiringly.

"It's very good of you to see me at short notice, Mr Standish – "

"Yes, yes, we've established that."

"– but I'm sure you know what newspaper deadlines are like."

"I know at least as much as I would ever care to know about newspapers, Miss, er – "

He opened his drawer again.

"Miss Schechter, but – "

"Well that's partly what made me approach you," lied Kate charmingly. "I know that you have suffered from some, well, unfortunate publicity here, and thought you might welcome the opportunity to talk about some of the more enlightening aspects of the work at the Woodshead Hospital." She smiled very sweetly.

"It's only because you come to me with the highest recommendation from my very good friend and colleague Mr, er – "

"Franklin, Alan Franklin," prompted Kate, to save the psychologist from having to open his drawer again. Alan Franklin was a therapist whom Kate had seen for a few sessions after the loss of her husband Luke. He had warned her that Standish, though brilliant, was also peculiar, even by the high standards set by his profession.

"Franklin," resumed Standish, "that I agreed to see you. Let me warn you instantly that if I see any resumption of this 'Something nasty in the Woodshead' mendacity appearing in the papers as a result of this interview I will, I will – "

"'– do such things –

'What they are yet I know not – but they shall be

'The terror of the Earth'," said Kate, brightly.

Standish narrowed his eyes.

"*Lear*, Act 2, Scene 4," he said. "And I think you'll find it's 'terrors' and not 'terror'."

"Do you know, I think you're right?" replied Kate.

Thank you, Alan, she thought. She smiled at Standish, who relaxed into pleased superiority. It was odd, Kate reflected, that people who needed to bully you were the easiest to push around.

"So you would like to know precisely what, Miss Schechter?"

"Assume," said Kate, "that I know nothing."

Standish smiled, as if to signify that no assumption could possibly give him greater pleasure.

"Very well," he said. "The Woodshead is a research hospital. We specialise in the care and study of patients with unusual or previously unknown conditions, largely in the psychological or psychiatric fields. Funds are raised in various ways. One of our chief methods is quite simply to take in private patients at exorbitantly high fees, which they are happy to pay, or at least happy to complain about. There is in fact nothing to complain about because patients who come to us privately are made fully aware of why our fees are so high. For the money they are paying, they are, of course, perfectly entitled to complain – the right to complain is one of the privileges they are paying for. In some cases we come to a special arrangement under which, in return for being made the sole beneficiaries of a patient's estate, we will guarantee to look after that patient for the rest of his or her life."

"So in effect you are in the business of giving scholarships to people with particularly gifted diseases?"

"Exactly. A very good way of expressing it. We are in the business of giving scholarships to people with particularly gifted diseases. I must make a note of that. Miss Mayhew!"

He had opened a drawer, which clearly contained his office intercom. In response to his summons one of the cupboards opened, and turned out to be a door into a side office – a feature which must have appealed to some architect who had conceived an ideological dislike of doors. From this office there emerged obediently a thin and rather blank-faced woman in her mid-forties.

"Miss Mayhew," said Mr Standish, "we are in the business of giving scholarships to people with particularly gifted diseases."

"Very good, Mr Standish," said Miss Mayhew, and retreated backwards into her office, pulling the door closed after her. Kate wondered if it was perhaps a cupboard after all.

"And we do have some patients with some really quite outstanding diseases at the moment," enthused the psychologist. "Perhaps you would care to come and see one or two of our current stars?"

"Indeed I would. That would be most interesting, Mr

Standish, you're very kind," said Kate.

"You have to be kind in this job," Standish replied, and flicked a smile on and off at her.

Kate was trying to keep some of the impatience she was feeling out of her manner. She did not take to Mr Standish, and was beginning to feel that there was a kind of Martian quality to him. Furthermore, the only thing she was actually interested in was discovering whether or not the hospital had accepted a new admission in the early hours of the morning, and if so, where he was and whether she could see him.

She had originally tried the direct approach but had been rebuffed by a mere telephone receptionist on the grounds that she didn't have a name to ask for. Simply asking if they had any tall, well-built, blond men in residence had seemed to create entirely the wrong impression. At least, she insisted to herself that it was entirely the wrong impression. A quick phone call to Alan Franklin had set her up for this altogether more subtle approach.

"Good!" A look of doubt passed momentarily over Mr Standish's face, and he summoned Miss Mayhew from out of her cupboard again.

"Miss Mayhew, that last thing I just said to you – "

"Yes, Mr Standish?"

"I assume you realised that I wished you to make a note of it for me?"

"No, Mr Standish, but I will be happy to do so."

"Thank you," said Mr Standish with a slightly tense look. "And tidy up in here please. The place looks a – "

He wanted to say that the place looked a mess, but was frustrated by its air of clinical sterility.

"Just tidy up generally," he concluded.

"Yes, Mr Standish."

The psychologist nodded tersely, brushed a non-existent speck of dust off the top of his desk, flicked another brief smile on and off at Kate and then escorted her out of his office into the corridor which was immaculately laid with the sort of beige carpet which gave everyone who walked on it electric shocks.

"Here, you see," said Standish, indicating part of the wall they were walking past with an idle wave of his hand, but not making it in any way clear what it was he wished her to see or what she was supposed to understand from it.

"And this," he said, apparently pointing at a door hinge.

"Ah," he added, as the door swung open towards them. Kate was alarmed to find herself giving a little expectant start every time a door opened anywhere in this place. This was not the sort of behaviour she expected of a worldly-wise New Yorker journalist, even if she didn't actually live in New York and only wrote travel articles for magazines. It still was not right for her to be looking for large blond men every time a door opened.

There was no large blond man. There was instead a small, sandy-haired girl of about ten years old, being pushed along in a wheelchair. She seemed very pale, sick and withdrawn, and was murmuring something soundlessly to herself. Whatever it was she was murmuring seemed to cause her worry and agitation, and she would flop this way then that in her chair as if trying to escape from the words coming out of her mouth. Kate was instantly moved by the sight of her, and on an impulse asked the nurse who was pushing her along to stop.

She squatted down to look kindly into the girl's face, which seemed to please the nurse a little, but Mr Standish less so.

Kate did not try to demand the girl's attention, merely gave her an open and friendly smile to see if she wanted to respond, but the girl seemed unwilling or unable to. Her mouth worked away endlessly, appearing almost to lead an existence that was independent of the rest of her face.

Now that Kate looked at her more closely it seemed that she looked not so much sick and withdrawn as weary, harassed and unutterably fed up. She needed a little rest, she needed peace, but her mouth kept motoring on.

For a fleeting instant her eyes caught Kate's, and the message

Kate received was along the lines of "I'm sorry but you'll just have to excuse me while all this is going on". The girl took a deep breath, half-closed her eyes in resignation and continued her relentless silent murmuring.

Kate leant forward a little in an attempt to catch any actual words, but she couldn't make anything out. She shot an enquiring look up at Standish.

He said, simply, "Stock market prices."

A look of amazement crept over Kate's face.

Standish added with a wry shrug, "Yesterday's, I'm afraid."

Kate flinched at having her reaction so wildly misinterpreted, and hurriedly looked back at the girl in order to cover her confusion.

"You mean," she said, rather redundantly, "she's just sitting here reciting yesterday's stock market prices?" The girl rolled her eyes past Kate's.

"Yes," said Standish. "It took a lip reader to work out what was going on. We all got rather excited, of course, but then closer examination revealed that they were only yesterday's which was a bit of a disappointment. Not that significant a case really. Aberrant behaviour. Interesting to know why she does it, but – "

"Hold on a moment," said Kate, trying to sound very interested rather than absolutely horrified, "are you saying that she is reciting – what? – the closing prices over and over, or – "

"No. That's an interesting feature of course. She pretty much keeps pace with movements in the market over the course of a whole day. Just twenty-four hours out of step."

"But that's extraordinary, isn't it?"

"Oh yes. Quite a feat."

"A *feat*?"

"Well, as a scientist, I have to take the view that since the information is freely available, she is acquiring it through normal channels. There's no necessity in this case to invent any supernatural or paranormal dimension. Occam's razor.

Shouldn't needlessly multiply entities."

"But has anyone seen her studying the newspapers, or copying stuff down over the phone?"

She looked up at the nurse, who shook her head, dumbly.

"No, never actually caught her at it," said Standish. "As I said, it's quite a feat. I'm sure a stage magician or memory man could tell you how it was done."

"Have you asked one?"

"No. Don't hold with such people."

"But do you really think that she could possibly be doing this deliberately?" insisted Kate.

"Believe me, if you understood as much about people as I do, Miss, er – you would believe anything," said Standish, in his most professionally reassuring tone of voice.

Kate stared into the tired, wretched face of the young girl and said nothing.

"You have to understand," said Standish, "that we have to be rational about this. If it was tomorrow's stock market prices, it would be a different story. That would be a phenomenon of an entirely different character which would merit and demand the most rigorous study. And I'm sure we'd have no difficulty in funding the research. There would be absolutely no problem about that."

"I see," said Kate, and meant it.

She stood up, a little stiffly, and brushed down her skirt.

"So," she said, and felt ashamed of herself, "who is your newest patient? Who has arrived most recently, then?" She shuddered at the crassness of the *non sequitur*, but reminded herself that she was there as a journalist, so it would not seem odd.

Standish waved the nurse and the wheelchair with its sad charge on their way. Kate glanced back at the girl once, and then followed Standish through the swing-doors and into the next section of corridor, which was identical to the previous one.

"Here, you see," said Standish again, this time apparently in relation to a window frame.

"And this," he said, pointing at a light.

He had obviously either not heard her question or was deliberately ignoring it. Perhaps, thought Kate, he was simply treating it with the contempt it deserved.

It suddenly dawned on her what all this *Here you see*, and *And this*ing was about. He was asking her to admire the quality of the decor. The windows were sashes, with finely made and beautifully painted beads; the light fittings were of a heavy dull metal, probably nickel-plated – and so on.

"Very fine," she said accommodatingly, and then noticed that this had sounded an odd thing to say in her American accent.

"Nice place you've got here," she added, thinking that that would please him.

It did. He allowed himself a subdued beam of pleasure.

"We like to think of it as a quality caring environment," he said.

"You must get a lot of people wanting to come here," Kate continued, plugging away at her theme. "How often do you admit new patients? When was the last –?"

With her left hand she carefully restrained her right hand which wanted to strangle her at this moment.

A door they were passing was slightly ajar, and she tried, unobtrusively, to look in.

"Very well, we'll take a look in here," said Standish immediately, pushing the door fully open, on what transpired to be quite a small room.

"Ah yes," Standish said, recognising the occupant. He ushered Kate in.

The occupant of the room was another non-large, non-blond person. Kate was beginning to find the whole visit to be something of an emotionally wearing experience, and she had a feeling that things were not about to ease up in that respect.

The man sitting in the bedside chair while his bed was being made up by a hospital orderly was one of the most deeply and disturbingly tousled people that Kate had ever seen. In fact it was only his hair that was tousled, but it was tousled to such an extreme degree that it seemed to draw all of his long face up into its distressed chaos.

He seemed quite content to sit where he was, but there was something tremendously vacant about his contentedness – he seemed literally to be content about nothing. There was a completely empty space hanging in the air about eighteen inches in front of his face, and his contentedness, if it sprang from anything, sprang from staring at that.

There was also a sense that he was waiting for something. Whether it was something that was about to happen at any moment, or something that was going to happen later in the week, or even something that was going to happen some little while after hell iced over and British Telecom got the phones fixed was by no means apparent because it seemed to be all the same to him. If it happened he was ready for it and if it didn't – he was content.

Kate found such contentedness almost unbearably distressing.

"What's the matter with him?" she said quietly, and then instantly realised that she was talking as if he wasn't there when he could probably speak perfectly well for himself. Indeed, at that moment, he suddenly did speak.

"Oh, er, hi," he said. "OK, yeah, thank you."

"Er, hello," she said, in response, though it didn't seem quite to fit. Or rather, what he had said didn't seem quite to fit. Standish made a gesture to her to discourage her from speaking.

"Er, yeah, a bagel would be fine," said the contented man. He said it in a flat kind of tone, as if merely repeating something he had been given to say.

"Yeah, and maybe some juice," he added. "OK, thanks." He then relaxed into his state of empty watchfulness.

"A very unusual condition," said Standish, "that is to say, we can only believe that it is entirely unique. I've certainly never heard of anything remotely like it. It has also proved virtually impossible to verify beyond question that it is what it appears to be, so I'm glad to say that we have been spared the embarrassment of attempting to give the condition a name."

"Would you like me to help Mr Elwes back to bed?" asked the orderly of Standish. Standish nodded. He didn't bother to waste words on minions.

The orderly bent down to talk to the patient.

"Mr Elwes?" he said quietly.

Mr Elwes seemed to swim up out of a reverie.

"Mmmm?" he said, and suddenly looked around. He seemed confused.

"Oh! Oh? What?" he said faintly.

"Would you like me to help you back to bed?"

"Oh. Oh, thank you, yes. Yes, that would be kind."

Though clearly dazed and bewildered, Mr Elwes was quite able to get himself back into bed, and all the orderly needed to supply was reassurance and encouragement. Once Mr Elwes was well settled, the orderly nodded politely to Standish and Kate and made his exit.

Mr Elwes quickly lapsed back into his trancelike state, lying propped up against an escarpment of pillows. His head dropped forward slightly and he stared at one of his knees, poking up bonily from under the covers.

"Get me New York," he said.

Kate shot a puzzled glance at Standish, hoping for some kind of explanation, but got none.

"Oh, OK," said Mr Elwes, "it's 541 something. Hold on." He spoke another four digits of a number in his dead, flat voice.

"What is happening here?" asked Kate at last.

"It took us rather a long time to work it out. It was only quite by the remotest chance that someone discovered it. That television was on in the room…"

He pointed to the small portable set off to one side of the bed.

"…tuned to one of those chat programme things, which happened to be going out live. Most extraordinary thing. Mr

Elwes was sitting here muttering about how much he hated the BBC – don't know if it was the BBC, perhaps it was one of those other channels they have now – and was expressing an opinion about the host of the programme, to the effect that he considered him to be a rectum of some kind, and saying furthermore that he wished the whole thing was over and that, yes, all right he was coming, and then suddenly what he was saying and what was on the television began in some extraordinary way almost to synchronise."

"I don't understand what you mean," said Kate.

"I'd be surprised if you did," said Standish. "Everything that Elwes said was then said just a moment later on the television by a gentleman by the name of Mr Dustin Hoffman. It seems that Mr Elwes here knows everything that this Mr Hoffman is going to say just a second or so before he says it. It is not, I have to say, something that Mr Hoffman would be very pleased about if he knew. Attempts have been made to alert the gentleman to the problem, but he has proved to be somewhat difficult to reach."

"Just what the shit is going on here?" asked Mr Elwes placidly.

"Mr Hoffman is, we believe, currently making a film on location somewhere on the west coast of America."

He looked at his watch.

"I think he has probably just woken up in his hotel and is making his early morning phone calls," he added.

Kate was gazing with astonishment between Standish and the extraordinary Mr Elwes.

"How long has the poor man been like this?"

"Oh, about five years I think. Started absolutely out of the blue. He was sitting having dinner with his family one day as usual when suddenly he started complaining about his caravan. And then shortly afterwards about how he was being shot. He then spent the entire night talking in his sleep, repeating the same apparently meaningless phrases over and over again and also saying that he didn't think much of the way they were written. It was a very trying time for his family, as you can imagine, living with such a perfectionist actor and not even realising it. It now seems very surprising how long it took them to identify what was occurring. Particularly when he once woke them all up in the early hours of the morning to thank them and the producer and the director for his Oscar."

Kate, who didn't realise that the day was still only softening her up for what was to come, made the mistake of thinking that it had just reached a climax of shock.

"The poor man," she said in a hushed voice. "What a pathetic state to be in. He's just living as someone else's shadow."

"I don't think he's in any pain."

Mr Elwes appeared to be quietly locked in a bitter argument which seemed to touch on the definitions of the words "points", "gross", "profits" and "limo".

"But the implications of this are *extraordinary* aren't they?" said Kate. "He's actually saying these things moments *before* Dustin Hoffman?"

"Well, it's all conjecture of course. We've only got a few clear instances of absolute correlation and we just haven't got the opportunity to do more thorough research. One has to recognise that those few instances of direct correlation were not rigorously documented and could more simply be explained as coincidence. The rest could be merely the product of an elaborate fantasy."

"But if you put this case next to that of the girl we just saw..."

"Ah, well we can't do that you see. We have to judge each case on its own merits."

"But they're both in the same world..."

"Yes, but there are separate issues. Obviously, if Mr Elwes here could demonstrate significant precognition of, for instance, the head of the Soviet Union or, better still, the President of the United States, then clearly there would be important defence issues involved and one might be prepared to stretch a point on the question of what is and what is not coincidence and fantasy, but for a mere screen actor – that is, a screen actor with no apparent designs on political office – I think that, no, we have to stick to the principles of rigorous science.

"So," he added, turning to leave, and drawing Kate with him, "I think that in the cases of both Mr Elwes and, er, what-was-her-name, the charming girl in the wheelchair, it may be that we are not able to be of much more help to them, and we may need the space and facilities for more deserving cases."

Kate could think of nothing to say to this and followed, seething dumbly.

"Ah, now here we have an altogether much more interesting and promising case," said Standish, forging on ahead through the next set of double doors.

Kate was trying to keep her reactions under control, but nevertheless even someone as glassy and Martian as Mr Standish could not help but detect that his audience was not absolutely with him. A little extra brusqueness and impatience crept into his demeanour, to join forces with the large quantities of brusqueness and impatience which were already there.

They paced down the corridor for a few seconds in silence. Kate was looking for other ways of casually introducing the subject of recent admissions, but was forced to concede to herself that you cannot attempt to introduce the same subject three times in a row without beginning to lose that vital quality of casualness. She glanced as surreptitiously as she could at each door they passed, but most were firmly closed, and the ones that were not revealed nothing of interest.

She glanced out of a window as they walked past it and noticed a van turning into a rear courtyard. It caught her attention in the brief instant that it was within her view because it very clearly wasn't a baker's van or a laundry van. Baker's vans and laundry vans advertise their business and have words like "Bakery" and "Laundry" painted on them, whereas this van was completely blank. It had absolutely nothing to say to anyone and it said it loudly and distinctly.

It was a large, heavy, serious-looking van that was almost on the verge of being an actual lorry, and it was painted in a uniform dark metallic grey. It reminded Kate of the huge gun-metal-grey freight lorries which thunder through Bulgaria and Yugoslavia on their way from Albania with nothing but the word "Albania" stencilled on their sides. She remembered wondering what it was that the Albanians exported in such an anonymous way, but when on one occasion she had looked it up, she found that their only export was electricity – which, if she remembered her high school physics correctly, was unlikely to be moved around in lorries.

The large, serious-looking van turned and started to reverse towards a rear entrance to the hospital. Whatever it was that the van usually carried, Kate thought, it was about either to pick it up or deliver it. She moved on.

A few moments later Standish arrived at a door, knocked at it gently and looked enquiringly into the room within. He then beckoned to Kate to follow him in.

This was a room of an altogether different sort. Immediately within the door was an ante-room with a very large window through which the main room could be seen. The two rooms were clearly sound-proofed from each other, because the ante-room was decked out with monitoring equipment and computers, not one of which but didn't hum loudly to itself, and the main room contained a woman lying in bed, asleep.

"Mrs Elspeth May," said Standish, and clearly felt that he was introducing the top of the bill. Her room was obviously a very good one – spacious and furnished comfortably and expensively. Fresh flowers stood on every surface, and the bedside table on which Mrs May's knitting lay was of mahogany.

She herself was a comfortably shaped, silver-haired lady of late middle age, and she was lying asleep half propped up in bed on a pile of pillows, wearing a pink woolly cardigan. After a moment it became clear to Kate that though she was asleep she was by no means inactive. Her head lay back peacefully with her eyes closed, but her right hand was clutching a pen which was scribbling away furiously on a large pad of paper which lay beside her. The hand, like the wheelchair girl's mouth, seemed to lead an independent and feverishly busy existence. Some small pinkish electrodes were taped to Mrs May's forehead just below her hairline, and Kate assumed that these were providing some of the readings which danced across the computer screens in the ante-room in which she and Standish stood. Two white-coated men and a woman sat monitoring the equipment, and a nurse stood watching through the window. Standish exchanged a couple of brief words with them on the current state of the patient, which was universally agreed to be excellent.

Kate could not escape the impression that she ought to know who Mrs May was, but she didn't and was forced to ask.

"She is a medium," said Standish a little crossly, "as I assumed you would know. A medium of prodigious powers. She is currently in a trance and engaged in automatic writing. She is taking dictation. Virtually every piece of dictation she receives is of inestimable value. You have not heard of her?"

Kate admitted that she had not.

"Well, you are no doubt familiar with the lady who claimed that Mozart, Beethoven and Schubert were dictating music to her?"

"Yes, I did hear about that. There was a lot of stuff in colour supplements about her a few years ago."

"Her claims were, well, interesting, if that's the sort of thing you're interested in. The music was certainly more consistent with what might be produced by each of those gentlemen quickly and before breakfast, than it was with what you would expect from a musically unskilled middle-aged housewife."

Kate could not let this pomposity pass.

"That's a rather sexist viewpoint," she said, "George Eliot was a middle-aged housewife."

"Yes, yes," said Standish testily, "but she wasn't taking

musical dictation from the deceased Wolfgang Amadeus. That's the point I'm making. Please try and follow the logic of this argument and do not introduce irrelevancies. If I felt for a moment that the example of George Eliot could shed any light on our present problem, you could rely on me to introduce it myself.

"Where was I?"

"I don't know."

"Mabel. Doris? Was that her name? Let us call her Mabel. The point is that the easiest way of dealing with the Doris problem was simply to ignore it. Nothing very important hinged on it at all. A few concerts. Second rate material. But here, here we have something of an altogether different nature."

He said this last in hushed tones and turned to study a TV monitor which stood among the bank of computer screens. It showed a close-up of Mrs May's hand scuttling across her pad of paper. Her hand largely obscured what she had written, but it appeared to be mathematics of some kind.

"Mrs May is, or so she claims, taking dictation from some of the greatest physicists. From Einstein and from Heisenberg and Planck. And it is very hard to dispute her claims, because the information being produced here, by automatic writing, by this...untutored lady, is in fact physics of a very profound order.

"From the late Einstein we are getting more and more refinements to our picture of how time and space work at a macroscopic level, and from the late Heisenberg and Planck we are increasing our understanding of the fundamental structures of matter at a quantum level. And there is absolutely no doubt that this information is edging us closer and closer towards the elusive goal of a Grand Unified Field Theory of Everything.

"Now this produces a very interesting, not to say somewhat embarrassing situation for scientists because the means by which the information is reaching us seems to be completely contrary to the meaning of the information."

"It's like Uncle Henry," said Kate, suddenly.

Standish looked at her blankly.

"Uncle Henry thinks he's a chicken," Kate explained.

Standish looked at her blankly again.

"You must have heard it," said Kate. "'We're terribly worried about Uncle Henry. He thinks he's a chicken.' 'Well, why don't you send him to the doctor?' 'Well, we would only we need the eggs.'"

Standish stared at her as if a small but perfectly formed elderberry tree had suddenly sprung unbidden from the bridge of her nose.

"Say that again," he said in a small, shocked voice.

"What, all of it?"

"All of it."

Kate stuck her fist on her hip and said it again, doing the voices with a bit more dash and Southern accents this time.

"That's brilliant," Standish breathed when she had done.

"You must have heard it before," she said, a little surprised by this response. "It's an old joke."

"No," he said, "I have not. We need the eggs. We need the *eggs*. We *need* the eggs. 'We can't send him to the doctor because *we need the eggs*.' An astounding insight into the central paradoxes of the human condition and of our indefatigable facility for constructing adaptive rationales to account for it. Good God."

Kate shrugged.

"And you say this is a *joke*?" demanded Standish incredulously.

"Yes. It's very old, really."

"And are they all like that? I never realised."

"Well – "

"I'm astounded," said Standish, "utterly astounded. I thought that jokes were things that fat people said on television and I never listened to them. I feel that people have been keeping something from me. Nurse!"

The nurse who had been keeping watch on Mrs May through

the window jumped at being barked at unexpectedly like this.

"Er, yes, Mr Standish?" she said. He clearly made her nervous.

"Why have you never told me any jokes?"

The nurse stared at him, and quivered at the impossibility of even knowing how to think about answering such a question.

"Er, well..."

"Make a note of it will you? In future I will require you and all the other staff in this hospital to tell me all the jokes you have at your disposal, is that understood?"

"Er, yes, Mr Standish – "

Standish looked at her with doubt and suspicion.

"You do know some jokes do you, nurse?" he challenged her.

"Er, yes, Mr Standish, I think, yes I do."

"Tell me one."

"What, er, now, Mr Standish?"

"This instant."

"Er, well, um – there's one which is that a patient wakes up after having, well, that is, he's been to, er, to surgery, and he wakes up and, it's not very good, but anyway, he's been to surgery and he says to the doctor when he wakes up, 'Doctor, doctor, what's wrong with me, I can't feel my legs.' And the doctor says, 'Yes, I'm afraid we've had to amputate both your arms.' And that's it really. Er, that's why he couldn't feel his legs, you see."

Mr Standish looked at her levelly for a moment or two.

"You're on report, nurse," he said.

"Yes, Mr Standish."

He turned to Kate.

"Isn't there one about a chicken crossing a road or some such thing?"

"Er, yes," said Kate, doubtfully. She felt she was caught in a bit of a situation here.

"And how does that go?"

"Well," said Kate, "it goes 'Why did the chicken cross the road?'"

"Yes? And?"

"And the answer is 'To get to the other side'."

"I see." Standish considered things for a moment. "And what does this chicken do when it arrives at the other side of the road?"

"History does not relate," replied Kate promptly. "I think that falls outside the scope of the joke, which really only concerns itself with the journey of the chicken across the road and the chicken's reasons for making it. It's a little like a Japanese *haiku* in that respect."

Kate suddenly found she was enjoying herself. She managed a surreptitious wink at the nurse, who had no idea what to make of anything at all.

"I see," said Standish once again, and frowned. "And do these, er, jokes require the preparatory use of any form of artificial stimulant?"

"Depends on the joke, depends on who it's being told to."

"Hmm, well I must say, you've certainly opened up a rich furrow for me, Miss, er. It seems to me that the whole field of humour could benefit from close and immediate scrutiny. Clearly we need to sort out the jokes which have any kind of genuine psychological value from those which merely encourage drug abuse and should be stopped. Good."

He turned to address the white-coated researcher who was studying the TV monitor on which Mrs May's scribblings were being tracked.

"Anything fresh of value from Mr Einstein?" he asked.

The researcher did not move his eyes from the screen. He replied, "It says 'How would you like your eggs? Poached or boiled?'"

Again, Standish paused.

"Interesting," he said, "very interesting. Continue to make a careful note of everything she writes. Come." This last he said to

Kate, and made his way out of the room.

"Very strange people, physicists," he said as soon as they were outside again. "In my experience the ones who aren't actually dead are in some way very ill. Well, the afternoon presses on and I'm sure that you are keen to get away and write your article, Miss, er. I certainly have things urgently awaiting my attention and patients awaiting my care. So, if you have no more questions – "

"There is just one thing, Mr Standish." Kate decided, to hell with it. "We need to emphasise that it's up to the minute. Perhaps if you could spare a couple more minutes we could go and see whoever is your most recent admission."

"I think that would be a little tricky. Our last admission was about a month ago and she died of pneumonia two weeks after admission."

"Oh, ah. Well, perhaps that isn't so thrilling. So. No new admissions in the last couple of days. No admissions of anyone particularly large or blond or Nordic, with a fur coat or a sledge-hammer perhaps. I mean, just for instance." An inspiration struck her. "A *re*-admission perhaps?"

Standish regarded her with deepening suspicion.

"Miss, er – "

"Schechter."

"Miss Schechter, I begin to get the impression that your interests in the hospital are not – "

He was interrupted at that moment by the swing-doors just behind them in the corridor being pushed open. He looked up to see who it was, and as he did so his manner changed.

He motioned Kate sharply to stand aside while a large trolley bed was wheeled through the doors by an orderly. A sister and another nurse followed in attendance, and gave the impression that they were the entourage in a procession rather than merely nurses about their normal business.

The occupant of the trolley was a delicately frail old man with skin like finely veined parchment.

The rear section of the trolley was inclined upwards at a very slight angle so that the old man could survey the world as it passed him, and he surveyed it with a kind of quiet, benevolent horror. His mouth hung gently open and his head lolled very slightly, so that every slightest bump in the progress of the trolley caused it to roll a little to one side or the other. Yet in spite of his fragile listlessness, the air he emanated was that of very quietly, very gently, owning everything.

It was the one eye which conveyed this. Each thing it rested on, whether it was the view through a window, or the nurse who was holding back the door so that the trolley could move through it without impediment, or whether it was on Mr Standish, who suddenly was all obsequious charm and obeisance, all seemed instantly gathered up into the domain ruled by that eye.

Kate wondered for a moment how it was that eyes conveyed such an immense amount of information about their owners. They were, after all, merely spheres of white gristle. They hardly changed as they got older, apart from getting a bit redder and a bit runnier. The iris opened and closed a bit, but that was all. Where did all this flood of information come from? Particularly in the case of a man with only one of them and only a sealed up flap of skin in place of the other.

She was interrupted in this line of thought by the fact that at that instant the eye in question moved on from Standish and settled on her. The grip it exerted was so startling that she almost yelped.

With the frailest of faint motions the old man signalled to the orderly who was pushing the trolley to pause. The trolley drew to a halt and when the noise of its rolling wheels was stilled there was, for a moment, no other noise to be heard other than the distant hum of an elevator.

Then the elevator stopped.

Kate returned his look with a little smiling frown as if to say, "Sorry, do I know you?" and then wondered to herself if in fact she did. There was some fleeting familiarity about his face, but she couldn't quite catch it. She was impressed to notice that though this was only a trolley bed he was in, the bed linen that his hands lay on was real linen, freshly laundered and ironed.

Mr Standish coughed slightly and said, "Miss, er, this is one of our most valued and, er, cherished patients, Mr – "

"Are you quite comfortable, Mr Odwin?" interrupted the Sister helpfully. But there was no need. This was one patient whose name Standish most certainly knew.

Odin quieted her with the slightest of gestures.

"Mr Odwin," said Standish, "this is Miss, er – "

Kate was about to introduce herself once more when she was suddenly taken completely by surprise.

"I know exactly who she is," said Odin in a quiet but distinct voice, and there was in his eye for a moment the sense of an aerosol looking meaningfully at a wasp.

She tried to be very formal and English.

"I'm afraid," she said stiffly, "that you have the advantage of me."

"Yes," said Odin.

He gestured to the orderly, and together they resumed their leisurely passage down the corridor. Glances were exchanged between Standish and the Sister, and then Kate was startled to notice that there was someone else standing in the corridor there with them.

He had not, presumably, appeared there by magic. He had merely stood still when the trolley moved on, and his height, or rather his lack of it, was such that he had simply hitherto been hidden behind it.

Things had been much better when he had been hidden.

There are some people you like immediately, some whom you think you might learn to like in the fullness of time, and some that you simply want to push away from you with a sharp stick. It was instantly apparent into which category, for Kate, the person of Toe Rag fell. He grinned and stared at her, or rather, appeared to stare at some invisible fly darting round her head.

He ran up, and before she could prevent him, grabbed hold of her right hand in his and shook it wildly up and down.

"I, too, have the advantage of you, Miss Schechter," he said, and gleefully skipped away up the corridor.

Chapter 12

The large, serious-looking grey van moved smoothly down the driveway, emerged through the stone gates and dipped sedately as it turned off the gravel and on to the asphalt of the public road. The road was a windy country lane lined with the wintry silhouettes of leafless oaks and dead elms. Grey clouds were piled high as pillows in the sky. The van made its stately progress away down the lane and soon was lost among its further twists and turns.

A few minutes later the yellow Citroën made its less stately appearance between the gates. It turned its splayed wheels up on to the camber of the lane and set off at a slow but difficult rate in the same direction.

Kate was rattled.

The last few minutes had been rather unpleasant. Standish was clearly an oddly behaved man at the best of times, but after their encounter with the patient named Odwin, he had turned unequivocally hostile. It was the frightening hostility of one who was himself frightened – of what, Kate did not know.

Who was she? he had demanded to know. How had she wheedled a reference out of Alan Franklin, a respected man in the profession? What was she after? What – and this seemed to be the big one – had she done to arouse the disapprobation of Mr Odwin?

She held the car grimly to the road as it negotiated the bends with considerable difficulty and the straight sections with only slightly less. The car had landed her in court on one occasion when one of its front wheels had sailed off on a little expedition of its own and nearly caused an accident. The police witness in court had referred to her beloved Citroën as "the alleged car" and the name had subsequently stuck. She was particularly fond of the alleged car for many reasons. If one of its doors, for instance, fell off she could put it back on herself, which is more than you could say for a BMW.

She wondered if she looked as pale and wan as she felt, but the rear-view mirror was rattling around under the seat so she was spared the knowledge.

Standish himself had become quite white and shaky at the very idea of anybody crossing Mr Odwin and had dismissed out of hand Kate's attempts to deny that she knew anything of him at all. If that were the case, he had demanded of her, why then had Mr Odwin made it perfectly clear that he knew her? Was she accusing Mr Odwin of being a liar? If she was then she should have a care for herself.

Kate did not know. The encounter with Mr Odwin was completely inexplicable to her. But she could not deny to herself that the man packed some kind of punch. When he looked at you you stayed looked at. But beneath the disturbing quality of his steady gaze had lain some even more disturbing undercurrents. They were more disturbing because they were undercurrents of weakness and fear.

And as for the other creature...

Clearly he was the cause of the stories that had arisen recently in the more extremely abhorrent sectors of the tabloid press about there being "Something Nasty in the Woodshead". The stories had, of course, been offensive and callously insensitive and had largely been ignored by everybody in the country except for those very few millions who were keen on offensive and callously insensitive things.

The stories had claimed that people in the area had been "terrorised" by some repulsively deformed "goblin-like" creature who regularly broke out of the Woodshead and committed an impressively wide range of unspeakable acts.

Like most people, Kate had assumed, insofar as she had thought about it at all, that what had actually happened was that some poor bewildered mental patient had wandered out of the grounds and given a couple of passing old ladies a bit of a turn, and that the slavering hacks of Wapping had done the rest. Now she was a little more shaky and a little less sure.

He – it – had known her name.

What could she make of that?

What she made of it was a wrong turning. In her preoccupation she missed the turning that would take her on to the main road back to London, and then had to work out what to do about it. She could simply do a three-point turn and go back, but it was a long time since she had last put the car into reverse gear, and she was frankly a bit nervous about how it would take to it.

She tried taking the next two right turns to see if that would set her straight, but she had no great hopes of this actually working, and was right not to have. She drove on for two or three miles, knowing that she was on the wrong road but at least, judging from the position of the lighter grey smear in the grey clouds, going in the right direction.

After a while she settled down to this new route. A couple of signposts she passed made it clear to her that she was merely taking the B route back to London now, which she was perfectly happy to do. If she had thought about it in advance, she would probably have chosen to do so anyway in preference to the busy trunk road.

The trip had been a total failure, and she would have done far better simply to have stayed soaking in the bath all afternoon. The whole experience had been thoroughly disturbing, verging on the frightening, and she had drawn a complete blank as far as her actual objective was concerned. It was bad enough having an objective that she could hardly bring herself to admit to, without having it completely fall apart on her as well. A sense of stale futility gradually closed in on her along with the general greyness of the sky.

She wondered if she was going very slightly mad. Her life seemed to have drifted completely out of her control in the last few days, and it was distressing to realise just how fragile her grip was when it could so easily be shattered by a relatively minor thunderbolt or meteorite or whatever it was.

The word "thunderbolt" seemed to have arrived in the middle of that thought without warning and she didn't know what to make of it, so she just let it lie there at the bottom of her mind, like the towel lying on her bathroom floor that she hadn't been bothered to pick up.

She longed for some sun to break through. The miles ground along under her wheels, the clouds ground her down, and she found herself increasingly thinking of penguins. At last she felt she could stand it no more and decided that a few minutes' walk was what she needed to shake her out of her mood.

She stopped the car at the side of the road, and the elderly Jaguar which had been following her for the last seventeen miles ran straight into the back of her, which worked just as well.

Chapter 13

With a delicious shock of rage Kate leapt, invigorated, out of her car and ran to harangue the driver of the other car who was, in turn, leaping out of his in order to harangue her.

"Why don't you look where you're going?" she yelled at him. He was a rather overweight man who had been driving wearing a long leather coat and a rather ugly red hat, despite the discomfort this obviously involved. Kate warmed to him for it.

"Why don't I look where *I'm* going?" he replied heatedly. "Don't you look in your rear-view mirror?"

"No," said Kate, putting her fists on her hips.

"Oh," said her adversary. "Why not?"

"Because it's under the seat."

"I see," he replied grimly. "Thank you for being so frank with me. Do you have a lawyer?"

"Yes I do, as a matter of fact," said Kate. She said it with vim and hauteur.

"Is he any good?" said the man in the hat. "I'm going to need one. Mine's popped into prison for a while."

"Well, you certainly can't have mine."

"Why not?"

"Don't be absurd. It would be a clear conflict of interest."

Her adversary folded his arms and leant back against the bonnet of his car. He took his time to survey the surroundings. The lane was growing dim as the early winter evening began to settle on the land. He then leant into his car to turn on his hazard warning indicators. The rear amber lights winked prettily on the scrubby grass of the roadside. The front lights were buried in the rear of Kate's Citroën and were in no fit state to wink.

He resumed his leaning posture and looked Kate up and down appraisingly.

"You are a driver," he said, "and I use the word in the loosest possible sense, i.e. meaning merely somebody who occupies the driving seat of what I will for the moment call – but I use the term strictly without prejudice – a car while it is proceeding along the road, of stupendous, I would even say verging on the superhuman, lack of skill. Do you catch my drift?"

"No."

"I mean you do not drive well. Do you know you've been all over the road for the last seventeen miles?"

"Seventeen miles!" exclaimed Kate. "Have you been following me?"

"Only up to a point," said Dirk. "I've tried to stay on this side of the road."

"I see. Well, thank you in turn for being so frank with me. This, I need hardly tell you, is an outrage. You'd better get yourself a damn good lawyer, because mine's going to stick red-hot skewers in him."

"Perhaps I should get myself a kebab instead."

"You look as if you've had quite enough kebabs. May I ask you why you were following me?"

"You looked as if you knew where you were going. To begin with at least. For the first hundred yards or so."

"What the hell's it got to do with you where I was going?"

"Navigational technique of mine."

Kate narrowed her eyes.

She was about to demand a full and instant explanation of this preposterous remark when a passing white Ford Sierra slowed down beside them.

The driver wound down the window and leant out. "Had a crash then?" he shouted at them.

"Yes."

"Ha!" he said and drove on.

A second or two later a Peugeot stopped by them.

"Who was that just now?" the driver asked them, in reference to the previous driver who had just stopped.

"I don't know," said Dirk.

"Oh," said the driver. "You look as if you've had a crash of some sort."

"Yes," said Dirk.

"Thought so," said the driver and drove on.

"You don't get the same quality of passers-by these days, do you?" said Dirk to Kate.

"You get hit by some real dogs, too," said Kate. "I still want to know why you were following me. You realise that it's hard for me not to see you in the role of an extremely sinister sort of a person."

"That's easily explained," said Dirk. "Usually I am. On this occasion, however, I simply got lost. I was forced to take evasive action by a large grey oncoming van which took a proprietorial view of the road. I only avoided it by nipping down a side lane in which I was then unable to reverse. A few turnings later and I was thoroughly lost. There is a school of thought which says that you should consult a map on these occasions, but to such people I merely say, 'Ha! What if you have no map to consult? What if you have a map but it's of the Dordogne?' My own strategy is to find a car, or the nearest equivalent, which looks as if it knows where it's going and follow it. I rarely end up where I was intending to go, but often I end up somewhere that I needed to be. So what do you say to that?"

"Piffle."

"A robust response. I salute you."

"I was going to say that I do the same thing myself sometimes, but I've decided not to admit that yet."

"Very wise," said Dirk. "You don't want to give away too much at this point. Play it enigmatic is my advice."

"I don't want your advice. Where were you trying to get before suddenly deciding that driving seventeen miles in the opposite direction would help you get there?"

"A place called the Woodshead."

"Ah, the mental hospital."

"You know it?"

"I've been driving away from it for the last seventeen miles and I wish it was further. Which ward will you be in? I need to know where to send the repair bill."

"They don't have wards," said Dirk. "And I think they would be distressed to hear you call it a mental hospital."

"Anything that distresses 'em is fine by me."

Dirk looked about him.

"A fine evening," he said.

"No it isn't."

"I see," said Dirk. "You have, if I may say so, the air of one to whom her day has not been a source of joy or spiritual enrichment."

"Too damn right, it hasn't," said Kate. "I've had the sort of day that would make St Francis of Assisi kick babies. Particularly if you include Tuesday in with today, which is the last time I was actually conscious. And now look. My beautiful car. The only thing I can say in favour of the whole shebang is that at least I'm not in Oslo."

"I can see how that might cheer you."

"I didn't say it cheered me. It just about stops me killing myself. I might as well save myself the bother anyway, with people like you so keen to do it for me."

"You were my able assistant, Miss Schechter."

"Stop doing that!"

"Stop doing what?"

"My name! Suddenly every stranger I meet knows my name. Would you guys please just quit knowing my name for one second? How can a girl be enigmatic under these conditions? The only person I met who didn't seem to know my name was the only one I actually introduced myself to. All right," she said, pointing an accusing finger at Dirk, "you're not supernatural, so just tell me how you knew my name. I'm not letting go of your tie till you tell me."

"You haven't got hold of – "

"I have now, buster."

"Unhand me!"

"Why were you following me?" insisted Kate. "How do you know my name?"

"I was following you for exactly the reasons stated. As for your name, my dear lady, you practically told me yourself."

"I did not."

"I assure you, you did."

"I'm still holding your tie."

"If you are meant to be in Oslo but have been unconscious since Tuesday, then presumably you were at the incredible exploding check-in counter at Heathrow Terminal Two. It was widely reported in the press. I expect you missed it through being unconscious. I myself missed it through rampant apathy, but the events of today have rather forced it on my attention."

Kate grudgingly let go of his tie, but continued to eye him with suspicion.

"Oh yeah?" she said. "What events?"

"Disturbing ones," said Dirk, brushing himself down. "Even if what you had told me yourself had not been enough to identify you, then the fact of your having also been today to visit the Woodshead clinched it for me. I gather from your mood of belligerent despondency that the man you were seeking was not there."

"What?"

"Please, have it," said Dirk, rapidly pulling off his tie and handing it to her. "By chance I ran into a nurse from your hospital earlier today. My first encounter with her was one which, for various reasons, I was anxious to terminate abruptly. It was only while I was standing on the pavement a minute or two later, fending off the local wildlife, that one of the words I had heard her say struck me, I may say, somewhat like a thunderbolt. The idea was fantastically, wildly improbable. But like most fantastically, wildly improbable ideas it was at least as worthy of consideration as a more mundane one to which the facts had been strenuously bent to fit.

"I returned to question her further, and she confirmed that a somewhat unusual patient had, in the early hours of the morning, been transferred from the hospital, apparently to the Woodshead.

"She also confided to me that another patient had been almost indecently curious to find out what had become of him. That patient was a Miss Kate Schechter, and I think you will agree, Miss Schechter, that my methods of navigation have their advantages. I may not have gone where I intended to go, but I think I have ended up where I needed to be."

Chapter 14

After about half an hour a hefty man from the local garage arrived with a pick-up truck, a tow-rope and a son. Having looked at the situation he sent his son and the pick-up truck away to deal with another job, attached the tow-rope to Kate's now defunct car and pulled it away to the garage himself.

Kate was a little quiet about this for a minute or two, and then said, "He wouldn't have done that if I hadn't been an American."

He had recommended to them a small local pub where he would come and look for them when he had made his diagnosis on the Citroën. Since Dirk's Jaguar had only lost its front right indicator light, and Dirk insisted that he hardly ever turned right anyway, they drove the short distance there. As Kate, with some reluctance, climbed into Dirk's car she found the Howard Bell book which Dirk had purloined from Sally Mills in the café, and pounced on it. A few minutes later, walking into the pub, she was still trying to work out if it was one she had read or not.

The pub combined all the traditional English qualities of

horse brasses, Formica and surliness. The sound of Michael Jackson in the other bar mingled with the mournful intermittence of the glass-cleaning machine in this one to create an aural ambience which perfectly matched the elderly paintwork in its dinginess.

Dirk bought himself and Kate a drink each, and then joined her at the small corner table she had found away from the fat, T-shirted hostility of the bar.

"I have read it," she announced, having thumbed her way by now through most of *Run Like the Devil*. "At least, I started it and read the first couple of chapters. A couple of months ago, in fact. I don't know why I still read his books. It's perfectly clear that his editor doesn't." She looked up at Dirk. "I wouldn't have thought it was your sort of thing. From what little I know of you."

"It isn't," said Dirk. "I, er, picked it up by mistake."

"That's what everyone says," replied Kate. "He used to be quite good," she added, "if you liked that sort of thing. My brother's in publishing in New York, and he says Howard Bell's gone very strange nowadays. I get the feeling that they're all a little afraid of him and he quite likes that. Certainly no one seems to have the guts to tell him he should cut chapters ten to twenty-seven inclusive. And all the stuff about the goat. The theory is that the reason he sells so many millions of copies is that nobody ever does read them. If everyone who bought them actually read them they'd never bother to buy the next one and his career would be over."

She pushed it away from her.

"Anyway," she said, "you've very cleverly told me why I went to the Woodshead; you haven't told me why you were going there yourself."

Dirk shrugged. "To see what it was like," he said, non-committally.

"Oh yes? Well, I'll save you the bother. The place is quite horrible."

"Describe it. In fact start with the airport."

Kate took a hefty swig at her Bloody Mary and brooded silently for a moment while the vodka marched around inside her.

"You want to hear about the airport as well?" she said at last.

"Yes."

Kate drained the rest of her drink.

"I'll need another one, then," she said and pushed the empty glass across at him.

Dirk braved the bug-eyedness of the barman and returned a minute or two later with a refill for Kate.

"OK," said Kate. "I'll start with the cat."

"What cat?"

"The cat I needed to ask the next-door neighbour to look after for me."

"Which next-door neighbour?"

"The one that died."

"I see," said Dirk. "Tell you what, why don't I just shut up and let you tell me?"

"Yes," said Kate, "that would be good."

Kate recounted the events of the last few days, or at least, those she was conscious for, and then moved on to her impressions of the Woodshead.

Despite the distaste with which she described it, it sounded to Dirk like exactly the sort of place he would love to retire to, if possible tomorrow. It combined a dedication to the inexplicable, which was his own persistent vice (he could only think of it as such, and sometimes would rail against it with the fury of an addict), with a pampered self-indulgence which was a vice to which he would love to be able to aspire if he could ever but afford it.

At last Kate related her disturbing encounter with Mr Odwin and his repellent minion, and it was as a result of this that Dirk remained sunk in a frowning silence for a minute afterwards. A large part of this minute was in fact taken up with an internal struggle about whether or not he was going to cave in and have a cigarette. He had recently foresworn them and the struggle was a regular one and he lost it regularly, often without noticing.

He decided, with triumph, that he would not have one, and then took one out anyway. Fishing out his lighter from the capacious pocket of his coat involved first taking out the envelope he had removed from Geoffrey Anstey's bathroom. He put it on the table next to the book and lit his cigarette.

"The check-in girl at the airport..." he said at last.

"She drove me mad," said Kate, instantly. "She just went through the motions of doing her job like some kind of blank machine. Wouldn't listen, wouldn't think. I don't know where they find people like that."

"She used to be my secretary, in fact," said Dirk. "They don't seem to know where to find her now, either."

"Oh. I'm sorry," said Kate immediately, and then reflected for a moment.

"I expect you're going to say that she wasn't like that really," she continued. "Well, that's possible. I expect she was just shielding herself from the frustrations of her job. It must drive you insensible working at an airport. I think I would have sympathised if I hadn't been so goddamn frustrated myself. I'm sorry, I didn't know. So that's what you're trying to find out about."

Dirk gave a non-committal type of nod. "Amongst other things," he said. Then he added, "I'm a private detective."

"Oh?" said Kate in surprise, and then looked puzzled.

"Does that bother you?"

"It's just that I have a friend who plays the double bass."

"I see," said Dirk.

"Whenever people meet him and he's struggling around with it, they all say the same thing, and it drives him crazy. They all say, 'I bet you wished you played the piccolo.' Nobody ever works out that that's what everybody else says. I was just trying to work out if there was something that everybody would always say to a private detective, so that I could avoid saying it."

"No. What happens is that everybody looks very shifty for a moment, and you got that very well."

"I see." Kate looked disappointed. "Well, do you have any clues – that is to say, any idea about what's happened to your secretary?"

"No," said Dirk, "no idea. Just a vague image that I don't know what to make of." He toyed thoughtfully with his cigarette, and then let his gaze wander over the table again and on to the book.

He picked it up and looked it over, wondering what impulse had made him pick it up in the first place.

"I don't really know anything about Howard Bell," he said.

Kate was surprised at the way he suddenly changed the subject, but also a little relieved.

"I only know," said Dirk, "that he sells a lot of books and that they all look pretty much like this. What should I know?"

"Well, there are some very strange stories about him."

"Like what?"

"Like what he gets up to in hotel suites all across America. No one knows the details, of course, they just get the bills and pay them because they don't like to ask. They feel they're on safer ground if they don't know. Particularly about the chickens."

"Chickens?" said Dirk. "What chickens?"

"Well apparently," said Kate, lowering her voice and leaning forward a little, "he's always having live chickens delivered to his hotel room."

Dirk frowned.

"What on earth for?" he said.

"Nobody knows. Nobody ever knows what happens to them. Nobody ever sees them again. Not," she said, leaning even further forward, and dropping her voice still further, "a single feather."

Dirk wondered if he was being hopelessly innocent and naïve.

"So what do people think he's doing with them?" he asked.

"Nobody," Kate said, "has the faintest idea. They don't even *want* to have the faintest idea. They just don't know."

She shrugged and picked the book up again herself.

"The other thing David – that's my brother – says about him is that he has the absolute perfect bestseller's name."

"Really?" said Dirk. "In what way?"

"David says it's the first thing any publisher looks for in a new author. Not, 'Is his stuff any good?' or, 'Is his stuff any good once you get rid of all the adjectives?' but, 'Is his last name nice and short and his first name just a bit longer?' You see? The 'Bell' is done in huge silver letters, and the 'Howard' fits neatly across the top in slightly narrower ones. Instant trade mark. It's publishing magic. Once you've got a name like that, then whether you can actually write or not is a minor matter. Which in Howard Bell's case is now a significant bonus. But it's a very ordinary name if you write it down in the normal way, like it is here you see."

"What?" said Dirk.

"Here on this envelope of yours."

"Where? Let me see."

"That's his name there, isn't it? Crossed out."

"Good heavens, you're right," said Dirk, peering at the envelope. "I suppose I didn't recognise it without its trade mark shape."

"Is this something to do with him, then?" asked Kate, picking it up and looking it over.

"I don't know what it is, exactly," said Dirk. "It's something to do with a contract, and it may be something to do with a record."

"I can see it might be to do with a record."

"How can you see that?" asked Dirk, sharply.

"Well, this name here is Dennis Hutch, isn't it? See?"

"Oh yes. Yes, I do," said Dirk, examining it for himself. "Er, should I know that name?"

"Well," said Kate slowly, "it depends if you're alive or not, I suppose. He's the head of the Aries Rising Record Group. Less famous than the Pope, I grant you, but – you know of the Pope I take it?"

"Yes, yes," said Dirk impatiently, "white-haired chap."

"That's him. He seems to be about the only person of note this envelope hasn't been addressed to at some time. Here's Stan Dubcek, the head of Dubcek, Danton, Heidegger, Draycott. I know they handle the ARRGH! account."

"The...?"

"ARRGH! Aries Rising Record Group Holdings. Getting that account made the agency's fortunes."

She looked at Dirk.

"You have the air," she stated, "of one who knows little of the record business or the advertising business."

"I have that honour," said Dirk, graciously inclining his head.

"So what are you doing with this?"

"When I manage to get it open, I'll know," said Dirk. "Do you have a knife on you?"

Kate shook her head.

"Who's Geoffrey Anstey, then?" she asked. "He's the only name not crossed out. Friend of yours?"

Dirk paled a little and didn't immediately answer. Then he said, "This strange person you mentioned, this 'Something Nasty in the Woodshead' creature. Tell me again what he said to you."

"He said, 'I, too, have the advantage of you, Miss Schechter.'" Kate tried to shrug.

Dirk weighed his thoughts uncertainly for a moment.

"I think it is just possible," he said at last, "that you may be in some kind of danger."

"You mean it's possible that passing lunatics may crash into me in the road? That kind of danger?"

"Maybe even worse."

"Oh yeah?"

"Yes."

"And what makes you think that?"

"It's not entirely clear to me yet," replied Dirk with a frown. "Most of the ideas I have at the moment have to do with things that are completely impossible, so I am wary about sharing them. They are, however, the only thoughts I have."

"I'd get some different ones, then," said Kate. "What was the Sherlock Holmes principle? 'Once you have discounted the impossible, then whatever remains, however improbable, must be the truth.'"

"I reject that entirely," said Dirk, sharply. "The impossible often has a kind of integrity to it which the merely improbable lacks. How often have you been presented with an apparently rational explanation of something which works in all respects other than one, which is just that it is hopelessly improbable? Your instinct is to say, 'Yes, but he or she simply wouldn't do that.'"

"Well, it happened to me today, in fact," replied Kate.

"Ah yes," said Dirk, slapping the table and making the glasses jump, "your girl in the wheelchair – a perfect example. The idea that she is somehow receiving yesterday's stock market prices apparently out of thin air is merely impossible, and therefore *must* be the case, because the idea that she is maintaining an immensely complex and laborious hoax of no benefit to herself is hopelessly improbable. The first idea merely supposes that there is something we don't know about, and God knows there are enough of those. The second, however, runs contrary to something fundamental and human which we do know about. We should therefore be very suspicious of it and all its specious rationality."

"But you won't tell me what you think."

"No."

"Why not?"

"Because it sounds ridiculous. But I think you are in danger. I think you might be in horrible danger."

"Great. So what do you suggest I do about it?" said Kate, taking a sip of her second drink, which otherwise had stayed almost untouched.

"I suggest," said Dirk seriously, "that you come back to London and spend the night in my house."

Kate hooted with laughter and then had to fish out a Kleenex to wipe tomato juice off herself.

"I'm sorry, what is so extraordinary about that?" demanded Dirk, rather taken aback.

"It's just the most wonderfully perfunctory pick-up line I've ever heard." She smiled at him. "I'm afraid the answer is a resounding 'no'."

He was, she thought, interesting, entertaining in an eccentric kind of way, but also hideously unattractive to her.

Dirk felt very awkward. "I think there has been some appalling misunderstanding," he said. "Allow me to explain that – "

He was interrupted by the sudden arrival in their midst of the mechanic from the garage with news of Kate's car.

"Fixed it," he said. "In fact there were nothing to fix other than the bumper. Nothing new that is. The funny noise you mentioned were just the engine. But it'll go all right. You just have to rev her up, let in the clutch, and then wait for a little bit longer than you might normally expect."

Kate thanked him a little stiffly for this advice and then insisted on allowing Dirk to pay the £25 he was charging for it.

Outside, in the car park, Dirk repeated his urgent request that Kate should go with him, but she was adamant that all she needed was a good night's sleep and that everything would look bright and clear and easily capable of being coped with in the morning.

Dirk insisted that they should at least exchange phone numbers. Kate agreed to this on condition that Dirk found another route back to London and didn't sit on her tail.

"Be very careful," Dirk called to her as her car grumbled out on to the road.

"I will," shouted Kate, "and if anything impossible happens, I promise you'll be the first to know."

For a brief moment, the yellow undulations of the car gleamed dully in the light leaking from the pub windows and stood out against the heavily hunched greyness of the night sky which soon swallowed it up.

Dirk tried to follow her, but his car wouldn't start.

Chapter 15

The clouds sank more heavily over the land, clenching into huge sullen towers, as Dirk, in a sudden excess of alarm, had to call out the man from the garage once again. He was slower to arrive with his truck this time and bad-tempered with drink when at last he did.

He emitted a few intemperate barks of laughter at Dirk's predicament, then fumbled the bonnet of his car open and subjected him to all kinds of muttered talk about manifolds, pumps, alternators and starlings and resolutely would not be drawn on whether or not he was going to be able to get the thing to go again that night.

Dirk was unable to get a meaningful answer, or at least an answer that meant anything to him, as to what was causing the rumpus in the alternator, what ailed the fuel pump, in what way the operation of the starter motor was being disrupted and why the timing was off.

He did at last understand that the mechanic was also claiming that a family of starlings had at some time in the past made their nest in a sensitive part of the engine's workings and had subsequently perished horribly, taking sensitive parts of the engine with them, and at this point Dirk began to cast about himself desperately for what to do.

He noticed that the mechanic's pick-up truck was standing nearby with its engine still running, and elected to make off with this instead. Being a slightly less slow and cumbersome runner than the mechanic he was able to put this plan into operation with a minimum of difficulty.

He swung out into the lane, drove off into the night and parked three miles down the road. He left the van's lights on, let down its tyres and hid himself behind a tree. After about ten minutes his Jaguar came hurtling round the corner, passed the van, hauled itself to an abrupt halt and reversed wildly back towards it. The mechanic threw open the door, leapt out and hurried over to reclaim his property, leaving Dirk with the opportunity he needed to leap from behind the tree and reclaim his own.

He spun his wheels pointedly and drove off in a kind of grim triumph, still haunted, nevertheless, by anxieties to which he was unable to give a name or shape.

Kate, in the meantime, had joined the dimly glowing yellow stream that led on eventually through the western suburbs of Acton and Ealing and into the heart of London. She crawled up over the Westway flyover and soon afterwards turned north up towards Primrose Hill and home.

She always enjoyed driving up alongside the park, and the dark night shapes of the trees soothed her and made her long for the quietness of her bed.

She found the nearest parking space she could to her front door, which was about thirty yards distant. She climbed out of the car and carefully omitted to lock it. She never left anything of value in it, and she found that it was to her advantage if people didn't have to break anything in order to find that out. The car had been stolen twice, but on each occasion it had been found abandoned twenty yards away.

She didn't go straight home but set off instead in the opposite direction to get some milk and bin liners from the small corner shop in the next street. She agreed with the gentle-faced Pakistani who ran it that she did indeed look tired, and should have an early night, but on the way back she made another small diversion to go and lean against the railings of the park, gaze into its darkness for a few minutes, and breathe in some of its cold, heavy night air. At last she started to head back towards her flat. She turned into her own road and as she passed the first street lamp it flickered and went out, leaving her in a small pool of darkness.

That sort of thing always gives one a nasty turn.

It is said that there is nothing surprising about the notion of, for instance, a person suddenly thinking about someone they haven't thought about for years, and then discovering the next day that the person has in fact just died. There are always lots of people suddenly remembering people they haven't thought about for ages, and always lots of people dying. In a population the size of, say, America the law of averages means that this particular coincidence must happen at least ten times a day, but it is none the less spooky to anyone who experiences it.

By the same token, there are light bulbs burning out in street lamps all the time, and a fair few of them must go pop just as someone is passing beneath them. Even so, it still gives the person concerned a nasty turn, especially when the very next street lamp they pass under does exactly the same thing.

Kate stood rooted to the spot.

If one coincidence can occur, she told herself, then another coincidence can occur. And if one coincidence happens to occur just after another coincidence, then that is just a coincidence. There was absolutely nothing to feel alarmed about in having a couple of street lamps go pop. She was in a perfectly normal friendly street with houses all around her with their lights on. She looked up at the house next to her, unfortunately just as the lights in its front window chanced to go out. This was presumably because the occupants happened to choose that moment to leave the room, but though it just went to show what a truly extraordinary thing coincidence can be it did little to improve her state of mind.

The rest of the street was still bathed in a dim yellow glow. It was only the few feet immediately around her that were suddenly dark. The next pool of light was just a few footsteps away in front of her. She took a deep breath, pulled herself together, and walked towards it, reaching its very centre at the exact instant that it, too, extinguished itself.

The occupants of the two houses she had passed on the way also happened to choose that moment to leave their front rooms, as did their neighbours on the opposite side of the street.

Perhaps a popular television show had just finished. That's what it was. Everyone was getting up and turning off their TV sets and lights simultaneously, and the resulting power surge was blowing some of the street lamps. Something like that. The resulting power surge was also making her blood pound a little. She moved on, trying to be calm. As soon as she got home she'd have a look in the paper to see what the programme had been that had caused three street lamps to blow.

Four.

She stopped and stood absolutely still under the dark lamp. More houses were darkening. What she found particularly alarming was that they darkened at the very moment that she looked at them.

Glance – *pop*.

She tried it again.

Glance – *pop*.

Each one she looked at darkened instantly.

Glance – *pop*.

She realised with a sudden start of fear that she must stop herself looking at the ones that were still lit. The rationalisations she had been trying to construct were now running around inside her head screaming to be let out and she let them go. She tried to lock her eyes to the ground for fear of extinguishing the whole street, but couldn't help tiny glances to see if it was working.

Glance – *pop*.

She froze her gaze down on to the narrow path forward. Most of the road was dark now.

There were three remaining street lamps between her and the front door which led to her own flat. Though she kept her eyes averted, she thought she could detect on the periphery of her vision that the lights of the flat downstairs from hers were lit.

Neil lived there. She couldn't remember his last name, but he was a part-time bass-player and antiques dealer who used to give her decorating advice she didn't want and also stole her milk – so her relationship with him had always remained at a slightly frosty level. Just at the moment, though, she was praying that he was there to tell her what was wrong with her sofa, and that his light would not go out as her eyes wavered from the pavement in front of her, with its three remaining pools of light spaced evenly along the way she had to tread.

For a moment she tried turning, and looked back the way she had come. All was darkness, shading off into the blackness of the park which no longer calmed but menaced her, with hideously imagined thick, knotted roots and treacherous, dark, rotting litter.

Again she turned, sweeping her eyes low.

Three pools of light.

The street lights did not extinguish as she looked at them, only as she passed.

She squeezed her eyes closed and visualised exactly where the lamp of the next street light was, above and in front of her. She raised her head, and carefully opened her eyes again, staring directly into the orange glow radiating through the thick glass.

It shone steadily.

With her eyes locked fast on it so that it burnt squiggles on her retina, she moved cautiously forward, step by step, exerting her will on it to stay burning as she approached. It continued to glow.

She stepped forward again. It continued to glow. Again she stepped, still it glowed. Now she was almost beneath it, craning her neck to keep it in focus.

She moved forward once more, and saw the filament within the glass flicker and quickly die away, leaving an after-image prancing madly in her eyes.

She dropped her eyes now and tried looking steadily forward, but wild shapes were leaping everywhere and she felt she was losing control. The next lamp she took a lunging run towards, and again, sudden darkness enveloped her arrival. She stopped there panting, and blinking, trying to calm herself again and get her vision sorted out. Looking towards the last street lamp, she thought she saw a figure standing beneath it. It was a large form, silhouetted with jumping orange shadows. Huge horns stood upon the figure's head.

She stared with mad intensity into the billowing darkness, and suddenly screamed at it, "Who are you?"

There was a pause, and then a deep answering voice said, "Do you have anything that can get these bits of floorboard off my back?"

Chapter 16

There was another pause, of a different and slightly disordered quality.

It was a long one. It hung there nervously, wondering which direction it was going to get broken from. The darkened street took on a withdrawn, defensive aspect.

"What?" Kate screamed back at the figure, at last. "I said... *what*?"

The great figure stirred. Kate still could not see him properly because her eyes were still dancing with blue shadows, seared there by the orange light.

"I was," said the figure, "glued to the floor. My father – "

"Did *you*...are *you*..." Kate quivered with incoherent rage, "are you responsible...for all *this*?" She turned and swept an angry hand around the street to indicate the nightmare she had just traversed.

"It is important that you know who I am."

"Oh yeah?" said Kate. "Well let's get the name down right now so I can take it straight to the police and get you done for breach of something wilful or other. Intimidation. Interfering with – "

"I am Thor. I am the God of Thunder. The God of Rain. The God of the High Towering Clouds. The God of Lightning. The God of the Flowing Currents. The God of the Particles. The God of the Shaping and the Binding Forces. The God of the Wind. The God of the Growing Crops. The God of the Hammer Mjollnir."

"Are you?" simmered Kate. "Well, I've no doubt that if you'd picked a slack moment to mention all that, I might have taken an interest, but right now it just makes me very angry. Turn the damn lights on!"

"I am – "

"I said turn the lights on!"

With something of a sheepish glow, the streetlights all came back on, and the windows of the houses all quietly illuminated themselves once more. The lamp above Kate popped again almost immediately. She shot him a warning look.

"It was an old light, and infirm," he said.

She simply continued to glare at him.

"See," he said, "I have your address." He held out the piece of paper she had given him at the airport, as if that somehow explained everything and put the world to rights.

"I – "

"Back!" he shouted, throwing up his arms in front of his face.

"What?"

With a huge rush of wind a swooping eagle dropped from out of the night sky, with its talons outspread to catch at him. Thor beat and thrashed at it until the great bird flailed backwards, turned, nearly crashed to the ground, recovered itself, and with great slow beats of its wings, heaved itself back up through the air and perched on top of the street lamp. It grasped the lamp hard with its talons and steadied itself, making the whole lamppost quiver very slightly in its grip.

"Go!" shouted Thor at it.

The eagle sat there and peered down at him. A monstrous creature made more monstrous by the effect of the orange light on which it perched, casting huge, flapping shadows on the nearby houses, it had strange circular markings on its wings. These were markings that Kate wondered if she had seen before, only in a nightmare, but then again, she was by no means certain that she was not in a nightmare now.

There was no doubt that she had found the man she was looking for. The same huge form, the same glacial eyes, the same look of arrogant exasperation and slight muddle, only this time his feet were plunged into huge hide boots, great furs, straps and thongs hung from his shoulders, a huge steel horned helmet stood on his head, and his exasperation was directed this time not at an airline check-in girl but at a huge eagle perched on a lamppost in the middle of Primrose Hill.

"Go," he shouted at it again. "The matter is beyond my power! All that I can do I have done! Your family is provided for. You I can do nothing more for! I myself am powerless and sick."

Kate was suddenly shocked to see that there were great gouges on the big man's left forearm where the eagle had got its talons into him and ripped them through his skin. Blood was welling up out of them like bread out of a baking tin.

"Go!" he shouted again. With the edge of one hand he scraped the blood off his other arm and flung the heavy drops at the eagle, which reared back, flapping, but retained its hold. Suddenly the man leapt high into the air and grappled himself to the top of the lamppost, which now began to shake dangerously under their combined weight. With loud cries the eagle pecked viciously at him while he tried with great swings of his free arm to sweep it from its perch.

A door opened. It was the front door of Kate's house and a man with grey-rimmed spectacles and a neat moustache looked out. It was Neil, Kate's downstairs neighbour, in a mood.

"Look, I really think – " he started. However, it quickly

became clear that he simply didn't know what to think and retreated back indoors, taking his mood, unsatisfied, with him.

The big man braced himself, and with a huge leap hurled himself through the air and landed with a slight, controlled wobble on top of the next lamppost, which bent slightly under his weight. He crouched, glaring at the eagle, which glared back.

"Go!" he shouted again, brandishing his arm at it.

"Gaarh!" it screeched back at him.

With another swing of his arm he pulled from under his furs a great short-handled sledge-hammer and hefted its great weight meaningfully from one hand to another. The head of the hammer was a roughly cast piece of iron about the size and shape of a pint of beer in a big glass mug, and its shaft was a stocky, wrist-thick piece of ancient oak with leather strapping bound about its handle.

"Gaaarrrh!" screeched the eagle again, but regarded the sledgehammer with keen-eyed suspicion. As Thor began slowly to swing the hammer, the eagle shifted its weight tensely from one leg to the other, in time to the rhythm of the swings.

"Go!" said Thor again, more quietly, but with greater menace. He rose to his full height on top of the lamppost, and swung the hammer faster and faster in a great circle. Suddenly he hurled it directly towards the eagle. In the same instant a bolt of high voltage electricity erupted from the lamp on which the eagle was sitting, causing it to leap with loud cries wildly into the air. The hammer sailed harmlessly under the lamp, swung up into the air and out over the darkness of the park, while Thor, released of its weight, wobbled and tottered on top of his lamppost, spun round and regained his balance. Flailing madly at the air with its huge wings, the eagle, too, regained control of itself, flew upwards, made one last diving attack on Thor, which the god leapt backwards off the lamppost to avoid, and then climbed up and away into the night sky in which it quickly became a small, dark speck, and then at last was gone.

The hammer came bounding back from out of the sky,

scraped flying sparks from the paving-stones with its head, turned over twice in the air and then dropped its head back to the ground next to Kate and rested its shaft gently against her leg.

An elderly lady who had been waiting patiently with her dog in the shadows beneath the street lamp, which was now defunct, sensed, correctly, that all of the excitement was now over and proceeded quietly past them. Thor waited politely till they had passed and then approached Kate, who stood with her arms folded watching him. After all the business of the last two or three minutes he seemed suddenly not to have the faintest idea what to say and for the moment merely gazed thoughtfully into the middle distance.

Kate formed the distinct impression that thinking was, for him, a separate activity from everything else, a task that needed its own space. It could not easily be combined with other activities such as walking or talking or buying airline tickets.

"We'd better take a look at your arm," she said, and led the way up the steps to her house. He followed, docile.

As she opened the front door she found Neil in the hall leaning his back against the wall and looking with grim pointedness at a Coca-Cola vending machine standing against the opposite wall and taking up an inordinate amount of space in the hallway.

"I don't know what we're going to do about this, I really don't," he said.

"What's it doing there?" asked Kate.

"Well, that's what I'm asking you, I'm afraid," said Neil. "I don't know how you're going to get it up the stairs. Don't see how it can be done to be perfectly frank with you. And let's face it, I don't think you're going to like it once you've got it up there. I know it's very modern and American, but think about it, you've got that nice French cherrywood table, that sofa which will be very nice once you've taken off that dreadful Collier Campbell covering like I keep on saying you should, only you won't listen, and I just don't see that it's going to fit in, not in either sense. And I'm not even sure that I should allow it, I mean it's a very heavy object and you know what I've said to you about the floors in this house. I'd think again, I really would, you know."

"Yes, Neil, how did it get here?"

"Well, your friend here delivered it just an hour or so ago. I don't know where he's been working out, but I must say I wouldn't mind paying his gym a visit. I said I thought the whole thing was very doubtful but he would insist and in the end I even had to give him a hand. But I must say that I think we need to have a very serious think about the whole topic. I asked your friend if he liked Wagner but he didn't respond very well. So, I don't know, what do you want to do about it?"

Kate took a deep breath. She suggested to her huge guest that he carry on upstairs and she would see him in just a moment. Thor lumbered past, and was an absurd figure mounting the stairs.

Neil watched Kate's eyes very closely for a clue as to what, exactly, was going on, but Kate was as blank as she knew how.

"I'm sorry, Neil," she said, matter-of-factly. "The Coke machine will go. It's all a misunderstanding. I'll get this sorted out by tomorrow."

"Yes, that's all very well," said Neil, "but where does all this leave me? I mean, you see my problem."

"No, Neil, I don't."

"Well, I've got this...thing out here, you've got that...person upstairs, and the whole thing is just a total disruption."

"Is there anything I can do to make anything any better?"

"Well it's not as easy as that, is it? I mean, I think you should just think about it a bit, that's all. I mean, all this. You told me you were going away. I heard the bath running this afternoon. What was I to think? And after you had gone on about the cat, and you know I won't work with cats."

"I know, Neil. That's why I asked Mrs Grey next door to look after her."

"Yes, and look what happened to her. Died of a heart attack. Mr Grey's very upset, you know."

"I don't think it had anything to do with me asking her if she would look after my cat."

"Well, all I can say is that he's *very* upset."

"Yes, Neil. His wife's died."

"Well, I'm not saying anything. I'm just saying I think you should think about it. And what on earth are we going to do about all this?" he added, re-addressing his attention to the Coca-Cola machine.

"I've said that I will make sure it's gone in the morning, Neil," said Kate. "I'm quite happy to stand here and scream very loudly if you think it will help in any way, but – "

"Listen, love, I'm only making the point. And I hope you're not going to be making a lot of noise up there because I've got to practise my music tonight, and you know that I need quiet to concentrate." He gave Kate a meaningful look over the top of his glasses and disappeared into his flat.

Kate stood and silently counted as much of one to ten as she could currently remember and then headed staunchly up the stairs in the wake of the God of Thunder, feeling that she was not in a mood for either weather or theology. The house began to throb and shake to the sound of the main theme of *The Ride of the Valkyries* being played on a Fender Precision bass.

Chapter 17

As Dirk edged his way along the Euston Road, caught in the middle of a rush hour traffic jam that had started in the late nineteen-seventies and which, at a quarter to ten on this Thursday evening, still showed no signs of abating, he thought he caught sight of something he recognised.

It was his subconscious which told him this – that infuriating part of a person's brain which never responds to interrogation, merely gives little meaningful nudges and then sits humming quietly to itself, saying nothing.

"Well of course I've just seen something I recognise," Dirk muttered mentally to his subconscious. "I drive along this benighted thoroughfare twenty times a month. I expect I recognise every single matchstick lying in the gutter. Can't you be a little more specific?" His subconscious would not be hectored though, and was dumb. It had nothing further to add. The city was probably full of grey vans anyway. Very unremarkable.

"Where?" muttered Dirk to himself fiercely, twisting round in his seat this way and that. "Where did I see a grey van?"

Nothing.

He was thoroughly hemmed in by the traffic and could not manoeuvre in any direction, least of all forward. He erupted from his car and started to jostle his way back through the jammed cars bobbing up and down to try and see where, if anywhere, he might have caught a glimpse of a grey van. If he had seen one, it eluded him now. His subconscious sat and said nothing.

The traffic was still not moving, so he tried to thread his way further back, but was obstructed by a large motorcycle courier edging his way forward on a huge grimy Kawasaki. Dirk engaged in a brief altercation with the courier, but lost it because the courier was unable to hear Dirk's side of the altercation; eventually Dirk retreated through the tide of traffic which now was beginning slowly to move in all lanes other than the one in which his car sat, driverless, immobile and hooted at.

He felt suddenly elated by the braying of the motor horns, and as he swayed and bobbed his way back through the snarled up columns of cars, he suddenly found that he reminded himself of the crazies he had seen on the streets of New York, who would career out into the road to explain to the oncoming traffic about the Day of Judgement, imminent alien invasions and incompetence and corruption in the Pentagon. He put his hands above his head and started to shout out, "The Gods are walking the Earth! The Gods are walking the Earth!"

This further inflamed the feelings of those who were beeping their horns at his stationary car, and quickly the whole rose through a crescendo of majestic cacophony, with Dirk's voice ringing out above it.

"The Gods are walking the Earth! The Gods are walking the Earth!" he hollered. "The Gods are walking the Earth! Thank you!" he added, and ducked down into his car, put it into Drive and pulled away, allowing the whole jammed mass at last to seethe easily forward.

He wondered why he was so sure. An "Act of God". Merely a chance, careless phrase by which people were able to dispose conveniently of awkward phenomena that would admit of no more rational explanation. But it was the chance carelessness of it which particularly appealed to Dirk because words used carelessly, as if they did not matter in any serious way, often allowed otherwise well-guarded truths to seep through.

An inexplicable disappearance. Oslo and a hammer: a tiny, tiny coincidence which struck a tiny, tiny note. However, it was a note which sang in the midst of the daily hubbub of white noise, and other tiny notes were singing at the same pitch. An Act of God, Oslo, and a hammer. A man with a hammer, trying to go to Norway, is prevented, loses his temper, and as a result there is an "Act of God".

If, thought Dirk, if a being were immortal he would still be alive today. That, quite simply, was what "immortal" meant.

How would an immortal being have a passport?

Quite simply, how? Dirk tried to imagine what might happen if – to pick a name quite at random – the God Thor, he of the Norwegian ancestry and the great hammer, were to arrive at the passport office and try to explain who he was and how come he had no birth certificate. There would be no shock, no horror, no loud exclamations of astonishment, just blank, bureaucratic impossibility. It wouldn't be a matter of whether anybody believed him or not, it would simply be a question of producing a valid birth certificate. He could stand there wreaking miracles all day if he liked but at close of business, if he didn't have a valid birth certificate, he would simply be asked to leave.

And credit cards.

If, to sustain for a moment the same arbitrary hypothesis, the God Thor were alive and for some reason at large in England, then he would probably be the only person in the country who did not receive the constant barrage of invitations to apply for an American Express card, crude threats by the same post to take their American Express cards away, and gift catalogues full of sumptuously unpleasant things, lavishly tooled in naff brown plastic.

Dirk found the idea quite breathtaking.

That is, if he were the only god at large – which, once you were to accept the first extravagant hypothesis, was hardly likely to be the case.

But imagine for a moment such a person attempting to leave the country, armed with no passport, no credit cards, merely the power to throw thunderbolts and who knew what else. You would probably have to imagine a scene very similar to the one that did in fact occur at Terminal Two, Heathrow.

But why, if you were a Norse god, would you be needing to leave the country by means of a scheduled airline? Surely there were other means? Dirk rather thought that one of the perks of being an immortal divine might be the ability to fly under your own power. From what he remembered of his reading of the Norse legends many years ago, the gods were continually flying all over the place and there was never any mention of them hanging around in departure lounges eating crummy buns. Admittedly, the world was not, in those days, bristling with air-traffic controllers, radar, missile warning systems and such like. Still, a quick hop across the North Sea shouldn't be that much of a problem for a god, particularly if the weather was in your favour, which, if you were the God of Thunder, you would pretty much expect it to be, or want to know the reason why. Should it?

Another tiny note sang in the back of Dirk's mind and then was lost in the hubbub.

He wondered for a moment what it was like to be a whale. Physically, he thought, he was probably well placed to get some good insights, though whales were better adapted for their lives of gliding about in the vast pelagic blueness than he was for his of struggling up through the Pentonville Road traffic in a weary old Jaguar – but what he was thinking of, in fact, was the whales' songs. In the past the whales had been able to sing to each other across whole oceans, even from one ocean to another because sound travels such huge distances underwater. But now, again because of the way in which sound travels, there is no part of the ocean that is not constantly jangling with the hubbub of ships' motors, through which it is now virtually impossible for the whales to hear each other's songs or messages.

So fucking what, is pretty much the way that people tend to view this problem, and understandably so, thought Dirk. After all, who wants to hear a bunch of fat fish, oh all right, mammals, burping at each other?

But for a moment Dirk had a sense of infinite loss and sadness that somewhere amongst the frenzy of information noise that daily rattled the lives of men he thought he might have heard a few notes that denoted the movements of gods.

As he turned north into Islington and began the long haul up past the pizza restaurants and estate agents, he felt almost frantic at the idea of what their lives must now be like.

Chapter 18

Thin fingers of lightning spread out across the heavy underside of the great clouds which hung from the sky like a sagging stomach. A small crack of fretful thunder nagged at it and dragged from it a few mean drops of greasy drizzle.

Beneath the sky ranged a vast assortment of wild turrets, gnarled spires and pinnacles which prodded at it, goaded and inflamed it till it seemed it would burst and drown them in a flood of festering horrors.

High in the flickering darkness, silent figures stood guard behind long shields, dragons crouched gaping at the foul sky as Odin, father of the Gods of Asgard, approached the great iron portals through which led to his domain and on into the vaulted halls of Valhalla. The air was full of the noiseless howls of great winged dogs, welcoming their master to the seat of his rule. Lightning searched among the towers and turrets.

The great, ancient and immortal God of Asgard was returning to the current site of his domain in a manner that would have surprised even him centuries ago in the years of the prime of his life – for even the immortal gods have their primes, when their powers are rampant and they both nourish and hold sway over the world of men, the world whose needs give them birth – he was returning in a large, unmarked grey Mercedes van.

The van drew to a halt in a secluded area.

The cab door opened and there climbed down from it a dull, slow-faced man in an unmarked grey uniform. He was a man who was charged with the work he did in life because he was not one to ask questions – not so much on account of any natural quality of discretion as because he simply could never think of any questions to ask. Moving with a slow, rolling gait, like a paddle being pulled through porridge, he made his way to the rear of the van and opened the rear doors – an elaborate procedure involving the co-ordinated manipulation of many sliders and levers.

At length the doors swung open, and if Kate had been present she might for a moment have been jolted by the thought that perhaps the van was carrying Albanian electricity after all. A haze of light greeted Hillow – the man's name was Hillow – but nothing about this struck him as odd. A haze of light was simply what he expected to see whenever he opened this door. The first time ever he had opened it he had simply thought to himself, "Oh. A haze of light. Oh well," and more or less left it at that, on the strength of which he had guaranteed himself regular employment for as long as he cared to live.

The haze of light subsided and coalesced into the shape of an old, old man in a trolley bed attended by a short little figure whom Hillow would probably have thought was the most evil-looking person he had ever seen if he had had a mind to recall the other people he had seen in his life and run through them all one by one, making the comparison. That, however, was harder than Hillow wished to work. His only concern at present was to assist the small figure with the decanting of the old man's bed on to ground level.

This was fluently achieved. The legs and wheels of the bed were a miracle of smoothly operating stainless steel technology. They unlocked, rolled, swivelled, in elaborately interlocked movements which made the negotiating of steps or bumps all part of the same fluid, gliding motion.

To the right of this area lay a large ante-chamber panelled in finely carved wood with great marble torch holders standing proudly from the walls. This in turn led into the great vaulted hall itself. To the left, however, lay the entrance to the majestic inner chambers where Odin would go to prepare himself for the encounters of the night.

He hated all this. Hounded from his bed, he muttered to himself, though in truth he was bringing his bed with him. Made to listen once again to all kinds of self-indulgent clap-trap from his bone-headed thunderous son who would not accept, could not accept, simply did not have the intelligence to accept the new realities of life. If he would not accept them then he must be extinguished, and tonight Asgard would see the extinction of an immortal god. It was all, thought Odin fractiously, too much for someone at his time of life, which was extremely advanced, but not in any particular direction.

He wanted merely to stay in his hospital, which he loved. The arrangement which had brought him to that place was of the sweetest kind and though it was not without its cost, it was a cost that simply had to be borne and that was all there was to it. There were new realities, and he had learned to embrace them. Those who did not would simply have to suffer the consequences. Nothing came of nothing, even for a god.

After tonight he could return to his life in the Woodshead indefinitely, and that would be good. He said as much to Hillow.

"Clean white sheets," he said to Hillow, who merely nodded, blankly. "Linen sheets. Every day, clean sheets."

Hillow manoeuvred the bed around and up a step.

"Being a god, Hillow," continued Odin, "being a god, well, it was unclean, you hear what I'm saying? There was no one who took care of the sheets. I mean really took care of them. Would you think that? In a situation like mine? Father of the Gods? There was no one, absolutely no one, who came in and said, 'Mr Odwin,'" – he chuckled to himself – "they call me Mr Odwin there, you know. They don't quite know who they're dealing with. I don't think they could handle it, do you, Hillow? But there was no one in all that time who came in and said, 'Mr Odwin, I have changed your bed and you have clean sheets.' No one. There was constant talk about hewing things and ravaging things and splitting things asunder. Lots of big talk of things being mighty, and of things being riven, and of things being in thrall to other things, but very little attention given, as I now realise, to the laundry. Let me give you an example..."

His reminiscences were for a moment interrupted, however, by the arrival of his vehicle at a great doorway which was guarded by a great sweaty splodge of a being who stood swaying, arms akimbo, in their path. Toe Rag, who had been preserving an intense silence as he stalked along just ahead of the bed, hurried forward and had a quick word with the sweating creature, who had to bend, red-faced, to hear him. Then instantly the sweaty creature shrank back with glistening obsequiousness into its yellow lair, and the sacred trolley rolled forward into the great halls, chambers and corridors from which great gusty echoes roared and fetid odours blew.

"Let me give you an example, Hillow," continued Odin. "Take this place for example. Take Valhalla..."

Chapter 19

Turning north was a manoeuvre which normally had the effect of restoring a sense of reason and sanity to things, but Dirk could not escape a sense of foreboding.

Furthermore it came on to rain a little, which should have helped, but it was such mean and wretched rain to come from such a heavy sky that it only increased the sense of claustrophobia and frustration which gripped the night. Dirk turned on the car wipers which grumbled because they didn't have quite enough rain to wipe away, so he turned them off again. Rain quickly speckled the windscreen.

He turned on the wipers again, but they still refused to feel that the exercise was worthwhile, and scraped and squeaked in protest. The streets turned treacherously slippery.

Dirk shook his head. He was being quite absurd, he told himself, in the worst possible way. He had allowed himself to become fanciful in a manner that he quite despised. He astounded himself at the wild fantasies he had built on the flimsiest amount of, well he would hardly call it evidence, mere conjecture.

An accident at an airport. Probably a simple explanation.

A man with a hammer. So what?

A grey van which Kate Schechter had seen at the hospital. Nothing unusual about that. Dirk had nearly collided with it, but again, that was a perfectly commonplace occurrence.

A Coca-Cola machine: he hadn't taken that into account.

Where did a Coca-Cola machine fit into these wild notions about ancient gods? The only idea he had about that was simply too ridiculous for words and he refused even to acknowledge it to himself.

At that point Dirk found himself driving past the house where, that very morning, he had encountered a client of his who had had his severed head placed on a revolving record turntable by a green-eyed devil-figure waving a scythe and a blood-signed contract who had then vanished into thin air.

He peered at it as he passed, and when a large dark-blue BMW pulled out from the kerb just ahead of him he ran straight into the back of it, and for the second time that day he had to leap out of his car, already shouting.

"For God's sake can't you look where you're going?" he exclaimed, in the hope of bagging his adversary's best lines from the outset. "Stupid people!" he continued, without pausing for breath. "Careering all over the place. Driving without due care and attention! Reckless assault!" Confuse your enemy, he thought. It was a little like phoning somebody up, and saying "Yes? Hello?" in a testy voice when they answered, which was one of Dirk's favourite methods of whiling away long, hot summer afternoons. He bent down and examined the palpable dent in the rear of the BMW, which was quite obviously, damn it, a brand new one. Blast and bugger it, thought Dirk.

"Look what you've done to my bumper!" he cried. "I hope you have a good lawyer!"

"I am a good lawyer," said a quiet voice which was followed

by a quiet click. Dirk looked up in momentary apprehension. The quiet click was only the sound of the car door closing.

The man was wearing an Italian suit, which was also quiet. He had quiet glasses, quietly cut hair, and though a bow-tie is not, by its very nature, a quiet object, the particular bow-tie he wore was, nevertheless, a very quietly spotted example of the genre. He drew a slim wallet from his pocket and also a slim silver pencil. He walked without fuss to the rear of Dirk's Jaguar and made a note of the registration number.

"Do you have a card?" he enquired as he did so, without looking up. "Here's mine," he added, taking one from his wallet. He made a note on the back of it. "My registration number," he said, "and the name of my insurance company. Perhaps you would be good enough to let me have the name of yours. If you don't have it with you, I'll get my girl to call you."

Dirk sighed, and decided there was no point in putting up a fight on this one. He fished out his wallet and leafed through the various business cards that seemed to accumulate in it as if from nowhere. He toyed for a second with the idea of being Wesley Arlott, an ocean-going yacht navigation consultant from, apparently, Arkansas, but then thought better of it. The man had, after all, taken his registration number, and although Dirk had no particular recollection of paying an insurance premium of late, he also had no particular recollection of not paying one either, which was a reasonably promising sign. He handed over a bona-fide card with a wince. The man looked at it.

"Mr Gently," he said. "Private investigator. I'm sorry, private *holistic* investigator. OK."

He put the card away, taking no further interest.

Dirk had never felt so patronised in his life. At that moment there was another quiet click from the other side of the car. Dirk looked across to see a woman with red spectacles standing there giving him a frozen half-smile. She was the woman he had spoken with over Geoffrey Anstey's garden wall this morning, and the man, Dirk therefore supposed, was probably her husband. He wondered for a second whether he should wrestle them to the ground and question them rigorously and violently, but he was suddenly feeling immensely tired and run down.

He acknowledged the woman in red spectacles with a minute inclination of his head.

"All done, Cynthia," said the man and flicked a smile on and off at her. "It's all taken care of."

She nodded faintly, and the two of them climbed back into their BMW and after a moment or two pulled away without fuss and disappeared away down the road. Dirk looked at the card in his hand. Clive Draycott. He was with a good firm of City solicitors. Dirk stuck the card away in his wallet, climbed despondently back into his car, and drove on back to his house, where he found a large golden eagle sitting patiently on his doorstep.

Chapter 20

Kate rounded on her guest as soon as they were both inside her flat with the door closed and Kate could be reasonably certain that Neil wasn't going to sneak back out of his flat and lurk disapprovingly half-way up the stairs. The continuing thumping of his bass was at least her guarantee of privacy.

"All right," she said fiercely, "so what is the deal with the eagle then? What is the deal with all the street lights? Huh?"

The Norse God of Thunder looked at her awkwardly. He had to remove his great horned helmet because it was banging against the ceiling and leaving scratch marks in the plaster. He tucked it under his arm.

"What is the deal," continued Kate, "with the Coca-Cola machine? What is the deal with the hammer? What, in short, is the big deal? Huh?"

Thor said nothing. He frowned for a second in arrogant irritation, then frowned in something that looked somewhat like embarrassment, and then simply stood there and bled at her.

For a few seconds she resisted the impending internal

collapse of her attitude, and then realised it was just going to go to hell anyway so she might as well go with it.

"OK," she muttered, "let's get all that cleaned up. I'll find some antiseptic."

She went to rummage in the kitchen cupboard and returned with a bottle to find Thor saying "No" at her.

"No what?" she said crossly, putting the bottle down on the table with a bit of a bang.

"That," said Thor, and pushed the bottle back at her. "No."

"What's the matter with it?"

Thor just shrugged and stared moodily at a corner of the room. There was nothing that could be considered remotely interesting in that corner of the room, so he was clearly looking at it out of sheer bloody-mindedness.

"Look, buster," said Kate, "if I can call you buster, what – "

"Thor," said Thor, "God of – "

"Yes," said Kate, "you've told me all the things you're God of. I'm trying to clean up your arm."

"Sedra," said Thor, holding his bleeding arm out, but away from her. He peered at it anxiously.

"What?"

"Crushed leaves of sedra. Oil of the kernel of the apricot. Infusion of bitter orange blossom. Oil of almonds. Sage and comfrey. Not this."

He pushed the bottle of antiseptic off the table and sank into a mood.

"Right!" said Kate, picked up the bottle and hurled it at him. It rebounded off his cheekbone leaving an instant red mark. Thor lunged forward in a rage, but Kate simply stood her ground with a finger pointed at him.

"You stay right there, buster!" she said, and he stopped. "Anything special you need for that?"

Thor looked puzzled for a moment.

"That!" said Kate, pointing at the blossoming bruise on his cheek.

"Vengeance," said Thor.

"I'll have to see what I can do," said Kate. She turned on her heel and stalked out of the room.

After about two minutes of unseen activity Kate returned to the room, trailed by wisps of steam.

"All right," she said, "come with me."

She led him into her bathroom. He followed her with a great show of reluctance, but he followed her. Kate had been trailed by wisps of steam because the bathroom was full of it. The bath itself was overflowing with bubbles and gunk.

There were some bottles and pots, mostly empty, lined up along a small shelf above the bath. Kate picked them up one by one and displayed them at him.

"Apricot kernel oil," she said, and turned it upside down to emphasise its emptiness. "All in there," she added, pointing at the foaming bath.

"Neroli oil," she said, picking up the next one, "distilled from the blossom of bitter oranges. All in there."

She picked up the next one. "Orange cream bath oil. Contains almond oil. All in there."

She picked up the pots.

"Sage and comfrey," she said of one, "and sedra oil. One of them's a hand cream and the other's hair conditioner, but they're all in there, along with a tube of Aloe Lip Preserver, some Cucumber Cleansing Milk, Honeyed Beeswax and Jojoba Oil Cleanser, Rhassoul Mud, Seaweed and Birch Shampoo, Rich Night Cream with Vitamin E, and a very great deal of cod liver oil. I'm afraid I haven't got anything called 'Vengeance', but here's some Calvin Klein 'Obsession'."

She took the stopper from a bottle of perfume and threw the bottle in the bath.

"I'll be in the next room when you're done."

With that she marched out, and slammed the door on him. She waited in the other room, firmly reading a book.

Chapter 21

For about a minute Dirk remained sitting motionless in his car a few yards away from his front door. He wondered what his next move should be. A small, cautious one, he rather thought. The last thing he wanted to have to contend with at the moment was a startled eagle.

He watched it intently. It stood there with a pert magnificence about its bearing, its talons gripped tightly round the edge of the stone step. From time to time it preened itself, and then peered sharply up the street and down the street, dragging one of its great talons across the stone in a deeply worrying manner. Dirk admired the creature greatly for its size and its plumage and its general sense of extreme air-worthiness, but, asking himself if he liked the way that the light from the street lamp glinted in its great glassy eye or on the huge hook of its beak, he had to admit that he did not.

The beak was a major piece of armoury.

It was a beak that would frighten any animal on earth, even

one that was already dead and in a tin. Its talons looked as if they could rip up a small Volvo. And it was sitting waiting on Dirk's doorstep, looking up and down the street with a gaze that was at once meaningful and mean.

Dirk wondered if he should simply drive off and leave the country. Did he have his passport? No. It was at home. It was behind the door which was behind the eagle, in a drawer somewhere or, more likely, lost.

He could sell up. The ratio of estate agents to actual houses in the area was rapidly approaching parity. One of their lot could come and deal with the house. He'd had enough of it, with its fridges and its wildlife and its ineradicable position on the mailing lists of the American Express company.

Or he could, he supposed with a slight shiver, just go and see what it was the eagle wanted. There was a thought. Rats, probably, or a small whippet. All Dirk had, to his knowledge, was some Rice Krispies and an old muffin, and he didn't see those appealing to this magisterial creature of the air. He rather fancied that he could make out fresh blood congealing on the bird's talons, but he told himself firmly not to be so ridiculous.

He was just going to have to go and face up to the thing, explain that he was fresh out of rats and take the consequences.

Quietly, infinitely quietly, he pushed open the door of his car, and stole out of it, keeping his head down. He peered at it from over the bonnet of the car. It hadn't moved. That is to say, it hadn't left the district. It was still looking this way and that around itself with, possibly, a heightened sense of alertness. Dirk didn't know in what remote mountain eyrie the creature had learnt to listen out for the sound of Jaguar car door hinges revolving in their sockets, but the sound had clearly not escaped its attention.

Cautiously, Dirk bobbed along behind the line of cars that had prevented him from being able to park directly outside his own house. In a couple of seconds all that separated him from the extraordinary creature was a small, blue Renault.

What next?

He could simply stand up and, as it were, declare himself. He would be saying, in effect, "Here I am, do what you will." Whatever then transpired, the Renault could probably bear the brunt.

There was always the possibility, of course, that the eagle would be pleased to see him, that all this swooping it had been directing at him had been just its way of being matey. Assuming, of course, that it was the same eagle. That was not such an enormous assumption. The number of golden eagles at large in North London at any one time was, Dirk guessed, fairly small.

Or maybe it was just resting on his doorstep completely by chance, enjoying a quick breather prior to having another hurtle through the sky in pursuit of whatever it is that eagles hurtle through the sky after.

Whatever the explanation, now, Dirk realised, was the time that he had simply to take his chances. He steeled himself, took a deep breath and arose from behind the Renault, like a spirit rising from the deep.

The eagle was looking in another direction at the time, and it was a second or so before it looked back to the front and saw him, at which point it reacted with a loud screech and stepped back an inch or two, a reaction which Dirk felt a little put out by. It then blinked rapidly a few times and adopted a sort of perky expression of which Dirk did not have the faintest idea what to make.

He waited for a second or two, until he felt the situation had settled down again after all the foregoing excitement, and then stepped forward tentatively, round the front of the Renault. A number of quiet, interrogative cawing noises seemed to float uncertainly through the air, and then after a moment Dirk realised that he was making them himself and made himself stop. This was an eagle he was dealing with, not a budgie.

It was at this point that he made his mistake.

With his mind entirely taken up with eagles, the possible

intentions of eagles, and the many ways in which eagles might be considered to differ from small kittens, he did not concentrate enough on what he was doing as he stepped up out of the road and on to a pavement that was slick with the recent drizzle. As he brought his rear foot forward it caught on the bumper of the car; he wobbled, slipped, and then did that thing which one should never do to a large eagle of uncertain temper, which was to fling himself headlong at it with his arms outstretched.

The eagle reacted instantly.

Without a second's hesitation it hopped neatly aside and allowed Dirk the space he needed to collapse heavily on to his own doorstep. It then peered down at him with a scorn that would have withered a lesser man, or at least a man that had been looking up at that moment.

Dirk groaned.

He had sustained a blow to the temple from the edge of the step, and it was a blow, he felt, that he could just as easily have done without this evening. He lay there gasping for a second or two, then at last rolled over heavily, clasping one hand to his forehead, the other to his nose, and looked up at the great bird in apprehension, reflecting bitterly on the conditions under which he was expected to work.

When it became clear to him that he appeared for the moment to have nothing to fear from the eagle, who was merely regarding him with a kind of quizzical, blinking doubt, he sat up, and then slowly dragged himself back to his feet and wiped and smacked some of the dirt off his coat. Then he hunted through his pockets for his keys and unlocked the front door, which seemed a little loose. He waited to see what the eagle would do next.

With a slight rustle of its wings it hopped over the lintel and into his hall. It looked around itself, and seemed to regard what it saw with a little distaste. Dirk didn't know what it was that eagles expected of people's hallways, but had to admit to himself that it wasn't only the eagle which reacted like that. The disorder was not that great, but there was a grimness to it which tended to cast a pall over visitors, and the eagle was clearly not immune to this effect.

Dirk picked up a large flat envelope lying on his doormat, looked inside it to check that it was what he had been expecting, then noticed that a picture was missing from the wall. It wasn't a particularly wonderful picture, merely a small Japanese print that he had found in Camden Passage and quite liked, but the point was that it was missing. The hook on the wall was empty. There was a chair missing as well, he realised.

The possible significance of this suddenly struck him, and he hurried through to the kitchen. Many of his assorted kitchen implements had clearly gone. The rack of largely unused Sabatier knives, the food processor and his radio cassette player had all vanished, but he did, however, have a new fridge. It had obviously been delivered by Nobby Paxton's felonious thugs, and he would just have to make the usual little list.

Still, he had a new fridge and that was a considerable load off his mind. Already the whole atmosphere in the kitchen seemed easier. The tension had lifted. There was a new sense of lightness and springiness in the air which had even communicated itself to the pile of old pizza boxes which seemed now to recline at a jaunty rather than an oppressive angle.

Dirk cheerfully threw open the door to the new fridge and was delighted to find it completely and utterly empty. Its inner light shone on perfectly clean blue and white walls and on gleaming chrome shelves. He liked it so much that he instantly determined to keep it like that. He would put nothing in it at all. His food would just have to go off in plain view.

Good. He closed it again.

A screech and a flap behind him reminded him that he was entertaining a visiting eagle. He turned to find it glaring at him from on top of the kitchen table.

Now that he was getting a little more accustomed to it, and had not actually been viciously attacked as he had suspected he might be, it seemed a little less fearsome than it had at first. It was still a serious amount of eagle, but perhaps an eagle was a slightly more manageable proposition than he had originally supposed. He relaxed a little and took off his hat, pulled off his coat, and threw them on to a chair.

The eagle seemed at this juncture to sense that Dirk might be getting the wrong idea about it and flexed one of its claws at him. With sudden alarm Dirk saw that it did indeed have something that closely resembled congealed blood on the talons. He backed away from it hurriedly. The eagle then rose up to its full height on its talons and began to spread its great wings out, wider and wider, beating them very slowly and leaning forward so as to keep its balance. Dirk did the only thing he could think to do under the circumstances and bolted from the room, slamming the door behind him and jamming the hall table up against it.

A terrible cacophony of screeching and scratching and buffeting arose instantly from behind it. Dirk sat leaning back against the table, panting and trying to catch his breath, and then after a while began to get a worrying feeling about what the bird was up to now.

It seemed to him that the eagle was actually dive-bombing itself against the door. Every few seconds the pattern would repeat itself – first a great beating of wings, then a rush, then a terrible cracking thud. Dirk didn't think it would get through the door, but was alarmed that it might beat itself to death trying. The creature seemed to be quite frantic about something, but what, Dirk could not even begin to imagine. He tried to calm himself down and think clearly, to work out what he should do next.

He should phone Kate and make certain she was all right.

Whoosh, thud!

He should finally open up the envelope he had been carrying with him all day and examine its contents.

Whoosh, thud!

For that he would need a sharp knife.

Whoosh, thud!

Three rather awkward thoughts then struck him in fairly quick succession.

Whoosh, thud!

First, the only sharp knives in the place, assuming Nobby's removal people had left him with any at all, were in the kitchen.

Whoosh, thud!

That didn't matter so much in itself, because he could probably find something in the house that would do.

Whoosh, thud!

The second thought was that the actual envelope itself was in the pocket of his coat which he had left lying over the back of a chair in the kitchen.

Whoosh, thud!

The third thought was very similar to the second and had to do with the location of the piece of paper with Kate's telephone number on it.

Whoosh, thud!

Oh God.

Whoosh, thud!

Dirk began to feel very, very tired at the way the day was working out. He was deeply worried by the sense of impending calamity, but was still by no means able to divine what lay at the root of it.

Whoosh, thud!

Well, he knew what he had to do now...

Whoosh, thud!

...so there was no point in not getting on with it. He quietly pulled the table away from the door.

Whoosh –

He ducked and yanked the door open, passing smoothly under the eagle as it hurtled out into the hallway and hit the opposite wall. He slammed the door closed behind him from inside the kitchen, pulled his coat off the chair and jammed the chair back up under the handle.

Whoosh, thud!

The damage done to the door on this side was both considerable and impressive, and Dirk began seriously to worry about what this behaviour said about the bird's state of mind, or what the bird's state of mind might become if it maintained this behaviour for very much longer.

Whoosh…scratch…

The same thought seemed to have occurred to the bird at that moment, and after a brief flurry of screeching and of scratching at the door with its talons it lapsed into a grumpy and defeated silence, which after it had been going on for about a minute became almost as disturbing as the previous batterings.

Dirk wondered what it was up to.

He approached the door cautiously and very, very quietly moved the chair back a little so that he could see through the keyhole. He squatted down and peered through it. At first it seemed to him that he could see nothing through it, that it must be blocked by something. Then, a slight flicker and glint close up on the other side suddenly revealed the startling truth, which was that the eagle also had an eye up at the keyhole and was busy looking back at him. Dirk almost toppled backwards with the shock of the realisation, and backed away from the door with a sense of slight horror and revulsion.

This was extremely intelligent behaviour for an eagle wasn't it? Was it? How could he find out? He couldn't think of any ornithological experts to phone. All his reference books were piled up in other rooms of the house, and he didn't think he'd be able to keep on pulling off the same stunt with impunity, certainly not when he was dealing with an eagle which had managed to figure out what keyholes were for.

He retreated to the kitchen sink and found some kitchen towel. He folded it into a wad, soaked it, and dabbed it first on his bleeding temple, which was swelling up nicely, and then on his nose which was still very tender, and had been a considerable size for most of the day now. Maybe the eagle was an eagle of delicate sensibilities and had reacted badly to the sight of Dirk's face in its current, much abused, state and had simply lost its mind. Dirk sighed and sat down.

Kate's telephone, which was the next thing he turned his attention to, was answered by a machine when he tried to ring it. Her voice told him, very sweetly, that he was welcome to leave a message after the beep, but warned that she hardly ever listened to them and that it was much better to talk to her directly, only he couldn't because she wasn't in, so he'd best try again.

Thank you very much, he thought, and put the phone down.

He realised that the truth of the matter was this: he had spent the day putting off opening the envelope because of what he was worried about finding in it. It wasn't that the idea was frightening, though indeed it was frightening that a man should sell his soul to a green-eyed man with a scythe, which is what circumstances were trying very hard to suggest had happened. It was just that it was extremely depressing that he should sell it to a green-eyed man with a scythe in exchange for a share in the royalties of a hit record.

That was what it looked like on the face of it. Wasn't it?

Dirk picked up the other envelope, the one which had been waiting for him on his doormat, delivered there by courier from a large London bookshop where Dirk had an account. He pulled out the contents, which were a copy of the sheet music of *Hot Potato*, written by Colin Paignton, Phil Mulville and Geoff Anstey.

The lyrics were, well, straightforward. They provided a basic repetitive bit of funk rhythm and a simple sense of menace and cheerful callousness which had caught the mood of last summer. They went:

Hot Potato,
Don't pick it up, pick it up, pick it up.
Quick, pass it on, pass it on, pass it on.

You don't want to get caught, get caught, get caught.
Drop it on someone. Who? Who? Anybody.
You better not have it when the big one comes.
I said you better not have it when the big one comes.
It's a Hot Potato.

And so on. The repeated phrases got tossed back and forward between the two members of the band, the drum machine got heavier and heavier, and there had been a dance video.

Was that all it was going to be? Big deal. A nice house in Lupton Road with polyurethaned floors and a broken marriage?

Things had certainly come down a long way since the great days of Faust and Mephistopheles, when a man could gain all the knowledge of the universe, achieve all the ambitions of his mind and all the pleasures of the flesh for the price of his soul. Now it was a few record royalties, a few pieces of trendy furniture, a trinket to stick on your bathroom wall and, whap, your head comes off.

So what exactly was the deal? What was the *Potato* contract? Who was getting what and why?

Dirk rummaged through a drawer for the breadknife, sat down once more, took the envelope from his coat pocket and ripped through the congealed strata of Sellotape which held the end of it together.

Out fell a thick bundle of papers.

Chapter 22

At exactly the moment that the telephone rang, the door to Kate's sitting-room opened. The Thunder God attempted to stomp in through it, but in fact he wafted. He had clearly soaked himself very thoroughly in the stuff Kate had thrown into the bath, then redressed, and torn up a nightgown of Kate's to bind his forearm with. He casually tossed a handful of softened oak shards away into the corner of the room. Kate decided for the moment to ignore both the deliberate provocations and the telephone. The former she could deal with and the latter she had a machine for dealing with.

"I've been reading about you," she challenged the Thunder God. "Where's your beard?"

He took the book, a one volume encyclopaedia, from her hands and glanced at it before tossing it aside contemptuously.

"Ha," he said, "I shaved it off. When I was in Wales." He scowled at the memory.

"What were you doing in Wales for heaven's sake?"

"Counting the stones," he said with a shrug, and went to stare out of the window.

There was a huge, moping anxiety in his bearing. It suddenly occurred to Kate with a spasm of something not entirely unlike fear, that sometimes when people got like that, it was because they had picked up their mood from the weather. With a Thunder God it presumably worked the other way round. The sky outside certainly had a restless and disgruntled look.

Her reactions suddenly started to become very confused.

"Excuse me if this sounds like a stupid question," said Kate, "but I'm a little at sea here. I'm not used to spending the evening with someone who's got a whole day named after them. What stones were you counting in Wales?"

"All of them," said Thor in a low growl. "All of them between this size..." he held the tip of his forefinger and thumb about a quarter of an inch apart, "...and this size." He held his two hands about a yard apart, and then put them down again.

Kate stared at him blankly.

"Well...how many were there?" she asked. It seemed only polite to ask.

He rounded on her angrily.

"Count them yourself if you want to know!" he shouted. "What's the point in my spending years and years and years counting them, so that I'm the only person who knows, and who will ever know, if I just go and tell somebody else? Well?"

He turned back to the window.

"Anyway," he said, "I've been worried about it. I think I may have lost count somewhere in Mid-Glamorgan. But I'm not," he shouted, "going to do it again!"

"Well, why on earth would you do such an extraordinary thing in the first place?"

"It was a burden placed on me by my father. A punishment. A penance." He glowered.

"Your father?" said Kate. "Do you mean Odin?"

"The All-Father," said Thor. "Father of the Gods of Asgard."

"And you're saying he's alive?"

Thor turned to look at her as if she was stupid.

"We are immortals," he said, simply.

Downstairs, Neil chose that moment to conclude his thunderous performance on the bass, and the house seemed to sing in its aftermath with an eerie silence.

"Immortals are what you wanted," said Thor in a low, quiet voice. "Immortals are what you got. It is a little hard on us. You wanted us to be for ever, so we are for ever. Then you forget about us. But still we are for ever. Now at last, many are dead, many dying," he then added in a quiet voice, "but it takes a special effort."

"I can't even begin to understand what you're talking about," said Kate, "you say that I, we – "

"You *can* begin to understand," said Thor, angrily, "which is why I have come to you. Do you know that most people hardly see me? Hardly notice me at all? It is not that we are hidden. We are here. We move among you. My people. Your gods. You gave birth to us. You made us be what you would not dare to be yourselves. Yet you will not acknowledge us. If I walk along one of your streets in this...world you have made for yourselves without us, then barely an eye will once flicker in my direction."

"Is this when you're wearing the helmet?"

"Especially when I'm wearing the helmet!"

"Well – "

"You make fun of me!" roared Thor.

"You make it very easy for a girl," said Kate. "I don't know what – "

Suddenly the room seemed to quake and then to catch its breath. All of Kate's insides wobbled violently and then held very still. In the sudden horrible silence, a blue china table lamp slowly toppled off the table, hit the floor, and crawled off to a dark corner of the room where it sat in a worried little defensive huddle.

Kate stared at it and tried to be calm about it. She felt as if cold, soft jelly was trickling down her skin.

"Did you do that?" she said shakily.

Thor was looking livid and confused. He muttered, "Do not make me angry with you. You were very lucky." He looked away.

"What are you *saying*?"

"I'm saying that I wish you to come with me."

"What? What about *that*?" She pointed at the small, befuddled kitten under the table which had so recently and so confusingly been a blue china table lamp.

"There's nothing I can do for it."

Kate was suddenly so tired and confused and frightened that she found she was nearly in tears. She stood biting her lip and trying to be as angry as she could.

"Oh yeah?" she said. "I thought you were meant to be a god. I hope you haven't got into my home under false pretences, I..." She stumbled to a halt, and then resumed in a different tone of voice.

"Do you mean," she said, in a small voice, "that you have been here, in the world, *all this time*?"

"Here, and in Asgard," said Thor.

"Asgard," said Kate. "The home of the gods?"

Thor was silent. It was a grim silence that seemed to be full of something that bothered him deeply.

"Where is Asgard?" demanded Kate.

Again Thor did not speak. He was a man of very few words and enormously long pauses. When at last he did answer, it wasn't at all clear whether he had been thinking all that time or just standing there.

"Asgard is also here," he said. "All worlds are here."

He drew out from under his furs his great hammer and studied its head deeply and with an odd curiosity, as if something about it was very puzzling. Kate wondered where she found such a gesture familiar from. She found that it instinctively made her want to duck. She stepped back very slightly and was watchful.

When he looked up again, there was an altogether new focus and energy in his eyes, as if he was gathering himself up to hurl himself at something.

"Tonight I must be in Asgard," he said. "I must confront my father Odin in the great hall of Valhalla and bring him to account for what he has done."

"You mean, for making you count Welsh pebbles?"

"No!" said Thor. "For making the Welsh pebbles not worth counting!"

Kate shook her head in exasperation. "I simply don't know what to make of you at all," she said. "I think I'm just too tired. Come back tomorrow. Explain it all in the morning."

"No," said Thor. "You must see Asgard yourself, and then you will understand. You must see it tonight." He gripped her by the arm.

"I don't want to go to Asgard," she insisted. "I don't go to mythical places with strange men. You go. Call me up and tell me how it went in the morning. Give him hell about the pebbles."

She wrested her arm from his grip. It was very, very clear to her that she only did this with his permission.

"Now please, go, and let me sleep!" She glared at him.

At that moment the house seemed to erupt as Neil launched into a thumping bass rendition of Siegfried's Rheinfahrt from Act 1 of *Götterdämmerung*, just to prove it could be done. The walls shook, the windows rattled. From under the table the sound of the table lamp mewing pathetically could just be heard.

Kate tried to maintain her furious glare, but it simply couldn't be kept up for very long in the circumstances.

"OK," she said at last, "how do we get to this place?"

"There are as many ways as there are tiny pieces."

"I beg your pardon?"

"Tiny things." He held up his thumb and forefinger again to indicate something very small. "Molecules," he added, seeming to be uncomfortable with the word. "But first let us leave here."

"Will I need a coat in Asgard?"

"As you wish."

"Well, I'll take one anyway. Wait a minute."

She decided that the best way to deal with the astonishing rigmarole which currently constituted her life was to be businesslike about it. She found her coat, brushed her hair, left a new message on her telephone answering machine and put a saucer of milk firmly under the table.

"Right," she said, and led the way out of the flat, locking it carefully after them, and making shushing noises as they passed Neil's door. For all the uproar he was currently making he was almost certainly listening out for the slightest sound, and would be out in a moment if he heard them going by to complain about the Coca-Cola machine, the lateness of the hour, man's inhumanity to man, the weather, the noise, and the colour of Kate's coat, which was a shade of blue that Neil for some reason disapproved of most particularly. They stole past successfully and closed the front door behind them with the merest click.

Chapter 23

The sheets which tumbled out on to Dirk's kitchen table were made of thick heavy paper, folded together, and had obviously been much handled.

He sorted them out, one by one, separating them from each other, smoothing them out with the flat of his hand and laying them out neatly in rows on the kitchen table, clearing a space, as it became necessary, among the old newspapers, ashtrays and dirty cereal bowls which Elena the cleaner always left exactly where they were, claiming, when challenged on this, that she thought he had put them there specially.

He pored over the papers for several minutes, moving from one to another, comparing them with each other, studying them carefully, page by page, paragraph by paragraph, line by line.

He couldn't understand a word of them.

It should have occurred to him, he realised, that the green-eyed, hairy, scythe-waving giant might differ from him not only in general appearance and personal habits, but also in such matters as the alphabet he favoured.

He sat back in his seat, disgruntled and thwarted, and reached for a cigarette, but the packet in his coat was now empty. He picked up a pencil and tapped it in a cigarette-like way, but it wasn't able to produce the same effect.

After a minute or two he became acutely conscious of the fact that he was probably still being watched through the keyhole by the eagle and he found that this made it impossibly hard to concentrate on the problem before him, particularly without a cigarette. He scowled to himself. He knew there was still a packet upstairs by his bed, but he didn't think he could handle the sheer ornithology involved in going to get it.

He tried to stare at the papers for a little longer. The writing, apart from being written in some kind of small, crabby and indecipherable runic script, was mostly hunched up towards the left-hand side of the paper as if swept there by a tide. The right-hand side was largely clear except for an occasional group of characters which were lined up underneath each other. All of it, except for a slight sense of indefinable familiarity about the layout, was completely meaningless to Dirk.

He turned his attention back to the envelope instead and tried once more to examine some of the names which had been so heavily crossed out.

Howard Bell, the incredibly wealthy bestselling novelist who wrote bad books which sold by the warehouse-load despite – or perhaps because of – the fact that nobody read them.

Dennis Hutch, record company magnate. Now that he had a context for the name, Dirk knew it perfectly well. The Aries Rising Record Group which had been founded on Sixties ideals, or at least on what passed for ideals in the Sixties, grown in the Seventies and then embraced the materialism of the Eighties without missing a beat, was now a massive entertainment conglomerate on both sides of the Atlantic. Dennis Hutch had stepped up into the top seat when its founder had died of a lethal overdose of brick wall, taken while under the influence of a Ferrari and a bottle of tequila. ARRGH! was also the record label on which *Hot Potato* had been released.

Stan Dubcek, senior partner in the advertising company with the silly name which now owned most of the British and American advertising companies which had not had names which were quite as silly, and had therefore been swallowed whole.

And here, suddenly, was another name that was instantly recognisable, now that Dirk was attuned to the sort of names he should be looking for. Roderick Mercer, the world's greatest publisher of the world's sleaziest newspapers. Dirk hadn't at first spotted the name with the unfamiliar "...erick" in place after the "Rod". Well, well, well...

Now here were people, thought Dirk suddenly, who had really got something. Certainly they had got rather more than a nice little house in Lupton Road with some dried flowers lying around the place. They also had the great advantage of having heads on their shoulders as well, unless Dirk had missed something new and dramatic on the news. What did that all mean? What was this contract? How come everybody whose hands it had been through had been so astoundingly successful except for one, Geoffrey Anstey? Everybody whose hands it had passed through had benefited from it except for the one who had it last. Who had still got it.

It was a hot potato...

You better not have it when the big one comes.

The notion suddenly formed in Dirk's mind that it might have been Geoffrey Anstey himself who had overheard a conversation about a hot potato, about getting rid of it, passing it on. If he remembered correctly the interview he had read with Pain, he didn't say that he himself had overheard the conversation.

You better not have it when the big one comes.

The notion was a horrible one and ran on like this: Geoffrey Anstey had been pathetically naïve. He had overheard this conversation, between – who? Dirk picked up the envelope and ran over the list of names – and had thought that it had a good dance rhythm. He had not for a moment realised that what he was listening to was a conversation that would result in his own hideous death. He had got a hit record out of it, and when the real hot potato was actually handed to him he had picked it up.

Don't pick it up, pick it up, pick it up.

And instead of taking the advice he had recorded in the words of the song...

Quick, pass it on, pass it on, pass it on.

...he had stuck it behind the gold record award on his bathroom wall.

You better not have it when the big one comes.

Dirk frowned and took a long, slow thoughtful drag on his pencil.

This was ridiculous.

He had to get some cigarettes if he was going to think this through with any intellectual rigour. He pulled on his coat, stuffed his hat on his head and made for the window.

The window hadn't been opened for – well, certainly not during his ownership of the house, and it struggled and screamed at the sudden unaccustomed invasion of its space and independence. Once he had forced it wide enough, Dirk struggled out on to the windowsill, pulling swathes of leather coat out with him. From here it was a bit of a jump to the pavement since there was a lower ground floor to the house with a narrow flight of steps leading down to it in the front. A line of iron railings separated these from the pavement, and Dirk had to get clear over these.

Without hesitating for a moment he made the jump, and it was in mid-bound that he realised he had not picked up his car keys from the kitchen table where he'd left them.

He considered as he sailed gracelessly through the air whether or not to execute a wild mid-air twist, make a desperate grab backwards for the window and hope that he might just manage to hold on to the sill, but decided on mature reflection that an error at this point might just conceivably kill him whereas the walk would probably do him good.

He landed heavily on the far side of the railings, but the tails of his coat became entangled with them and he had to pull them off, tearing part of the lining in the process. Once the ringing shock in his knees had subsided and he had recovered what little composure the events of the day had left him with, he realised that it was now well after eleven o'clock and the pubs would be shut, and he might have a longer walk than he had bargained for to find some cigarettes.

He considered what to do.

The current outlook and state of mind of the eagle was a major factor to be taken into account here. The only way to get his car keys now was back through the front door into his eagle-infested hallway.

Moving with great caution he tip-toed back up the steps to his front door, squatted down and, hoping that the damn thing wasn't going to squeak, gently pushed up the flap of the letter-box and peered through.

In an instant a talon was hooked into the back of his hand and a great screeching beak slashed at his eye, narrowly missing it but scratching a great gouge across his much abused nose.

Dirk howled with pain and lurched backwards, not getting very far because he still had a talon hooked in his hand. He lashed out desperately and hit at the talon, which hurt him considerably, dug the sharp point even further into his flesh and caused a great, barging flurry on the far side of the door, each tiniest movement of which tugged heavily in his hand.

He grabbed at the great claw with his free hand and tried to tug it back out of himself. It was immensely strong, and was shaking with the fury of the eagle, which was as trapped as he was. At last, quivering with pain, he managed to release himself, and pulled his injured hand back, nursing and cuddling it with the other.

The eagle pulled its claw back sharply, and Dirk heard it

flapping away back down his hallway, emitting terrible screeches and cries, its great wings colliding with and scraping the walls.

Dirk toyed with the idea of burning the house down, but once the throbbing in his hand had begun to subside a little he calmed down and tried, if he could, to see things from the eagle's point of view.

He couldn't.

He had not the faintest idea how things appeared to eagles in general, much less to this particular eagle, which seemed to be a seriously deranged example of the species.

After a minute or so more of nursing his hand, curiosity – allied to a strong sense that the eagle had definitely retreated to the far end of the hall and stayed there – overcame him, and he bent down once more to the letter-box. This time he used his pencil to push the flap back upwards and scanned the hallway from a safe position a good few inches back.

The eagle was clearly in view, perched on the end of the bannister rail, regarding him with resentment and opprobrium, which Dirk felt was a little rich coming from a creature which had only a moment or two ago been busily engaged in trying to rip his hand off.

Then, once the eagle was certain that it had got Dirk's attention, it slowly raised itself up on its feet and slowly shook its great wings out, beating them gently for balance. It was this gesture that had previously caused Dirk to bolt prudently from the room. This time, however, he was safely behind a couple of good solid inches of wood and he stood, or rather, squatted his ground. The eagle stretched its neck upwards as well, jabbing its tongue out at the air and cawing plaintively, which surprised Dirk.

Then he noticed something else rather surprising about the eagle, which was that its wings had strange, un-eaglelike markings on them. They were large concentric circles.

The differences of coloration which delineated the circles

were very slight, and it was only the absolute geometric regularity of them which made them stand out as clearly as they did. Dirk had the very clear sense that the eagle was showing him these circles, and that that was what it had wanted to attract his attention to all along. Each time the bird had dived at him, he realised as he thought back, it had then started on a strange kind of flapping routine which had involved opening its wings right out. However, each time it had happened Dirk had been too busily engaged with the business of turning round and running away to pay this exhibition the appropriate attention.

"Have you got the money for a cup of tea, mate?"

"Er, yes thank you," said Dirk, "I'm fine." His attention was fully occupied with the eagle, and he didn't immediately look round.

"No, I meant can you spare me a bob or two, just for a cup of tea?"

"What?" This time Dirk looked round, irritably.

"Or just a fag, mate. Got a fag you can spare?"

"No, I was just going to go and get some myself," said Dirk.

The man on the pavement behind him was a tramp of indeterminate age. He was standing there, slightly wobbly, with a look of wild and continuous disappointment bobbing in his eyes.

Not getting an immediate response from Dirk, the man dropped his eyes to the ground about a yard in front of him, and swayed back and forth a little. He was holding his arms out, slightly open, slightly away from his body, and just swaying. Then he frowned suddenly at the ground. Then he frowned at another part of the ground. Then, holding himself steady while he made quite a major realignment of his head, he frowned away down the street.

"Have you lost something?" said Dirk.

The man's head swayed back towards him.

"Have I *lost* something?" he said in querulous astonishment. "Have I *lost* something?"

It seemed to be the most astounding question he had ever heard. He looked away again for a while, and seemed to be trying to balance the question in the general scale of things. This involved a fair bit more swaying and a fair few more frowns. At last he seemed to come up with something that might do service as some kind of answer.

"The sky?" he said, challenging Dirk to find this a good enough answer. He looked up towards it, carefully, so as not to lose his balance. He seemed not to like what he saw in the dim, orange, street-lit pallor of the clouds, and slowly looked back down again till he was staring at a point just in front of his feet.

"The ground?" he said, with evident great dissatisfaction, and then was struck with a sudden thought.

"Frogs?" he said, wobbling his gaze up to meet Dirk's rather bewildered one. "I used to like...frogs," he said, and left his gaze sitting on Dirk as if that was all he had to say, and the rest was entirely up to Dirk now.

Dirk was completely flummoxed. He longed for the times when life had been easy, life had been carefree, the great times he'd had with a mere homicidal eagle, which seemed now to be such an easygoing and amiable companion. Aerial attack he could cope with, but not this nameless roaring guilt that came howling at him out of nowhere.

"What do you want?" he said in a strangled voice.

"Just a fag, mate," said the tramp, "or something for a cup of tea."

Dirk pressed a pound coin into the man's hand and lunged off down the street in a panic, passing, twenty yards further on, a builder's skip from which the shape of his old fridge loomed at him menacingly.

Chapter 24

As Kate came down the steps from her house she noticed that the temperature had dropped considerably. The clouds sat heavily on the land and loured at it. Thor set off briskly in the direction of the park, and Kate trotted along in his wake.

As he strode along, an extraordinary figure on the streets of Primrose Hill, Kate could not help but notice that he had been right. They passed three different people on the way, and she saw distinctly how their eyes avoided looking at him, even as they had to make allowance for his great bulk as he passed them. He was not invisible, far from it. He simply didn't fit.

The park was closed for the night, but Thor leapt quickly over the spiked railings and then lifted her over in turn as lightly as if she had been a bunch of flowers.

The grass was damp and mushy, but still worked its magic on city feet. Kate did what she always did when entering the park, which was to bob down and put the flats of her hands down on the ground for a moment. She had never quite worked out why she did this, and often she would adjust a shoe or pick up a piece of litter as a pretext for the movement, but all she really wanted was to feel the grass and the wet earth on her palms.

The park from this viewpoint was simply a dark shoulder that rose up before them, obscuring itself. They mounted the hill and stood on the top of it, looking over the darkness of the rest of the park to where it shaded off into the hazy light of the heart of London which lay to the south. Ugly towers and blocks stuck yobbishly up out of the skyline, dominating the park, the sky, and the city.

A cold, damp wind moved across the park, flicking at it from time to time like the tail of a dark and broody horse. There was an unsettled, edgy quality to it. In fact the night sky seemed to Kate to be like a train of restless, irritable horses, their traces flapping and slapping in the wind. It also seemed to her as if the traces all radiated loosely from a single centre, and that the centre was very close by her. She reprimanded herself for absurd suggestibility, but nevertheless, it still seemed that all the weather was gathered and circling around them, waiting on them.

Thor once more drew out his hammer, and held it before him in the thoughtful and abstracted manner she had seen a few minutes before in her flat. He frowned, and seemed to be picking tiny invisible pieces of dust off it. It was a little like a chimpanzee grooming its mate, or – that was it! – the comparison was extraordinary, but it explained why she had tensed herself so watchfully when last he had done it. It was like Jimmy Connors minutely adjusting the strings of his racquet before preparing to serve.

He looked up sharply once again, drew his arm back, turned fully once, twice, three times, twisting his heels heavily in the mud, and then hurled his hammer with astonishing force up to the heavens.

It vanished almost instantly into the murky haze of the sky. Damp flashes sparked deep within the clouds, tracking its path in a long parabola through the night. At the furthest extent of the parabola it swung down out of the clouds, a distant tiny pinpoint moving slowly now, gathering and redirecting its momentum for the return flight. Kate watched, breathless, as the speck crept behind the dome of St Paul's. It then seemed almost as if it had halted altogether, hanging silently and improbably in the air, before gradually beginning to increase microscopically in size as it accelerated back towards them.

Then, as it returned, it swung aside in its path, no longer describing a simple parabola, but following instead a new path which seemed to lie along the perimeter of a gigantic Möbius strip which took it round the other side of the Telecom Tower. Then suddenly it was swinging back in a path directly towards them, hurtling out of the night with impossible weight and speed like a piston in a shaft of light. Kate swayed and nearly dropped in a dead faint out of its path, when Thor stepped forward and caught it with a grunt.

The jolt of it sent a single heavy shudder down into the earth, and then the thing was resting quietly in Thor's grip. His arm quivered slightly and was still.

Kate felt quite dizzy. She didn't know exactly what it was that had just happened, but she felt pretty damn certain that it was the sort of experience that her mother would not have approved of on a first date.

"Is this all part of what we have to do to go to Asgard?" she said. "Or are you just fooling around?"

"We will go to Asgard...now," he said.

At that moment he raised his hand as if to pluck an apple, but instead of plucking he made a tiny, sharp turning movement. The effect was as if he had twisted the entire world through a billionth part of a billionth part of a degree. Everything shifted, was for a moment minutely out of focus, and then snapped back again as a suddenly different world.

This world was a much darker one and colder still.

A bitter, putrid wind blew sharply, and made every breath gag in the throat. The ground beneath their feet was no longer the soft muddy grass of the hill, but a foul-smelling, oozing slush. Darkness lay over all the horizon with a few small exceptional fires dotted here and there in the distance, and one great blaze of light about a mile and a half away to the southeast.

Here, great fantastical towers stabbed at the night; huge pinnacles and turrets flickered in the firelight that surged from a thousand windows. It was an edifice that mocked reason, ridiculed reality and jeered wildly at the night.

"My father's palace," said Thor, "the Great Hall of Valhalla, where we must go."

It was just on the tip of Kate's tongue to say that something about the place was oddly familiar when the sound of horses' hooves pounding through the mud came to them on the wind. At a distance, between where they stood and the Great Hall of Valhalla, a small number of flickering torches could be seen jolting towards them.

Thor once more studied the head of his hammer with interest, brushed it with his forefinger and rubbed it with his thumb. Then slowly he looked up, again he twisted round once, then twice and a third time and then hurled the missile into the sky. This time, however, he continued to hold on to its shaft with his right hand, while with his left he held Kate's waist in his grasp.

Chapter 25

Cigarettes clearly intended to make themselves a major problem for Dirk tonight.

For most of the day, except for when he'd woken up, and except for again shortly after he'd woken up, and except for when he had just encountered the revolving head of Geoffrey Anstey, which was understandable, and also except for when he'd been in the pub with Kate, he had had absolutely no cigarettes at all.

Not one. They were out of his life, foresworn utterly. He didn't need them. He could do without them. They merely nagged at him like mad and made his life a living hell, but he decided he could handle that.

Now, however, just when he had suddenly decided, coolly, rationally, as a clear, straightforward decision rather than merely a feeble surrender to craving, that he would, after all, have a cigarette, could he find one? He could not.

The pubs by this stage of the night were well closed. The late night corner shop obviously meant something different by "late night" than Dirk did, and though Dirk was certain that he could convince the proprietor of the rightness of his case through sheer linguistic and syllogistic bravado, the wretched man wasn't there to undergo it.

A mile away there was a 24-hour filling station, but it turned out just to have sustained an armed robbery. The plate glass was shattered and crazed round a tiny hole, police were swarming over the place. The attendant was apparently not badly injured, but he was still losing blood from a wound in his arm, having hysterics and being treated for shock, and no one would sell Dirk any cigarettes. They simply weren't in the mood.

"You could buy cigarettes in the blitz," protested Dirk. "People took a pride in it. Even with the bombs falling and the whole city ablaze you could still get served. Some poor fellow, just lost two daughters and a leg, would still say 'Plain or filter-tipped?' if you asked him."

"I expect you would, too," muttered a white-faced young policeman.

"It was the spirit of the age," said Dirk.

"Bug off," said the policeman.

And that, thought Dirk to himself, was the spirit of this. He retreated, miffed, and decided to prowl the streets with his hands in his pockets for a while.

Camden Passage. Antique clocks. Antique clothes. No cigarettes.

Upper Street. Antique buildings being ripped apart. No sign of cigarette shops being put up in their place.

Chapel Market, desolate at night. Wet litter wildly flapping. Cardboard boxes, egg boxes, paper bags and cigarette packets – empty ones.

Pentonville Road. Grim concrete monoliths, eyeing the new spaces in Upper Street where they hoped to spawn their horrid progeny.

King's Cross station. They must have cigarettes, for heaven's sake. Dirk hurried on down towards it.

The old frontage to the station reared up above the area, a great yellow brick wall with a clock tower and two huge arches fronting the two great train sheds behind. In front of this lay the one-storey modern concourse which was already far shabbier than the building, a hundred years its senior, which it obscured and generally messed up. Dirk imagined that when the designs for the modern concourse had been drawn up the architects had explained that it entered into an exciting and challenging dialogue with the older building.

King's Cross is an area where terrible things happen to people, to buildings, to cars, to trains, usually while you wait, and if you weren't careful you could easily end up involved in a piece of exciting and challenging dialogue yourself. You could have a cheap car radio fitted while you waited, and if you turned your back for a couple of minutes, it would be removed while you waited as well. Other things you could have removed while you waited were your wallet, your stomach lining, your mind and your will to live. The muggers and pushers and pimps and hamburger salesmen, in no particular order, could arrange all these things for you.

But could they arrange a packet of cigarettes, thought Dirk, with a mounting sense of tension. He crossed York Way, declined a couple of surprising offers on the grounds that they did not involve cigarettes in any immediately obvious way, hurried past the closed bookshop and in through the main concourse doors, away from the life of the street and into the safer domain of British Rail.

He looked around him.

Here things seemed rather strange and he wondered why, but he only wondered this very briefly because he was also wondering if there was anywhere open selling cigarettes and there wasn't.

He sagged forlornly. It seemed to him that he had been playing catch-up with the world all day. The morning had started in about as disastrous a way as it was possible for a morning to start, and he had never managed to get a proper grip on it since. He felt like somebody trying to ride a bolting horse, with one foot in a stirrup and the other one still bounding along hopefully on the ground behind. And now even as simple a thing as a cigarette was proving to be beyond his ability to get hold of.

He sighed and found himself a seat, or at least, room on a bench.

This was not an immediately easy thing to do. The station was more crowded than he had expected to find it at – what was it? he looked up at the clock – one o'clock in the morning. What in the name of God was he doing on King's Cross station at one o'clock in the morning, with no cigarette and no home that he could reasonably expect to get into without being hacked to death by a homicidal bird?

He decided to feel sorry for himself. That would pass the time. He looked around himself, and after a while the impulse to feel sorry for himself gradually subsided as he began to take in his surroundings.

What was strange about it was seeing such an immediately familiar place looking so unfamiliar. There was the ticket office, still open for ticket sales, but looking sombre and beleaguered and wishing it was closed.

There was the W.H.Smith, closed for the night. No one would be needing any further newspapers or magazines tonight, except for purposes of accommodation, and old ones would do just as well for sleeping under.

The pimps and hookers, drug-pushers and hamburger salesmen were all outside in the streets and in the hamburger bars. If you wanted quick sex or a dirty fix or, God help you, a hamburger, that was where you went to get it.

Here were the people that nobody wanted anything from at all. This was where they gathered for shelter until they were periodically shooed out. There was something people wanted from them, in fact – their absence. That was in hot demand, but not easily supplied. Everybody has to be somewhere.

Dirk looked from one to another of the men and women shuffling round or sitting hunched in seats or struggling to try and sleep across benches that were specifically designed to prevent them from doing exactly that.

"Got a fag, mate?"

"What? No, I'm sorry. No, I haven't got one," replied Dirk, awkwardly patting his coat pockets in embarrassment, as if to suggest the making of a search which he knew would be fruitless. He was startled to be summoned out of his reverie like this.

"Here you are, then." The old man offered him a beat-up one from a beat-up packet.

"What? Oh. Oh – thanks. Thank you." Momentarily taken aback by the offer, Dirk nevertheless accepted the cigarette gratefully, and took a light from the tip of the cigarette the old man was smoking himself.

"What you come here for then?" asked the old man – not challenging, just curious.

Dirk tried to look at him without making it seem as if he was looking him up and down. The man was wildly bereft of teeth, had startled and matted hair, and his old clothes were well mulched down around him, but the eyes which sagged out of his face were fairly calm. He wasn't expecting anything worse than he could deal with to happen to him.

"Well, just this in fact," said Dirk, twiddling the cigarette. "Thanks. Couldn't find one anywhere."

"Oh ah," said the old man.

"Got this mad bird at home," said Dirk. "Kept attacking me."

"Oh ah," said the man, nodding resignedly.

"I mean an actual bird," said Dirk, "an eagle."

"Oh ah."

"With great wings."

"Oh ah."

"Got hold of me with one of its talons through the letter-box."

"Oh ah."

Dirk wondered if it was worth pursuing the conversation much further. He lapsed into silence and looked around.

"You're lucky it didn't slash at you with its beak as well," said the old man after a while. "An eagle will do that when roused."

"It did!" said Dirk. "It did! Look, right here on my nose. That was through the letter-box as well. You'd scarcely believe it! Talk about grip! Talk about reach! Look at what it did to my hand!"

He held it out for sympathy. The old man gave it an appraising look.

"Oh ah," he said at last, and retreated into his own thoughts.

Dirk drew his injured hand back.

"Know a lot about eagles, then, do you?"

The man didn't answer, but seemed instead to retreat still further.

"Lot of people here tonight," Dirk ventured again, after a while.

The man shrugged. He took a long drag on his cigarette, half-closing his eyes against the smoke.

"Is it always like this? I mean, are there always so many people here at night?"

The man merely looked down, slowly releasing the smoke from his mouth and nostrils.

Yet again, Dirk looked around. A man a few feet away, not so old-looking as Dirk's companion but wildly deranged in his demeanour, had sat nodding hectically over a bottle of cooking brandy all this time. He slowly stopped his nodding, screwed with difficulty a cap on to the bottle, and slipped it into the pocket of his ragged old coat. An old fat woman who had been fitfully browsing through the bulging black bin liner of her possessions began to twist the top of it together and fold it.

"You'd almost think that something was about to happen," said Dirk.

"Oh ah," said his companion. He put his hands on his knees,

bent forward and raised himself painfully to his feet. Though he was bent and slow, and though his clothes were dirt-ridden and tattered, there was some little power and authority there in his bearing.

The air which he unsettled as he stood, which flowed out from the folds of his skin and clothes, was richly pungent even to Dirk's numbed nostrils. It was a smell that never stopped coming at you – just as Dirk thought it must have peaked, so it struck on upwards with renewed frenzy till Dirk thought that his very brain would vaporise.

He tried not to choke, indeed he tried to smile courteously without allowing his eyes to run as the man turned to him and said, "Infuse some blossom of the bitter orange. Add some sprinklings of sage while it is still warm. This is very good for eagle wounds. There are those who will add apricot and almond oil and even, the heavens defend us, sedra. But then there are always those that will overdo things. And sometimes we have need of them. Oh ah."

With that he turned away once more and joined the growing stream of pathetic, hunched and abused bodies that were heading for the front exit from the station. In all about two, maybe three dozen were leaving. Each seemed to be leaving separately, each for his or her entirely independent reasons, and not following too fast the one upon the other, and yet it was not hard to tell, for anyone who cared to watch these people that no one cared to watch or see, that they were leaving together and in a stream.

Dirk carefully nursed his cigarette for a minute or so and watched them intently as one by one they left. Once he was certain that there were no more to go, and that the last two or three of them were at the door, he dropped the cigarette and ground it out with his heel. Then he noticed that the old man had left behind his crumpled cigarette packet. Dirk looked inside and saw that there were still two bedraggled cigarettes left. He pocketed it, stood up, and quietly followed at a distance that he thought was properly respectful.

Outside on the Euston Road the night air was grumbling and unsettled. He loitered idly by the doorway, watching which way they went – to the west. He took one of the cigarettes out and lit it and then idled off westwards himself, around the taxi rank and towards St Pancras Street.

On the west side of St Pancras Street, just a few yards north of the Euston Road, a flight of steps leads up to the forecourt of the old Midland Grand Hotel, the huge, dark gothic fantasy of a building which stands, empty and desolate, across the front of St Pancras railway station.

Over the top of the steps, picked out in gold letters on wrought-iron-work, stands the name of the station. Taking his time, Dirk followed the last of the band of old tramps and derelicts up these steps, which emerged just to the side of a small, squat, brick building which was used as a car-park. To the right, the great dark hulk of the old hotel spread off into the night, its roofline a vast assortment of wild turrets, gnarled spires and pinnacles which seemed to prod at and goad the night sky.

High in the dim darkness, silent stone figures stood guard behind long shields, grouped around pilasters behind wrought-iron railings. Carved dragons crouched gaping at the sky as Dirk Gently, in his flapping leather coat, approached the great iron portals which led to the hotel, and to the great vaulted train shed of St Pancras station. Stone figures of winged dogs crouched down from the top of pillars.

Here, in the bridged area between the hotel entrance and the station booking hall, was parked a large unmarked grey Mercedes van. A quick glance at the front of it was enough to tell Dirk that it was the same one which had nearly forced him off the road several hours earlier in the Cotswolds.

Dirk walked into the booking hall, a large space with great panelled walls along which were spaced fat marble columns in the form of torch holders.

At this time of night the ticket office was closed – trains do not run all night from St Pancras – and beyond it the vast chamber of the station itself, the great Victorian train shed, was shrouded in darkness and shadow.

Dirk stood quietly secluded in the entrance to the booking hall and watched as the old tramps and bag ladies, who had entered the station by the main entrance from the forecourt, mingled together in the dimness. There were now many more than two dozen of them, perhaps as many as a hundred, and there seemed to be about them an air of repressed excitement and tension.

As they moved about it seemed to Dirk after a while that, though he had been surprised at how many of them there had been when he first arrived, there seemed now to be fewer and fewer of them. He peered into the gloom trying to make out what was happening. He detached himself from his seclusion in the entrance to the booking hall and entered the main vault, but kept himself nevertheless as close to the side wall as possible as he ventured in towards them.

There were definitely fewer still of them now, a mere handful left. He had a distinct sense of people slipping away into the shadows and not re-emerging from them.

He frowned at them.

The shadows were deep but they weren't that deep. He began to hurry forward, and quickly threw all caution aside to reach the small remaining group. But by the time he reached the centre of the concourse where they had been gathered there were none remaining at all and he was left whirling round in confusion in the middle of the great, dark, empty railway station.

Chapter 26

The only thing which prevented Kate screaming was the sheer pressure of air rushing into her lungs as she hurtled into the sky.

When, a few seconds later, the blinding acceleration eased a little, she found she was gulping and choking, her eyes were stinging and streaming to the extent that she could hardly see, and there was hardly a muscle in her body which wasn't gibbering with shock as waves of air pummelled past her, tearing at her hair and clothes and making her knees, knuckles and teeth batter at each other.

She had to struggle with herself to suppress her urge to struggle. On the one hand she absolutely certainly did not want to be let go of. Insofar as she had any understanding at all of what was happening to her she knew that she did not want to be let go of. On the other hand the physical shock of it was facing some stiff competition from her sheer affronted rage at being suddenly hauled into the sky without warning. The result of this was that she struggled rather feebly and was angry at herself for doing so. She ended up clinging to Thor's arm in the most abject and undignified way.

The night was dark, and the blessing of this, she supposed, was that she could not see the ground. The lights she had seen dotted here and there in the distance now swung sickeningly away beneath her, but her instincts would not identify them as representing ground. Already the flickering beacons which shone from the insanely turreted building she had glimpsed seconds before this outrage occurred were swaying away behind her now at an increasing distance.

They were still ascending.

She could not struggle, she could not speak. She could probably, if she tried, bite the stupid brute's arm, but she contented herself with the idea of this rather than the actual deed.

The air was bad and rasped in her lungs. Her nose and eyes were streaming, and this made it impossible for her to look forward. When she did try it, just once, she caught a momentary blurred glimpse of the head of the hammer streaking out through the dark air ahead of them, of Thor's arm grasping its stunted handle and being pulled forward by it. His other arm was gripped around her waist. The strength of him defied her imagination but did not make her any the less angry.

She got the feeling that they were now skimming along just beneath the clouds. Every now and then they would be buffeted by damp clamminess, and breathing would become yet harder and more noxious. The wet air tasted bitter, and deadly cold, and her streaming wet hair lashed and slammed about her face

She decided that the cold was definitely going to kill her, and after a while was convinced that she was beginning to lose consciousness. In fact she realised she was actually trying to lose consciousness but she couldn't. Time slipped into a greyness though, and she was less aware of how much of it was passing.

At last she began to sense that they were slowing and that they were beginning to curve back downwards. This precipitated fresh waves of nausea and disorientation in her, and she felt that her stomach was being slowly turned through a mangle.

The air was, if anything, getting worse. It smelled worse, tasted more acrid and seemed to be getting a great deal more turbulent. They were definitely slowing now, and the going was becoming more and more difficult. The hammer was clearly pointing downwards now, and finding its way along rather than surging ahead.

Down still further they went, battling through the thickening clouds that swirled round them till it seemed that they must now reach all the way down to the ground.

Their speed had dropped to the point where Kate felt able to look ahead now, though the acridity of the air was such that she was only able to manage a very brief glance. In the moment that she glanced, Thor released the hammer. She couldn't believe it. He released it only for a fraction of a second, just to change his grip on the thing, so that they were now hanging from the shaft as it flew slowly forward, rather than being pulled along by it. As he redistributed his weight into this new posture he hoisted Kate firmly upwards as if pulling up a sock. Down they went, and down further and further.

There was now a roaring crashing sound borne in on them by the wind from up ahead, and suddenly Thor was running, leaping over rocky, sandy scrubland, dancing through the knotted tussocks, and finally pounding and drumming his feet to a halt.

They stood still at last, swaying, but the ground on which they stood was solid.

Kate breathed for a few seconds, bending over to catch her breath. She then pulled herself up to her full height and was about to deliver a full account of her feelings concerning these events at the top of her voice, when she suddenly got an alarming sense of where she was standing.

Though the night was dark, the wind whipping at her and the pungent smell of it told her that some kind of sea was very close by. The sound of wild crashing breakers told her that in fact it was more or less beneath her, that they were standing very near to the edge of a cliff. She gripped the arm of the insufferable god who had brought her here and hoped, vainly, that it hurt him.

As her reeling senses began gradually to calm down she noticed that there was a dim light spreading away before her, and after a while she realised that this was coming off the sea.

The whole sea was glowing like an infection. It was rearing itself up in the night, lunging and thrashing in a turmoil of itself and then smashing itself to pieces in a frenzy of pain against the rocks of the coast. Sea and sky seethed at each other in a poisonous fury.

Kate watched it speechlessly, and then became aware of Thor standing at her shoulder.

"I met you at an airport," he said, his voice breaking up in the wind. "I was trying to get home to Norway by plane." He pointed out to sea. "I wanted you to see why I couldn't come this way."

"Where are we? What is this?" asked Kate fearfully.

"In your world, this is the North Sea," said Thor and turned away inland again, walking heavily and dragging his hammer behind him.

Kate pulled her wet coat close around her and hurried after him.

"Well, why didn't you just fly home the way we just did but in, well, in our world?"

The rage in her had subsided into vague worries about vocabulary.

"I tried," responded Thor, still walking away.

"Well, what happened?"

"I don't want to talk about it."

"What on earth's the point of that?"

"I'm not going to discuss it."

Kate shuddered in exasperation. "Is this godlike behaviour?" she shouted. "It bothers you so you won't talk about it?"

"Thor! Thor! Is it you?"

This last was a thin voice trailing over the wind. Kate peered into the wind. Through the darkness a lantern was bobbing towards them from behind a low rise.

"Is that you, Thor?" A little old lady came into view, holding a lantern above her head, hobbling enthusiastically. "I thought that must be your hammer I saw. Welcome!" she chirruped. "Oh, but you come in dismal times. I was just putting the pot on and thinking of having a cup of something and then perhaps killing myself, but then I said to myself, just wait a couple of days longer, Tsuliwa…, Tsuwila…, Swuli…, Tsuliwaënsis – I can never pronounce my own name properly when I'm talking to myself, and it drives me hopping mad, as I'm sure you can imagine, such a bright boy as I've always maintained, never mind what those others say, so I said to myself, Tsuliwaënsis, see if anyone comes along, and if they don't, well, then might be a good time to think about killing myself. And look! Now here you are! Oh, but you are welcome, welcome! And I see you've brought a little friend. Are you going to introduce me? Hello, my dear, hello! My name's Tsuliwaënsis and I won't be at all offended if you stutter."

"I…I'm, er, Kate," said Kate, totally flummoxed.

"Yes, well I'm sure that will be all right," said the old woman sharply. "Anyway, come along if you're coming. If you're going to hang around out here all night I may as well just get straight on with killing myself now and let you get your own tea when you're quite ready. Come along!"

She hurried on ahead, and in a very few yards they reached a terrible kind of ramshackle structure of wood and mud which looked as if it had become unaccountably stuck while half-way through collapsing. Kate glanced at Thor, hoping to read some kind of reaction from him to give her a bearing on the situation, but he was occupied with his own thoughts and was clearly not about to share them. There seemed to her to be a difference in the way he moved, though. In the brief experience she had of

him he seemed constantly to be struggling with some internal
and constrained anger, and this, she felt, had lifted. Not gone
away, just lifted. He stood aside to allow her to enter
Tsuliwaënsis's shack, and brusquely gestured her to go in. He
followed, ducking absurdly, a few seconds later, having paused
for a moment outside to survey what little could be seen of the
surrounding landscape.

Inside was tiny. A few boards with straw for a bed, a
simmering pot hung over a fire, and a box tucked away in the
corner for sitting on.

"And this is the knife I was thinking of using, you see," said
Tsuliwaënsis, fussing around. "Just been sharpening it up nicely,
you see. It comes up very nice if you get a nice sweeping action
with the stone, and I was thinking here would be a good place,
you see? Here on the wall, I can stick the handle in this crack so
it's held nice and firm, and then just go *fling!* And fling myself
at it. *Fling!* You see? I wonder, should it be a little lower, what
do you think, my dear? Know about these things, do you?"

Kate explained that she did not, and managed to sound
reasonably calm about it.

"Tsuliwaënsis," said Thor, "we have come not to stay but
to...Tsuli – please put the knife down."

Tsuliwaënsis was standing looking up at them quite chirpily,
but she was also holding the knife, with its great heavy sweeping
blade, poised over her own left wrist.

"Don't mind me, dears," she said, "I'm quite comfortable. I
can just pop off any time I'm ready. Happy to. These times are
not to live in. Oh, no. You go off and be happy. I won't disturb
your happiness with the sound of me screaming. I'll hardly
make a sound with the knife as you go." She stood quivering
and challenging.

Carefully, almost gently, Thor reached out and drew the knife
away and out of her shaking hand. The old woman seemed to
crumple as it went, and all the performance faded out of her. She
sat back in a heap on her box. Thor squatted down in front of

her, slowly drew her to him and hugged her. She gradually seemed to come back to life, and eventually pushed him away telling him not to be so stupid, and then made a bit of a fuss of smoothing out her hopelessly ragged and dirty black dress.

When once she had composed herself properly she turned her attention to Kate and looked her up and down.

"You're a mortal, dear, aren't you?" she said at last.

"Well...yes," said Kate.

"I can tell it from your fancy dress. Oh, yes. Well, now you see what the world looks like from the other side, don't you, dear? What do you think then?"

Kate explained that she did not yet know what to think. Thor sat himself down on the floor and leant his big head back against the wall, half-closing his eyes. Kate had the sense that he was preparing himself for something.

"It used to be things were not so different," continued the old woman. "Used to be lovely here, you know, all lovely. Bit of give and take between us. Terrible rows, of course, terrible fights, but really it was all lovely. Now?" She let out a long and tired sigh, and brushed a bit of nothing much off the wall.

"Oh, things are bad," she said, "things are very bad. You see things get affected by things. Our world affects your world, your world affects our world. Sometimes it is hard to know exactly what that effect is. Very often it is hard to like it, either. Most of them, these days, are difficult and bad. But our worlds are so nearly the same in so many ways. Where in your world you have a building there will be a structure here as well. Maybe it will be a small muddy hillock, or a beehive, or an abode like this one. Maybe it will be something a little grander, but it will be something. You all right, Thor, dear?"

The Thunder God closed his eyes and nodded. His elbows lay easily across his knees. The ragged strips of Kate's nightgown bound about his left forearm were limp and wet. He idly pushed them off.

"And where there is something which is not dealt with

properly in your world," the old lady prattled on, "as like as not it will emerge in ours. Nothing disappears. No guilty secret. No unspoken thought. It may be a new and mighty god in our world, or it may be just a gnat, but it will be here. I might add that these days it is more often a gnat than a new and mighty god. Oh, there are so many more gnats and fewer immortal gods than once there were."

"How can there be fewer immortals?" asked Kate. "I don't want to be pedantic about it, but – "

"Well, there's being immortal, dear, and then again there's being immortal. I mean, if I could just get this knife properly secured and then work up a really good fling, we'd soon see who was immortal and who wasn't."

"Tsuli..." admonished Thor, but didn't open his eyes to do it.

"One by one we're going, though. We are, Thor. You're one of the few that care. There's few enough now that haven't succumbed to alcoholism or the onx."

"What is that? Some kind of disease?" asked Kate. She was beginning to feel cross again. Having been dragged unwillingly from her flat and hurled across the whole of East Anglia on the end of a hammer, she was irritated at being then just abandoned to a conversation with an insanely suicidal old woman while Thor just sat and looked content with himself, leaving her to make an effort she was not in a mood to make.

"It's an affliction, dear, which only gods get. It really means that you can't take being a god any more, which is why only gods get it you see."

"I see."

"In the final stages of it you simply lie on the ground and after a while a tree grows out of your head and then it's all over. You rejoin the earth, seep into its bowels, flow through its vital arteries, and eventually emerge as a great pure torrent of water, and as like as not get a load of chemical waste dumped into you. It's a grim business being a god nowadays, even a dead god.

"Well," she said, patting her knees. Her eyes hovered on

Thor, who had opened his eyes but was only using them to stare at his own knuckles and fingertips. "Well, I hear you have an appointment tonight, Thor."

"Hmm," grunted Thor, without moving.

"I hear you've called together the Great Hall for the Challenging Hour, is that right?"

"Hmm," said Thor.

"The Challenging Hour, hmm? Well, I know that things have not been too good between you and your father for a long time. Hmm?"

Thor wasn't going to be drawn. He said nothing.

"I thought it was quite dreadful about Wales," continued Tsuliwaënsis. "Don't know why you stood for it. Of course I realise that he's your father and the All-Father which makes it difficult. But, Odin, Odin – I've known him for so long. You know that he made a deal once to sacrifice one of his own eyes in exchange for wisdom? Of course you do, dear, you're his son, aren't you? Well, what I've always said is he should stand up and make a fuss about that particular deal, demand his eye back. Do you know what I mean by that, Thor? And that horrible Toe Rag. There's someone to be careful of, Thor, very careful indeed. Well, I expect I shall hear all about it in the morning, won't I?"

Thor slid his back up the wall and stood up. He clasped the old woman warmly by the hands and smiled a tight smile, but said nothing. With a slight nod he gestured to Kate that they were leaving. Since leaving was what she most wanted in all the world to do she resisted the temptation to say "Oh yeah?" and kick up a fuss about being treated like this. Meekly she bade a polite farewell to the old woman and made her way out into the murky night. Thor followed her.

She folded her arms and said, "Well? Where now? What other great social events have you got in store for me this evening?"

Thor prowled around a little, examining the ground. He

pulled out his hammer, and weighed it appreciatively in his hands. He peered out into the night, and swung the hammer a couple of times, idly. He swung himself round a couple of times, again not hard. He loosed the hammer, which bounded off into the night and split open a casually situated rock a couple of dozen yards away and then bounded back. He caught it easily, tossed it up into the air and caught it easily again.

Then he turned to her and looked her in the eye for the first time.

"Would you like to see something?" he asked.

Chapter 27

A gust of wind blew through the huge vaults of the empty station and nearly provoked in Dirk a great howl of frustration at the trail that had so suddenly gone cold on him. The cold moonlight draped itself through the long ranges of glass panels that extended the length of the St Pancras station roof.

It fell on empty rails, and illuminated them. It fell on the train departures board, it fell on the sign which explained that today was a Blue Saver Day and illuminated them both.

Framed in the archway formed by the far end of the vaulted roof were the fantastical forms of five great gasometers, the supporting superstructures of which seemed in their adumbrations to be tangled impossibly with each other, like the hoops of an illusionist's conjuring trick. The moonlight illuminated these as well, but Dirk it did not illuminate.

He had watched upwards of a hundred people or so simply vanish into thin air in a way that was completely impossible. That in itself did not give him a problem. The impossible did not bother him unduly. If it could not possibly be done, then obviously it had been done impossibly. The question was how?

He paced the area of the station which they had all vanished from, and scanned everything that could be seen from every vantage point within it, looking for any clue, any anomaly, anything that might let him pass into whatever it was he had just seen a hundred people pass into as if it was nothing. He had the sense of a major party taking place in the near vicinity, to which he had not been invited. In desperation he started to spin around with his arms outstretched, then decided this was completely futile and lit a cigarette instead.

He noticed that as he had pulled out the packet, a piece of paper had fluttered from his pocket, which, once the cigarette was burning well, he stooped to retrieve.

It was nothing exciting, just the bill he had picked up from the stroppy nurse in the café. "Outrageous," he thought about each of the items in turn as he scanned down them, and was about to screw it up and throw it away when a thought struck him about the general layout of the document.

The items charged were listed down the left hand side, and the actual charges down the right.

On his own bills when he issued them, when he had a client, which was rare at the moment, and the ones he did have seemed unable to stay alive long enough to receive his bills and be outraged by them, he usually went to a little trouble about the items charged. He constructed essays, little paragraphs to describe them. He liked the client to feel that he or she was getting his or her money's worth in this respect at least.

In short, the bills he issued corresponded in layout almost exactly to the wad of papers with indecipherable runic scripts which he had been unable to make head or tail of a couple of hours previously. Was that helpful? He didn't know. If the wad was not a contract but a bill, what might it be the bill for? What services had been performed? They must certainly have been intricate services. Or at least, intricately described services. Which professions might that apply to? It was at least something to think about. He screwed up the café bill and moved off to throw it into a bin.

As it happened, this was a fortuitous move.

It meant that he was away from the central open space of the station, and near a wall against which he could press himself inconspicuously when he suddenly heard the sound of two pairs of feet crossing the forecourt outside.

In a few seconds, they entered the main part of the station, by which time Dirk was well out of sight round the angle of a wall.

Being well out of sight worked less well for him in another respect, which was that for a while he was unable to see the owners of the feet. By the time he caught a glimpse of them, they had reached exactly the same area where a few minutes previously a small horde of people had, quietly and without fuss, vanished.

He was surprised by the red spectacles of the woman and the quietly tailored Italian suit of the man, and also the speed with which they themselves then immediately vanished.

Dirk stood speechless. The same two damn people who had been the bane of his life for the entire day (he allowed himself this slight exaggeration on the grounds of extreme provocation) had now flagrantly and deliberately disappeared in front of his eyes.

Once he was quite certain that they had absolutely definitely vanished and were not merely hiding behind each other, he ventured out once more into the mysterious space.

It was bafflingly ordinary. Ordinary tarmacadam, ordinary air, ordinary everything. And yet a quantity of people that would have kept the Bermuda triangle industry happy for an entire decade had just vanished in it within the space of five minutes.

He was deeply aggravated.

He was so deeply aggravated that he thought he would share the sense of aggravation by phoning someone up and aggravating them – as it would be almost certain to do at twenty past one in the morning.

This wasn't an entirely arbitrary thought – he was still anxious concerning the safety of the American girl, Kate Schechter, and had not been at all reassured to have been answered by her machine when last he had called. By now she should surely be at home and in bed asleep, and would be reassuringly livid to be woken by a meddling phone call at this time.

He found a couple of coins and a working telephone and dialled her number. He got her answering machine again.

It said that she had just popped out for the night to Asgard. She wasn't certain which parts of Asgard they were going to but they would probably swing by Valhalla later, if the evening was up to it. If he cared to leave a message she would deal with it in the morning if she was still alive and in the mood. There were some beeps, which rang on in Dirk's ear for seconds after he heard them.

"Oh," he said, realising that the machine was currently busy taping him, "good heavens. Well, I thought the arrangement was that you were going to call me before doing anything impossible."

He put the phone down, his head spinning angrily. Valhalla, eh? Was that where everybody was going to tonight except him? He had a good mind to go home, go to bed and wake up in the grocery business.

Valhalla.

He looked about him once again, with the name Valhalla ringing in his ears. There was no doubt, he felt, that a space this size would make a good feasting hall for gods and dead heroes, and that the empty Midland Grand Hotel would be almost worth moving the shebang from Norway for.

He wondered if it made any difference knowing what it was you were walking into.

Nervously, tentatively, he walked across and through the space in question. Nothing happened. Oh well. He turned, and stood surveying it for a moment or two while he took a couple of slow drags on the cigarette he had got from the tramp. The space didn't look any different.

He walked back through it again, this time a little less tentatively, but with slow positive steps. Once again, nothing happened, but then just as he was moving out of it at the end he half fancied that he half heard a half moment of some kind of raucous sound, like a burst of white noise on a twisted radio dial. He turned once more, and headed back into the space, moving his head carefully round trying to pick up the slightest sound. For a while he didn't catch it, then suddenly there was a snatch of it that burst around him and was gone. A movement and another snatch. He moved very, very slowly and carefully. With the most slight and gentle movements, trying to catch at the sound he moved his head round what seemed like a billionth part of a billionth part of a degree, slipped behind a molecule and was gone.

He had instantly to duck to avoid a great eagle swooping out of the vast space at him.

Chapter 28

It was another eagle, a different eagle. The next one was a different eagle too, and the next. The air seemed to be thick with eagles, and it was obviously impossible to enter Valhalla without getting swooped on by at least half a dozen of them. Even eagles were being swooped on by eagles.

Dirk threw up his arms over his head to fend off the wild, beating flurries, turned, tripped and fell down behind a huge table on to a floor of heavy, damp, earthy straw. His hat rolled under the table. He scrambled after it, stuffed it back firmly on his head, and slowly peered up over the table.

The hall was dark, but alive with great bonfires.

Noise and woodsmoke filled the air, and the smells of roasting pigs, roasting sheep, roasting boar, and sweat and reeking wine and singed eagle wings.

The table he was crouched behind was one of countless slabs of oak on trestles that stretched in every direction, laden with steaming hunks of dead animals, huge breads, great iron beakers slopping with wine and candles like wax anthills. Massive sweaty figures seethed around them, on them, eating, drinking, fighting over the food, fighting in the food, fighting with the food.

A yard or so from Dirk, a warrior was standing on top of a table fighting a pig which had been roasting for six hours, and he was clearly losing, but losing with vim and spirit and being cheered on by other warriors who were dousing him down with wine from a trough.

The roof – as much of it as could be made out at this distance, and by the dark and flickering light of the bonfires – was made of lashed-together shields.

Dirk clutched his hat, kept his head down and ran, trying to make his way towards the side of the hall. As he ran, feeling himself to be virtually invisible by reason of being completely sober and, by his own lights, normally dressed, he seemed to pass examples of every form of bodily function imaginable, other than actual teeth-cleaning.

The smell, like that of the tramp in King's Cross station, who must surely be here participating, was one that never stopped coming at you. It grew and grew until it seemed that your head had to become bigger and bigger to accommodate it. The din of sword on sword, sword on shield, sword on flesh, flesh on flesh was one that made the eardrums reel and quiver and want to cry. He was pummelled, tripped, elbowed, shoved and drenched with wine as he scurried and pushed through the wild throng, but arrived at last at a side wall – massive slabs of wood and stone faced with sheets of stinking cow hide.

Panting, he stopped for a moment, looked back and surveyed the scene with amazement.

It was Valhalla.

Of that there could be absolutely no question. This was not something that could be mocked up by a catering company. And the whole seething, wild mass of carousing gods and warriors and their caroused-at ladies, with their shields and fires and boars did seem to fill a space that must be something approaching the size of St Pancras station. The sheer heat that rose off it all seemed as if it should suffocate the flocks of deranged eagles which thrashed through the air above them.

And maybe it was. He was by no means certain that a flock of enraged eagles which thought that they might be suffocating would behave significantly differently from many of the eagles he was currently watching.

There was something he had been putting off wondering while he had fought his way through the mass, but the time had come to wonder it now.

What, he wondered, about the Draycotts?

What could the Draycotts possibly be doing here? And where, in such a mêlée, could the Draycotts possibly be?

He narrowed his eyes and peered into the heaving throng, trying to see if he could locate anywhere a pair of red designer spectacles or a quiet Italian suit mingling out there with the clanging breastplates and the sweaty leathers, knowing that the attempt was futile but feeling that it should be made.

No, he decided, he couldn't see them. Not, he felt, their kind of party. Further reflections along these lines were cut short by a heavy short-handled axe which hurtled through the air and buried itself with an astounding thud in the wall about three inches from his left ear and for a moment blotted out all thought.

When he recovered from the shock of it, and let his breath out, he thought that it was probably not something that had been thrown at him with malicious intent, but was merely warriorly high spirits. Nevertheless, he was not in a partying mood and decided to move on. He edged his way along the wall in the direction which, had this actually been St Pancras station rather than the hall of Valhalla, would have led to the ticket office. He didn't know what he would find there, but he reckoned that it must be different to this, which would be good.

It seemed to him that things were generally quieter here, out on the periphery.

The biggest and best of the good times seemed to be

concentrated more strongly towards the middle of the hall, whereas the tables he was passing now seemed to be peopled with those who looked as if they had reached that season in their immortal lives when they preferred to contemplate the times when they used to wrestle dead pigs, and to pass appreciative comments to each other about the finer points of dead pig wrestling technique, than actually to wrestle with one again themselves just at the moment.

He overheard one remark to his companion that it was the left-handed three-fingered flat grip on the opponent's sternum that was all-important at the crucial moment of finally not quite falling over in a complete stupor, to which his companion responded with a benign "Oh ah."

Dirk stopped, looked and backtracked.

Sitting hunched in a thoughtful posture over his iron plate, and clad in heavily stained and matted furs and buckles which were, if anything, more rank and stinking than the ensemble Dirk had last encountered him in, was Dirk's companion from the concourse at King's Cross station.

Dirk wondered how to approach him. A quick backslap and a "Hey! Good party. Lot of energy," was one strategy, but Dirk didn't think it was the right one.

While he was wondering, an eagle suddenly swooped down from out of the air and, with a lot of beating and thrashing, landed on the table in front of the old man, folded its wings and advanced on him, demanding to be fed. Easily, the old man pulled a bit of meat off a bone and held it up to the great bird, which pecked it sharply but accurately out of his fingers.

Dirk thought that this was the key to a friendly approach. He leant over the table and picked up a small hunk of meat and offered it in turn to the bird. The bird attacked him and went for his neck, forcing him to try and beat the savage creature off with his hat, but the introduction was made.

"Oh ah," said the man, shooed the eagle away, and shifted a couple of inches along the bench. Though it was not a fulsome invitation, it was at least an invitation. Dirk clambered over the bench and sat down.

"Thank you," said Dirk, puffing.

"Oh ah."

"If you remember, we – "

At that moment the most tremendous reverberating thump sounded out across Valhalla. It was the sound of a drum being beaten, but it sounded like a drum of immense proportions, as it had to be to make itself heard over the tumult of noise with which the hall was filled. The drum sounded three times, in slow and massive beats, like the heartbeat of the hall itself.

Dirk looked up to see where the sound might have come from. He noticed for the first time that at the south end of the hall, to which he had been heading, a great balcony or bridge extended across most of its width. There were some figures up there, dimly visible through the heat haze and the eagles, but Dirk had a sense that whoever was up there presided over whoever was down here.

Odin, thought Dirk. Odin the All-Father must be up on the balcony.

The sound of the revels died down quickly, though it was several seconds before the reverberations of the noise finally fell away.

When all was quiet, but expectant, a great voice rang out from the balcony and through the hall.

The voice said, "The time of the Challenging Hour is nearly at an end. The Challenging Hour has been called by the great God Thor. For the third time of asking, where is Thor?"

A murmuring throughout the hall suggested that nobody knew where Thor was and why he had not come to make his challenge.

The voice said, "This is a very grave affront to the dignity of the All-Father. If there is no challenge before the expiration of the hour, the penalty for Thor shall be correspondingly grave."

The drum beat again three times, and the consternation in the hall increased. Where was Thor?

"He's with some girl," said a voice above the rest, and there were loud shouts of laughter, and a return to the hubbub of before.

"Yes," said Dirk, quietly, "I expect he probably is."

"Oh ah."

Dirk had supposed that he was talking to himself and was surprised to have elicited a response from the man, though not particularly surprised at the response that had been elicited.

"Thor called this meeting tonight?" Dirk asked him.

"Oh ah."

"Bit rude not to turn up."

"Oh ah."

"I expect everyone's a bit upset."

"Not as long as there's enough pigs to go round."

"Pigs?"

"Oh ah."

Dirk didn't immediately know how to go on from here.

"Oh ah," he said, resignedly.

"It's only Thor as really cares, you see," said the old man. "Keeps on issuing his challenge, then not being able to prove it. Can't argue. Gets all confused and angry, does something stupid, can't sort it out and gets made to do a penance. Everybody else just turns up for the pigs."

"Oh ah." Dirk was learning a whole new conversational technique and was astonished at how successful it was. He regarded the man with a new-found respect.

"Do you know how many stones there are in Wales?" asked the man suddenly.

"Oh ah," said Dirk warily. He didn't know this joke.

"Nor do I. He won't tell anybody. Says count 'em yourself and goes off in a sulk."

"Oh ah." He didn't think it was a very good one.

"So this time he hasn't even turned up. Can't say I blame him. But I'm sorry, because I think he might be right."

"Oh ah."

The man lapsed into silence.

Dirk waited.

"Oh ah," he said again, hopefully.

Nothing.

"So, er," said Dirk, going for a cautious prompt, "you think he might be right, eh?"

"Oh ah."

"So. Old Thor might be right, eh? That's the story," said Dirk.

"Oh ah."

"In what way," said Dirk, running out of patience at last, "do you think he might be right?"

"Oh, every way."

"Oh ah," said Dirk, defeated.

"It's no secret that the gods have fallen on hard times," said the old man, grimly. "That's clear for all to see, even for the ones who only care about the pigs, which is most of 'em. And when you feel you're not needed any more it can be hard to think beyond the next pig, even if you used to have the whole world there with you. Everyone just accepts it as inevitable. Everyone except Thor, that is. And now he's given up. Hasn't even bothered to turn up and break a pig with us. Given up his challenge. Oh ah."

"Oh ah," said Dirk.

"Oh ah."

"So, er, Thor's challenge then," said Dirk tentatively.

"Oh ah."

"What was it?"

"Oh ah."

Dirk lost his patience entirely and rounded on the man.

"What was Thor's challenge to Odin?" he insisted angrily.

The man looked round at him in slow surprise, looked him up and down with his big sagging eyes.

"You're a mortal, aren't you?"

"Yes," said Dirk testily, "I'm a mortal. Of course I'm a mortal. What has being a mortal got to do with it?"

"How did you get here?"

"I followed you." He pulled the screwed up, empty cigarette packet out of his pocket and put it on the table. "Thanks," he said, "I owe you."

It was a pretty feeble type of apology, he thought, but it was the best he could manage.

"Oh ah." The man looked away.

"What was Thor's challenge to Odin?" said Dirk, trying hard to keep the impatience out of his voice this time.

"What does it matter to you?" the old immortal said bitterly. "You're a mortal. Why should you care? You've got what you want out of it, you and your kind, for what little it's now worth."

"Got what we want out of what?"

"The deal," said the old immortal. "The contract that Thor claims Odin has entered into."

"Contract?" said Dirk. "What contract?"

The man's face filled with an expression of slow anger. The bonfires of Valhalla danced deeply in his eyes as he looked at Dirk.

"The sale," he said darkly, "of an immortal soul."

"What?" said Dirk. He had already considered this idea and discounted it. "You mean a man has sold his soul to him? What man? It doesn't make sense."

"No," said the man, "that wouldn't make sense at all. I said an immortal soul. Thor says that Odin has sold his soul to Man."

Dirk stared at him with horror and then slowly raised his eyes to the balcony. Something was happening there. The great drum beat out again, and the hall of Valhalla began to hush itself once more. But a second or third drumbeat failed to come. Something unexpected seemed to have occurred, and the figures on the balcony were moving in some confusion. The Challenging Hour was just expiring, but a challenge of some kind seemed to have arrived.

Dirk beat his palms to his forehead and swayed where he sat as all kinds of realisations finally dawned on him.

"Not to Man," he said, "but to *a* man, and *a* woman. A lawyer and an advertiser. I said it was all her fault the moment I saw her. I didn't realise I might actually be right." He rounded on his companion urgently. "I have to get up there," he said, "for Gods' sake, help me."

Chapter 29

"O…ddddiiiiiiiinnnnnn!!!!!"

Thor let out a bellow of rage which made the sky shake. The heavy clouds let out a surprised grunt of thunder at the sheer volume of air that moved beneath them. Kate started back, white with fear and shock, with her ears ringing.

"Toe *Rag!!!!!!*"

He hurled his hammer to the ground right at his very feet with both hands. He hurled it this short distance with such astounding force that it hit and rebounded into the air up to about a hundred feet.

"Ggggrrrraaaaaaaaaah!!!!!!" With an immense explosion of air from his lungs he hurled himself up into the air after it, caught it just as it was beginning to drop, and hurled it straight back down at the ground again, catching it again as it bounded back up, twisting violently round in mid-air and hurling it with all the force he could muster out to sea before falling to the ground himself on his back, and pounding the earth with his ankles, elbows and fists in an incredible tattoo of rage.

The hammer shot out over the sea on a very low trajectory. The head went down into the water and planed through it at a constant depth of about six inches. A sharp ripple opened slowly but easily across its surface, extending eventually to about a mile as the hammer sliced its way through it like a surgeon's knife. The inner walls of the ripple deepened smoothly in its wake, falling away from the sheer force of the hammer, till a vast valley had opened in the face of the sea. The walls of the valley wobbled and swayed uncertainly, then folded up and crashed together in crazed and foaming tumult. The hammer lifted its head and swung up high into the air. Thor leapt to his feet and watched it, still pounding his feet on the ground like a boxer, but like a boxer who was perhaps about to precipitate a major earthquake. When the hammer reached the top of its trajectory, Thor hurled his fist downwards like a conductor, and the hammer hurtled down into the crashing mass of sea.

That seemed to calm the sea for a moment in the same way that a smack in the face will calm a hysteric. The moment passed. An immense column of water erupted out of the smack, and seconds later the hammer exploded upwards out of its centre, pulling another huge column of water up from the middle of the first one.

The hammer somersaulted at the top of its rise, turned, spun, and rushed back to its owner like a wildly over-excited puppy. Thor caught at it, but instead of stopping it he allowed it to carry him backwards, and together they tumbled back through the rocks for about a hundred yards and scuffled to a halt in some soft earth.

Instantly, Thor was back on his feet again. He turned round and round, bounding from one leg to the other with strides of nearly ten feet, swinging the hammer round him at arm's length. When he released it again it raced out to sea once more, but this time it tore round the surface in a giant semicircle, causing the sea to rear up around its circumference to form for a moment a gigantic amphitheatre of water. When it fell forward it crashed like a tidal wave, ran forward and threw itself, enraged, against the short wall of the cliff.

The hammer returned to Thor, who threw it off again instantly in a great overarm. It flew into a rock, hitting off a fat angry spark. It bounded off further and hit a spark off another rock, and another. Thor threw himself forward on to his knees, and with each rock the hammer hit he pounded the ground with his fist to make the rock rise to meet the hammer. Spark after spark erupted from the rocks. The hammer hit each successive one harder and harder, until one spark provoked a warning lick of lightning from the clouds.

And then the sky began to move, slowly, like a great angry animal uncoiling in its lair. The pounding sparks flew faster and heavier from the hammer, more lightning licks arced down to meet them from the sky, and the whole earth was beginning to tremble in something very like fearful excitement.

Thor hauled his elbows up above his head and then thrust them hard down with another ringing bellow at the sky.

"O...ddddiiiiiiiinnnnnnn!!!!!"

The sky seemed about to crack open.

"Toe Raaaaaggggggggg!!!!!!!!"

Thor threw himself into the ground, heaving aside about two skipsful of rocky earth. He shook with expanding rage. With a deep groan the whole of the side of the cliff began slowly to lean forward into the sea as he pushed and shook. In a few seconds more it tumbled heavily into the seething torment beneath it as Thor clambered back, seized a rock the size of a grand piano and held it above his head.

Everything seemed still for a fleeting moment.

Thor hurled the rock into the sea.

He regained his hammer.

"O...!" he bellowed.

"...Ddddddddinnnnnnnnnnn!!!!!!!!!!"

His hammer cracked down.

A torrent of water erupted from the ground, and the sky

exploded. Lightning flickered down like a white wall of light for miles along the coast in either direction. Thunder roared like colliding worlds and the clouds vomited rain that shattered the ground. Thor stood exulting in the torrent.

A few minutes later and the violence abated. A strong and steady rain continued to fall. The clouds were cleansing themselves and the weak rays of the early morning light began to find their way through the thinning cover.

Thor trudged back up from where he had been standing, slapping and washing the mud from his hands. He caught at his hammer when it flew to him.

He found Kate standing watching him, shivering with astonishment, fear and fury.

"What was *that* all about?" she yelled at him.

"I just needed to be able to lose my temper properly," he said. When this didn't seem to satisfy her he added, "A god can show off once in a while can't he?"

The huddled figure of Tsuliwaënsis came hurrying out through the rain towards them.

"You're a noisy boy, Thor," she scolded, "a noisy boy."

But Thor was gone. When they looked, they guessed that he must be the tiny speck hurtling northwards through the clearing sky.

Chapter 30

Cynthia Draycott peered over the balcony at the scene below them with distaste. Valhalla was back in full swing.

"I hate this," she said, "I don't want this going on in my life."

"You don't have to, my darling," said Clive Draycott quietly from behind her, with his hands on her shoulders. "It's all going to be taken care of right now, and it's going to work out just fine. Couldn't be better in fact. It's just what we wanted. You know, you look fantastic in those glasses? They really suit you. I mean really. They're *very* chic."

"Clive, it was meant to have been taken care of originally. The whole point was that we weren't to be troubled, we could just do it, deal with it, and forget about it. That was the whole point. I've put up with enough shit in my life. I just wanted it to be good, 100 per cent. I don't want all this."

"Exactly. And that's why this is so perfect for us. So perfect. Clear breach of contract. We get everything we wanted now, and we're released from all obligations. Perfecto. We come out of it smelling of roses, and we have a life that is just 100 per cent

good. 100 per cent. And clean. Just exactly as you wanted it.
Really, it couldn't be better for us. Trust me."

Cynthia Draycott hugged herself irritably.

"So what about this new...person? Something else we have to
deal with."

"It'll be so easy. *So* easy. Listen, this is nothing. We either
cut him in to it, or we cut him *right* out. It'll be taken care of
before we leave here. We'll buy him something. A new coat.
Maybe we'll have to buy him a new house. Know what that'll
cost us?" He gave a charming laugh. "It's nothing. You won't
ever even need to think about it. You won't ever even need to
think about not thinking about it. It's...that...easy. OK?"

"Hm."

"OK. I'll be right back."

He turned and headed back into the ante-chamber of the hall
of the All-Father, smiling all the way.

"So, Mr..." he made a show of looking at the card again
"...Gently. You want to act for these people do you?"

"These immortal gods," said Dirk.

"OK, gods," said Draycott. "That's fine. Perhaps you'll do a
better job than the manic little hustler I had to deal with first
time out. You know, he's really quite a little character, our Mr
Rag, Mr *Rag*. You know, that guy was really quite amazing. He
did everything he could, tried every oldest trick in the book to
freak me out, and give me the run-around. You know how I deal
with people like that? Simple. I ignore it. I just...ignore it. If he
wants to play around and threaten and screech, and shovel in
five hundred and seventeen subclauses that he thinks he's going
to catch me out on, that's OK. He's just taking up time, but so
what? I've got time. I've got plenty of time for people like Mr
Rag. Because you know what the really crazy thing is? You
know what's *really* crazy? The guy cannot draw up an actual
contract to save his life. Really. To save...his...life. And I tell
you something, that's fine by me. He can thrash around and spit
all he likes – when he gets tired I just reel him in. Listen. I draw

up contracts in the record business. These guys are just minnows by comparison. They're primitive savages. You've met them. You've dealt with them. They're primitive savages. Well, aren't they? Like the Red Indians. They don't even know what they've got. You know, these people are lucky they didn't meet some real shark. I mean it. You know what America cost? You know what the whole United States of America actually *cost?* You don't, and neither do I. And shall I tell you why? The sum is so negligible that someone could tell us what it was and two minutes later we would have forgotten. It would have gone clean out of our minds.

"Now, compared with that, let me tell you, I am *providing*. I am *really* providing. A private suite in the Woodshead Hospital? Lavish attention, food, sensational quantities of linen. *Sensational*. You could practically buy the United States of America at today's prices for what that's all costing. But you know what? I said, if he wants the linen, let him have the linen. Just let him have it. It's fine. The guy's earned it. He can have all the linen...he...wants. Just don't fuck with me is all.

"Now let me tell you, this guy has a nice life. A *nice* life. And I think that's what we all want, isn't it. A nice life. This guy certainly did. And he didn't know how to have it. None of these guys did. They're just kind of helpless in the modern world. It's kind of tough for them and I'm just trying to help out. Let me tell you how naïve they are, and I mean *naïve*.

"My wife, Cynthia, you've met her, and let me tell you, she is the best. I tell you, my relationship with Cynthia is *so good –* "

"I don't want to hear about your relationship with your wife."

"OK. That's fine. That's absolutely fine. I just think maybe it's worth you getting to know a few things. But whatever you want is fine. OK. Cynthia's in advertising. You know that. She is a senior partner in a major agency. Major. They did some big campaign, really big, a few years back in which some actor is playing a god in this commercial. And he's endorsing something, I don't know, a soft drink, you know, tooth rot for kids.

And Odin at this time is just a down and out. He's living on
the streets. He simply can't get anything together, because he's
just not adapted for this world. All that power, but he doesn't
know how to make it work for him here, today. Now here's the
crazy part.

"Odin sees this commercial on the television and he thinks to
himself, 'Hey, I could do that, I'm a god.' He thinks maybe he
could get paid for being in a commercial. And you know what
that would be. Pays even less than the United States of America
cost, you follow me? Think about it. Odin, the chief and fount of
all the power of all of the Norse gods, *thinks he might be able to
get paid for being in a television commercial to sell soft drinks*.

"And this guy, this *god*, literally goes out and tries to find
someone who'll let him in a TV commercial. *Pathetically* naïve.
But also greedy – let's not forget greedy.

"Anyway, he happens to come to Cynthia's attention. She's
just a lowly account executive at the time, doesn't pay any
attention, thinks he's just a whacko, but then she gets kind of
fascinated by how odd he is, and I get to see him. And you know
what? It dawns on us he's for real. The guy is for real. A real
actual god with the whole panoply of divine powers. And not
only a god, but like, the main one. The one all the others depend
on for their power. And he wants to be in a commercial. Let's
just say the word again shall we? A *commercial*.

"The idea was dumbfounding. Didn't the guy know what he
had? Didn't he realise what his power could get him?

"Apparently not. I have to tell you, this was the most
astounding moment in our lives. A…stoun…ding. Let me tell
you, Cynthia and I have always known that we were, well,
special people, and that something special would happen to us,
and here it was. Something special.

"But look. We're not greedy. We don't want all that power,
all that wealth. And I mean, we're looking at the world here.
The whole…fucking…world. We could own the world if we
wanted to. But who wants to own the world? Think of the

trouble. We don't even want huge wealth, all those lawyers and accountants to deal with, and let me tell you, *I'm* a lawyer. OK, so you can hire people to look after your lawyers and accountants for you, but who are those people going to be? Just more lawyers and accountants. And you know, we don't even want the responsibility for it all. It's too much.

"So then I have this idea. It's like you buy a big property, and then you sell on what you don't want. That way you get what you want, and a lot of other people get what they want, only they get it through you, and they feel a little obligated to you, and they remember who they got it through because they sign a piece of paper which says how obligated they feel to you. And money flows back to pay for our Mr Odin's very, very, very expensive private medical care.

"So we don't have much, Mr Gently. One or two modestly nice houses. One or two modestly nice cars. We have a very nice life. Very, very nice indeed. We don't need much because anything we need is always made available to us, it's taken care of. All we demanded, and it was a very reasonable demand in the circumstances, was that we didn't want to know any more about it. We take our modest requirements and we bow out. We want nothing more than absolute peace and absolute quiet, and a nice life because Cynthia's sometimes a little nervous. OK.

"And then what happens this morning? Right on our own doorstep. Pow. It's disgusting. I mean it is really a disgusting little number. And you know how it happened?

"Here's how it happened. It's our friend Mr Rag again, and he's tried to be a clever tricky little voodoo lawyer. It's so pathetic. He has fun trying to waste my time with all his little tricks and games and run-arounds, and then he tries to faze me by presenting me with a bill for his time. That's nothing. It's work creation. All lawyers do it. OK. So I say, I'll take your bill. I'll take it, I don't care what it is. You give me your bill and I'll see it's taken care of. It's OK. So he gives it to me.

"It's only later I see it's got this tricky kind of subtotal thing in it. So what? He's trying to be clever. He's given me a hot potato. Listen, the record business is full of hot potatoes. You just get them taken care of. There are always people happy to take care of things for you when they want to make their way up the ladder. If they're worthy of their place on the ladder, well, they'll get it taken care of in return. You get a hot potato, you pass it on. I passed it on. Listen, there were a lot of people who are *very* happy to get things taken care of for me. Hey, you know? It was really funny seeing how far and how fast that particular potato got passed on. That told me a lot about who was bright and who was not. But then it lands up in my back garden, and that's a penalty clause job I'm afraid. The Woodshead stuff is a *very* expensive little number, and I think your clients may have blown it on that particular score. We have the whip hand here. We can just cancel this whole thing. Believe me, I have everything I could *possibly* want now.

"But listen, Mr Gently. I think you understand my position. We've been pretty frank with each other and I've felt good about that. There are certain sensitivities involved, of course, and I'm also in a position to be able to make a lot of things happen. So perhaps we can come to any one of a number of possible accommodations. Anything you want, Mr Gently, it can be made to happen."

"Just to see you dead, Mr Draycott," said Dirk Gently, "just to see you dead."

"Well fuck you, too."

Dirk Gently turned and left the room and went to tell his new client that he thought they might have a problem.

Chapter 31

A little while later a dark-blue BMW pulled quietly away from the otherwise deserted forecourt of St Pancras station and moved off up the quiet streets.

Somewhat dejected, Dirk Gently put on his hat and left his newly acquired and newly relinquished client who said that he wished to be alone now and maybe turn into a rat or something like some other people he could mention.

He closed the great doors behind him and walked slowly out on to the balcony overlooking the great vaulted hall of gods and heroes, Valhalla. He arrived just as the last few stragglers of the revels were fading away, presumably to emerge at the same moment in the great vaulted train shed of St Pancras station. He stayed staring for a while at the empty hall, in which the bonfires now were just fading embers.

It then took the very slightest flicker of his head for him to perform the same transition himself, and he found himself standing in a gusty and dishevelled corridor of the empty Midland Grand Hotel. Out in the great dark concourse of St

Pancras station he saw again the last stragglers from Valhalla shuffling away and out into the cold streets of London to find benches that were designed not to be slept on, and to try to sleep on them.

He sighed and tried to find his way out of the derelict hotel, a task that proved more difficult than he anticipated, as immense and as dark and as labyrinthine as it was. He found at last the great winding gothic staircase which led all the way down to the huge arches of the entrance lobby, decorated with carvings of dragons and griffins and heavy ornamental ironwork. The main front entrance was locked as it had been for years, and eventually Dirk found his way down a side corridor to an exit manned by a great sweaty splodge of a man who guarded it at night. He demanded to know how Dirk had gained entrance to the hotel and refused to be satisfied by any of his explanations. In the end he had simply to allow Dirk to leave, since there was little else he could do.

Dirk crossed from this entrance to the entrance into the station booking hall, and then into the station itself. For a while he simply stood there looking around, and then he left via the main station entrance, and descended the steps which led down on to the St Pancras Road. As he emerged on to the street he was so surprised not to be instantly swooped upon by a passing eagle that he tripped and stumbled and was run over by the first of the early morning's motorcycle couriers.

Chapter 32

With a huge crash, Thor surged through the wall at the far end of the great hall of Valhalla and stood ready to proclaim to the assembled gods and heroes that he had finally managed to break through to Norway and had found a copy of the contract Odin had signed buried deep in the side of a mountain, but he couldn't because they'd all gone and there was no one there.

"There's no one here," he said to Kate, releasing her from his huge grip, "they've all gone."

He slumped in disappointment.

"Wh – " said Kate.

"We'll try the old man's chambers," said Thor and hurled his hammer up to the balcony, with themselves in tow.

He stalked through the great chambers, ignoring Kate's pleas, protests and general abuse.

He wasn't there.

"He's here somewhere," said Thor angrily, trailing his hammer behind him.

"Wh – "

"We'll go through the world divide," he said, and took hold of Kate again. They flicked themselves through.

They were in a large bedroom suite in the hotel.

Litter and scraps of rotting carpet covered the floors, the windows were grimy with years of neglect. Pigeon droppings were everywhere, and the peeling paintwork made it look as if several small families of starfish had exploded on the walls.

There was an abandoned trolleybed in the middle of the floor in which an old man lay in beautifully laundered linen, weeping from his one remaining eye.

"I found the contract, you bastard," raged Thor, waving it at him. "I found the deal you did. You *sold* all our power to…to a lawyer and a…an advertiser and, and all sorts of other people. You stole our power! You couldn't steal all of mine because I'm too strong, but you kept me bewildered and confused, and made bad things happen every time I got angry. You prevented me getting back home to Norway by every method you could, because you knew I'd find *this*! You and that poison dwarf Toe Rag. You've been abusing and humiliating me for years, and – "

"Yes, yes, we know all that," said Odin.

"Well…Good!"

"Thor – " said Kate.

"Well I've shaken all that off now!" shouted Thor.

"Yes, I see – "

"I went somewhere I could get good and angry in peace, when I knew you'd be otherwise occupied and expecting me to be here, and I had a hell of a good shout and blew things up a bit, and I'm all right now! And I'm going to tear this up for a start!"

He ripped right through the contract, threw the pieces in the air and incinerated them with a look.

"Thor – " said Kate.

"And I'm going to put right all the things you made happen so I'd be afraid of getting angry. The poor girl at the airline check-in desk that got turned into a drink machine. Woof! Wham! She's back! The jet fighter that tried to shoot me down when I was flying to Norway! Woof! Wham! It's back! See, I'm back in control of myself!"

"My table lamp," said Kate quietly.

"And Kate's table lamp! It shall be a small kitten no more! Woof! Wham! Thor speaks and it is so! What was that noise?"

A ruddy glow was spreading across the London skyline.

"Thor, I think there's something wrong with your father."

"I should bloody well hope so. Oh. What's wrong? Father? Are you all right?"

"I have been so very, very foolish and unwise," wept Odin, "I have been so wicked and evil, and – "

"Yes, well that's what I think, too," said Thor and sat on the end of his bed. "So what are we going to do?"

"I don't think I could live without my linen, and my Sister Bailey, and…It's been so, so, so long, and I'm so, so old. Toe Rag said I should kill you, but I…I would rather have killed myself. Oh, Thor…"

"Oh," said Thor. "I see. Well. I don't know what to do now. Blast. Blast everything."

"Thor – "

"Yes, yes, what is it?"

"Thor, it's very simple what you do about your father and the Woodshead," said Kate.

"Oh yes? What then?"

"I'll tell you on one condition."

"Oh really? And what's that?"

"That you tell me how many stones there are in Wales."

"What!" exclaimed Thor in outrage. "Away from me! That's years of my life you're talking about!"

Kate shrugged.

"No!" said Thor. "Anything but that! Anyway," he added sullenly, "I told you."

"No you didn't."

"Yes I did. I said I lost count somewhere in Mid-Glamorgan. Well, I was hardly going to start again, was I? Think, girl, think!"

Chapter 33

Beating a path through the difficult territory to the north-east of Valhalla – a network of paths that seemed to lead only to other paths and then back to the first paths again for another try – went two figures, one a big, stupid, violent creature with green eyes and a scythe which hung from its belt and often seriously impeded its progress, the other a small crazed creature who clung on to the back of the bigger one, manically urging him on while actually impeding his progress still further.

They attained at last a long, low, smelly building into which they hurried shouting for horses. The old stable master came forward, recognised them and, having heard already of their disgrace, was at first disinclined to help them on their way. The scythe flashed through the air and the stable master's head started upwards in surprise while his body took an affronted step backwards, swayed uncertainly, and then for lack of any further instructions to the contrary keeled over backwards in its own time. His head bounded into the hay.

His assailants hurriedly lashed up two horses to a cart and

clattered away out of the stable yard and along the broader thoroughfare which led upwards to the north.

They made rapid progress up the road for a mile, Toe Rag urging the horses on frantically with a long and cruel whip. After a few minutes, however, the horses began to slow down and to look about them uneasily. Toe Rag lashed them all the harder, but they became more anxious still then suddenly lost all control and reared in terror, turning over the cart and tipping its occupants out on the ground, from which they instantly sprang up in a rage.

Toe Rag screamed at the terrified horses and then, out of the corner of his eye, caught sight of what had so disturbed them.

It wasn't so terrifying. It was just a large, white, metal box, upturned on a pile of rubbish by the roadside and rattling itself.

The horses were rearing and trying to bolt away from the big white rattling thing but they were impossibly entangled in their traces. They were only working themselves up into a thrashing lather of panic. Toe Rag quickly realised that there would be no calming them until the box was dealt with.

"Whatever it is," he screeched at the green-eyed creature, "kill it!"

Green-eye unhooked his scythe from his belt once more and clambered up the pile of rubbish to where the box was rattling. He kicked it and it only rattled the more. He got his foot behind it and with a heavy thrust shoved it away down the heap. The big white box slithered a foot or so then turned over and toppled to the ground. It rested there for a moment and then a door, finally freed, flew open. The horses screamed in fear.

Toe Rag and his green-eyed thug approached the thing with worried curiosity, then staggered back in horror as a great and powerful new god erupted from its innards.

Chapter 34

The following afternoon, at a comfortable distance from all these events, set at a comfortable distance from a well-proportioned window through which the afternoon light was streaming, lay an elderly one-eyed man in a white bed. A newspaper sat like a half-collapsed tent on the floor, where it had been hurled two minutes before.

The man was awake but not glad to be. His exquisitely frail hands lay slightly curled on the pure white linen sheets and quivered very faintly.

His name was variously given as Mr Odwin, or Wodin, or Odin. He was – is – a god, and furthermore he was a confused and startled god.

He was confused and startled because of the report he had just been reading on the front page of the newspaper, which was that another god had been cutting loose and making a nuisance of himself. It didn't say so in so many words of course, it merely described what had happened last night when a missing jet fighter aircraft had mysteriously erupted under full power from out of a house in North London into which it could not conceivably have been thought to have fitted. It had instantly lost its wings and gone into a screaming dive and crashed and exploded in a main road. The pilot had managed to eject during the few seconds he had had in the air, and had landed, shaken, bruised, but otherwise unharmed, and babbling about strange men with hammers flying over the North Sea.

Luckily, because of the time at which the inexplicable disaster had occurred, the roads were almost deserted, and apart from massive damage to property, the only fatalities to have occurred were the as yet unidentified occupants of a car which was thought to have been possibly a BMW and possibly blue, though because of the rather extreme nature of the accident it was rather hard to tell.

He was very, very tired and did not want to think about it, did not want to think about last night, did not want to think of anything other than linen sheets and how wonderful it was when Sister Bailey patted them down around him as she had just now, just five minutes ago, and again just ten minutes before that.

The American girl, Kate something, came into his room. He wished she would just let him sleep. She was going on about something being all fixed up. She congratulated him on having extremely high blood pressure, high cholesterol levels and a very dicky heart, as a consequence of which the hospital would be very glad to accept him as a lifelong patient in return for his entire estate. They didn't even care to know what his estate was worth, because it would clearly be sufficient to cover a stay as brief as his was likely to be.

She seemed to expect him to be pleased, so he nodded amiably, thanked her vaguely and drifted, drifted happily off to sleep.

Chapter 35

The same afternoon Dirk Gently awoke, also in hospital, suffering from mild concussion, scrapes and bruises and a broken leg. He had had the greatest difficulty in explaining, on admittance, that most of his injuries had been caused by a small boy and an eagle, and that really, being run over by a motorcycle courier was a relatively restful experience since it mostly involved lying down a lot and not being swooped on every two minutes.

He was kept under sedation – in other words, he slept – for most of the morning, suffering terrible dreams in which Toe Rag and a green-eyed, scythe-bearing giant made their escape to the north-east from Valhalla, where they were unexpectedly accosted and consumed by a newly created, immense Guilt God which had finally escaped from what looked suspiciously like an upturned refrigerator on a skip.

He was relieved to be woken at last from this by a cheery, "Oh it's you, is it? You nicked my book."

He opened his eyes and was greeted by the sight of Sally

Mills, the girl he had been violently accosted by the previous day in the café, for no better reason than that he had, prior to nicking her book, nicked her coffee.

"Well, I'm glad to see you took my advice and came in to have your nose properly attended to," she said as she fussed around him. "Pretty roundabout way you seem to have taken, but you're here and that's the main thing. You caught up with the girl you were interested in did you? Oddly enough, you're in the very bed that she was in. If you see her again, perhaps you could give her this pizza which she arranged to have delivered before checking herself out. It's all cold now, but the courier did insist that she was very adamant it should be delivered.

"I don't mind you nicking the book, really, though. I don't know why I buy them really, they're not very good, only everyone always does, don't they? Somebody told me there's a rumour he had entered into a pact with the devil or something. I think that's nonsense, though I did hear another story about him which I much preferred. Apparently he's always having these mysterious deliveries of chickens to his hotel rooms, and no one dares to ask why or even guess what it is he wants them for, because nobody ever sees a single scrap of them again. Well, I met somebody who knows exactly what he wants them for. The somebody I met once had the job of secretly smuggling the chickens straight back out of his rooms again. What Howard Bell gets out of it is a reputation for being a very strange and demonic man and everybody buys his books. Nice work if you can get it is what I say. Anyway, I expect you don't want to have me nattering to you all afternoon, and even if you do I've got better things to do. Sister says you'll probably be discharged this evening so you can go to your own home and sleep in your own bed, which I'm sure you'll much prefer. Anyway, hope you feel better, here's a couple of newspapers."

Dirk took the papers, glad to be left alone at last.

He first turned to see what The Great Zaganza had to say about his day. The Great Zaganza said, "You are very fat and stupid and persistently wear a ridiculous hat which you should be ashamed of."

He grunted slightly to himself about this, and turned to the horoscope in the other paper.

It said, "Today is a day to enjoy home comforts."

Yes, he thought, he would be glad to get back home. He was still strangely relieved about getting rid of his old fridge and looked forward to enjoying a new phase of fridge ownership with the spanking new model currently sitting in his kitchen at home.

There was the eagle to think about, but he would worry about that later, when he got home.

He turned to the front page to see if there was any interesting news.